W9-BUE-368

Toxic Game

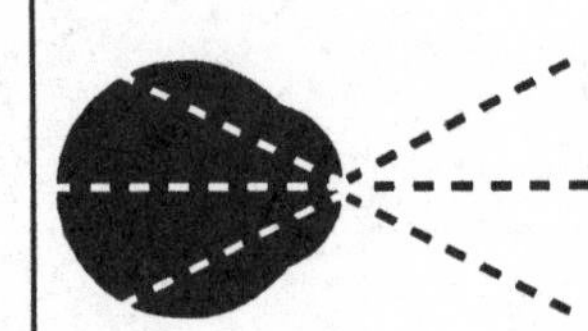

TOXIC GAME

CHRISTINE FEEHAN

THORNDIKE PRESS
A part of Gale, a Cengage Company

Farmington Hills, Mich • San Francisco • New York • Waterville, Maine
Meriden, Conn • Mason, Ohio • Chicago

GhostWalker.
Thorndike Press, a part of Gale, a Cengage Company.

Thorndike Press® Large Print Romance.
The text of this Large Print edition is unabridged.
Other aspects of the book may vary from the original edition.
Set in 16 pt. Plantin.

LIBRARY OF CONGRESS CIP DATA ON FILE.
CATALOGUING IN PUBLICATION FOR THIS BOOK
IS AVAILABLE FROM THE LIBRARY OF CONGRESS

ISBN-13: 978-1-4328-6208-4 (hardcover alk. paper)

Published in 2019 by arrangement with Berkley, an imprint of Penguin Publishing Group, a division of Penguin Random House LLC

Printed in Mexico
1 2 3 4 5 6 7 23 22 21 20 19

For my Shylah, a fierce
but kindhearted warrior.
This one's for you.

FOR MY READERS

Be sure to go to christinefeehan.com/members/ to sign up for my private book announcement list and download the free ebook of *Dark Desserts.* Join my community and get firsthand news, enter the book discussions, ask your questions and chat with me. Please feel free to email me at Christine@christinefeehan.com. I would love to hear from you.

ACKNOWLEDGMENTS

This book was incredibly interesting to write and gave me a few problems here and there. I had the help of quite a few people. First, I have to thank Shari Kaiser, PhD; Molly Ohainele, PhD; and Erin Garcia, PhD. They were extraordinarily thoughtful to take the time out of very busy schedules to answer my questions about hemorrhagic viruses. Any mistake is mine, as they did their best to make me understand what a hot virus is and just how incredibly frightening one can be should it find its way into the population. Sheila English, Kathie Firzlaff and Cheryl Wilson, thank you for your work double-checking the facts and making certain everything written was in keeping with things that could actually happen. Sheila English, thank you for helping me with villages and research for Sumatra that was especially difficult to uncover. Thanks to Domini Walker for her help with the final edits, and Brian for keeping me on track through all the craziness!

THE GHOSTWALKER SYMBOL DETAILS

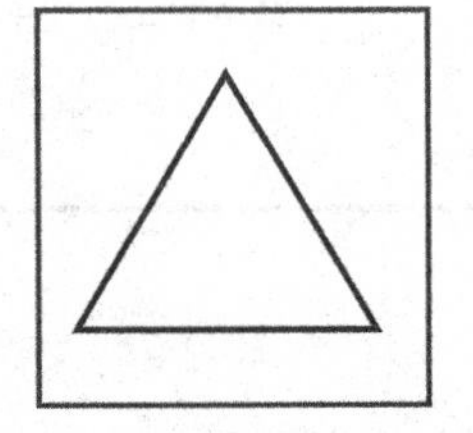

SIGNIFIES
shadow

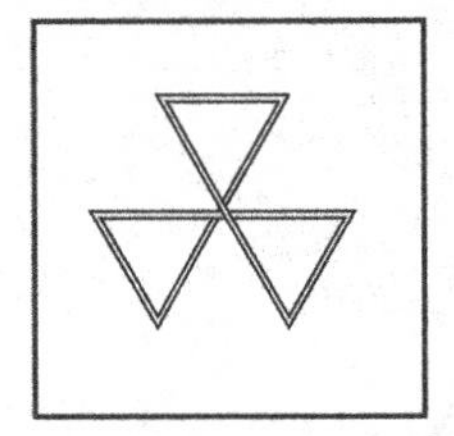

SIGNIFIES
protection against evil forces

SIGNIFIES
the Greek letter psi, which is used by parapsychology researchers to signify ESP or other psychic abilities

SIGNIFIES
qualities of a knight—loyalty, generosity, courage and honor

SIGNIFIES
shadow knights who protect against evil forces using psychic powers, courage and honor

nox noctis est nostri

THE GHOSTWALKER CREED

We are the GhostWalkers, we live in the shadows
The sea, the earth, and the air are our domain
No fallen comrade will be left behind
We are loyalty and honor bound
We are invisible to our enemies
and we destroy them where we find them
We believe in justice and we protect our country
and those unable to protect themselves
What goes unseen, unheard, and unknown are GhostWalkers
There is honor in the shadows and it is us
We move in complete silence whether in jungle or desert
We walk among our enemy unseen and unheard
Striking without sound and scatter to the winds

before they have knowledge of our existence
We gather information and wait with endless patience
for that perfect moment to deliver swift justice
We are both merciful and merciless
We are relentless and implacable in our resolve
We are the GhostWalkers and the night is ours

1

"Hot as hell!" Barry Font yelled, wiping the sweat from his face. He looked around him at the crew he was transporting straight into the hot zone. He hadn't meant the strip of land they were setting the helicopters down in. They all knew it was bad. The last rescue attempt had been ambushed. Three dead, two wounded, and the helicopter had barely made it out.

The temperature was at least ninety degrees with 99 percent humidity and gusting winds that took that heat and shoved it right down your throat — and this was at night. His skin felt wet and sticky all the time. He wanted to strip himself bare and lie under the helicopter's rotor blades just to get some relief.

They dropped down out of the mountains, the helicopters running low enough to make his gut tighten as they skimmed along the lowlands heading toward the forest. They were sitting ducks making that run, and this area was infamous for frequent ground-to-air fire. With the Milisi Separatis Sumatra terrorist cell active and firing at anything, every man in the choppers was at risk. Gunners grimly watched out their doors on either side, but that didn't make him feel any less like he had a target painted on his back. Strangely, it wasn't the run that was scaring the crap out of him. He felt like he was trapped in a cage surrounded by predators.

The Air Force pararescue team didn't seem affected by anything as mundane as the heat or terrorists. The crazy thing was, they were mostly officers. Doctors. *What the hell?* As a rule, Barry thought most officers were a joke. These men had seen combat and looked as tough as nails. He'd never flown them anywhere before and hadn't known what to expect.

His crew had taken men into all sorts of combat situations, but he'd never seen a team like the one he was bringing in. He didn't even know how to explain their difference. It wasn't like he could name one single thing about them that made them stand out in his mind. They just gave off a dangerous vibe. Being with them really did feel as if he were inside a tiger's cage, surrounded by the big cats. They were that still, that menacing, and yet they hadn't said or done anything to warrant his nerves or the shiver of dread creeping down his spine at the sight of them.

They sat stoically while the helicopter swayed and jerked, bumping like it was in the rockiest terrain. They moved with the craft as if seasoned veterans of helicopter travel. Sweat trickled down faces — well, all but one. He looked at the man sitting at the very end of the jump seat. Dr. Draden Freeman, a gifted surgeon, was a fucking model, not a tough-as-nails soldier about to be dropped into the hottest zone in Indonesia.

Freeman had dark brown hair that was thick and wavy. At six-two he was all muscle, without an ounce of fat. His eyes were a dark blue and held an intensity; when he flicked Barry a careless glance at his remark, Barry's gut reacted as if punched. The man had rugged good looks that had catapulted him into stardom in the modeling world. Ordinarily, Barry and the crew would have been making fun of him behind his back, but no one did — especially after one of those smoldering, scary glances. Not one single bead of sweat marred his good looks.

"Five minutes out." The call came from

the front via his radio.

Barry held up five fingers and the five men in the helicopter barely reacted. The helicopter was coming in with guns ready, knowing they wouldn't have much time to retrieve the wounded U.S. Rangers, Kopassus or civilians. The gunners were in position and tension mounted.

Members of the WHO, the World Health Organization, had come at the request of the government to examine the remains of the dead at a small village, Lupa Suku, in a remote part of Sumatra. Every man, woman and child had died of what appeared to be a very fast-acting and deadly virus, possibly a dreaded hemorrhagic one. Before they could set up their equipment, the WHO members had been attacked by a small terrorist cell known to the government.

The Milisi Separatis Sumatra, or MSS as the government referred to them, had sprung up in the last few years. They were growing fast and were well funded. Their goal seemed to be similar to that of most other terrorist cells — to take down the government. They were now suspected of having chosen the small village of Lupa Suku to test a hemorrhagic virus, but where it came from and how they got it, no one knew, but they needed to find out fast.

The rain forest of Sumatra was rich in plants and wildlife, although over the years even that had been shrinking significantly. The trees were thick, the taller dipterocarp shooting up to the sky providing shade, vines climbing them and flowers wrapping around them. Mangrove roots pulled sediment from the river leaving large areas of peat swamps with rich nutrients at their edges promoting thicker growth. The village of Lupa Suku was surrounded by the forest and tucked in just far enough from the river to be a perfect target.

The government had sent in their special forces, the Kopassus, to rescue the single WHO representative still alive. The Kopassus were known worldwide as tough soldiers able to stack up against any army. They were well trained and very skilled. They'd been ambushed as they were trying to aid the wounded man. A small force of U.S. Rangers had been called to aid the Kopassus who were pinned down, some reportedly badly wounded. The Rangers were then attacked and pinned down as well.

It began to look as if Lupa Suku had been sacrificed in order to draw the Indonesian soldiers into fighting a guerrilla-style war on the terrorists' home turf. Whatever the rumor, there were wounded men needing aid and six of them were soldiers of the United States. Now, this team was going to try to bring those soldiers out of the hot zone — along with any Kopassus and the remaining single living representative of the WHO.

"Two minutes."

Barry held up two fingers and the team moved, readying themselves for a quick departure.

"Ten minutes is all you've got and then we have to get into the air," Barry reminded them. "If we can't hold our position, we'll come back around for you."

Freeman flicked him a quick glance. It was one of those looks that seemed to burn a hole right through him. Barry shivered, not liking those eyes on him. They were intelligent, focused — almost too focused. They didn't blink, and it felt like death looking at him.

The team leader, Dr. Joe Spagnola, gave him a quick look as well. It pretty much said, "You maggot, if you leave one of my men behind, don't ever go to sleep because I'll be coming for you." At least Barry interpreted the look that way.

Joe Spagnola ignored the way the helicopter crew was looking at his team. He didn't look at them or his own men, but instead, reached telepathically to his GhostWalker unit. GhostWalkers were enhanced psychically as well as physically. The first they'd signed on for; the last, not so much. Still, they were classified soldiers and they did their jobs, no matter how fucked-up that was.

Each branch of the service had one GhostWalker team consisting of ten members. The first team experimented on had a few major problems. Some needed anchors to drain away the psychic energy that adhered to them like magnets. Others had brain bleeds. Every subsequent team had fewer flaws until Whitney, the doctor performing the experiments, had rolled out his prize group, the Pararescue Team. They might have what Whitney considered fewer flaws, but they also had more genetic enhancements than any of them cared for.

He leaves us, we'll be finding him and his candy-ass crew when we get out of here. Joe's voice slid into their minds.

Draden's gaze shifted, just for one moment to Barry Font and then over to his fellow teammate, Malichai Fortunes.

There's a hundred and fifty volcanoes in Indonesia, Malichai, their fact man, informed them all telepathically. *We can shove his ass out of the helicopter right into one of them if he tries leaving any of us behind.*

Draden let amusement slide into his eyes for a moment but didn't let it show on his face. Malichai had been spouting all kinds of facts about the rain forest and the wildlife at risk there. That was his way in a dangerous situation, and all members of the team just let him carry on.

The enhancements made them predators any way you looked at it. Hunters. They were very good at their jobs. They looked like soldiers. Doctors. Officers. But they were much more than that and anyone in close confines with them felt that difference sooner rather than later. All of them could smell the fear the helicopter crew were giving off and that fear had nothing to do with flying into a hot zone. No, Barry and the crew were used to that sort of danger — they just didn't like their passengers.

Draden could give a rat's ass if he was liked or not. He had a job to do. They were going into enemy territory to bring out the wounded and make certain they stayed alive until they got them back to the hospitals.

The helicopter set down with a jarring thump and Draden was out fast, running with his fellow teammates in the dark toward the southern tip of the tree line. Deliberately, they'd chosen to fly in at three in the morning, when the enemy was least likely to be at its sharpest. The sound of the rotors was loud in the night, something that couldn't be helped. He knew the noise would draw the enemy. That couldn't be helped either. They just needed a few minutes.

The terrorist cell had set their trap with live bait. They knew the terrain and had chosen it carefully. The MSS had the advantage, especially when the Indonesian government had wounded soldiers waiting for help. They knew the authorities would send their elite, and it was a chance to mow them down.

Draden fanned out to his left while Gino Mazza went right, both flanking the others as Joe went down on one knee and flashed the tiny blue light in each direction three times. They received a response from the west. Instantly, they were up and running again toward the returned signal.

Thirty feet from the thickest brush, they spread out even farther, running in absolute silence as only GhostWalkers could. Joe, Malichai and Diego Campo dropped down, their weapons ready, while Draden and

Gino continued forward. Draden slipped into the cover of the brush, a place he was at home.

He found their contact ten feet in, crouched down in the thick buttresses of a dipterocarp tree. "How many wounded?" Draden asked, his voice a thread of sound.

"Fifteen."

Draden gave a mental shake of his head. Fifteen was a lot of wounded. They had room in the three helicopters, but maybe not the time to get them all in. "Anyone besides you who can help get them to the choppers?"

"Two others."

That wasn't good either.

"Enemy?"

"No idea of their numbers. They seem to come and go. At least we think they're gone and the moment we move, they open fire."

Draden nodded. "Any of you sick?"

The Ranger shook his head. "The only one to go near the village was Dr. Henderson and he was in full hazmat gear. We stayed out of there. Henderson wants the village burned."

Draden turned and signaled the others in. They came like wraiths, sliding out of the night in complete silence. Draden gave him the number of wounded telepathically while

Joe tapped his watch.

Move fast, gentlemen. We don't have time to triage here. Get them into the choppers.

Joe didn't sound alarmed, but Draden felt it nevertheless. They had about eight minutes, and getting to the wounded would eat up another minute or two.

The Ranger was already on his feet, so they followed him through the thick forest to a small dip in the terrain hidden by brush and the buttresses of wide tree trunks. The Kopassus looked grim, two dead, three of them badly wounded, but guns steady as rocks. One was still standing and ready to pack out his teammates, already gathering their weapons. The Rangers were in similar straits, one dead, the others in various states of badly wounded or just broken and bloody. Those with lighter injuries were gathering up their teammates to pack them out. The WHO doctor, clearly in bad shape, staggered as he stood. None of them looked as if they could walk more than a few steps.

The GhostWalkers were all business. Gino took the worst Ranger, slapping field dressings on the wounds to keep him from bleeding out while he ran with the man to the choppers. The Kopassus followed with one of his fellow team members. Joe took a Ranger and Diego a Kopassus. Malichai took the civilian. One of the Rangers staggered to his feet.

"I can walk out."

Draden nodded and waved him after the others. He moved from wounded man to wounded man, giving them water and seeing to the worst of their wounds, all the while listening for any changes in the sounds of the night that would indicate members of the MSS had returned at the sound of the helicopters.

Gino was back, hoisting another Ranger onto his back. The Kopassus soldier returned with him and took another of the wounded. The Indonesian didn't look in good shape, but he wasn't leaving anyone behind. They wanted to pack their dead with them as well, not leave them behind, but the dead had to go last. Joe, Diego and Malichai all had taken the next round of wounded and were gone, disappearing into the darkness, when Draden felt his first prickle of unease.

He crouched low and signaled to the remaining soldiers for absolute silence. The remaining men showed why they were considered elite. In spite of their wounds, they immediately went into survival mode, weapons ready, sliding deeper into the depression for cover. Draden moved away from them, toward the north. There were no sounds of insects. Not even the continual drone of cicadas or loud croaks of tree frogs. For a moment, the forest had gone unnaturally quiet, signaling something was moving into it that didn't belong.

He was part of the forest and could read every sign. He moved fast, slipping through brush without a whisper of sound. Sinking into the thick foliage, he waited. A man emerged from a small group of trees, heading stealthily toward the encampment of wounded. Draden saw another fifteen feet from him, and a third man the same distance out as the terrorists moved in unison toward the small group of soldiers.

Draden waited until the nearest terrorist had passed him and then rose up swiftly, catching him around the head, his hand muffling any sound as he plunged his knife into the base of the skull before lowering the man to the ground. The forest floor was thick with vegetation and cushioned the fall of the rifle. Draden was already melting into the dark, making his way across the expanse to the next man in line.

As the terrorist turned his head toward where the fallen man should have been, Draden was on him, repeating the kill, and slipping away. Behind him, more of the terrorists were emerging into the kill zone. They were filtering through the trees and shrubbery, making little sound, coming up toward the encampment where the remaining wounded waited to be transported.

Draden took the third man on their front line and then glanced down at his watch. He needed to buy Joe and the others an extra couple of minutes to pack out the last of the wounded. Then he'd have to double-time it back to the choppers so they could get out of there before the MSS had time to get real firepower set up.

He reached up, leapt, caught the branches of a durian tree and pulled himself up, waiting for the next line of soldiers to pass in front of him. Although he was aware of every second ticking by, he was patient. The moment the five men crept through the darkness, he dropped down, so he was between the MSS filtering through the forest. They were creeping stealthily toward the helicopters, trying to insert themselves between the choppers and the remaining wounded soldiers.

MSS coming at you, Draden warned his team. *I'll buy some time.*

Draden moved much faster, risking being seen by one of the terrorists behind him as he cut down first one and then a second in that line. Glancing at his watch, he ran toward a third, his knife stabbing deep into the base of the skull as he shot past. He held on to the hilt of the knife, so that as he ran, it spun his victim around before the blade came free. He threw a balanced throwing knife sideways into the neck of another as he sprinted out of the protection of the trees.

We're in. We're away, Joe reported. *Circling to bring you home.*

Coming in on the run.

The last of the helicopters had lifted from the ground, gunners providing cover for him, spraying the tree line to keep the terrorists from taking aim at Draden. Diego and Malichai used automatics to aid the gunners as Joe and Gino worked on the wounded. A rope was dropped down as the chopper circled back. Draden kept running as gunfire erupted from the cover of the forest. Bullets spat around him.

The chopper came slipping out of the sky toward him, coming in low, the rope flying like a slinky tail. Behind him, the forest went strangely silent. No gunfire. He didn't stop. He leapt for the rope, his gloved hands catching hold, the jerk so strong it nearly pulled his arms out of their sockets. Still, his enhanced strength allowed him to hang on while the chopper began to climb.

He was twenty feet up when he felt the sting in his thigh, and his heart stuttered with instant awareness. He glanced down to see a dart protruding from his muscle and knew why the terrorists' weapons had gone silent. They had a sniper, and he wasn't armed with a bullet. He was armed with a virus. If Draden went up into the helicopter, he was condemning everyone in it to the same death as those in the village. Without real conscious thought, he let go of the rope, dropping out of the sky and back to earth.

Virus injection. It was the best information he could give them, so they would know to leave him behind.

Malichai was staring down at him, their eyes meeting as he fell away. He saw Malichai practically dive from the helicopter, but Diego caught him, holding him back. Draden landed in a crouch, his enhanced DNA allowing his legs to act like springs to absorb the shock. He somersaulted forward and stood up, facing the forest, his arms spread wide. Let them shoot him if they wanted, but if they didn't, he was infecting the bastards. He began walking toward the edge of all those trees and brush.

Draden. What the hell happened? Joe's voice slipped into his mind. It was faded, as if the distance was already too far. He heard the helicopter circling back so Joe would be able to reach him. He pictured Joe holding a weapon on the crew. He could get that intense.

By the time he reached the trees, the MSS members had faded away, leaving him to die however the villagers had. He'd seen the reports the Indonesian government had shared with the WHO. It was one of the reasons his team had been in the region. Two team members were two of the leading scientists developing treatments, therapies and pharmaceuticals in the field of viruses.

Infected with the virus.

Draden had taken the time to finish both his doctorate and MD, to be an asset to others on his team. He'd dabbled in biochemistry but finished his undergrad degree, a BS in genetics. Stanford offered a dual MD and PhD program and he'd taken advantage of that. He'd gotten his MD as an infectious disease doctor and his PhD in microbiology and immunology. He found it ironic that he would be dying of a weaponized virus after all that work to earn his degrees. Determined to be of some use, he decided to record everything he could about his symptoms, along with any suppositions he might have before he put a bullet in his head. He'd leave final conclusions for them.

Tell Trap and Wyatt I'll leave behind a recording. Don't know if they can use whatever I find, but they should be able to remotely access my recorder without touching the device.

I'm sorry, man. Trap and Wyatt may have ideas.

Draden knew, just from the earlier reports, that their ideas would be too late. The virus acted too fast. He would be dead before Joe had time to make it back to the States.

I'll torch the village. He hoped he'd get that done fast so he could hunt the terrorists who were infecting people and then using them as bait to kill more. He wanted to kill as many of the bastards as possible before the virus took hold and left him too sick to go after them.

He could hear the chopper circling back around a second time. *Hope you didn't put a gun to their heads.* He injected humor he wasn't really feeling into his voice.

Maybe if we get you back we can find the treatment before it's too late, Malichai said.

Too fast acting. Can't chance infecting all of you. We all signed up for a one-way ticket when we joined the GhostWalkers. It's just my turn.

Fuck! Gino hissed.

I'll take out as many of the cell as I can

before I go down, Draden said, meaning it. He was going to make sure as many of them were dead as possible. Not because they'd infected him, but because they'd infected an entire village to use as a trap. *Joe, someone has to find out where this is coming from.*

I will, Joe promised.

Get the wounded out of here, there's not much you can do for me. Some of those injuries were severe.

Damn it, Draden. That was Gino.

He didn't feel as bad as they did. He didn't have much of a future anyway. *Just pissed I wasted all that time going to school instead of partying.*

Yeah, cuz you're such a party animal, Malichai said with an attempt at sarcastic humor. His voice was tight. The feeling in his mind — sorrow.

Tell Nonny she's the best. He should have told the old woman that himself. Wyatt Fontenot's grandmother had taken the entire team into her home. She'd cared for them as she would her own. He hadn't had that kind of affection from anyone since his foster mother had died when he was so young. He hadn't known anyone else was capable of loving others the way the woman he called mother had until he met Nonny.

He should have told her, and he hadn't, not once. He was surprised at the emotion welling up. Yeah, he should have told her. She'd mourn for him, and it shouldn't have shocked him that his teammates would as well, but it did.

We can pick you up, take you back and try one of the treatments. I know they're not sanctioned yet, but some have worked when a virus is detected early enough, Gino said.

We don't know anything about this one yet and we can't take the chance, you all know that, he objected, because he could infect every one of them and when they landed, every doctor and nurse waiting to help the wounded. He wasn't having that on his conscience.

You have anywhere from a few days to twenty.

Joe, don't make this worse. Get the hell out of here and make certain every single one of the wounded survives.

There was the briefest of hesitations, but Joe was the commanding officer for a reason. He had to make the tough decisions. *You have my word. Damn honor serving with you, Draden.*

The others murmured similar sentiments. He didn't reply. What was there to say? He had never considered himself a sentimental man. In fact, he tried not to feel much at all, but living in Louisiana with his GhostWalker Team, emotions had crept in whether he wanted them to or not. He'd learned at a very early age that it was better to push feelings aside and use logic for every decision. Emotions fucked things up in ways that could be very, very bad.

Still, there was Trap. The man was a genuine crazy-ass genius with Asperger's. Super-high IQ and wealthy as all hell. Didn't have a clue about social cues. Draden had been the one to clue him in as often as possible. Trap didn't let many people in and neither did Draden, but they'd been there for each other.

Tell Trap he's the best. He'll do fine. Tell him — He broke off, shocked that he was choking up. He loved the man like a brother. *Shit.*

I got it, Joe said.

Draden let the forest close around him as the sound of the helicopter faded into the distance. He wasn't worried about being alone. He was used to it. He'd been alone most of his life, even in the midst of a crowd. He could handle that, no problem. He began to move fast toward the village of the dead. It was very small, only a few families, many related to one another. He was a very fast runner, but that would spread the virus through his bloodstream much quicker. Still, it might not be a bad idea just to get it over with. He played with that idea as he jogged, his animal senses flaring out to uncover anyone that might have been left behind to keep an eye on him.

He pulled up the facts about the village and region they'd been briefed on. The village's name, Lupa Suku, meant Forgotten Tribe and he thought it very apt from everything he'd read about them. The village was so remote, it wasn't even considered a sub-district of Rambutan. He knew that driving southeast from Palembang the thirty-four and some miles to Rambutan, villages along the road were more and more scarce. Eventually, that road became nothing more than a muddy broad path lined on either side by trees and brush. A few cars and buses shared the road with bikes and animals until it disappeared.

So remote, Lupa Suku could only be reached by bike, boat or animals such as a domestic ox. It was impossible during the wet season to get any motorized vehicle through. Heavy items tended to get stuck in the thick mud, so it was necessary to move everything via water. Most used a small boat to access the village via the Banyuasin River.

According to the briefing given by the representative of the Indonesian government, primary trade consisted of fish and rice. There was a small copper mine that was kept a secret by the locals. The copper was mined by hand a little at a time as they had no modern machinery. The government had turned a blind eye, acting as though they knew nothing about that little mine or the fact that the villagers traded the copper to poachers who came to the area looking for exotic birds. Money meant little to the villagers, so they tended to barter for the things they needed.

Draden figured bartering was how the terrorists had introduced the virus. It was possible that the virus had occurred some other way, via bugs or animals, but he doubted it. The WHO had been trying to find a source, but the fact that the nearby terrorist cell had used the dead villagers for an ambush, killing nearly all the WHO doctors and their workers, tended to make him believe they were responsible.

The terrorist cell was organized for being fairly new. Their job was to topple the government and unlike others targeting police officers, they had chosen to undermine the people's confidence in their government by introducing a hot virus. Draden and his team believed the village was their first large test. There had to have been other smaller experiments.

Lupa Suku was the perfect village to test the virus on. The people preferred to do their trading via boat, didn't allow outsiders to come to their village without a good reason or an invitation. They were secretive, mostly, the government thought, because they had the copper mine and didn't want outsiders to know about it. They were very self-sufficient and lived in accord with the animals in the forest. Very peaceful, they used their weapons only for protection.

During the times of the year when the rain made it very difficult to travel, the tribe went weeks without being seen by others. Lupa Suku was located a quarter mile inland of the river and couldn't be seen by passersby traveling on the water, which, again, made them a perfect target. The village kept boats docked and a sentry to watch over the area and call out should there be trouble. A virus would go unseen by the sentry.

Draden moved through the forest with confidence. He knew at least one or two of the MSS would have been left behind to observe him and tell the others what he was up to. He intended to burn the village and then go hunting them. He would kill as many as possible, leaving one alive to follow back to the main MSS village.

Trap and Wyatt, like Draden, were very familiar with hemorrhagic viruses. All three had worked on combining antibodies to target specific strains of Ebola. The antibodies had successfully saved monkeys that had been infected within twenty-four hours, but as the disease progressed, the success rate had dwindled. They had been in discussions, long into the nights, on how to raise those chances for those who were in the more advanced stages of the diseases.

From his studies into most hot viruses, Draden knew he didn't have long before he would be feeling the effects. His death would be a horrible one. He had a gun, and he was going out that way for sure. He just had to make certain he didn't wait so long that his body was too ravaged by the disease to be able to make the rational decision to use a bullet. He'd seen the effects of hemorrhagic viruses on a human being and his mind shied away from his gruesome future.

Even so, he picked up the pace, winding his way along the narrow animal trails he found leading through the forest toward Lupa Suku. He knew he had to be cautious, traveling fast the way he was. There were other dangers in the forest besides the MSS.

There were only about five hundred Sumatran tigers left and one of them had chosen the area around the village as its territory. The people of the village considered it an honor and lived in harmony with the big cat. According to the reports Draden had read, the tiger had showed up when a palm mill threatened its former habitat and the peat swamp near Lupa Suku had lured the endangered animal to claim new territory. The village made an agreement with the local poachers to leave the tiger alone in exchange for trading their copper exclusively with them. Even with that agreement in place, traps were set for poachers looking for tigers or other rare animals. Draden couldn't afford to be caught in one of them.

Heavy vegetation surrounded Lupa Suku. Tall dipterocarp trees joined at the top to gather into a canopy. Climbing their trunks were woody, thick-stemmed lianas and dozens of species of epiphytes. Orchids and ferns also lived on the trunks and derived their nourishment from the air.

Flowers were everywhere, and the exotic plants and vines were surprisingly colorful. Several trees and brush held the colored flowers up and out. Cicada trees lined a path from the water to the inland village, more trees forming a barrier to the peat swamp, the flowers threatening to blossom at any moment.

Draden drank in his surroundings with both appreciation and sorrow. The beautiful path led to a village that should have been thriving. Instead, it was now a path to certain death. The stench was unbelievable. The WHO camp had been set up a distance away from Lupa Suku, but still within sight. He could see that members of the MSS had ransacked the camp after killing the workers and doctors. Some lay dead in their hazmat suits. He went right past their camp and entered the village.

It was eerily silent. A pit had been dug and the bodies had already been placed inside of it for cremation by the WHO. Even the fuel was sitting there in cans. It would burn hot and fast. Draden made a quick circuit of the village to make certain no bodies had been left behind before he doused all buildings with the accelerant and then the bodies in the pit. He lit the entire thing on fire and then backed away from the terrible heat.

He was fortunate that it wasn't raining, although the forest around Lupa Suku was saturated. He moved into deeper forest, away from the flames shooting into the air, going farther inland so that the sentries the MSS had left behind would have to actively search for him.

He covered his passing through the peat swamp, using trees to travel in rather than making his way across the wet ground. He found a nice place to wait — the branches of a hardwood tree. Around him were aromatic spice trees, but this one had a nice crotch where several branches met at the main trunk, providing him with a semi-comfortable place to rest.

Draden remained very still and quiet so that all around him the insects and rodents in the forest once more became active. They made for good sentries. He drank water he'd retrieved from one of the fallen Rangers' packs while he studied the forest around him. Fig trees were abundant, mass-producing enough fruit twice a year to feed many of the forest's inhabitants, including the endangered helmeted hornbill. The forests were rich in valuable hardwood and he saw the evidence of that all around him. The tree he'd chosen was in the middle of a grove of exotic fruit trees that attracted a tremendous amount of wildlife.

Colorful birds were everywhere. He identified scarlet-rumped trogon and the red-naped trogon. Eventually, he spotted the

Asian paradise flycatcher and a blue-throated bee-eater. He'd already seen the blue-eared kingfisher when he'd been closer to the river. He looked for the rarest of the birds, the helmeted hornbill, wanting a sign of good luck, but there were none to be seen. This was a place poachers often came to trap birds to sell in other countries as there were so many sought-after species. That, in turn, could mean there were traps set by the villagers.

Farther out from the fruit trees was a small grouping of *Cinnamomum burmanni* trees. This village had everything it needed, not only to survive, but to thrive. The cinnamon in the bark could be harvested and traded as well as used by the villagers.

Draden took his time studying the layout of the forest floor. Once the members of the MSS came, he would have to move fast, kill most and then track one back to their nest. He wanted to know where every trap might be, so he didn't get caught in one. After mapping out the forest floor in every direction as far as he could see, he marked the places he thought a trap most likely would be set.

He closed his eyes and studied the effects of the virus on his body. He could find none. His guess was, going off incubation for the Ebola and Marburg viruses, he had two to twenty days to find the home of the MSS terrorists and kill them. As far as he was concerned, that gave him plenty of time to get his job done.

He might have dozed off but when the insects stopped their continuous droning, his eyes were quartering the forest floor for his prey. Two men approached from the direction of the burning village. He could smell the smoke, but the glow of the flames had died down. If the fire had licked at the surrounding trees and brush, it hadn't spread far, at least it didn't appear as though it had, thanks to the level of saturation from the continuous rain. There was nothing he could do even if the flames had found the trees and brush. Lupa Suku had to be burned for the good of the country.

Both men studied the ground, searching for signs that Draden had come this way. They were Indonesian and appeared to be used to tracking in the forest. They didn't hesitate as they moved through the dense vegetation. They were quiet and appeared to listen to the warnings of the animals and insects. Neither spotted him sitting up in the tree. He watched them for a few minutes, getting a feel for them. They talked back and forth in hushed tones, pointing out a bruised leaf and a crushed frond of fern as evidence of his passing. Since he hadn't come from that direction, he knew he wasn't the one leaving behind the signs for them to follow. Idly, he wondered who had.

He let them nose around right under the tree he sat in. Neither looked up. Not once. Their eyes were trained on the ground as they cast back and forth for any kind of a track. One squatted suddenly and pointed to the ground where Draden was certain a trap had been placed for any poachers. The trap was uncovered, proving him right.

It was hot. Rain began to fall, a steady drizzle that hit the leaves of the canopy and filtered down to the forest floor. Light was streaking through the sky, turning the rain to an eerie silver. This was a far cry from his modeling days. He waited until the guerrillas pointed in the opposite direction of the village and started to walk that way.

Very calmly, he put a bullet through the head of one and the shoulder of the second. It was deliberate and fast, a quick one-two, squeezing the trigger as he switched aim. One crumpled to the ground while the second jerked sideways, nearly went down but forced himself to stumble behind the thick buttresses of a dipterocarp tree.

Draden remained absolutely still. The two bullets had been fired fast. The sound of the gunshots had been loud, reverberating through the forest and quieting the insects. It didn't take long for the cacophony to start up again. In short time, the frogs began to join in. Mice scurried through the leaves. Beetles and ants found the dead body and the pool of blood that coated the debris on the ground. The forest returned to normal that quickly, as if the violence had never been.

The man he'd wounded would need immediate care if he wanted to live. Infections were almost a foregone conclusion in the high humidity and vast array of insects of the rain forest. As a native, the wounded man would know that. He would have to make his way back to the nest, the home of the Milisi Separatis Sumatra.

Draden didn't move, staying as still as any predator with his gaze fixed on his prey. No muscle moved. He didn't take his eyes from the man. He could just make out a part of his thigh and boot. The MSS member was stoic, but the pain had to be excruciating. Draden had made certain the shoulder was shattered. He went for maximum pain. He'd also put the man's dominant arm out of commission.

The man held out for over an hour. He had to have been worried about blood loss at that point. Draden was. He didn't want the man to bleed out on him and die. It would be far easier to follow him back to the nest than to backtrack.

2

The home of the Milisi Separatis Sumatra was a good distance from the river, and Draden found it an hour after the sun rose. It was still close enough that they could use the river for escaping or traveling. They had established themselves in a village of similar size to Lupa Suku, which Draden found a little ironic. One village they had captured, keeping the occupants prisoners, treating them almost as slaves, while another they'd annihilated with a hemorrhagic virus.

The people in both villages were Indonesian, the same as the members of the MSS. The cell wanted to overthrow the government and to do that, they were hurting their own people. Draden had never seen the logic in that, how they could convince themselves that what they were doing was justified because they believed in the end game. As far as he was concerned, the MSS was a band of murderers.

He spent most of the day studying them. He wanted to be able to identify every single member and hopefully learn their habits quickly. He was good at detail. He watched them from each direction, circling around the tight cluster of houses until he knew their routines. The man he'd wounded had been taken to a small infirmary just on the outskirts on the western side. He observed a man being dragged out of one of the homes and taken forcibly to the small makeshift hospital.

Draden waited until nightfall before he entered the village. He kept his hands gloved and wore a mask over his mouth and nose to be safe. He didn't plan on infecting the residents, but he did plan on killing as many of the terrorists as he possibly could in one night. The village was heavily guarded, everyone stirred up after the man he'd shot stumbled back into their camp. MSS members had been easy to identify, running around, shoving weapons at people and shouting orders. They had doubled the guard around the village, allowing Draden to spot every position they used to protect their home turf.

He noted each member, paying attention to faces and identifying marks. None of them made any attempt to hide themselves.

If anything, they wanted the villagers to recognize them in order to pay deference to them. Some were aggressive and belligerent toward the people, and others ignored them or were more courteous. It didn't matter to Draden what they were like. They had committed mass murder and clearly had been hoping, by infecting Draden, that they would kill many more.

He needed to know where the virus had originated. How they had gotten it. By the time darkness fell he was ready for warfare and had a plan. Ignoring the rain, he slipped past the guard and made his way to the infirmary first. He told himself it was to take out the man who had tried to kill his teammates, but he knew it was to check on the villager they'd dragged from his home. He was most likely the closest thing the inhabitants of the village had to a doctor.

Most of the houses were very small and built from an amalgamation of any type of materials possible, including wood, mud and rusty corrugated tin. Some were built on stilts with thatched roofs. All electricity was powered by forest water rather than government power lines, and the people relied on agriculture to survive. They grew their crops, harvested them and sold them, mostly utilizing the river for their farmer's market. Like Lupa Suku, they were just isolated enough to be a perfect village for the MSS to infiltrate and then take over.

Draden peered through the dirty window. He could see the man he had shot lying on a cot, moaning and rolling back and forth in obvious pain. Two others, clearly his friends, tried to get him to drink water and let them look at whatever the "doctor" had done to him. The "doctor" lay on the floor in a pool of blood. Clearly, the village healer had been out of his depth trying to work on a shattered shoulder.

The three men were grouped close together. Calmly, Draden opened the door to the infirmary, and as they looked up, he threw a knife into the one whose gun hung by a shoulder strap. The second knife took the guard who had laid his weapon on the end of the bed. Both blades hit dead center on the carotid artery running prominently in their necks.

He closed the door behind him, crossed the room and shoved both dead men aside with his foot. It was only when Draden loomed over the man on the bed like the grim reaper that he realized anything was wrong. He opened his mouth to yell, but Draden slammed a blade deep into his throat and then wiped the blood on his shirt. He recovered his throwing knives and went to the door.

Thanks to his enhancements, he had excellent hearing, and he detected no footsteps nor the sound of voices. That didn't mean he was in the clear. He snapped off the yellow light, so pale as to be almost nonexistent. That was a way the members of the MSS gave their locations away: they used electricity after dark when the villagers didn't.

Cautiously opening the door, he slipped out into the cover of darkness. Above all other things, GhostWalkers were enhanced to be able to disappear into the night, fade into darkness and remain undetected by an enemy no matter how close they got to him — or her. Draden used his abilities to move like a wraith through the village, finding the home of the one he'd watched commanding the others.

Unlike most of the houses that had been built from every kind of material and even pieces of machinery they'd found or traded for, this house was more modern although very small. It was made of hardwood with a sloping thatched roof. The structure appeared a little lopsided, but it was sound and in much better shape than all of the other homes. Presumably the head of the village resided there.

Draden made his way through the buildings with porches held up by sticks of wood that looked as if they would snap in two if anyone of weight stepped on the planks. There was a small stick fence that went nowhere in front of the house. Three severed heads were stuck on taller poles and they'd obviously been there for a while. They looked grotesque, even in the dark, and Draden was certain this was the village elder, his wife and most probably his grown son. The commander of the MSS was inside, and the heads served as a warning to the people that he was in charge and any resistance would be met with swift retaliation.

Draden made his way around the strange little half fence and gained the porch. He moved from window to window, peering into the rooms. There were only four. The main room, the sleeping room, bathroom and a kitchen. The rooms ran right into one another with ornate tapestries hanging in the archways to separate each space. He could see the commander dragging something heavy to the door.

Draden pressed himself tight against the side of the house. He didn't go up to the roof but remained absolutely still as the leader of the MSS opened the door and dragged a body out. It was a young woman. She was naked. Dead. He could see she'd been strangled. Most likely she'd been the wife of the young man whose head was on the fence.

The commander shoved her away from the door, rolling her body toward the edge of the planked decking as if it were garbage. A long sword was in his hand and he lifted it high and brought it down on her neck. The blade was so sharp it severed the woman's head. He spit and shoved the body with his foot in an effort to roll it off the deck.

When she didn't go off, he grunted, propped the sword up by the door, opened his pants and peed, the stream going over the body and then to the ground below. He turned, looked right at Draden, and then was back inside, shutting the door. Draden could hear him moving around, his footsteps going toward the sleeping room.

The GhostWalker followed him around on the outside wall. The sides of the house jutted out to nearly touch the end of the outside planking, making it difficult for a big man to traverse the narrow passageway, so Draden clung to the side of the house like a giant spider.

Once in the sleeping chamber, the commander stripped and stretched out on the thin woven mattress. He cursed a couple of times, clearly not used to the hard floor the elder had preferred to sleep on. Finally, he lay on his back, hands behind his head, staring up at the ceiling.

Draden once again studied the layout of the room. He had excellent night vision thanks to the doctor genetically altering him when he was physically enhanced. The cat DNA edited into his genes made for some useful improvements. He measured the room in his mind, mapping it out, and then he used the wall again to navigate his way back to the front porch.

It shouldn't have surprised him that the commander had murdered the elder and his family, including the woman he had obviously forced into his bed after killing her husband, but it did. This man had orchestrated the murder of an entire village, so it stood to reason he wouldn't mind killing any of those in the little self-sufficient settlement.

Draden picked up the sword and, ignoring the front door, went under the house. Pushing the sword forward with one hand, he used his elbows and toes to make his way to the exact spot where the mattress was, although he could have crawled on his hands and knees easily. The floorboards were extremely thin. The planks forming the porch had bowed under his weight when he walked on them, threatening to break.

His strength was enormous, and so was the burning need to kill this man. He'd felt this way on more than one occasion. The drive was an actual need, like breathing, consuming him, almost taking him out of his body so that the rage was a separate entity. He was calm. Air moved in and out of his lungs steadily. He had become the perfect killing machine.

His entire focus was on his target. Nothing existed at that moment but the man lying on a palliasse a woman had made with her own two hands for her husband. Draden visualized her killer so clearly that the floor seemed to drop away and he stared through the boards and woven pad to the backside of the commander.

Taking a breath, he let his rage loose, the need that was living and breathing inside of him. Using every ounce of his strength, Draden slammed the sword straight up through the wood and thin cushion and right through the back of the man's neck, severing his spine. The blade sliced through wood, straw, flesh and bone, burying itself to the hilt. Draden kept his hand on the hilt, waiting to make certain the commander was dead before he rolled to the edge of the porch, leaving the sword in place.

He slipped out of the village so he could take out the guards. There were plenty of them. They surrounded the little community from every vantage point. In each of the four corners there were two guards posted. He knew they were in communication. The modern technology and weapons, in spite of the fact that the commander had a sword — which Draden was positive had belonged to the elder — told him the MSS was well funded. Whoever had begun this movement had recruited locals who knew their way around the forest and a weapon.

Draden exterminated the forest-side guards one by one. He wanted more than one escape route. The terrorist cell was prepared for escape or defense by water. Boats were docked on the riverside. The village was inland, but only by a mile. He ran nightly, and he was fast. With his enhanced speed, he could cover that mile in well under three minutes even in the forested terrain.

He killed the two on the north corner next, leaving the bodies where they lay. He searched them for weapons and radios, taking whatever he found or destroying it. For a moment he was uneasy, feeling eyes on him. It should have been impossible to spot him, but he went to ground, going with his gut, rolling away from the bodies toward the next guard and staying as low as possible.

Once he was a distance from the two kills, he used the military crawl to make his way to the next guard. The man was watching the forest in front of him, just as he'd been told. He was careful, but the village was at his back. He thought the danger was the river and anything coming at them through the trees, so he scanned continually, never once considering that the enemy he feared was behind him, already creeping so close that if he stepped back, he'd step right into him. Draden rose up like the ghost he was, directly behind the guard, one hand covering his mouth while the other slammed the blade deep into the base of his skull, severing the spinal cord.

Two guards had been stationed at each of the four corners around the village. Between each set of corner guards were five men. Draden managed to take out two of the corners and all five of the guards between two of them. That left at least fourteen more guards. He was a machine, not feeling the grueling effects on his muscles as he made the slow crawl between targets, but the longer he was in the field, moving from kill to kill, the more he felt eyes on him.

Uneasy, he paused just as he was coming up on the third corner, the one also facing the river. The rain was steady now, falling in fine drops little more than a mist, so that a gray veil seemed to be descending over the forest. He could use that to conceal himself and hunt for whoever was shadowing him. He tried to "feel" the energy. He could always feel an enemy long before he came upon one, but this time he didn't seem to ever be close enough to get a feel for whoever was watching.

He gained ground under cover of the darkness, coming up on the two soldiers who were clearly uneasy. They continually tried to raise the other guards, their voices reflecting their growing fear. Unlike the others, they turned, going back to back, weapons ready while they talked frantically into their radios, now raising the alarm that too many of the guards weren't answering.

Shylah Cosmos lay in the slight depression that afforded her some cover, puzzling out the identity of the lone man ruthlessly cutting down the guards of the Milisi Separatis Sumatra. He was not just good; he was a freaking killing machine. He could have been a robot programmed to kill. There didn't appear to be one wasted motion. He didn't seem to need rest. He just flowed across the ground, like a dark wraith in the night, like a ghost . . .

She gasped and shoved her knuckles into her mouth, biting down to keep from making a sound. He had to be a GhostWalker. She was looking at a legitimate GhostWalker. The real deal. He was that good. That smooth. So quiet he couldn't be real. He looked more a predator, more an animal flowing across the ground than a human. She blinked several times to keep her focus. She'd been following him ever since she'd caught a shadow sliding into the village and then the infirmary.

He'd gone right into the enemy stronghold without so much as a flinch. He could really have been a ghost for all the MSS members noticed him as he walked among them. No way could Shylah not have noticed him. He had a distinctive build. He seemed larger than life, but maybe it was because she was watching him do the impossible. In one night he had made at least twenty-five kills single-handedly. That was impressive. Four in the village, three of the four corners, and that was two guards each. Across the back of the village, in front and down one side, were five each. He might have made more kills had the guards not been in continual contact with one another.

She knew that the soldiers would try to raise their commander, and she knew that he was already dead. She'd seen the Ghost-Walker do the impossible and kill him. She knew it was a clean kill because she'd actually gotten into the house to see with her own eyes. Up close, the kill had been grisly, the sword blade slicing cleanly through the man's throat. The dead commander was staring up at the ceiling, eyes wide open, the blade protruding. The eyes made her sick to her stomach and she'd had to turn away. Still, as deaths went, she considered it the perfect ending for a man like that, although she would have liked to have known he suffered before he went.

Shylah had seen the effects of the virus on the people of Lupa Suku and she was certain the commander had access to the virus and had infected the villagers with it. She'd been tracking the three virologists who had created the virus for some time and her search had brought her here to Sumatra. There had been five incidents that she knew of to date, all occurring right around the Banyuasin River. The first three had been small and could have been easily overlooked, but she'd been sent in as soon as the first incident had been recorded.

A fisherman on the Banyuasin River had found three men dead, their bodies bloated and ravaged by some horrible disease, but each in a different dwelling. The three men had makeshift camps they'd used as a base to hunt and fish. They hadn't been together, nor did they seem to have had any contact with one another when she'd traced their movements, yet all three men had died the same way.

The fisherman who'd found the bodies had called the authorities and they'd made a report. Dr. Whitney immediately had been notified that an unknown virus appearing to be hemorrhagic had killed three random people, men who made their living on the river. Unfortunately, Whitney suspected his three missing virologists had created the virus and she'd been sent in to confirm. More, Whitney was certain the three were testing the virus, or showing buyers what it could do. He feared the virus had been offered for sale to the MSS and they had used it on the unsuspecting forgotten tribe.

She'd been angry when she saw the ravaged remains of a once peaceful and thriving community. The people of Lupa Suku had been passive and had lived in accord with the forest and the animals there. They were self-sufficient and loyal to one another. They didn't deserve to die the way they had, callously thrown away for someone's gain. Whatever the agenda of the MSS, it shouldn't have mattered more than those people.

She had to admit she was still angry — angry enough that she felt satisfaction when she spotted that shadow of death flowing through the village taking no prisoners. She'd followed him, very careful to make sure that he hadn't spotted her and turned that bloodthirsty knife on her. Now she lay in the dirt and rotting vegetation, with ants and spiders crawling around her and over her, watching him. Every muscle in her body was in knots.

She had a bad feeling and wanted to shout at him to get out of there, to run away. Or dissolve in the way of ghosts. He'd taken too many lives and he didn't seem to want to stop. The alarm had gone out and now the rest of the group would be actively looking for him, especially once they tried to rouse their commander and found him dead. That would happen at any moment.

The GhostWalker had to know he was blown. He *had* to. She wasn't supposed to make her presence known. She had a job to do and she couldn't do it if anyone knew about her. She was supposed to stay off the radar. She couldn't be seen backing the man who had killed so many members of the MSS.

He was not going to stop. She could only watch in silence as the shadow rose up almost at the two guards' feet. His thirsty knife slashed across one throat and then the other. It happened so fast neither man probably ever saw him. Neither had turned his head toward him before the second throat had been cut and the shadow had gone to ground.

Watching the two MSS realize they were dead, that the life was draining from them as blood poured onto the ground, was something out of a horror movie. She couldn't look away. She was wholly mesmerized by the way they stared at each other in silent terror, and then slowly crumpled to the ground like empty gunnysacks.

Gunfire erupted, pulling her attention back to the assassin. She couldn't see him, just the blaze of orange and blue muzzle blasts as several guards opened fire around the station where their two fallen comrades had gone down. She thought they were firing blindly, but then she saw him. He was running along a deer trail that led straight toward her — and the river.

He took her breath away. He was solid, all muscle and she could see, even with the veil of gray rain, that his muscles rippled deliciously as he ran. His tee was plastered on him, so that he might as well not have been wearing one. She could see his body moving effortlessly, even when he leapt over fallen tree trunks and smaller brush.

He didn't carry anything with him, so if he had a war bag, he'd stashed it somewhere. Did that mean he'd come to the encampment armed with only a knife? He was heading for the river and a small army of very angry MSS soldiers chased after him. He was fast though, like that machine she'd named him before.

Shylah scooted back as he came close, but there was no way to move as he veered away from a particularly large tree trunk and headed straight for the depression where she was secreted. Bullets thunked into the bark, sending splinters flying into the air, but she could only watch in fascination as the man loomed over her.

Holy cow, he was the hottest man she'd ever seen in her life. The thing of fantasies, movie star quality. Or a rock star. Someone a woman could spend hours just staring at.

She had all of three seconds because he never broke stride, vaulting over her easily. There wasn't even the sound of heavy breathing and he was sprinting full out. Her heart beat way too fast and it wasn't because half the MSS army was chasing him. In real life, men like that didn't exist.

He disappeared around a bend in the trail, and she rolled down and away from the guards trailing him. They were still a little farther out, and she had every confidence that she could get away without being seen. *He* had seen her. For one moment, their eyes locked. His were blue, but that was far too mundane to describe them. Almost a pure dark blue, a true navy. She'd seen them for a second, but it didn't matter with her enhanced vision. She would dream about those eyes for the rest of her life.

She scrambled on all fours down to the little tunnel small animals had made in the brush and crawled inside. She was fast, sliding almost on the bare ground along the worn, very narrow path that led to the river. This was a game trail, one smaller animals used when they were nervous, which was all the time. It was the fastest way to the river and the safest for her. She went fast, hearing the guards running, still firing their guns, although she doubted if they could even see the GhostWalker.

She burst out from the tunnel just before the bank of the river, coming to an upright position, still moving. Boats were tied up and several of the MSS were rushing up the embankment, firing steadily, over and over at the running GhostWalker. It was his poor luck that other members of the MSS had returned at such an unexpected hour.

She saw the GhostWalker's head jerk back and then his body was in the water. The guards continued to shoot at him as he went under. Shylah didn't hesitate but kept on running so that she went right to the edge and dove. She was nowhere near as good in the water as her friend Bellisia, whom she had known and trained with her entire life. Still, she was a strong swimmer and could stay underwater for long periods of time. She wasn't without her own enhancements.

She swam to the spot where she saw him go under. Bullets streaked through the water, raining down as more soldiers from the village joined those who had come from the river. The streaks looked silver in the murky, dark water. She went deeper, grateful for her enhanced vision but still unable to see very far in front of her. Her foot kicked him, and she grabbed. He was a dead weight and her heart sank. There was no time to examine him, she had to get him — and herself — away from the rapidly firing guards.

Shylah knew they couldn't see her, but they were so angry, they kept shooting blindly into the water. She struck out strongly for the other side of the river. It wasn't terribly wide, well within her range, even toting dead weight with one hand. There was a slight bend in the river and she went with the current, letting it help her sweep around that bend as she continued to pull for the bank.

To her dismay, it was much steeper on that side. She rolled the GhostWalker over so he was faceup and kept swimming, trying to find a place to drag him even partially onto land. Time slowed down, and a part of her wanted to panic. Then it was there, an embankment that stretched to the very edge of the river. She made for it, redoubling her efforts at speed.

The moment she had him half in, half out of the water, she rolled him to his side to try to clear his lungs and then listened for breathing and heartbeat. There appeared to be neither. She began CPR immediately, fitting her mouth over his, blowing air into his lungs and then doing chest compressions.

Come on, ghost man. You want this. You

want to live. I know you do. Breathe for me. Take a breath. She wasn't about to lose him. She listened a second time, checked his pulse, breathed for him. For both of them. All the while she listened for sounds of the MSS, just in case they had leapt into their boats and tried to sweep both sides of the river for his body.

There was a wound on his temple. She had given it a cursory examination. The bullet had shaved skin off his head, probably knocked him unconscious, or when he dove, he'd hit a rock. Either way, he'd lost consciousness in the river and his lungs were full of water. She wasn't letting him drown. When she brushed the blood from the side of his temple, more welled up and her heart leapt. Beneath her hand he stirred. Coughed. Water bubbled up. She turned him onto his side and he coughed again, more water draining from his lungs.

She turned her head toward the river, listening for the sound of the angry terrorists hunting them. Without warning, a giant hand wrapped around her throat and she was slammed down into the dirt. The GhostWalker rose above her, his face a mask of fury.

"What the *fuck* did you just do?"

Her heart accelerated to the point where

she thought it might explode. He was so strong there was no breaking his hold. She caught at his wrist, but it felt like she wrapped her fingers around steel. There was no talking. No way words could escape from that grip. He turned his head away and coughed more. He spat water and looked toward the river, clearly listening for the enemy.

He'd been dead. Well, he would have been dead had she not given him CPR, yet he had come out of it fully cognizant. Completely aware.

He turned his head back toward her and those dark, navy-colored eyes bore down into hers. She stayed very still, trying to keep her body relaxed. If she didn't tense up, it was possible he would relax his grip and she'd be able to break free. She wasn't certain that would do much good; she'd seen him run and he was the fastest she'd ever seen.

"Did you give me CPR?" It was a demand.

She tried to nod. His lashes swept down for a brief moment, and she saw despair etched deeply into his face. Her heart ceased to beat and then began to pound as sudden knowledge filled her. She knew he was infected. She didn't know how, but it was that look on his face. The way his hold on her throat gentled. He shook his head and moved back away from her.

"We have to get out of here." His voice was a mere whisper of sound.

"You've been exposed to the virus, haven't you?" Now her heart was wild. Out of control. She was terrified. She'd seen the horrific way the men and women had died. She knew, but she still needed his confirmation.

He caught her hand and rose, pulling her with him. Her arms and legs suddenly felt like spaghetti. There was a strange roaring in her head. Chaos reigned in her brain. She began to hyperventilate. The virus. He was infected with the virus and she'd put her mouth over his and breathed into his lungs. Her fingers had wiped at the blood on his temple. She had his blood on her at that very moment.

His fingers tightened around her upper arm. "We have to move. Right now."

The urgency in his voice caught at her. She was an elite, highly trained soldier. It didn't matter if the worst had happened; she would deal with it later. She straightened her spine, looked into those eyes of his and nodded.

Her reward was instant. His expression softened, and he gave her a quick nod of approval and then began to jog, still holding her arm, forcing her to go with him down the embankment.

What are you doing? They're going to be on the river in boats. Without thinking she went to telepathy because the women she'd trained with all could speak mind to mind.

They'll be expecting us on this side. We're going back in and crossing to the other side. There was a place where the forest came right down to the edge of the water. We'll cross there so they won't be able to track us.

She hadn't expected the intimacy of his voice in her head. It had a smoothness to it that gave way now and then to gravel. The way he moved in her mind stole something from her. She liked that little nod of approval he'd given her as if she were his equal just because she hadn't given into the hysteria welling up.

She didn't object, and he didn't slow down, his fingers never leaving her arm, so she didn't slow either. She was worried about his injury. It had to hurt even though he was the smoothest runner she'd ever met.

I'm Shylah Cosmos. Well, Shylah is the name my sisters gave me. I dislike my real name with a passion. Peony. Who is named Peony?

Draden Freeman. I believe I know your

sisters. Bellisia and Zara? Did Whitney send you here? And there's nothing wrong with Peony.

She almost stopped jogging she was so shocked. He knew Bellisia and Zara? *Are they alive? They left separately on missions and we never heard from them again. And there* is *something wrong with being named Peony, so never call me that.*

Whitney knows they're alive. He came after them even after he said he'd let them go.

Dr. Peter Whitney had found her in an orphanage. Zara and Bellisia had been found the same way. Whitney had chosen them because he had a talent for recognizing others with undeveloped psychic abilities. He brought the infants to one of his many secret military facilities to experiment on them. He considered them throwaways. In his quest to find the perfect supersoldier, he experimented on the girls and when he thought he'd perfected what he was looking for, he psychically and genetically enhanced the soldiers in his GhostWalker program.

Are they okay?

They were both sent to China. Bellisia and Zara thought you had been too. But yes, they're alive and well.

They were nearing the last of the shore before the embankment began to rise. She could barely make out the rising bank. The rain had gone from light to a steady downpour, making it very difficult to see. There was no moon. Even with her enhanced vision, the rain hammered at her face, making her blink so much she couldn't focus on what was ahead. Draden didn't seem to have the same problem. He kept moving forward, heading straight for that last little bit of shore.

We're going in, he warned her.

He still hadn't let her go, and for the first time it occurred to her that he was making certain she couldn't escape. She was even more sure when he pulled her right into the water with him.

I swim better with two arms. Shylah tested her theory.

If you're Shylah, sister to Bellisia and Zara, you can swim with your hands tied behind your back.

That was true. She'd done it on more than one occasion. It was part of their training.

I'm not going anywhere. I'm not about to take the chance of infecting anyone else with this virus. I was here to try to track the source. Whitney is an asshole, but he definitely doesn't want a hemorrhagic virus let loose on any country, let alone the United States.

Swim with me, we'll sort it out on the other

side. I'm not losing you in the river. Tell me if you have to go up for air.

She doubted if he could lose her. He was too omnipotent. Invincible. Even with having to do CPR on him after his injury, there was a part of her that thought it was possible he would have miraculously come back to life without her. And she wouldn't have to go to the surface for air. She could breathe shallowly, let one tiny bit of air out at a time and last for a very long time if needed.

She used her legs, kicking strongly. She helped with her one free arm, but he essentially was a bullet in the water, speeding through like an otter to the other side. When their feet touched the bottom, they were in the mangrove forest, the roots rising all around them in the brackish water.

We have to get into the trees before they see us. Try not to make a sound.

That annoyed her. She was no amateur. She'd been observing the members of the MSS for some time without detection. *You didn't have a clue I was anywhere near you.* She couldn't keep the snippy note out of her tone.

Shylah didn't want to think about the virus and her exposure to it or what it meant. Death. Certain death. She could deal with dying, it was the *how.* Death from this particular hemorrhagic virus had looked horrific.

Don't. We'll figure that out later. Right now we need to make the few feet into the forest. They will come after us and that's what we want, just not right now.

She noticed he didn't apologize for thinking she was an idiot and needed a warning when in enemy territory. *Why do we want them to come after us?*

Because we're going to turn the tables on them and kill as many as possible.

She remained silent, and this time made certain he was completely out of her mind. She didn't want to chance him reading her thoughts. She knew all the members of the MSS were to blame for what had happened to the people of Lupa Suku. Intellectually, she knew. She was fine with the GhostWalker killing the commander of the terrorist cell. She'd seen the atrocities he'd committed. She didn't mind Draden killing the guards — after all, he had to escape. She wasn't in the least opposed to killing — that would make her a hypocrite — but she wasn't certain he could stop killing. The death toll was already so high.

Draden remained crouched half in and half out of the mangroves, making himself smaller by keeping his lower half in the water. Roots protruded, rising up like sentries. He was still enough that someone looking through the driving rain might think he was part of the trees rather than a human.

You didn't kill all those guards to escape. She knew it came out somewhere between an accusation and a little bit of awe. *You wanted them dead. All of them.*

He glanced back at her over his shoulder, his incredible eyes moving over her face. Seeing her. Focusing on her. The way he looked at her made her heart begin to accelerate. *Holy cow, Draden. You should be outlawed. If those guards were women, you would just have to look at them like that and they'd worship at your feet.* She tried going for humor, but it was too close to the truth for her to inject laughter into her mind.

He gave her a faint grin that raised her temperature about a hundred degrees. The flash of his white teeth, that mouth, the way his face softened just for a moment to let humor escape, had butterfly wings fluttering in her stomach. Maybe other places too but she wasn't acknowledging them. She'd lost her chance for that to ever happen. She would die with no experiences. None.

I don't see you worshipping yet, Shylah.

She had been enhanced as a soldier, trained as one, and she was going to die as one. Draden was right, they couldn't take the chance of infecting anyone else. Still, she really didn't want to die that way. If they were going to wage war on the enemy and she wasn't killed in battle, she was saving her last bullet for herself. In spite of her grim thoughts, she couldn't help but appreciate his sense of humor.

Not yet but give it time. I'm totally susceptible to good looks. On the other hand, I don't like bossy men, so if you want worshipping from me, you'll have to keep your mouth closed and let me boss you.

That fantasy mouth smiled. The kind of smile that could melt the panties off a nun. *Holy cow.* He could completely *own* a woman with that smile. He clearly appreciated her sense of humor, although she meant what she said. The GhostWalker was just a little too dominant for someone like her.

Good to know. About the talking too much. I'm not known for that, but I'll be much more careful.

She loved that he could tease her when they were in such a dire situation. It was a great distraction from the sound of voices coming toward them on the water. She could see the faint, distorted lights shining through the sheets of rain.

Go under. Stay under until I tell you otherwise. Don't make a sound.

Shylah obediently sank beneath the brackish water. *That is a prime example of what I was just saying. Your order of not making noise was unnecessary. I'm a soldier and I don't need you telling me what to do.*

Every soldier needs a commander and it looks like I'm yours.

You're a soldier. You need a commander. What makes you the boss? I'm bigger than you are, Draden said, his voice just a little arrogant.

Shylah refrained from answering. What was the point? He *was* bigger.

3

It took what seemed like forever for the boat filled with the Milisi Separatis Sumatra soldiers to move down the river and go around the long curve. Shylah had no problem staying underwater, even when it was murky, and she had no idea what was in the water with her. She could see with her enhanced vision, so if anything did come at her, she would know. The roiling in her stomach wasn't that. The knots and growing terror weren't from anything creepy in the water, holding her breath too long or the fact the hottest and most lethal man in the world was pressing his thigh against hers. It was knowledge. Time. The clock ticking.

She couldn't keep her mind on the soldiers making their way down the river, searching for signs of them. It was the fact that she had time to think. This gorgeous man, Draden Freeman, had somehow been infected with the hemorrhagic virus that had killed an entire village. It would kill him and eventually kill her. She had to cut herself off from every human being . . .

Stop thinking about it.

That voice. When it slipped into her mind, he poured in after it. Heat. Filling every space in her mind unexpectedly. She was lonely. How could she not be? But she was someone who knew she was intelligent. She had amazing skills, taught from childhood. Whitney had tried to undermine her self-worth, but Shylah knew better than to let him succeed.

She believed in herself and her dedication to her country. That was hers, not something Whitney could take from her, but self-esteem didn't make her any less lonely. Before, growing up, she'd had her two best friends, Bellisia and Zara. Then they were gone, and she was by herself. She would die that way . . .

Stop.

His fingers settled around her arm and he gently pulled her into him. The way he did it centered her, his touch a whisper against her skin, no more, yet she found herself tucked in close to his body. There was heat just like in her mind, as if inside Draden was a fire, burning hot and out of control, threatening to consume both of them.

She didn't know where she got that image, but it was there in her mind, which meant he got the same one. *This is embarrassing.*

Why? I am hot right now. I want to kill every single one of those fuckers. Most of the time rage for me is ice, but not this time. They killed every man, woman and child in that village. Those people were peaceful. They tried to live their lives in the best way possible, not asking for anything from anyone. You bet I'm hot.

Put that way, she understood. *They were testing the virus. I've been tracking the men who created it.*

He pulled out of her mind abruptly. She knew because she felt bereft. Starkly alone. The feeling was raw and ugly after having him there with her. She wanted him back, and that wasn't an intelligent response. She needed to stand on her own two feet at all times. That was what made her strong. Depending on someone else only made for weakness. With what was coming, she couldn't afford to be weak.

Do you know who they are? Their identity?

He was back, sliding into her mind so easily, as if they had been communicating telepathically for years. She could tell he was one of the rare anchors. He could draw psychic energy to him, so others wouldn't overload on it.

Whitney employs several top scientists. Most have their own labs scattered around the world. He oversees every project, gives his consent or nixes experiments. He's the banker, so if he doesn't approve, it isn't done.

At least, that was in theory. Shylah knew differently now. *Three of Whitney's protégés worked together in his laboratory in France, but they broke away and set up a remote lab here in Indonesia. Two were Americans and one was Indonesian. Whitney talked about them often and how brilliant they were. In the last few months, he's been angry with them.*

Do you know where their remote lab here is located?

She nodded. *It's several miles from here. They're gone and have been for a couple of days.*

I'll need to see it, if we can get there without infecting anyone.

I can take you there.

Do you know what the fight was about, the one that created a big enough rift that would cause the three scientists to leave Whitney and his endless supply of money?

Whitney nixed their project. They wanted to create new viruses as weapons. Whitney was violently opposed to the idea. He's all about creating supersoldiers, not destroying the world with a pandemic.

His scientists have gone rogue and you were sent here . . .

To kill them and destroy their work. It wasn't exactly sexy telling a gorgeous man that you came to kill someone, let alone three someones. Shylah was a weapon. She had no problem with killing the three men responsible for the creation of such a horrific virus as the one that had been visited on the people of Lupa Suku.

The Milisi Separatis Sumatra had to have gotten the virus from them.

Draden tapped her thigh. Up high. Her heart nearly stopped.

The boat's around the curve. You stay here, and I'll go see how many of them I can take out. It shouldn't take me long. If I haven't come back . . .

I'm going with you.

That isn't necessary. I work better alone.

That hurt, especially as he'd been treating her as a fellow soldier. *Doesn't matter how well you work alone. I'm better that way too, but we can't take chances. With two of us going after those in the boat, we'll get all of them.*

His fingers tightened around her arm. *Let's do it then. You follow my orders.*

She took a breath and went under again, allowing him to pull her toward deeper water in the middle of the river. *Why should I take orders from you?*

Are you an officer?

I should be. Whitney wouldn't allow that.

Amusement flooded her mind. *A man after my own heart. Keep the little rebels in the kitchen.*

Watch yourself, hotshot. You may be the best-looking man on earth, but I'm behind you wielding a very large knife and I'm not afraid to use it.

Bloodthirsty wench. At least you have a knife. Kitchenware, presumably.

He powered through the water like a rocket. The boat with the MSS members was chugging along slowly, spotlighting both banks in an effort to find where Shylah and Draden had come out of the water. It would probably be smarter to allow the terrorists to think they had drowned, but already, they were close to catching up. She could feel the vibrations of the engine.

You wish it was kitchenware, soldier. It's big enough to be a machete and twice as sharp. I could give you a little nick, so you could test how sharp.

Woman, save it for the enemy. There was a small pause. *You ever do this before?*

She'd gone up against Whitney's supersoldiers when he wanted to test her and his newest model soldiers. It was either be victorious or die. Whitney's experiments were useless to him if they couldn't perform to his expectations.

Yes. In the water as well as out. I'm not Bellisia, but I do all right. She preferred to drop from above and kill whenever possible. That didn't mean she couldn't come out of the water. She was genetically enhanced, and that meant Whitney had thought about whatever she might need. *Don't worry about me, Draden. I can keep up.*

For the first time, his fingers slipped from her arm. Strangely, whereas she'd wanted his hand off her, now she felt as though she was completely alone again, and Whitney was testing her. She didn't like the feeling and wanted Draden back.

We're coming up on the boat. You take the left, closest to the bank. There are six targets. Three on each side. The spotter has to be taken out immediately. He's on your side. I'll take out the commander. The four will begin shooting. If you're hit, go to deep water and hunker down. I'll come for you. I'm a doctor so . . .

I've been infected with the virus. A quick death is preferable to that kind of death.

Maybe. Don't count me out. I want to see their lab. In any case, one step at a time. Take the spotter and then the one on the far end of the boat. Don't work your way down the line. Middle man is the weakest.

How would he know that? They'd been underwater the entire time the boat chugged past. He'd been talking to her. He couldn't have seen those in the boat. She hadn't.

You didn't look. It's no big deal. If you think you can't do this, you need to tell me.

Was that exasperation in his voice? She wanted to kick him. It wasn't like she was having the best day of her life, and it was a perfectly normal question. *Men like you are the reason I like to work alone. I didn't say I couldn't do this, nor did I imply I was worried about doing it. What's the countdown?*

Prickly, aren't you? I was just looking out for you. Are you in position?

Shylah had to swim just under the boat to keep from being seen. It wasn't difficult as the boat was really going slow. The spotter had his light high and pointed to the shore, so they could examine the bank for any sign of them emerging.

On go. Three. Two. One. Go.

He didn't believe in playing around. She surged out of the water, plunged her blade through the spotter's heart and then sank below the surface before the body had time to fall. She swam toward the front of the boat and her next target.

Draden had taken the commander, yanking him into the water, stabbing him through the throat and heart, letting him go and slitting the throat of the man closest to him. Shylah's foot kicked a body as she rocketed up and stabbed her target just as he let loose a barrage of bullets where Draden had disappeared beneath the surface.

Her breath caught in her throat, terrified that Draden might be hit and she'd be left alone with the virus eating her internal organs, turning them to mush. She pushed away from the boat and went back under before her target toppled over the side, almost onto her. She dove deeper, swimming to the end of the boat again. Draden was coming around, converging on her target as well. All three of his were down, leaving only one more.

She couldn't help but admire how fast and efficient he was. He had a head injury and yet he didn't so much as hesitate. He'd killed three of the MSS members in seconds and had swept around the boat to provide a distraction. He hit the back of the boat with the hilt of his knife, deliberately scraping.

Her target turned toward the noise, shooting blindly into the dark, murky water toward the sound.

The moment he turned, firing his weapon, she shot out of the water, slashing at the back of his thighs, deep cuts that took him down. He retained his weapon, shooting into the air as he fell. She was behind him, holding herself out of the water with one hand, knife ready with the other. As he went to his knees and then fell forward, she slammed the blade deep into the back of his neck, severing the spinal cord.

The gunfire will draw others. Hurry, Shylah. We have to go. They're already close.

Draden caught her arm and yanked her down almost before she could take a breath. He took her to the deeper water, settling into thick layers of sediment, anchoring her beside him with his hands on her waist. The current tugged at her. Something hit Draden, but she couldn't see what it was, only felt the movement of his body.

She could hear the sound of an engine now, as a second boat chugged through the water with more MSS seeking to find their comrades. They could hear the voices of the soldiers calling out to the dead.

Are we going after them? She didn't want to, but she would if Draden thought it was a good idea. She was tired. Very tired. And scared. Very scared.

They're on alert. I have no doubt that we could take them, but why risk injury? We have a plan. Let's stick to it.

She was glad someone had a plan. She didn't. Her plan had gone to hell the moment she realized he was infected and she probably was as well. She closed her eyes and let herself relax. There was nothing else to do. They had killed six more MSS members. It was a large group. The recruiting had been heavy. Whitney had been watching them for some time and knew they had serious funding. He was trying to find out who was the moneyman because their goal wasn't just to take down the government in Indonesia, they were targeting anyone American. That meant if they were testing the virus, they were considering introducing it into the States.

She knew Whitney was angry with himself. He had absolute faith in himself and his ability to find the right people to work for him. In this case, he'd been wrong. The three men he'd mentored were far more interested in money than in patriotism.

He's been getting it wrong lately, Draden said softly in her mind, proving he was adept at using telepathy and once she'd given him the pathway, he could use it at will.

Shylah was unsure how she felt about that, but right now, she wanted the comfort of his presence, filling those lonely places. She shivered. It wasn't that she was cold. Her body seemed to adapt to any climate easily, but she was afraid. Something kept bumping Draden and then it hit her in the back. She had braided her hair before she'd gone to the village the terrorists had taken over, but part was loose now, strands coming out of the weave. Whatever bumped them tangled in her hair and pulled.

She reached back and batted at it. Her hand swiped across a large object and her heart sank. She knew immediately it was a body. The first reaction was to surface. To get away from it. The dead man came floating around her with the current. Its foot seemed to be caught in branches so that the body just bobbed there under the water, faceup. Eyes staring. Heart pounding, she tried to turn her head from those accusing eyes, but the body couldn't move, and she couldn't look away.

Draden's arm swept around her, dragged her right into him, one hand pressing her face into his chest. *You're all right. You did good.*

I'm not all right, she denied, trying to keep the sob and the belligerence from her voice. She didn't know which was worse. *I'm going to die and I'm going to do it in a really ugly way. Worse, I'll probably die before I can find the three men who cooked this abomination up and let it loose on the world. The least I could do before I die is contribute by getting their location to Whitney or someone else who could deal with them.*

I've got two friends who are proven in this type of crisis who are good at finding immune and drug therapies that help with hot viruses. They're military and will have the full confidence and cooperation of our government. Anything at all. They need to find answers fast. We have a chance. It's a small one, but still, it's a chance. Depends on incubation. If Whitney's virologists left their remote lab on the run, the three of them probably left behind enough notes for me to send my friends. Trap Dawkins and Wyatt Fontenot are considered two of the leading minds in the field.

Shylah kept her eyes closed. She could still feel the horrible dead body scraping at her with his hands. She wanted to scream. Instead, she burrowed closer into Draden. *I don't know if you're telling me that to keep me from losing it, but thank you. I appreciate it.*

I don't believe in giving false hope. It's a

slim chance, but they may be able to help us. If it's too late for us, maybe others. You ready to get out of here?

She was *so* ready. *Absolutely.*

We're going to swim back around the curve to where we were before. That's the best place to exit the river and they've looked at it twice now.

That meant pushing past the dead body. A tiny shudder went through her. His arms tightened around her. *Keep your eyes closed.*

I hate being all girly. It's just that I spent some time with dead bodies and they had their eyes open, and I've never quite gotten over it. She could kill when she needed to, but the eyes of the dead were a problem for her. She'd been careful when viewing his handiwork on the commander of the MSS not to give his glassy eyes more than a quick glance. She could look at bodies all day, even those covered in blood, but staring at dead eyes really got to her.

How old were you?

He was moving, slowly unfolding his long legs. She had long legs and as he unfolded his, she mirrored what he was doing, straightening very slowly. All the while she kept her eyes closed and her head tight against his chest.

Eight. It was a really bad night.

Eight? What in the hell was an eight-year-old doing surrounded by dead bodies?

Whitney wanted us tough and immune to girlish squeamishness. It's a little ironic that he gave me nightmares, and I still have trouble looking at the dead. I can kill, but then I can't look at my handiwork if their eyes are open. Makes a lot of sense, doesn't it?

There was a sense of comfort being wrapped up in his arms. He was calm in the middle of a terrifying experience. He was a rock she could cling to. She hoped she was doing the same for him but felt like she was failing miserably.

I think you're pretty brave, Shylah. Let's stretch out, heads turned away from the dead guy. Keep your eyes closed and let me haul you around him. Once we're away, I'll let you know. He made certain every hair from her head was unwrapped from the dead man's fingers.

Do dead guys freak you out when they stare at you? She almost hoped so.

Not dead guys, he admitted. *Needles do. I fucking hate needles.*

She frowned. *You're a doctor.*

He was towing her through the water. Around something large. She kept her eyes closed tight and stayed as relaxed as possible, so she wasn't a hindrance.

Exactly. I work with a group of men who would give me a rash of shit like you wouldn't believe if they knew. So, if you meet them, keep your mouth shut.

She liked that he acted as if it were possible she might meet his teammates. *You have to work with needles every day.*

True, but they aren't usually going into me. I don't mind looking at them, or using them on other people, but don't want them in me. We're clear. Let's get around that bend, then we'll only have a few hundred yards to go before we can head for the shallows.

They began to swim toward the spot where the bank wasn't steep, all the while hugging the bottom of the river as they neared the bend. They picked up speed once they were certain they were a good distance from the most recent boat. Around that curve an explosion blasted through the water. The only thing that really saved them was they were already a good distance away from the blast site.

Draden didn't hesitate. He was already able to touch down in the shallower water and he reached down, plucked her out of the river and tossed her onto the bank. *Run for the trees.*

Shylah struggled to her feet and had already covered half the distance when the second explosion hit, rocking the ground slightly as if a seismic event were taking place. She didn't look but trusted her partner to be right on her heels. When she reached the first line of trees, she halted and turned back.

Draden wasn't just out of the water, he was directly behind her. She hadn't heard a single sound, not even labored breathing. He swerved to avoid running into her, caught her hand and kept going without slowing down, taking her with him. Water poured off both of them and she tried not to think about how polluted it might be. She really shouldn't worry about things like that, not when she had given Draden mouth to mouth. She'd tried to save his life and in doing so had condemned herself to death.

She wasn't afraid of dying. She had always contemplated ending her life. She detested always going back to Whitney's compound and giving him power over her. This was too much though, living minute by minute knowing every second the virus was turning her insides to mush.

Shylah. Stop. Don't think about it yet. That's a few steps from now. You need to be running in the lead. We didn't have time to wipe out our tracks so they're going to be on to us. Even if they don't find us tonight, they'll be back in force tomorrow. We need a place to rest. I presume you have a camp.

She hesitated, which when she thought about it, was rather stupid. Secrecy had been drilled into her. The only partners she'd ever worked with were Bellisia and Zara. But that was early on when Whitney had thought to create a team of female soldiers capable of taking out the enemy easily. There had been five of them back then.

Two had died during that first trial, attempting to escape. Deserting — that was how Whitney had seen it. Because of their actions, none of the girls could be trusted. She'd never been allowed to work with her friends again. Whitney had sent them out individually, holding the others as hostages, threatening to harm them if the one in the field dared to desert. Bellisia, Zara and Shylah had talked it over, encouraging one another to leave if they ever got the chance. Two of them had done just that. Shylah had been very alone ever since.

Without a word, Shylah ran around Draden to take the lead position. She had a very good sense of direction and her feet always seemed to find the places to set down without making noise. It had been that way as long as she could remember. She wasn't too hot or too cold, no matter where she was, even with her clothes and body soaking wet. Her shoes squished a little, but that was the only real sound she made as she ran.

She listened for Draden, wondering if he made the weird little squelching noises, but couldn't hear him. She refused to look over her shoulder. Instead, she played a game with herself, listening intently for things such as breathing, his footfall, the whisper of his clothing. Occasionally she thought she felt water drops raining down on her back, but that would mean he was actually running in her exact steps, and how could he at night? In the dark? With a head injury.

It can't be good for you running with a head injury.

I'll make it.

And you had an open wound. You don't know what's in that water. You could easily get an infection.

He was silent, and she shook her head, embarrassed as realization dawned. The last thing he had to worry about was infection, not when he'd been exposed to the virus.

I'm sorry, that was stupid. I just wasn't thinking.

No worries.

How are you with jumping? Climbing? She

preferred the arboreal highway. It was one place the terrorists rarely checked. Not like Whitney's supersoldier teams she'd had to go up against. They *always* checked. They knew Whitney used genetic enhancements and they weren't about to forget to check the trees.

Lead the way.

Did he sound tired? Sick? Probably more like a man with a head injury. He'd killed a lot of men tonight. Moving that fast, exerting that much energy, had to have taken a toll. Just watching him had taken a toll on her.

Coming up on the tree we need. The first branch is about six feet off the ground. It's strong. We climb another ten feet and go from there.

She'd made the jump countless times and maybe she was showing off a bit for him. He seemed so good at everything and she was ashamed of panicking when the dead guy had stared at her. He had shared he hated needles, but she didn't really believe him. No one who hated needles that much would choose to be a doctor, would they? She didn't slow down or hesitate, she flung herself at the branch, swung up and moved quickly out of the way.

Draden didn't hesitate either. He was up

almost before she was. She didn't indulge in watching the way his muscles moved under his wet shirt but began climbing immediately. They had a good head start on the MSS chasing them. They'd been so quiet she doubted if the soldiers could have followed by sound. They probably had left a few tracks and she knew some of the recruits had been local trackers.

Shylah concentrated on climbing the tree and finding the long, thick branch that stretched out toward another tree. *I have better balance without my shoes. Give me a minute.* She took them off and tied them around her neck. They were very wet and heavy. She hated the feeling.

Without a word, Draden reached over her shoulder and took the hiking boots from her.

You don't have to do that.

He indicated for her to continue. So much for being a badass soldier he would admire. She turned resolutely toward the next branch. She had extraordinary balance and she picked up the pace, not wanting to be caught anywhere in the forest during daylight hours. She knew the terrorists would swarm through the interior searching for them. They'd not only lost their commander, but far too many men.

I do admire you.

Her breath caught in her throat. *You heard that, did you? I seem to be making a pretty big fool of myself.*

I'm not very fond of too many people, but since I know one of your secrets, I'll let you in on one of mine. I like flowers. Peonies were a favorite.

That's bullshit. She couldn't help but smile. Draden was the real deal. A GhostWalker. One who could take apart the enemy in seconds. The last thing he would know was anything about flowers.

Peonies are beautiful perennials. A classic, really. Every garden should have them. They're dependable, have a timeless, elegant beauty and will bloom with very little attention. He was silent for a moment while she switched branches and he followed. *Like you.*

Her heart stuttered. He said the most outrageous thing in that voice of his, matter-of-fact as if he weren't delivering the best compliment she'd ever had in her life.

Did your mother garden? she asked. He knew a lot about flowers, or he was very good at making things up.

Eliza loved flowers and planted them all around the place we lived. I remember the smell of them. And yes, she particularly loved what she called the classics, so we had peonies. After she was gone, I worked for a nursery that grew flowers and sold them to flower shops. I liked getting my hands in the dirt. There were rows of flowers, and the peonies had a delicate perfume that called to me. Some of the other flowers had nice scents, but I couldn't work in the rows for too long without the smell being overpowering. I could work in the rows of peonies forever.

He'd given her a piece of himself so casually, throwing the information out there as if it didn't matter when she knew it did. From what she knew of them, none of the GhostWalkers were the kind of men to reveal personal information about themselves or anyone else. She thought it odd that he referred to his mother by her first name, but she didn't pry.

I've never smelled a peony, she admitted. *Whitney grows flowers, but most of them are exotic.*

Classics are far better than exotics. Nothing rivals a cut peony. Seriously. They have a beauty about them no other flower has. And longevity. They look delicate and elegant, but they're strong survivors.

She knew he was trying to tell her not to give up. She wouldn't. It wasn't in her nature. *Maybe I'm more like a peony than I realized.*

I saw the resemblance immediately. He paused. *Perhaps not the scent at this precise moment.*

Shylah muffled the laughter welling up. She ran along the branches, switching from one tree to the next in the way a cat might. She knew when to duck to avoid getting hit with other branches and several times she forgot to warn Draden. He read the route in her mind and had no problem maneuvering, making her believe he had been genetically engineered even better than she had been.

They covered several miles before she began the descent to the forest floor. They were inland, away from the river. She would rather rely on the trees instead of water as an escape route.

You set up camp quite a distance from the MSS.

It was an observation, not a judgment. Shylah liked the way Draden seemed to reserve his conclusions until he had the facts. *I've never met a man like you before.*

Have you met a lot of men?

I was in one of Whitney's compounds. Sometimes he moved us from place to place. There were always soldiers around us. Yes, there were a lot of men.

From the tone of your voice, I'm grateful you

don't think I'm anything like the others.

Shylah stopped the continual flow of conversation in the branches of a thick dipterocarp tree, holding on to the limb above her while she took her time scanning the area carefully.

It was an observation, Shylah admitted. *A good one. If I'm going to die a really ugly death, it's nice to like the person I'm going to share that with.* She made every effort to sound impersonal. He was dying too. She wasn't looking for sympathy.

Let's hope my friend Trap is as brilliant as I think he is.

She glanced at him. He was looking at the forest floor, toward their back trail. No one could have followed them through the arboreal highway other than another trained GhostWalker. That was one of the many reasons she chose to go high.

"I think we're safe enough to talk out loud," she decided. A part of her wanted to continue to use telepathy and keep him in her mind, but it felt too intimate. "The reason my camp is a good distance away is because I wasn't looking for the terrorists. I was looking for the three virologists who designed the virus as a weapon. I thought they would have set up shop in the city, but they didn't." She began the climb down to the forest floor. "They felt safer out here and thought their experiments wouldn't draw any notice."

Draden followed her lead, staying just behind, climbing instead of jumping across the expanse — and she had the feeling he was very capable of jumping long distances without getting hurt. She liked that he didn't try to take over because they were away from the danger of those hunting them.

"You found them out here? In the middle of nowhere? You aren't even close to the river."

Shylah made the jump to the ground. It was a good twenty feet, but her legs acted like springs absorbing the shock. Draden landed right beside her. She glanced up at him. The wound on his head was still leaking.

"I hid right out in the open. There's a forest ranger cabin just up ahead. I've been using it. If a ranger should come along, I'd come up with an excuse. It's really got all the amenities, including a shower. I lucked out."

He flashed her a heart-stopping grin. "It was a bold move."

She couldn't help but smile as she put on her boots. He was really beautiful. If she was going to die, it wasn't a bad deal to die looking at him. She didn't bother to hide her tracks. She wanted anyone nosing around to think the forest ranger was in residence. Anyone in that area was most likely up to no good.

Poachers were in abundance, going after the rarest species protected in the rain forest: sun bears, clouded leopards, Sumatran tigers, rhinoceroses, orangutans and even elephants. Nothing seemed to be sacred, not even the birds, especially the rarest species. The forest rangers dismantled the traps poachers set and tracked them through the remaining viable rain forest. They also looked for signs of illegal logging.

"I've dismantled a few traps myself."

He shot her another look, but this said she was taking chances and he didn't like it. She knew she was, but she pretended she was just solidifying her cover, pretending to be a ranger.

"Do you think that was wise? Poachers can be very dangerous. They kill these animals for money."

She shrugged and led him along a narrow path to the small structure set in the middle of a grove of tall trees. He touched her shoulder, signaling for her to halt before she stepped into the open.

Wait here. Give me just a minute to check it out. No one's been here. I can tell.

Indulge me. I'd just feel better if I scouted around. It's a habit. Call it OCD.

Shylah knew better, but she nodded. She was suddenly very exhausted and if she'd been alone she would have allowed herself a very big breakdown. Instead, she forced her mind away from the fact that she had been exposed to the virus. He seemed to have great faith in his friend. She wished she could as well.

She kept her eyes on him as he moved out into the open area between the brush, trees and the forest ranger's cabin. What in the world was a man with his looks doing in the GhostWalker program? He could make his living as a movie star. Or maybe just charge money for women to look at him. He'd probably make even more money if he . . .

Before you go any further, I'm still connected to you telepathically. There was humor in his voice and amusement poured into her mind, inviting her to share his laughter.

She found herself doing just that instead of being embarrassed. It was the way he laughed at himself. *You* are *very good-looking.*

So I've been told. I used to model men's clothes. Just in case you saw some of the ads and were about to ask.

Of course he'd modeled men's clothes. Who better? Any woman seeing him in jeans and a shirt, or a particular suit, would rush out to buy those items for her man. Now that she saw him up close, she recognized him from the magazines.

Hunting terrorists is a far cry from modeling.

And much more fun. He paused dramatically. *Fulfilling. I should have said fulfilling. I'm sure that's what I meant.*

She laughed out loud even though she knew she was supposed to be silent in case there was someone waiting to kill them. *Cameras don't try to kill you. Terrorists do.*

Everyone tries to kill me. Doesn't much matter which world I'm in. I seem to bring that out in people. Did you see those boats filled with men trying to do me in?

She knew he was going for humor, but she turned his words over and over in her mind. What did he mean by *it doesn't much matter which world I'm in*? He moved with the stealth of a jungle cat. She had quite a bit of cat in her and could easily see as well as him. His body was fluid, every muscle working in a perfect show of strength.

I like you the way you are right now, although I'd understand if you wish you were still modeling and very, very far from here.

He had gained the porch of the cabin after circling around it, studying it from every angle. *I think you're safe to come on in. Actually, my beautiful little peony, I wouldn't rather be modeling. I understand this world a hell of a lot better than I did that one.*

She wanted to ask him what that meant and why, but she didn't want to force him to be personal. She wouldn't have liked him doing that to her. *Are you going to actually call me Peony?* She liked the *my* and the *beautiful.*

His soft laughter brushed intimately at the walls of her mind. *Take the shower first.*

Not a chance. The hot water takes time.

She went up the two stairs leading to the porch. He waited there for her, his hand on the door. She was tall, but he was much taller. "It's going to be strange talking out loud to you."

"You just don't want me in your head." He pushed open the door and indicated for her to go inside.

Shylah did so, automatically scenting the air much like a cat would. No one had been there in her absence. "I don't mind you in my head. I refuse to be embarrassed for thinking the truth. You have to know how good-looking you are. Fortunately for you, you seem to have brains and humor to go along with your looks."

"Which is the most important to you?" He followed her in and closed the door. The moment the door was closed, he pulled off his shirt. "Brains, humor or looks?"

For a moment she lost her train of thought and could only stare at all his muscles with her mouth open. When he burst out laughing, she did too.

"Ordinarily, I would say your intellect. Right now, we need brains to figure out how to get out of the mess we're in. I don't much care for turning to mush as a way to die. On the other hand, since we're probably going to suffer endlessly while we're dying, I'd say a sense of humor, because who wants a whiny partner when you're suffering? Then you take your shirt off like that, so the choices are ridiculously tough."

His white teeth flashed at her again with his perfect smile.

"Do women just walk up to you and say they want to have your baby?"

"Why? Are you considering it?"

She nodded. "Absolutely I am. I think you have a duty to the human race to procreate."

"Take your clothes off."

4

Shylah burst out laughing just as Draden hoped she would. He liked her. He didn't pay attention to many people and the ones he had, hadn't been worth his time.

"We're both dripping all over the floor. I should have been the one to tell you to get your clothes off." She indicated the single door leading to another room. The cabin was small but designed to meet every need with its small kitchen, bedroom and living quarters all sharing the same space. "There's the bathroom."

Draden's eyebrow shot up. "Indoor plumbing?" He was reacting to her. The woman was sexy, lethal and very confident. The sound of her laughter was enticing. Intriguing. It played along his nerve endings and sent an electrical current running through his bloodstream. He was on the verge of death and he'd never felt more alive.

"And hot water. Go take a shower, but hurry."

He opened his mouth to protest. He wanted her to take the shower first. Before he could say a word, she shook her head.

"Don't say it's because I'm a girl. You've got a nasty wound on your head. If a miracle happens and we survive the virus, you don't want to die of a simple infection. Just hurry."

Could she be any more wonderful? He flashed a cocky grin. "I was going to suggest we conserve hot water and shower together."

"I'll just bet you were." She pointed to the closed door.

He forced himself to walk across the small room, looking sulky. Who knew the ridiculous expressions and poses from his modeling days would come in handy? They made her laugh, and for him, that was what counted.

The water felt wonderful. It only took a few minutes to heat up and Draden didn't care how it was done, only that he had access to it. Cold didn't bother him so if he'd had to take a cold shower, he would have been okay with it, but he wanted time to consider what to do while he could. Right now, his brain was working, spitting out his chances — and hers — over and over. He needed to stop the offending loop and start working on the problem.

Shylah had obviously been tracking the madmen who had decided to start a pandemic for their own personal reasons and she probably knew more than she realized — or was telling him. After her shower, he would question her, get as many facts as possible so they had a shot at surviving the virus. It was a slim chance, but there was one. If anything, he needed to save her. She was one in a million, and who knew he would find her here in the rain forest?

He didn't have clean clothes with him, so he wrapped himself in a towel and stepped out with a grin on his face, knowing she appreciated his body far more than he did. The smile faded when he saw her wrapped in a towel. She had long legs. Beautiful legs. Her hair was out of its braid and she sent him a quick shy smile before stepping around him to enter the shower. He'd been as brief as possible in order to save the hot water for her, but after catching that little glimpse, he decided if they were going to be staying, they should share that shower.

I'm reading your thoughts.

Her laughter teased his senses, something that had never happened before, and left him a little uncomfortable. She was turning the tables on him, staying connected.

I guess it's a two-way street.

Still — she was sober again — *I'd prefer some privacy. I need to fall apart, just a little bit. It isn't that I mind knowing I'm going to die; it's the how. I saw the results of this virus and it wasn't pretty.*

Her honesty was killing him. *I understand.* He did. And he didn't have that much hope to give her. He was doing his best not to think too hard on what was to come.

He made certain their minds were totally apart before he allowed himself to contemplate what they were facing. He was definitely infected. That dart had been all about killing him and those he came into contact with. He had to find out if the terrorists had more of the virus. That meant he couldn't take his peony with him. The things he might have to do to get that information weren't for her. She had enough to contend with.

He stood at the window, staring out into the forest, contemplating the fact that he might have to kill Shylah Cosmos. He liked her. Most people, man or woman, would have been freaking out, knowing they were exposed to the virus. Most would have tried running to civilization and hospitals in the hopes they could be saved. Had she done that, he would have killed her. Once she'd opened a pathway between their two minds, he'd deliberately kept it open, needing to know her thoughts. If she planned to run, he had to know.

He'd considered killing her when he first realized she had performed CPR on him, when he saw the realization on her face that she was most likely infected. She hadn't panicked the way he'd expected. It had thrown her, but she'd remained clear-headed. She'd worked with him in the river against their common enemy. She thought herself squeamish, but even when the dead man had stared at her, she hadn't bailed. She'd forced herself to stay still, not giving away their position.

Yeah. He liked her. He could even admit he was attracted to her. He'd never had any shortage of women, but that was all physical. A release. Nothing more. He found it ironic that when he was going to die, he met a woman. Maybe *the* woman. She was smart. Funny. Brave. And damned good-looking. She laughed at herself. In the middle of the worst nightmare possible, she laughed at herself.

And made him laugh too.

Draden rinsed out his clothes and hung them on the porch to dry. It was hot enough that, despite the humidity, it shouldn't take too long. The ranger had left a change of clothes, but they were too small. There was no way to improvise. His head hurt like a mother, so he sat on the mattress and laid his head against the wall, closing his eyes. Just for a minute.

He had to be prepared to take care of Shylah. She was just now allowing herself to fully realize the implications of being infected. If she tried to run . . . He shut down the possibility of that. He knew, if she was suffering, he would have no problem ending her life, but to kill her because she was afraid . . . Maybe there was another way, he just had to think of it.

"Draden."

That voice. Soft. Gentle. Magical. She had a magical voice. He tried to answer her, but his head pounded, trying to drown out the music of her voice.

"Draden. I'm going to wash that cut again and butterfly stitch it. It's nasty and needs to be taken care of. Please don't hit me or anything."

He forced his lashes to lift. She was close. Her face right next to his. Her mouth. That perfect bow of a mouth. Full lips. She had a smattering of freckles across her nose. Long lashes and dark chocolate eyes. He caught her hand before she touched his face, shaking his head.

"Wait. We don't know for certain if you're infected. I hate that you saved my life and because of that you're at risk. You should wear a mask. You can't leave, but maybe if we're careful, we can reduce the risk to you." He wasn't giving her the best of chances, but again, there was a possibility. Unless Trap and Wyatt could come up with something, she was as good as dead.

She smiled at him, sitting on the edge of the bed looking like a million dollars. "This was my choice, Draden. You aren't responsible. I didn't have to dive into that river after you. The MSS was on your tail and I still interfered. I blew my cover by going in after you. I could have died right then from a bullet."

"Shylah, there's a big difference between taking a bullet and being infected with a hemorrhagic virus."

She shrugged. "Whitney plants viruses in us to force us to return home. The three virologists who cooked up this crap worked for him, created viruses aimed at killing us if we 'defected.' I knew sooner or later I wouldn't return, and I'd die from whatever they put in me. According to Whitney, we would die a very painful and horrible death, yet I always knew I would choose to live free for a while, even if it was only for a couple of weeks, and I'd die that painful and horrible death. So don't kick yourself too hard. None of this is on you."

"I could fall in love with you." He meant it to sound humorous, but it was too close to the truth. She refused to play the victim. His entire life had been one serious fucked-up fiasco. Now, at the end of it, he'd finally met a woman he admired.

"Since no one's ever fallen in love with me, I think now's a good time. I can go out knowing someone thought I was worth that."

She turned her head away from him, so he couldn't see her expression, but her tone caught at his heart. He hadn't known he had a heart, but it was evident by the way it ached for her that it was there somewhere. She already had a small tray ready with the tape and gauze and she turned back, looking at the wound, not at him. Her hands were gentle as she smeared on antibiotic ointment and then began to close the laceration.

"You've got quite a lump here."

"Do you get afraid coming to a place like this on your own?" He'd been curious to know. She seemed confident. Very self-sufficient. He'd never minded being on his own and it seemed like she was the same.

"I live in a prison," Shylah reminded. "It might resemble a military barracks, but my entire life has been in one of Whitney's compounds. We moved occasionally, but in the end, it was always the same no matter where we were. Getting out feels like freedom. At first, when he split us up, it was a little nerve-wracking to go out on my own, but I got used to it."

She smoothed the pad of her finger around the injury. "All done. I'll fix us something to eat and then you should get some sleep. You have to be exhausted." She got up and washed her hands. His heart sank knowing that regular soap and water wasn't going to help if the virus was transmitted via blood or from Shylah breathing for him.

"You know where the lab they used is?"

"Yes. I can show it to you. You'll be able to see it from the roof of this cabin. That's why I was so excited to find a ranger cabin here. They put their makeshift lab where they did because it gave them access to the Internet via satellite. Don't get too excited. They had already developed the virus in the laboratory Whitney supplied for them. Whitney became aware of what they were doing, and they had to make a run for it."

He nearly came up off the bed. He could communicate with Trap and Wyatt directly. "I want you to show me their lab." He knew Joe would never abandon him and sooner or later a satellite would be put in place for him to communicate, but if there was one already there, he needed to speed things up. The faster the military — and Trap and Wyatt — had data, the more the odds lengthened in their favor.

"Are you going in your towel? Don't be crazy, Draden, you're going to have to pace yourself. You really are injured. I'll fix some food, and then you rest. Your clothes will be dry, and we can go. Give it a couple of hours."

Draden was used to going his own way. His team consisted of a group of mavericks. They were cohesive when they needed to be, but their strength was their individual thinking. Many of their enhancements enabled them to do their jobs better alone than in a group. The idea had been that the GhostWalkers easily could do teamwork or perform alone. It was clear Shylah had those same skills because she worked seamlessly with him yet could strike out on her own.

"That makes sense," he conceded, mostly because there was worry in her voice. He hadn't experienced that in a very long time, but he hated losing a single minute. His head needed to stop pounding, and he was exhausted. If he closed his eyes for a couple of hours, it couldn't hurt anything. "Talk to me while you fix food," he ordered. "Tell me about these men."

"Two are brothers, Tyler and Cameron Williams. They're from the United States. Mississippi to be exact. The third man, Agus Orucov, is from Sumatra. They met in college and became friends. Whitney recruited them with the promise of big money. Their purpose, as far as I could make out, was solely to develop the viruses that would kill each of us."

Draden was never surprised that like-minded people always found one another. He'd learned that lesson at a very early age. He slid down on the bed and closed his eyes against the morning light, all the better to concentrate on the magic of her voice. He found her soothing. She reminded him of Wyatt's grandmother, Grace Fontenot. She was no-nonsense, but still all woman with that ability to nurture that he seemed to have been born without.

"I'm listening."

She pulled out a cooking pot and went to the gas stove. It was hooked up to a large canister the rangers must truck in after the rainy season when a vehicle could get back in the area. Within minutes, the aroma of food was tantalizing. He hadn't realized he was hungry.

"I don't know what went wrong between them. Maybe Whitney wasn't paying them what they thought they were worth or something else. It wouldn't surprise me, the way they argued, that it had to do with money. In any event, the three virologists wanted to go in a different direction with the viruses than what Whitney wanted. At least that's what he claimed. Whitney could very well have decided he wanted a weapon once they'd created it. Or he could have had them working on it all along. Who knows? He always had them develop an antiserum to what he put inside us . . ."

"Wait." Draden's eyes flew open and he waited until she half spun around to look at him. "Shylah, there has to be a therapy, antibodies that work against it. They wouldn't have worked on a virus like this one in what amounts to primitive conditions unless they believed they were immune."

She frowned and shook her head. "They definitely developed the virus in Whitney's lab, but they weren't completely finished or why have a lab here? More, Whitney was convinced they hadn't come up with a vaccine or antiserum."

"Could it be this is where they were trying to develop the therapies to counter it? Or the vaccine?"

She stared down into the small cooking pot, seeming mesmerized by stirring the contents. "They're brilliant men or Whitney never would have recruited them," she finally said. "Which means you've got to be right. They would have come up with a vaccine or some sort of protection before they took a chance of testing the virus or releasing it. I haven't been inside the lab, but I looked through the windows."

For some reason that got to him. He didn't know too many women who would trudge through a forest filled with exotic and rare, but dangerous animals, with terrorists close, hunting three men to assassinate them. His body stirred at the thought of her courage. She took his breath away. It was a cliché, but so damned true he could barely think with wanting her.

"I'm not much of a lab person. I wasn't schooled to work with viruses, so I stayed out of the hut. I didn't want to tip them off that I had found them."

"Can you describe what's inside?"

"I definitely saw a couple of computers, a

Bunsen burner. Microscope. There was a small freezer and fridge. A hood. None of the elaborate safety features that were in the laboratory in the compound."

"I need to go there. If they have a computer, they definitely are using a satellite."

"We have it here intermittently." She turned toward him, spoon in the air. "Why would they feel they had to test it on the village?"

"I can't imagine wiping out an entire village of people, so I don't have an answer for you."

She turned back to her cooking. "I've been trying to puzzle that out. Do you have any ideas? Especially *that* village. At first, I thought it was because it was remote enough to contain the virus, but even the choices of the first two fishermen found dead made no sense . . . unless —" She broke off completely, paying attention to the mixture in the cooking pot.

"Unless what?" he prompted. He liked that she gave the questions thought. That she actually saw the mysteries and worked at solving them.

"The three of them were furious with Whitney. What is the one thing above all else he holds as his greatest accomplishment?"

He frowned, sitting up straighter. "The GhostWalker program."

"Exactly. Whitney defied humanity by getting female orphans and conducting experiments on them. He knew if those experiments came to light he would be forever branded among the worst mad scientists of all time, but he did it because he believes that strongly in his GhostWalker program. Suppose this is all about revenge. The three of them despise Whitney, but along the way, they must have had personal demons, men or women who wronged them in some way."

Draden took a deep breath and let it out slowly, turning over and over what she'd said. For once, the pounding in his head receded as he considered that she might be right. "If that's the case, why use the MSS?"

"Money. Whitney has friends in high places. His first retaliation would be to freeze their bank accounts. They would need money to operate. Sell the virus but have them use it on the village of Orucov's choice. He probably used it on the individuals himself. If Orucov had ties to Lupa Suku, we're on the right track. I can use the satellite to get the information from Whitney."

He didn't want help from Whitney, not in any way, but this virus was too dangerous to worry about where information came from. "We can't waste time, Shylah. If this is about vengeance and not money, we're going to have to move fast. The three are already gone. That means they could be anywhere."

"We can't move anywhere, Draden." Her voice was soothing.

He felt her touch his mind, and instantly there was the flow of information between them. She was looking to see if he intended trying to follow the three into a populated area. If he was she intended to stop him.

She flushed, color creeping up her neck to her face. "I'm sorry." She ducked her head.

He flashed her a grin. "I told you I was falling in love with you, and I wasn't far off the mark. You're extraordinary. Don't feel bad because you want to protect the population, sweetheart. I was, with regret, thinking the same way."

She divided the food into two bowls. He didn't ask what it was, but it smelled edible.

"I guess that makes us a pair of serial killers," she teased and brought his bowl to him.

He kept his head down. As serial killers went, he could have been labeled one. He wished he had more remorse for those he'd killed, but he didn't. They were in his sights for a reason. Anyone able to annihilate an entire village of peaceful people didn't deserve to share the earth with others. But then some would say he didn't have the right to judge.

"That bother you?"

"What?" She perched on the end of the bed rather than at the small table that she'd been using as a desk.

"Don't pretend you weren't in my head. That I think that way. That I don't let the deaths of men like that tear me up at night."

"It doesn't tear me up, so why should I judge you more harshly than I do myself? I wasn't sent here to talk them into going home to Daddy. I was sent to kill them. I might cry over the people in that village, I might even obsess over them, but you won't catch me crying over the deaths of the ones who orchestrated that."

Draden shook his head. "Why the hell did it take me this long to find you?"

She sent him a small smile and indicated the bowl he held. "You won't be singing that same tune when you taste that. It's calories and it contains all the vitamins you need, but Whitney didn't believe tasting good was a prerequisite for food in the field."

He studied the expression on her face, but more importantly, he stayed connected to her, reading the sorrow for the villagers in her mind. She didn't compartmentalize the way he did. He could feel anger. Rage even. Ice-cold fury. But he could push the sight of them aside. He could look at them as something other than fellow human beings, mainly because he wasn't certain he looked at himself as a human being. It was clear his little peony couldn't do that.

There was kindness in her and compassion. Two characteristics he didn't have. Or at least, not in abundance. He was the perfect killing machine. He didn't need to feel bad. Once unleashed, set on a course, he followed it until it was done. He knew why he was wiping out the MSS. To him, it wasn't political. He wasn't a political man.

The MSS had murdered an entire village of their own people. Those people had been peaceful, doing their best to live on their own, not asking anything of anyone. He didn't care why the MSS had targeted them or what the overall agenda was. The terrorists had committed an atrocity against humanity and had to be stopped because they would continue to do so. That was a good enough reason to wipe them out, and he didn't give a damn whether others agreed with him or not.

Then along came his little peony.

"Stop it. Stop calling me that. And don't think of me as that." She gave him the most adorable little frown.

"Peony?"

"It sounds awful."

"Did you ever look up the flower?" He took his first bite and nearly choked. "Woman. Are you fucking trying to kill me? Why didn't you warn me?"

She burst out laughing. "Don't be such a baby. I did warn you, and you deserve it for calling me Peony. And you already asked me that."

He watched her eat two spoonsful of the thick broth. He was going to have to suck it up and eat the disgusting stuff because she wasn't besting him, not over food. "I didn't call you peony as in your name. I called you 'my peony' as in the flower." It bothered him that he'd repeated himself. He didn't do things like that, but his brain felt chaotic.

She rolled her eyes at him, and his heart did a weird stuttering thing. She was potent. Beautiful. Lethal. Funny.

"Shit, Shylah, we've got to figure this virus crap out. I figured I'd kill as many of those bastards as possible, record what I could for Wyatt and Trap and then put a bullet in my head. Along comes this woman that I didn't think was a possibility in my life and we're both supposed to fucking die, which isn't happening by the way. What kind of crap is that?" His head was throbbing, and his body felt hot. Fatigue ate at him and every muscle hurt. She sat there looking unaffected.

She was amazing as far as he was concerned, everything he ever could have wanted in a woman, and he barely knew her. She'd been taken by Whitney as an infant and been experimented on. He'd raised her as a soldier and a piece of property, yet she retained such incredible kindness and compassion. She loved her friends, embracing them as deeply as possible, as if they were siblings.

He had every advantage. Hard times maybe, but he'd created his own isolation and hell. He had teammates who accepted him for who he was. He had freedom and money and gifts. She wanted to live life to the fullest whenever she could, to experience every moment. He'd read that in her mind, yet he'd been the opposite, nearly throwing every opportunity away.

"You do know that the only reason you're feeling that way is because of the extreme circumstances. We're both going to die." She regarded him over the bowl. "Seriously, Draden, we're attracted to each other because we're in this mess together."

"I haven't accepted that we're going to die. I'm a fighter, Shylah. I'll fight until there's no reasonable way I can get out of knowing it's over."

"Keep eating. You might want it over." She shot him a little grin.

His heart did that strange stuttering thing again. Looking her in the eye, he ate a spoonful of the mixture. It was hot. Wet. Tasted like . . .

"Vomit?" Shylah suggested. "We took a vote once and included Whitney's supersoldiers. Vomit won, although quite a few other colorful suggestions were written in."

He could imagine her laughing with her sisters over the idea of a poll on the field rations Whitney sent them out with. She knew how to have fun in the worst circumstances.

"Yeah, I'm voting for that," Draden agreed, but doggedly ate the stuff. They needed their strength and if Whitney'd had some nutritionist concoct the crap, it probably did its job.

"If we get a chance to use the satellite, I'll get word back to Whitney to send someone after the three I'm hunting, because they need to die."

"I'll double the odds in our favor by alerting the GhostWalkers. If you're right and we're a target, all of the teams need to know.

One of them is located in San Francisco. That would be a disaster."

"I know you're going back to the village the MSS have taken over and that you intend to kill more of them. I'm going with you." She took his bowl along with hers over to the sink.

He liked the way she moved. She was quiet. An asset hunting prey, especially in the forest. "I'm going to have to find out if they have any more of the virus. They managed to shoot me with a dart. I can't assume that was all they had. They wouldn't need much."

She looked at him over her shoulder. Just that little movement, a turn of her head, her hair sliding around her shoulders, falling in waves now that it was dry, the profile of her face, with her long lashes and straight little nose — that was all it took. She might think it was because they both were going to die, but he knew better, and he knew he'd been robbed of the greatest gift he could have had.

"I'm going with you. If they get you, Draden . . ."

"They won't."

"We don't get to take a chance on something like this. This virus has the potential of doing as much damage in the world as

Ebola or Marburg. You know that."

She was right. *Damn it.* He didn't have to like it, but she was definitely right. "I'm going to have to take a prisoner and interrogate them, sweetheart. It won't be pretty. For one thing, I'm in a fucking foul mood and for another, we just plain don't have the time to be nice about it." If his body was anything to go by, he might not even have the time for that.

"I'm aware of that. I know some things are necessary."

"Not for you. I can live with what I have to do. You can't live with interrogation."

Her laughter slipped out again. "Draden, we're not going to live. You don't have to worry so much about that."

"Indulge me then, Shylah. I don't want to die with you looking at me as if I'm a monster. You can stay back and if something goes wrong, you'll be there to protect me."

"I can do that."

That simple. Who knew he would find a woman who would be a perfect partner; when he asked for something important to him, she gave it to him. "Just how lethal are you? Bellisia can kill with just one bite. I think Zara has venom under her fingernails. You must be able to kill without a gun or knife."

"I excel with both." She rinsed the bowls and set them out to dry, turning toward him and resting her hip against the sink. "I'm not too bad in hand-to-hand either."

"Are you bragging?"

She flashed another grin. "Just letting my partner know he doesn't have to worry about looking out for me. And yes, Whitney gave me an extra weapon or two. I'm good in trees. I have a healthy dose of cat in me." Her eyes met his. "I can see the same in you."

He nodded. "Most of us do."

"I also have the *Hadronyche formidabilis* venom in me. Another tree dweller, but much smaller than a cat."

"A spider?" Draden guessed.

"Right the first time. The northern tree funnel-web spider. Whitney got a little creative with the venom."

"And I put my hands on you."

"I wasn't about to kill you after I saved you. And by that time, I knew we were both infected. I figured you might have to shoot me."

He winced at the thought. She was the last person in the world he wanted to kill. "Do you have control of the venom?"

She nodded. "I work at things until I get them right. I can make my eyebrows dance."

She showed him, raising first one and then the other over and over, a little smile on her face. He wanted to kiss her. The desire hit him unexpectedly hard.

"That took practice," she said. "I won't tell you all the other things I've practiced, but I will say, I have great tongue control." She gave him an impish grin and sauntered out to the front porch to check his clothes.

Draden stared after her. In the short time he'd spent with her, while the hemorrhagic virus was busy replicating itself in his body, slowly killing him, he'd felt more alive than he'd ever been. She'd even managed to bring his heart to life. She was magnificent. Women like that shouldn't die of some man-made weapon just because the designers were pissed at someone. That wasn't going to happen. He could figure it out.

He stared at the door knowing he should get his ass up, that she was doing all the work, but he was exhausted. He didn't want to close his eyes, because they only had so much time. If he didn't do anything else, he wanted to save her. He also wanted to spend every minute he could in her company. He still believed he had a good chance of saving her, but then, for his own sanity, he had to believe that. He doubted that he would live through this given the injection they'd given him, but as long as he could save her, he could accept that he had to go out in a violent, horrific way as atonement for his sins.

She stepped back inside minus his clothes. "A few more minutes and they'll be ready. I can make coffee if you think that will help."

"Coffee always helps." He thought looking at her helped. "My head is pounding. Hurts like a son of a bitch."

Instantly she looked sympathetic. "I can feel it," she admitted as she filled a coffeepot. "There's aspirin here in the first aid kit the rangers keep." After putting the coffeepot on the stove, she rummaged through a bag that was just to the right of the bed, in a small, doorless closet. She brought him the aspirin and a glass of water.

While he washed down the medicine, her fingers slipped into his hair. His heart accelerated in a way he was beginning to associate with her. She had strong fingers, but she was gentle, stroking little caresses along his scalp, making him understand why cats purred. He had enough cat in him that he wanted to purr under her ministrations.

"No one's ever done this for me before." He was dying, so what the hell did he have to be embarrassed about? He could tell her anything.

"Done what?"

Her fingers never stopped moving, finding a rhythm and massaging deeper so that the jackhammer piercing his skull grew quiet.

"Taken care of me like this. I grew up on my own, finding my own way. I remember scrounging for food after my foster mother died. One of my teammates, Wyatt Fontenot, has a grandmother. We all call her Nonny. She was the first person who ever cooked a meal for me after that. She cooked for all of us, but she noticed if you liked a particular thing. She'd make that meal, and you knew she did it for you. She was the first after I lost my foster mother." He kept his head down.

Her fingers kept moving. "So, you're saying my meal wasn't your first and you've already compared my cooking to hers."

He was grateful she was turning to humor when he was revealing a very personal part of his past. He didn't allow his memories to be painful. They were just facts to him and he treated them that way, but she had that compassion in her and wouldn't view them the same way.

"Yeah, sweetheart, that's what I'm saying. But you're the first to ever have your fingers in my hair."

"Really?" The note of surprise in her voice

was genuine.

He glared up at her. "Woman, are you secretly calling me a liar?"

"I was thinking, if you hadn't so abruptly ripped our connection to shreds, you would have known that this is another thing you should be charging for. Along with that list we're making . . ."

"What list?" Her fingers were truly driving him crazy. They felt better than anything he could ever remember, yet they also wreaked havoc with his body — and his brain. He couldn't think straight, which was why he had broken their connection.

"The list I was making of things you could charge for, so you would always know you had plenty of money. Things like just sitting there and allowing women to stare at you. You could charge more for actual touching, like this, the privilege of giving you a scalp massage."

Laughter welled up. Real laughter. She was good for him. He hadn't known he could want to laugh, let alone do it. The sound of it startled him. Deep. Raw. He laughed with conviction because this woman was treasure — pure gold. She thought he should be the one charging.

"You think it's a privilege to give me a scalp massage?"

"Yes. Because you didn't ask for it. You were reluctant to let me close to you. In any case, what is wrong with the women you were with, that they didn't have their hands in your hair?"

"I wouldn't let them. Modeling and all that. It went with the image, but I didn't want their hands all over me." Putting their hands in his hair had felt like the women were taking something from him. He couldn't explain it to her, only that his sexual partners had felt grasping, trying to take the only thing he had left to him to earn a living — his looks. Later, when he had joined the GhostWalkers, habit had fed that weird revulsion. The feel of Shylah's hands on him was completely singular and produced an entirely different emotion.

She didn't reply but gave him a faint smile as she left him to get the coffee. He wanted to catch her wrist and pull her back to him, but he didn't. He just watched her because he couldn't take his eyes off of her.

"Stop staring at me."

"I'm trying to decide if I'm having hallucinations and you're really an angel — or witch. Either one, I can't tell yet."

"Given my personality, come down on the side of witch. There's very little angelic about me. You were in my mind, you know."

He wanted to be in her mind again. He liked being there. He liked her in his mind. He hadn't really known he was lonely until she'd filled him with her presence. Then, when she wasn't there, he'd felt bereft.

"Shylah, I intend to find a way to save your life. I don't want you getting too close to me, especially when the symptoms start manifesting themselves. Wear a mask when you're close."

"We already talked about this and I made myself clear," she said, her voice quiet. "There's no sugar, so you're going to have to drink it black."

"Black is perfect, and you're not listening to me. I'm telling you I'm going to save your life. You just have to cooperate a little bit."

She turned to face him, her eyes going a dark chocolate and drifting slowly over his face. Very slowly and deliberately, she put his cup down on the counter. One foot in front of the other, she crossed the room to him.

"Shylah." He said her name cautiously. She was so close now he could see those freckles scattered like kisses across her face.

She put a knee to the bed and leaned in, one hand curling around the nape of his neck, the other curving over his shoulder. Her mouth found his. His stomach knotted with tension. Blood rushed in a hot path straight to his groin. His mind screamed a warning. Shouted at him, warring with his body. His hands came up to grasp her, whether to push her away or pull her closer, he wasn't certain.

Her lips were soft. Sinful. Temptation itself. Her tongue licked along the seam of his mouth, then she poured into his mind and it was the most intimate thing he'd ever experienced.

I'm with you. Every step of the way. Open your mouth.

He obeyed, but he didn't know why. It was wrong, and she was taking away her last protection. Then her tongue stroked along his, a delicate dance, a promise that he would never be alone again. He wouldn't die alone. She would be right there with him. Everything about it was wrong and he knew that, but he couldn't help himself. Every bit of iron will, every bit of discipline went right out the window.

He pulled her into his arms and kissed her like she was his and had been for years. Like he was a man dying and she was his greatest love. He felt like she was. Shylah Cosmos. His only little peony. His delicate flower. Dependable. Long-lived. She'd tied her fate to his. Now, if he wanted to save her, he was going to have to figure out how to save himself.

5

Draden and Shylah approached the little hut that Agus Orucov and the Williams brothers had used while they were in the forest. The position of the small hut was perfect: It was set in a little clearing surrounded by trees, but the trees were far enough from the structure to allow for uninterrupted satellite access.

He wasn't too worried that the MSS would find them — he was certain the terrorists would stay close to the river — but he wasn't going to take chances. He'd already allowed Shylah to tie her fate irrevocably to his. He was crouched low in the brush, studying the hut, perfectly still, every muscle locked in place. He could have approached using the slow-motion movements of the leopard, but instead, he lifted his hand and touched his lips with his fingers.

He glanced to his side where his little

peony was right there with him. She lay stretched out in the dirt, her gaze fixed intently on the hut. She had perfect lips. They were naturally pink and full, and she had a habit of making a little moue with them, which he loved. Now he'd tasted her. The best thing he'd ever tasted in his life was homemade strawberry lemonade from the bayou. She had the faint taste of sass and sweet. Lethal and homey. The combination was deadly to a man like him.

Will you stop? There was a faint hint of laughter, but mostly exasperated embarrassment.

You kissed me, gave me that obsession. Now you're just going to have to live with the consequences. That's the way it works. You always have to pay the piper. You've got yourself a bona fide stalker.

She gave the mental equivalent of a sniff. *I was the one doing the kissing. I think I turned the tables on you.*

She had. It had been the last thing he'd expected from her. She was a little quirky, but very focused when she was onto something. She was also way out of his league. Classy. Beautiful. Smart. Funny. Every trait he could ever want, yet stubborn as hell. She wasn't going to accept leadership or . . .

Call it what it is, handsome. It's dictatorship.

I get that from Whitney and pay him the least amount of attention possible. I'm not going to rely on someone else when I have perfectly good judgment.

It didn't show good judgment to kiss me when I'm infected with a hemorrhagic virus.

Her amusement slipped into his mind and wrapped around his heart. *Occasionally I have lapses, and you have to admit, you're pretty irresistible.*

He had an urgent desire to kiss her again. This kiss wouldn't be so damned sweet either. He held himself in check.

Whitney must love having you. You've got to be an enormous asset to him.

The humor faded from her mind. *There's no pleasing Whitney, and after a while I gave up trying. I truly don't care that he thinks I'm flawed. I sometimes get so focused that I can't see or hear what's going on around me. That drives him insane because no soldier can survive that way.*

Yet he sends you out alone on one of the most dangerous assignments imaginable.

She gave the mental equivalent of a shrug. *I'm good at what I do, and I like the freedom of working alone. Whitney treated Zara the worst. I hope whoever she ends up with loves her like crazy.*

He does. Gino can't breathe without that

woman. He looks at her like the sun rises with her. He hadn't understood that look until he was in Shylah's mind. He liked just looking at her. She had the kind of face that lit up when she was happy or excited. Her frown was the cutest thing he'd ever seen. And those freckles . . . He could spend a lifetime kissing every one of them.

Stop, crazy man.

The laughter in her voice teased at every one of his senses.

I'm so glad she's found someone like that, she added. *Tell me about him. Will he take care of her? Will he see how special she is? She needs a family, Draden. She's so brilliant, but she wasn't cut out for this way of life. Whitney despised her for that, even though she kept him well ahead of everyone else. She's the best industrial spy ever created.*

Gino watches over her and is quite willing to put himself on the line for her, against anyone. She was sent to China and Cheng caught her and tortured her. She never broke. Never gave up the GhostWalkers. There was admiration in his voice because it was impossible not to admire Zara. *Gino's building her a research center along with the house they both want. He plans to travel with her if she speaks anywhere. Otherwise, she'll be staying home, protected by Gino and our team.*

He understands her?

I believe he does. She looks to him often in uncomfortable situations and he immediately takes the weight off her shoulders. He's that kind of man, and I think it's what she needs and wants.

Shylah smiled, lifting the binoculars to her eyes. *And Bellisia?*

That girl is a different kettle of fish. He smirked at his own joke and she made a small sound in his mind, letting him know she got it. Bellisia had toxin from the blue-ringed octopus in her, and she was fast in the water and could stay under for very long periods of time. *She's a warrior woman like Trap's wife, Cayenne. She's married to Ezekiel, one of my teammates. He's crazy about her. More than once she's been an asset to us.*

Cayenne?

He knew what she was doing, delaying the inevitable of going inside. Getting the information about her friends and the other women because she believed they were going to die. Not entering the hut gave them a few more minutes to believe there was hope that they could find a therapy that would work against the hemorrhagic virus.

Cayenne was one of Whitney's mess-ups. At least one of his people who oversaw the experiments decided she was a mess-up, and he scheduled her for termination. She's very spiderish. She can weave webs and kill with a bite.

That gave him pause. He waited, but Shylah didn't volunteer any information. It occurred to him that Cayenne had been considered a failed experiment, yet Shylah had been given similar traits. *Cayenne was developed in a dish. The dose of spider was fairly hefty. Can you weave a web if you want to do it?*

No one has ever asked me that, besides Whitney. I told him no. He was using silk to try to build armor for his supersoldiers. Do you know how much silk that is?

Cayenne said they forcibly removed it from her at times.

If he was going to terminate Cayenne, who clearly is an asset to you and was to him, why would he keep me?

I don't think Whitney gave the termination order. I think Cayenne was his protégé's experiment and she scared the crap out of the man. He's dead, by the way. Whitney didn't shed any tears. He was going to kill three little girls and Wyatt's wife, Pepper, as well. The three children, not even two years old, are Wyatt and Pepper's girls. Whitney wasn't too happy with his protégé for that order either.

Poor little babies. I'm glad they're safe now.

He wasn't so certain, not with Whitney's three rogue virologists on the loose. *You didn't answer the question. You told Whitney no, but you didn't tell me one way or the other if you can spin a web.*

Yes. I can spin silk.

That's awesome. He poured admiration into his voice. She was sensitive about the ability to make a web because she thought it made her appear less than human. He thought that skill made her even more lethal, and she was kick-ass already.

I miss them. I hope we do have satellite capability, so I can at least say good-bye to Bellisia and Zara and see for myself that they're happy and safe.

Why, Shylah? She'd condemned herself to death. Not just any death — she'd seen what hemorrhagic viruses did to the human body. He wanted to shake her. He wanted to kiss her. Mostly, he wanted to pull her into his arms and hold her, comfort her, although at that precise moment, he might need more comforting than she did. *Why did you kiss me, practically guaranteeing that you won't get out of this?*

I feel the same way about you that you do me, Draden. Maybe in another time or place, I wouldn't admit that to you, but now it seems rather silly to pretend I don't feel that same attraction. No way would you let me die alone. I see that in your mind. You weren't pushing so hard to save yourself, but to save me. That resolve you have, that driving need to save me, to see me through this, I have that same feeling for you.

God. She was so courageous. There was no beating around the bush with her, she just came out and gave him her truth. He glanced down at her again. She hadn't moved. Hadn't taken her eyes from the hut. She lay perfectly still without moving a muscle. That was the cat in her. She could probably keep it up for hours.

I'm telling you, woman, you're everything I could ever want. Thank you. Doing this together is easier. We can look out for symptoms and know the other is willing to provide the bullet if it gets too bad. He hoped it was him. He didn't want her to have to do him and then herself. *We're going to find a way. I want to get in there and see if I can contact Trap and Wyatt. They may be able to help.*

It looks clear. I don't see tracks and I can't smell anything to indicate someone's here.

She pushed off the ground and Draden reached down to help her up. *Is it safe to talk?*

She didn't want to be in his head when they entered the hut. He couldn't blame her. They both had to face their greatest fears. Once inside, they would know if they had any kind of a chance to defeat the virus. He held out his hand to her. She hesitated, just for a moment, and then her chin went up and she sent him a brief, humorless smile and held out hers.

"Yeah, sweetheart, we can talk."

Draden closed his fingers around her much smaller hand. She moved gracefully, all fluid like a cat flowing across the ground. They didn't bother to hide. Neither of their warning systems had gone off and both were confident that they were alone there in the forest.

He had an unfamiliar . . . no, not just unfamiliar — completely alien desire to protect her. He wanted to wrap her up and keep her so close to him that she was wearing his skin. He needed to keep her safe and his reluctance to enter the hut was centered around the fact that he didn't want anything happening to her — certainly not for her to die of a horrific virus. He was grateful she'd been the one to ask for privacy. He didn't want her to think he didn't believe she was his full partner and could handle what had happened to them every bit as well as he could. He might very well lose his mind when the symptoms began to show up. It was early yet and being infected didn't seem real.

They strolled through the clearing as if they were lovers walking through a park. He was aware of everything. The birds singing. The sound of cicadas droning on and on. Rodents scurrying in the vegetation. The wind whispering through the trees. The way the scent of her was so delicate, almost elusive. It could have been that he'd spent the happiest days of his youth in the nursery, after his mother died, far from everyone, breathing in the perfume of peonies, and Shylah's natural fragrance reminded him of the flowers he associated with that time.

He'd had a shit life, and not of his own making, in the beginning. He'd learned rage at such a young age, and how to push everyone away from him. He didn't trust, and he really hadn't learned — nor had he wanted to until he'd found the GhostWalkers. He'd been betrayed by just about everyone he'd ever known, including Dr. Whitney. He'd been lucky enough to find a home with Team Four of the GhostWalkers in the Pararescue Unit. In his life, those men had been the first he'd ever given his allegiance to, and that had been hard-won.

He realized Shylah'd had the same shit life, thrown away by her parents and sold to a doctor who believed that all experiments on throwaway female children were justifiable, no matter what he did to them. Draden had grown cold and something had broken inside of him. Shylah had grown warm and strong, refusing to let Whitney's evil poison her.

He stopped abruptly, just outside the door of the hut, and turned to her, framing her face with his hands. Her skin felt petal soft. Her bone structure delicate. She looked elegant, there in the forest in her camouflage cargo pants, a gun in her side holster, hair braided and wound into an intricate figure eight, and those long lashes fanning her cheeks. She would tempt a saint, and he was far from that. Even acknowledging he was physically attracted and that attraction was strong, he knew he just plain liked her. Admired her. He didn't admire many people, especially women. Too many had come at him for all the wrong reasons.

Draden knew he shouldn't, but he touched her mind, just to see if she was falling apart. To his shock, she wasn't. He expected to hear screaming. Crying. She knew she was going to die. She resolved to save a bullet for herself — and for him, if he was too far gone to do so for himself. She also was certain he would do the same.

He'd almost forgotten she'd been raised military. He'd joined the GhostWalker program knowing he'd be put into situations where there was no way out. He'd joined anyway. He believed serving one's country was a decent way to go. All along, he knew he'd been the one to make the choice and he had his reasons.

Shylah hadn't been given a choice, but she'd been raised military and she was as much a patriot as he was. She also knew she was going to die at some point. She had resolved to get away from Whitney, and that meant death. That was the price. Still, she was willing to pay for her freedom, but she wanted to choose how and when. She'd chosen. It was that simple. There weren't going to be hysterics. Once she'd gotten past the initial shock, she had made up her mind to be his partner and get as many desires checked off the list as possible — just as he had done.

"I'm going to kiss you." He needed to kiss her before he opened Pandora's box. Once he saw what was in the hut, he'd know if there was a chance for her. Strangely, his heart pounded as he waited for her answer.

Shylah continued to stare into his eyes,

taking him somewhere he'd never been, but it was a place he was willing to go. He'd felt physical attraction when he was with other women. He'd never felt like this — wanting to know everything about her. Everything. Her opinions. Her friends. What she liked or didn't like. He'd never cared, and he'd never shared anything about himself with other women. He wanted Shylah to see past his physical appearance to *him.* He needed her to care who he was.

"I was hoping you would."

Her velvet-soft tone stroked his cock like the touch of fingers. That soft voice wrapped around his heart and squeezed like a fist. Those eyes, like the darkest night, sin and temptation, called to him. He bent his head. He didn't have to go too far because she was tall enough for him to reach without stooping down.

Her arms slid around his neck, a slide of petal-soft skin. That familiar delicate scent enveloped him. Then her lips were under his. Cool. Firm. Soft. So inviting. His tongue demanded entry and she parted her lips and let him take her over. As a teen, working in the nursery, he had eaten his share of peonies. He'd become a little addicted to the taste of the flower. The petals were mild, but as a whole, they had a distinctly different flavor. If it was an acquired taste, he'd managed to develop a need for it.

That faint, elusive wintergreen was there, and he chased it. Cool heated fast. He nearly crushed her, pulling her into his arms, locking her there while he fed on her mouth. While he poured everything he was feeling but couldn't say into her. His body recognized her. Knew her. Needed her. Every cell. He'd never been so acutely focused on another human being.

Heat coursed like molten lava through his veins, spreading through his body, moving straight to his groin until he was full and aching, pressed tightly against her. She knew, but it didn't stop her from responding, kissing him back, giving him everything. In that moment, he felt like he belonged. He had a home. A woman. He had it all. Right there in the middle of a forest, with a virus eating his insides, he had it all.

Draden lifted his head just inches from her tempting mouth. "Did you practice kissing? Because I think that's your greatest weapon."

"If I said yes, you'd start wondering who I practiced with since we despised Whitney's supersoldiers." There was mischief in her eyes and teasing in her tone.

He laughed. He stood outside a hut where madmen had brought a virus that potentially could wipe out mankind, that virus eating away at him, but he was laughing. Because of her. Shylah Cosmos. She was so damned beautiful, inside and out, that he was shocked she would even look at him.

"That was totally unfair. Now, just because you said that, I'm going to have this image in my head and I'll not be able to get it out." He ran his thumb over her lips, listening to his heart pounding in his ears. Roaring really. For her.

"I can't help it if you took that all wrong and now you're perving on the idea of women practicing — with each other." Her eyes were wickedly laughing at him. She leaned into him, her tongue sliding over the seam of his lips. "Let's get this done. I'm wiped out and need sleep, and you're pretty exhausted as well."

He kissed her again. Instantly he was swept up in her fire. Flames licked at his body and electricity sparked and crackled in his bloodstream. Little whips of lightning struck his cock over and over as he indulged himself with that heated taste he was already so addicted to. He wasn't as careful this time, taking it up a notch, needing that burn to consume him. He wanted the fire. The flames. That lightning striking him, sending his body into a frenzy for her.

He was more alive in that moment than he had ever been. He devoured her, getting a little high off the taste of her. The owner of the nursery had shown him that peonies could be candied, and that sweet taste would linger in his mouth after he consumed the exotic garnishes in numbers. He felt that way now, kissing her, tasting candied peonies and knowing they were all for him.

He pressed his forehead against hers, drawing in air, looking down at her flushed face and the sweep of her long lashes. "I'm not certain you're entirely sane for making the decision to risk your life like you did, but thank you. In the short time I've known you, you've given me the best experiences I've ever had."

He would never have admitted such a thing if he hadn't known they were dying. She deserved to know she made his life so much better. That she was special. Exceptional. "You look like an innocent angel, Shylah, but you kiss like fucking sin."

Her eyes danced at him, lighting her face. Her skin was pale and creamy, her freckles a dust of gold. That fist inside him closed tightly around his heart and squeezed hard.

She got to him every time.

"You ready for this?"

She nodded. "If we can raise your unit, do you think I could speak with Bellisia and Zara? Tell them good-bye."

It was the first time her voice broke, and that got to him. He swept his arm around her shoulders and brought her in close to him. "Sure, but I'm going to ask them about this habit the three of you developed, practicing your skills on one another."

Color swept up her face, but she laughed, just like he hoped. "I didn't say that, and don't you *dare* say something like that on an open channel."

He laughed. "I like that you think I would. It might keep you in line. You're always tempting me when I have work to do."

He got exactly what he'd hoped for. Shylah laughed and smacked his chest with the flat of her hand.

Draden kissed the top of her head and then took the lead, moving up the stairs to the door of the hut. He pushed open the door with two fingers. He didn't have gloves, so he used a wad of paper towels he'd gotten from the ranger's cabin, but wasn't certain why. He was already infected. Habit maybe. Stepping in front of Shylah might protect her from a bullet, but not from the virus he was certain he shared with her. Still, he did it. He couldn't help needing to shield her.

He looked around the hut. It was very typical of the remote labs the Navy set up when helping the WHO contain an outbreak of Ebola. He was very familiar with the Navy's solar-powered lab in a box, and knew he was looking at one. The three virologists had set up the field lab just as they would have had they been assigned to help the WHO with the outbreaks.

Ebola, he was well aware, had killed over eleven thousand people in six countries. As recently as the year before there had been an outbreak in the Congo and another outbreak had just been reported, not more than a week earlier. Looking at the extremely well-put-together field lab, Draden wondered if these three men had worked on any of those outbreaks. It was certainly possible with Whitney's ties to the military.

"They brought a solar-powered lab in a box with them and quite a few hazmat suits along with gloves. You have to wear three layers of gloves. They have air respirators. See where the remains of the suits they've used have been incinerated? In that barrel? They clearly have been taking precautions to make certain they didn't get infected."

Draden tried to keep the little sneer from his voice. It was there in his mind. "These men, for whatever reason, allowed an entire village to die," he murmured aloud. "For what? Money? I detest the fact that they would trade a few dollars for human lives." At the same time, the hazmat equipment meant the virologists weren't vaccinated, and that wasn't good.

Shylah shrugged. "I've never had money one way or the other, so I certainly don't understand it."

"I have," Draden confessed. "I grew up on the streets and had to fight for everything I ever got. In the end, some woman who owned a modeling agency saw me and turned my life around, at least monetarily. Then I found I had just traded one jungle for another. I thought having money was the answer, but believe me, sweetheart, it isn't."

"Power?" Shylah guessed.

"I don't understand the need to feel powerful, to hold life and death over others. I'm a soldier and I have to kill enemies. That's a fact of the life I'm in and I do it. I'm good at it. But I certainly don't think of myself as a god, making decisions like that. Most of the time it's kill or be killed. Some of the time, it's save the world, like now,"

Draden said.

"Whitney craves power," Shylah said. "He definitely has the idea that he's superior to all others and that entitles him to make life-and-death decisions. I imagine the three virologists he hired got sick of him always putting them down. Intellectually, they had to believe they were his equals. I didn't hear that, Bellisia did. We often practiced hiding in plain sight. She was doing that near their laboratory, and they had taken a break and all of them were very angry with Whitney."

"Did she overhear that they wanted to create weapons instead of viruses that would specifically target your immune systems?"

She shook her head. "Whitney told me that."

"Did she report the conversation to Whitney?"

Shylah leveled her gaze on him. "Seriously? It was us against Whitney. We never told him anything unless it got us something we needed. We weren't protecting them either; they were our enemy. As far as we knew they were the ones coming up with the viruses Whitney planted in us to force us back to him."

"Were you aware they were working on a hemorrhagic virus?"

"How would I know that? I'm no scientist," Shylah denied. "I don't know the first thing about viruses. And, honestly, I don't want to."

Draden went still, anger beginning a slow burn through his mind. What the hell had Whitney been thinking, sending her into a mess she couldn't possibly understand or protect herself adequately from?

"Are you saying you'd never seen the results of the Ebola or Marburg viruses on human beings?"

"We keep up on the latest news. I heard a few years ago when Africa got hit so hard and then when there was a scare in the United States, but that was all until this latest news of the small outbreak in the Congo again."

He forced himself to breathe. He wanted to strangle Whitney with his bare hands. "Why the hell would Whitney send you into this situation?" Draden was furious. "You aren't in the least equipped to deal with a hemorrhagic virus, one that could start a pandemic if let loose in a crowded populated area. He had no right to send you, Shylah."

"I wasn't sent to deal with the virus. That wasn't my job." Her brown eyes didn't flinch away from his. Almost defiant. No remorse. "I'm a tracker. A very good one."

"A tracker?" he prompted, but he was certain he knew what it meant. He could track anything or anyone. He had an acute sense of smell and his eyesight was phenomenal. His hearing was exceptional and even when he was running full out, he was aware of everything around him in relationship to him.

"I can track anything. In this case, the three wayward scientists. You save lives, and I take them."

Draden stared at her in utter shock. It was the last thing he expected her to say. He knew she'd been sent after the three virologists, but it didn't occur to him that was her regular job. He had thought she was experienced with viruses so she'd drawn the short straw as an assassin. To call herself a tracker meant she was elite. She was Whitney's assassin. Given her personality, that was insane. She was too compassionate for that kind of work. It wasn't a façade. He'd been in her mind. He saw how empathetic she was.

"All of Whitney's creations are assassins, especially the ones he's been working on lately." He struggled to make sense of what she was telling him.

"Yes, but the genetic altering he did on me makes me singularly equipped to be the one he sends out when it's needed. I have more cat DNA than most, specifically tiger."

Instantly he stiffened. Knowing. Not wanting to know. "What the hell else do you have in you?" He refused to let his mind come up with any possibilities. He kept wiping the slate clean as fast as answers surged in.

"I'm a cocktail of things. I run fast, not like Zara, but where she is superfast, I can go all day."

He didn't want to tell her that Zara was no longer superfast. Her feet had been damaged when she'd been tortured, and she would never have that ability again.

"Eyesight, hearing, my ability to smell, all of my senses are heightened. My hair acts the same way a cat's whiskers do. All that enables me to be very good at hunting prey."

He had those same traits. Whitney liked to pair females with males. He didn't want to think the man had paired them, but it was just too much of a coincidence. He turned away from her, looking back at the room. "I think, with what we have to do, those traits will come in handy." He'd discuss it with her later, but right now, he wanted to put it out of his head. He did so, focusing on the equipment.

"They left in a hurry. Why, I wonder?" He

crossed the room to the freezer. A case lay on top of it with the lid open. It was heavily padded with three cutouts in the dense foam. He touched the case. "Have you ever seen this before?"

She nodded. "That's what Whitney was looking for. He showed me a picture of the outside of it. It acts like a freezer, and they carried the virus out in it."

"The tube is very, very tiny. Only two spaces in the freezing foam. Assuming they sold one to the MSS, they most likely have the other vial."

She shook her head and pointed to one of three hazardous waste cans. It was empty other than a single empty ampule.

"They used what they had in one vial while working with it, which meant they had a minuscule amount, but it doesn't take much at all to wreak havoc. A drop in the air. If they've already perfected the virus, then they had to be looking for a way to be immune to it." He looked around at the various hazard bags he could see into.

"Here's the computer." Shylah flipped the switch. "It's powering up."

He continued to look around the room at the equipment. There was a tiny freezer and refrigerator, Bunsen burner, a variety of graduated pipettes with disposable tips and conical tubes. He paced through the small space looking at everything, trying to recreate what the three virologists were doing out in the middle of a forest. Nitrile gloves, the computer, an electron microscope, glass slides, centrifuge and the all-important hood, which meant they were actively testing the virus. The suits and respirators were next to the wall where a small washing station had been set up.

"We're up and running," Shylah reported.

Draden immediately switched his attention to the computer. The notes were right there in plain sight. No passwords, nothing to protect their work. They'd left in such a hurry they hadn't destroyed anything at all. Again, he didn't have the answer for why they would do that, but he was going to figure it out. Just not this minute.

He hit up Trap Dawkins, the smartest man he knew, ringing him, uncaring of the distance. Trap answered almost immediately, his face swimming into view. He didn't say a word but waited until he saw Draden's face. There was no visible change of expression, but his breath hitched and his eyes lit up.

"Draden. Who did you sell your soul to in order to get online? You doing okay?"

"No signs yet, but I'm fuckin' tired. I'm

sending you all kinds of data in the hopes that you can find me a therapy to counter this thing. I think the three bastards working on it were also working on a vaccine. Their original job with Whitney was to create viruses to infect the girls Whitney needed to keep under his control. Each virus was a designer, threatening a particular woman. He then had an antiserum he could inject into them if the capsule broke open and infected them. They hadn't perfected the last with this virus, nor had they come up with a vaccine. At least, that's what it looks like to me."

"What happened to your head?"

"Got shot and then I knocked myself out diving into a river. Bellisia and Zara's friend, Shylah Cosmos, rescued me. Whitney sent her here to kill the three men. They worked for him and developed this shit. I'm sending you an audio file as well, explaining everything. I've got their notes here. I'll work here when I can, but I have more faith in your ability to find a therapy in time, at least for Shylah. She gave me CPR and she's infected as well. We can't go after these men ourselves, and they have to be stopped."

"I'm here in Indonesia. In Sumatra. The military set up a lab for me. Wyatt and Joe are with me. I'm bringing in Louisiana and

Ezekiel."

Others crowded around Trap. Draden found himself grinning, which he never would have done before. He leaned into Shylah. "He'll hate that. He doesn't like to be in close proximity of anyone other than Cayenne, his wife. Especially if they're touching him."

He put his arm around her and drew her into view of the camera. "The three virologists are Tyler and Cameron Williams from Mississippi and Agus Orucov from here in Sumatra. They worked for Whitney developing the viruses to kill the girls if they didn't get back to their handlers fast enough. We think they will be targeting the GhostWalkers, so alert all teams and be very careful."

"Will do," Trap said. "Are you showing any signs of infection yet?"

The screen split, and Ezekiel was there with a few of the other GhostWalkers and Bellisia and Zara in the background.

"It's early," Draden hedged. "I'm going to take a sample of both of our blood. This place has a remote lab set up. It's done too well. Obviously these three men, or at least the Williams brothers, have worked in the field before. Everything is contained, but they left in a hurry. I need to find out why."

"I need to know what's happening with

your blood as soon as possible, Draden," Trap said. "In the meantime, send me everything you've got. I'll look over the notes, everything you're sending me now and I'll be working out of there to increase our times. Wyatt and I will divide it up and come at it from two different angles. We'll share with every other military lab with good people so we up the chances of coming up with a therapy. We're running against the clock."

"I'm aware." The fact that Trap had already flown out told Draden he knew time was flying by. "Zeke, is it possible for Shylah to talk to Zara and Bellisia? She's been a trouper through this entire thing. She'd like to see them if possible."

"Draden." Trap's breath hissed out in a protest. "We don't have time for sentiment."

"You don't," Draden said when Shylah tried to pull away from him. He locked her in place to his side. "We do. We both need this contact, Trap. Have Nonny explain it to you sometime."

"After. I'll have her do that after," Trap said. "I have a million questions."

"Hold on to them. Zeke, please get Bellisia and Zara."

"We're here," Zara said off-camera.

She shouldered her way through the wall

of GhostWalkers. Like Shylah, she was tall. Bellisia was very tiny and she followed in Zara's wake. Zeke hovered, his hands on Bellisia's shoulders to give her support. Gino, Zara's husband, was standing behind Trap and Wyatt, still in Indonesia with the rest of his unit.

Zara sank into a seat and Bellisia stood very close to her. The three women stared at one another. Shylah put her hand up to the screen. Her two "sisters" followed suit. A fine tremor ran through Shylah's body. Draden felt it and wanted to pull her onto his lap, but was concerned she wouldn't like it in front of everyone.

"I was worried," Shylah whispered. "I had no idea if you were alive or dead."

"Alive," Bellisia said. "This is my husband." She leaned back and circled Ezekiel's neck with one arm, pulling his head down so the camera picked him up. "He's wonderful, Shylah, and so smart. Too smart. Trap is off-the-charts crazy smart and so is Wyatt. They'll figure this out. I know they will."

"Hi, Ezekiel," Shylah said. "I'm so glad you're taking good care of Bellisia. She's an amazing woman."

"I think so too," Ezekiel said. His gaze moved over Draden and then Shylah. "You two hang in there. We're going to get you out of this."

"Regardless, I'll record everything for you, all symptoms as they come up. I have a bitch of a headache right now," Draden admitted, "but that's probably from the blow to the head."

Shylah immediately turned toward him, her fingers gently sliding over the bump there. "You need to lie down, Draden." She turned back to the screen. "Whoever is in charge needs to order him to rest."

"That would be me," Ezekiel said. "Or Joe. I'll be here to defend the home, Draden. Joe's there to be the liaison between you and the labs. He'll collect your blood daily and bring you supplies. We're working things out."

"What about the MSS?"

"The Kopassus is ringing the ranger station. They'll allow you through to pick off the members of the terrorist cell, but they'll make certain the MSS don't come to you. We'll use a helicopter to drop what you need and collect the blood samples. So far the MSS hasn't come this far into the interior of the forest. They're staying close to the river."

"Sounds good."

"If you get run-down, that won't help. You have to be strong enough to fight this mother off, you understand me?"

With his team rallying to help them, Draden felt hope. Not a lot of it, but if the three virologists thought they could manufacture antibodies to fight the virus, then his extremely intelligent teammates could as well. He had no doubt that Trap — one of the smartest men on the planet — could do it; it was just a matter of whether or not he could do it in time.

"Yes, sir. I'll be resting, and then we're going to go after more of the MSS members. I managed to take a few of them out, including their commander. We need to know if they have any of the virus left. If they do, it has to be recovered and destroyed."

"Don't get killed."

"I don't intend to."

Shylah hadn't said a word, but he knew she wanted to talk to Zara. He sat back in his chair and indicated for her to speak.

"Zara, I was hoping you made it out of Cheng's place. I planned on taking care of these men and then coming to get you. Draden told me his team rescued you."

"That's right." Zara nodded her head. "Zeke, Gino and the others came for me. Gino and I are married. I wish you could meet him. He's there in Sumatra with Joe and the others. He's absolutely a rock for me."

"It's good that you have him." Shylah's hand, under the tabletop, slipped into Draden's.

"I'm here, princess," Gino said, moving in front of Trap. "Good to meet you, Shylah. Zara and Bellisia talk about you all the time."

Draden looked at her. She was trying very hard not to cry, but he could see that was going south fast. "We're going to be breaking up soon," he reported, warning the others they would need to go.

"I love you both so much," Shylah said. "Please be happy. For me, be happy." She turned away from the computer, backed away and hurried out of the room.

Draden hurriedly sent the files to Trap. "I'll try to contact you tomorrow around the same time. Keep an eye out because if I can, it will be sooner."

"Done," Trap said. "We're on this, Draden."

He counted on that.

6

Shylah was so embarrassed that she'd fallen apart. She hadn't realized how emotional she'd be when she actually saw Zara and Bellisia. They both were in tears, neither even trying to stop the emotions, although the tears just ran silently down their faces. Maybe they weren't even aware of it. She was happy for them that they'd found partners. If they felt anything like she did when she was in Draden's company, she was certain they were going to live very happy lives.

It was strange thinking that she'd only known Draden a few hours, when already she was fiercely protective of him and liked being in his company. She wasn't that fond of men. She'd really only been exposed to Whitney, his guards and his supersoldiers, none of whom were very nice.

When any of the women left the compound, they were given an injection to make them sleep, so they weren't aware where Whitney embedded the virus capsules in their bodies, but also so they wouldn't know how to get in and out of his compound. She knew the last part was so the women couldn't lead the authorities back to Whitney. They always had an appointed place where they met their handlers, so they could be given the necessary injection to counter the virus if they were late. Otherwise, Whitney removed the capsule once they were back.

She took in several deep breaths and forced herself to look around at the trees swaying in the wind. It wasn't as if she could get blown away, but the gusts felt strong. She took another deep breath and automatically checked their surroundings. Stepping off the low porch she circled the small hut the virologists had been using, making certain they were safe.

Her partner was inside working, and she needed to do her part. She was a very good guard and scout. She needed a little space from Draden. Making certain they were still very much alone was a good way to give herself time to sort out her feelings.

She'd told Draden that he was feeling attraction toward her because they were in an extreme situation and she'd honestly believed that at first, mainly because she wasn't prone to physical attraction toward any man. With Draden it was off the charts. More importantly, so was her emotional attachment to him. That had formed very fast. Too fast for her liking.

She was very self-sufficient. She didn't depend on others, not even Bellisia and Zara. She was comfortable being alone. She didn't like to be touched. There was a plethora of reasons why Draden and she didn't work, yet she hated not being in his mind. She actually had to use discipline to keep from constantly touching his mind.

Shylah liked him. A lot. More than a lot, and she wondered why. What made him so different? She'd watched him single-handedly take out a large number of the enemy. He had handled himself admirably when he'd found out he'd been injected with the virus. He'd been matter-of-fact when he told her what his team had been doing and how he'd cut himself loose. He seemed more concerned with finding a way to fight the virus off for her than for him.

"Okay, fine. I'm crushing hard," she admitted to the cicadas and frogs. "Very, very hard." She had to go back into that horrible little cabin where the evidence of her fate was all around her. She could handle that as long as she didn't have to look at the sorrow in Bellisia's and Zara's eyes.

Resolutely, she pushed open the cabin door. Draden was sitting on a stool, his eye to a microscope, and there was a frown on his face. He glanced up. "Come look at this, Shylah." His eye went back to the scope.

She couldn't help the smile welling up. She'd been outside thinking of him and daydreaming, acting like a lovesick idiot, and he was so far from her it wasn't funny. She could tell his mind was consumed with whatever he was looking at.

"What is it?"

"Blood. There were samples in the freezer. All are clearly from the same donor. There's no name on the vials, but there's a number. P-001×1. The second is P-001×2. They're numbered up to five."

Shylah frowned at him. "Is there something special about the blood?"

"Each different species has different cell surface proteins in their red blood cells."

She raised an eyebrow at him but came to stand beside him. He moved his head just enough to give her access to the microscope. She peered in. What she saw was cool, but she didn't understand it. She looked up at him for a better explanation.

"Put simply, we can't use animal blood on humans because our bodies would reject it. What you're looking at is neither animal nor human, but some kind of combination of both. I've only seen this in GhostWalker blood."

She went still. "One of us? Wait. They used us for some kind of base for a virus?"

"I can't tell what they used to create the virus. It stands to reason, if they were creating viruses aimed specifically at each woman where you were, and I presume at Whitney's other facilities, that they would start with specific blood. I'm hoping Trap or one of the other military virologists might figure it out."

"That makes sense." She really hated the idea, but it was a fact that Whitney paid the three scientists to construct viruses to kill them if they tried to escape.

"Have you ever seen what an actual filovirus looks like? *Filo* is thread. The virus presents in a few different ways. It can look like spaghetti or a snake, if you will. It can appear hooked, or spherical, even like the number six." He frowned, clearly trying to describe it to her. "Like filigree. It's distinctive."

"Okay." She got the picture but didn't know how the blood he was looking at, which had none of what he described in it, was in any way related.

"Filoviruses cannot replicate themselves. They have to find another way, another cell in order to replicate and survive. They work by attaching themselves to the membrane of the cell. The cells have a receptor that allows the virus to attach itself. Once the virus attaches to the cell membrane it moves inside the cell to the cytoplasm and starts to replicate."

Shylah shook her head but waved her hand to indicate he needed to keep going. She had no idea what he was talking about.

"Picture the receptor as a three-dimensional configuration that fits the virus perfectly. If the shape of that design is changed even slightly, the virus can't attach itself to that cell."

Shylah wasn't certain she needed to know how the virus worked. She just needed to know it was out there, let loose on an unsuspecting mass of people. Those people had been innocently going about their daily lives and three men had decided they would, for money, unleash hell on the world. That was what she needed to know, and those three men needed to be hunted, found and exterminated.

Draden wrapped his arm around her waist

and pulled her closer. "Pay attention, sweetheart. I'm actually going somewhere with this. We can't transfuse from one species to the other, which is a protection against the transfer of viruses. In other words, animals can get sick with illnesses specific to them, but they don't pass those on to us. There are exceptions. You can give a pig a cold. There are some species of monkey that can transfer an illness to a human and vice versa. But generally, it doesn't happen."

Shylah looked at him and then at the smear of blood on the slide. She still didn't see where he was going with it, but it was important to him and he was explaining it in a way she could understand and not want to pull her hair out.

"I'm listening, Draden, but you know, this isn't my thing. I'm here for a very different reason than you are."

He looked up at her, and her heart accelerated. His face was so perfectly masculine. A gorgeous man. Everything about him. Those eyes of his, darker blue than the deepest sea, his hair spilling across his forehead, that strong jaw and aristocratic nose. He was breathtaking. More, he looked at her as if he thought she was beautiful and someone to respect, even admire.

"That isn't true, Shylah, not anymore.

You're here with me because you chose to save my life and in doing that, the virus got a foothold in you. I want to take your blood. I've already taken mine. They'll be able to see how advanced the virus is in each of us. While I'm explaining this, I may as well take your blood and get started."

"I thought you didn't like needles." She stepped back, rubbing her arm for no reason at all other than anticipation.

He flashed her a grin that made butterflies take flight in her stomach, and her sex actually fluttered. She ignored that and sent up a silent prayer he had stayed out of her mind. He didn't need to know he sent her body into meltdown mode.

"I detest them, but we need this done." He took her arm, his touch so gentle it turned her heart over.

"I'm okay with you taking my blood." Shylah felt as if she had to reassure him. He was such a mixture, tough as nails and lethal, but with her, unfailingly a gentleman, tender and sweet, looking out for her so carefully. She knew he was more upset that she had the virus and was all but condemned to death than that he shared that same fate.

His gaze flicked from her arm to her face, his eyes smiling. His mouth curved, and that combination of eyes and lips set her heart pounding and her sex pulsing with need all over again. "The thing about that blood I was examining is that the virus didn't attach to the surface of the protein cell as it should have. I checked it multiple times. I read their notes on it. I've only examined two of the samples and a different virus was used in each case. The virus wasn't able to attach to the surface of the cell."

He deftly pulled the needle from her arm. She hadn't felt it go in.

"What does that mean?"

"I'm not certain, because I don't know where the blood came from. Does the P stand for prisoner? X1 and X2 usually would mean times one or times two, but that doesn't make any sense. In their notes, all three men refer to the blood they're testing as belonging to P-001 and then indicating times one up to five. Each was studying the blood separately from the other, so this particular GhostWalker was important to them."

"How would they get blood from one of you?"

"Shylah."

The way he said her name made her heart pound. Her body went instantly still, as if he were a predator and every cell in her told her she needed to go into prey mode and find a way to hide. She refused. She lifted her chin and faced him, not willing to be a victim. This death was her choice and she'd made it because of this man. She wouldn't hide anything from him because he refused to hide from her.

"What is it that I'm not getting?"

"I think this blood is yours. The *P* is for Peony. I think they were studying it because, aside from the obvious, something in you is quite extraordinary."

She had to get past the "aside from the obvious." In the middle of a discussion on why three maniacs considered her blood worth spending copious amounts of time studying, she couldn't very well encourage him to tell her what about her was so obviously extraordinary.

"I'm not sure what you mean." She didn't want to know. Her breath felt as though it was trapped in her lungs and she couldn't reach the air.

For the first time, when he was discussing anything to do with the virus, his expressionless mask slipped and excitement and interest slid over his perfect masculine features, enhancing them even more. "Joe will be picking all this up and taking it to Trap. He'll be able to make sense of this.

He'll have their notes, but it looks to me like they began developing stronger and stronger viruses in order to infect you. The viruses they designed were specifically targeting each individual. Bellisia and Zara could be infected. You couldn't. At least the viruses they tried in those samples didn't work."

Shylah frowned at him. "I was aware Whitney had the Williams brothers and Orucov design viruses to kill each of us. That's the reason he hired them. He made us very aware of that." Silently she was chanting, trying to change what she knew was coming. Was she responsible in some way? Had those three men created something to kill her and in doing so killed an entire village of people?

"Not just the three of you. He had other girls or women in other facilities that he needed to control. He did that through creating viruses and planting the capsules in the women. The viruses had to be ones the women could fight off, if necessary, at least for a short period of time. I've only looked at two samples, but I'm sending them all to Trap," he reiterated. "He'll share with anyone he needs to share with. Bellisia was in China too long, she was trapped through no fault of her own. The capsule dissolved, and she got sick. Her handlers gave her an injection to counter the effects of the virus."

A small burst of anger radiated out of her. "Whitney is such a bastard. Is Bellisia all right? No lasting effects?"

"She's fine. You saw her. She's very happy."

For a minute, Shylah lost her resolve. Bellisia and Zara were going to live long and happy lives. They'd probably have children. She was going to die a horrible death, right here in this place with a man she barely knew.

"Shylah."

He said her name softly and she heard the whisper of caring. Of affection. The sound slipped over her skin, stroking and caressing. She raised her head and forced a smile. If she had to die, she'd chosen this man to die with. *She* had made that choice. Not Whitney. And she was still resolved. Draden was a good man. The best as far as she was concerned. She would not regret her choice.

"I'm good, Draden. Keep going. Tell me everything you think." She meant it, and the ring of sincerity was in her tone.

For a moment his eyes searched hers, and then he nodded, seeing she was telling the truth. She could have loved him for just that moment when he looked as if he would have taken her into his arms and comforted her if she needed it.

"I think the Williams brothers and Orucov had a difficult time creating a virus that would kill you, so they began to experiment in places they shouldn't. They created a simplistic filovirus, one they thought they could reverse. If the virus wasn't able to attach, they would continue constructing one until they got the results they wanted. I think they developed this virus, but before they could test it and find a counter, they had a falling-out with Whitney. The point is, if the three creators of the virus think there's a chance to find a therapy against this virus with your blood, there's a chance for you."

Draden rubbed at his temples and she knew immediately that his head was pounding. He hadn't had any sleep and he'd been shot, although the bullet just grazed him. The fall into the water where he'd hit his head very hard had caused the most damage. In any case, she'd heard enough and wanted out of that lab. She didn't want to think that the virus in any way had anything to do with her, but deep down, she knew his conjecture could be right.

She laid her hand on his arm. "You're exhausted, Draden. You can sleep for a couple of hours and get back to this. I mean it. You're not going to do either of us any good if you're so run-down the virus takes hold too fast. You know that. You spent all night wreaking havoc with the MSS. You've talked to your team and they're on it."

"Whose satellite are we using? It doesn't appear to be geosynchronous. When I pulled it up, there was a time schedule."

"I don't know if Whitney's virologists were using something different, but we're using a military one. Whitney had it moved into place, but we can only have it at various times. I have a satellite phone to contact him if I need data or aid, but there's only certain times I can do that."

"You should have told me."

"I didn't think it mattered. We're both infected and we're not leaving this area or coming into contact with any other human we can infect."

"I'm killing terrorists," he pointed out.

"I realize that. I will be too." She pointed toward the freezer.

He ignored her and paced across the room to another machine. She just managed not to roll her eyes when he inserted a tube of blood.

"We're going to have to kill them from a distance or make certain our mouths and noses are covered and we're wearing gloves the next time we go after them. Not just any gloves, the gloves from this lab. And that has to be after we get a little sleep. I want to make certain they don't have any more of that virus on hand."

"Did you expect to find antibodies in the blood you were examining?" Clearly, he was going to work a little longer. If he needed to bounce his ideas off her, she had to have a clearer understanding of what he was looking for.

"They did. The Williams brothers and Orucov. The three of them. Why do you suppose they left in such a hurry? They didn't even try to cover their tracks. Could they have spotted you?"

"That's just insulting. I was trained in the military. They are civilians and have no real idea of self-defense. They lived in their lab. They stuck together and didn't have outside friends. No way did they spot me. They were gone just before I got here. Maybe even the same day."

"Why do you think that?"

She watched him as he went from his machine back to the computer and entered information. He was fast on a keyboard, she noted. Very fast. His hands fascinated her. He glanced at her over his shoulder, reminding her she'd been asked a question.

"When I looked through the window, it appeared as if they were coming right back, not as if they'd made a hasty departure. I spent a day setting up in the ranger station and watching the hut through my binoculars. That night I set up a blind in two different trees on either side of the hut, but they hadn't come back to the hut and it looked as if they were gone. In the morning I tracked them to the village where the terrorists are located. The tracks were fresh and led directly to the village. That was why I was doing surveillance there when you decided to strike."

"You're fearless, aren't you?" He hesitated a minute. "You're very good, Shylah. I ran right at you, and very few things get past me when I'm in hunting mode. I didn't see you until I was practically on top of you."

"You thought about killing me. I saw it on your face."

"Then why didn't you kill me immediately?" He looked as if he might shake her.

"We clearly were on the same team. You killed over a dozen of the bastards and I wasn't about to reward you by killing you. They deserved it." She kept her voice mild, but she felt very strongly about it. The moment she had spotted him, moving like a deadly shadow from guard to guard, to the commander's house, the little infirmary, everything in her rose up to protect him. He had been magnificent. He had done what she wanted to do.

Her orders were clear. Find her targets and take them out. She couldn't deviate from that, not even to retaliate against the Milisi Separatis Sumatra, no matter how much she wanted to. Personal retribution wasn't allowed, not when the stakes were so high. "Why didn't you? You could have killed me. You jumped right over me."

He'd cleared her by several feet and had done it with ease. He hadn't even been breathing that hard. She could run, not like Zara had been able to, but she could run when she had to. He'd made it look easy.

Draden turned away from her, staring down at his machine. "You were the most beautiful woman I'd ever seen."

When he said things like that so casually, he stole little pieces of her heart. No one had ever talked to her like that. She had freckles. That was girl-next-door, not beautiful. She wasn't exotic, a real beauty, like Zara, or tiny and perfect like Bellisia. She thought of herself as gangly, all arms and legs. For the longest time she was a string, thin and long with a mop of wild, untamable hair and eyes too big for her face. Her skin was so white she probably blinded people if she showed her tummy, and then there was always the freckles. No amount of makeup was going to cover them up completely, so she didn't bother trying.

It had taken forever for her to get any kind of a figure, a butt and breasts. They came late in her teens, very late. Now, she couldn't complain, but she'd been lying in the dirt on her belly, partially covered with debris and plants. She could lie still for hours, so still, the surrounding wildlife eventually crawled or slithered over her as well. Creepy, crawly things normally left her alone and very few spooked her.

"I'm ready. Let's go get some sleep," Draden announced, before she could reply to his compliment.

She didn't really know what to say. Being attracted to him was out of her field of expertise. He held out his hand to her as they went out the door and without thinking she took it. His fingers instantly closed around hers. He was strong, but careful. He didn't crush her, but instead, folded her hand with his snug around it, to his chest. He held it as if her hand was the most treasured thing he possessed.

It was silly to feel a thrill just at hand-holding, but it was a new experience for her.

It was clear Draden liked taking her hand and walking close to her. She hadn't thought she would like it; before no one ever touched her, or they'd find themselves on the floor, but it was totally different with Draden.

"I love the night." She looked around her. So much of the day had already passed. She should have forced him to go to sleep earlier. He looked very tired, and his skin color was off and he was very clammy. Tiny beads of sweat dotted his forehead. She had the feeling he was standing from sheer will. Alarm skittered down her spine. She didn't want to lose him. More, she didn't want to be the one to put a bullet in his head. She would — for mercy — but everything in her rebelled against it. She forced air through her lungs. "Darkness falls fast in the forest."

Night creatures were beginning to stir. Owls flitted from tree to tree, looking for a perfect place to wait out their prey. Rodents and lizards scurried in the thick vegetation, rustling leaves as they sought food. The frogs called, and the cicadas sang. To Shylah, there was harmony in the forest's song — it was rich and teeming with life.

"I believe you'd like where I live," Draden said. "Louisiana is beautiful. I don't think a lot of people appreciate it for what it is. The people have had to carve out their livings under difficult conditions, but for most of them, it's been worth it."

She glanced up at his face. Ordinarily, when Draden spoke, he sounded matter-of-fact. Casual even, no matter the subject. Without him being aware, animation had slipped in. His face lit up. That face that was unbelievably handsome was even more so.

"You obviously love the swamp."

He nodded. "I have real freedom there. I can run when I have to, and I can just take a boat on the river and there's peace, Shylah. Such peace. I could see us there. A house, the pier. Right on the river. Which means we'd have to contend with flooding, but every day we'd have that beauty."

Her heart turned over. He'd included her, and he didn't make a thing of it. He just made her feel like she was that important to him.

"What's the weather like there?"

"Like this, actually. Hot and humid. Thunderstorms. Wild lightning. The occasional hurricane." He grinned down at her, and for the first time, he looked very young. A mischievous boy up to no good, inviting her to participate with him.

"I do like storms. And hot and humid. I've never actually been near a hurricane and I think I'd prefer to keep it that way. I'm going to make a run for it if one comes our way." She entered into the fun of sharing his world. She'd never be there in person, but she'd have this with him. It would have to be enough. She refused to feel sorry for herself when she'd made the choice.

They walked up the stairs to the ranger's cabin together. Brushing up against Draden as he lifted his foot to take the next stair, she felt a tremor run through his body. It was barely there, but she was acutely tuned to him, aware of his every movement, his every response.

She slipped her arm around his waist. She didn't look it, but she was incredibly strong, strong enough to lend a little of that strength to him without being obvious about it. She did it casually and leaned into him just a little, gripping his belt as if it were the most natural thing in the world to do. Draden did small things that tipped her off to the fact that he was protective of her. He wouldn't like her to see weakness in him.

"I know what you're doing."

She burst out laughing. "So much for being sneaky. And I thought I was so clever." But she didn't let go of his belt and she didn't pull away.

He tugged open the door and indicated for her to go ahead of him. She did what she always did. She scented the air and checked to make certain the few lines of silk hadn't been broken. She had them at each window, the front door and back. Those were her alarms. No one would notice a few random spiderwebs.

While she ascertained the webs were intact, she took advantage of the genetic code of a large cat Whitney had edited into her DNA to ensure no one had gotten past her first alarm. The fine hairs on her body read the air, sending her information the way the whiskers on a cat would. It was habit to check and recheck. That was what kept her alive. She used every sense to try to discover an enemy. Only when she was positive no one had entered the ranger's cabin in their absence, did she step inside and help him over to the bed.

Draden sank down onto it. "Thanks. My head is hurting like a son of a bitch."

Shylah frowned. "What does that mean? 'Hurting like a son of a bitch.' I don't understand. That's like saying 'break a leg' to someone about to perform. It doesn't make sense." Her frown instantly turned to laughter. "I drove Whitney so crazy when he would try to explain that kind of thing to me. If it didn't make sense, there was no explanation." She tried hard not to see that he was running a temperature. She didn't want him to be sick.

Draden started to untie his boots, and Shylah, heart pounding, crouched down to do it for him. She ignored his resistance and kept talking, acting like they were an old married couple and she'd been taking his boots on and off for years.

"When I realized it made him nuts that I couldn't get it when he used idiotic sayings, I really refused to understand them. He goes ballistic if you challenge him. I did on more than one occasion."

Draden gave up trying to push her hands away. He sat straight and stared down at her. His blue eyes were vivid and seemed to see right through her. She kept her head down after the initial glance up. She was feeling too warm. Her body not quite her own. That made her uneasy and very nervous. She could handle any enemy, no matter what form it might take, but the things she felt for Draden were new and unsettling.

Shylah concentrated on removing the boots. Like her, he carried numerous weapons on him. She handed them to him without looking up. Each time his fingers brushed hers, a small wave of heat slid through her bloodstream.

"I'm going to lower the shades so it's darker in here and if, later, we light the lamp, no one can see in." She could tell his eyes hurt in spite of night falling. "Not that I think anyone's out there. Most people avoid the station. There were poachers, but I made certain they left and didn't come near this place again."

"That surprises me."

"What does?"

"That you engaged with them. You know better."

She did. There was no reprimand in his voice, merely curiosity. He was so right. She was on an extremely important mission — one that had to succeed — and yet she'd done things outside the constraints of her job. She should never have exposed herself to the terrorists by diving into the river and saving Draden. She certainly shouldn't have gone anywhere near the poachers. For one, they were dangerous.

"Did they see you? Did they know they were fighting a woman?"

"No." She'd been careful not to be seen. "I wanted them to think the ranger was in residence, so they'd clear out. It worked."

"How?"

"I made it clear I was using lethal force, that my bullets could kill. The poachers ran, but two were caught in traps. The others helped to free them and by the time they got into dense forest, they ran right into spiderwebs, great thick funnels of sticky silk. They had to wonder what kind of spider would weave a web of that size."

A slow smile formed on his face and took every drop of air out of the room. "I wish I could have seen that."

She hadn't realized she'd been waiting for him to chastise her. Yell. Call her stupid the way Whitney always did. Instead, he looked as if he would have enjoyed watching the results of her little antics.

"I am enjoying seeing your antics," he said, confirming he was also picking the images out of her mind. "Why did you choose to let the terrorists see you? That was a massive risk."

She shrugged and told the truth. "You were magnificent." She was dying anyway. She might as well tell him the truth. It might have embarrassed her for him to know how much she admired him at any other time, but it wouldn't matter after they both were gone. "I'd never seen anyone like you before."

He looked disappointed in her and it took

a second for her to comprehend. He thought she was referring to his looks. Most of his life, he'd probably been judged on his looks.

"You went through that village like a ghost. A phantom. The coolest harbinger of death there ever was. Every time I blinked, it seemed you'd killed an enemy." The words tumbled over one another as she explained. "You were a thing of absolute beauty. I watched with my heart in my throat and every single time you moved between sentries, I was certain you'd give yourself away, but you didn't. They had no idea you were anywhere near them even when you slipped up behind them and I could see you."

The tension slid out of Draden and he pulled his tee off with one hand. His belt was next. She held her breath a moment, but he didn't go any further.

"I can't believe you watched me the entire time and I didn't spot you."

There was admiration in his tone. Exhaustion. She studied his face. "Is the headache bad?" She sat on the edge of the bed and removed her shoes as well. "Let me see if I can help."

"The Marburg and Ebola virus symptoms often start with a headache."

Her stomach lurched. She didn't want to

hear that. "It's too soon and in any case, this virus is manmade, designed by three very narcissistic men. It isn't Marburg or Ebola. You got hit in the head and you've been running around like a maniac ever since." She spoke with authority, although she had no idea how soon symptoms usually started.

"You're right, but I haven't slowed down at all, which means it could take hold faster — maybe," he qualified. "It isn't going to start like a normal virus; they injected me with a large dose. I've got it, Shylah."

"Here." Ignoring his declaration, she scooted to the top of the bed and sat, stretching out her legs. "Put your head in my lap. Zara sometimes got headaches and I'd rub her temples for her. This might help."

Draden hesitated. "You do know I'm physically attracted to you."

She did know. It was obvious. He wasn't a small man and she could see the evidence. "I have to admit, I'm equally as attracted to you. What has that got to do with me soothing a headache?" Her heart pounded as she made the admission.

She'd been raised in the dormitory with the other girls. They'd trained and been educated there. The only men they were around were guards, or supersoldiers, teams sent to kill them if they couldn't do their jobs. Shylah had learned to be very good at her job, so good, Whitney sent her out of the compound. Then she hunted men to kill them. She certainly hadn't been attracted to them. She spent more time with Whitney than any other man and if he was any example of what a man was, she wanted no part of that.

"Nothing, sweetheart. I just didn't want you to be startled if certain parts of my anatomy rise to the occasion." There was humor in his voice as he stretched out on his back, head in her lap, his body sprawled across the mattress.

Shylah closed her eyes and pushed her fingers into all that thick, wild hair. "Someone besides Whitney gave you amazing genetics."

There were one or two heartbeats too long before he answered. "I suppose they did. I don't remember them, so I wouldn't know what they looked like or if I took after them."

Shylah sighed. "I never met either of mine. Father or mother. I was abandoned, from what Whitney tells me, and someone took me to the orphanage where he found me. Were you turned over to an orphanage?"

"I was traded for money because my birth mother wanted drugs. I was four at the time, and I can tell you, my life from birth to four was no picnic. She sold me to a woman who wanted kids, but couldn't have them, at least that was what she told me before she died. I didn't care. I thought of her as my mother. She was amazing and sweet. The best."

"What did she look like?" Shylah took her cue from him, speaking of the woman in the past tense.

"She was pretty, at least I thought so. Sweet face. Dark hair until it all fell out. She read to me all the time. Sometimes I think I dreamt her up, but then I remember the songs she sang. They were all learning songs. The alphabet, colors, numbers. She taught me to read. She listened to everything I said and taught me the importance of education."

Shylah loved the sound of his voice. He didn't say it, but there was love there. The woman he was telling her about was truly the one he regarded as his mother. Her fingers moved to his temples, stroked along the orbital sockets and back up to his temples, hoping to ease the headache pounding at his skull.

Until it all fell out. Had she gone through

chemotherapy? Shylah didn't ask. Instead, she waited, hoping he would volunteer the information. She had the feeling not too many people knew about the woman who had bought a child.

"What was her name?"

"Eliza. She was probably about forty, but I didn't notice her age. I don't recall a single time when she raised her voice to me. There was a lot of laughter. Storytelling." For a moment his voice stumbled as if he'd choked on something. "I never let myself think about it, but there was love there. If I know anything about that emotion, Eliza taught it to me."

His ridiculously long lashes lifted and those dark, navy blue eyes were staring at her, moving over her face as if memorizing every line. "She was kind and compassionate, like you are, Shylah. I'd forgotten that. I let her fade into the background, and she never should have been put there. It hurt to remember her too closely."

Shylah could hardly bear to look into those eyes. Draden didn't seem to allow himself to feel his emotions, but she could see them, stark and raw reflected in his gaze. Remembering Eliza did hurt him, but at the same time, he was allowing a flood of good memories in — and she had the feeling he needed those memories to balance out other things that had happened to him.

"She sounds lovely."

He nodded, and his lashes swept down, preventing access to his deepest emotions. Shylah knew she sounded wistful. She'd read about mothers, seen television shows and movies that portrayed the matriarch who doted on her children.

"I never pictured myself with a family," Draden said, reaching up, his hand covering hers, so that her fingers stilled, pressing into his temple. "But meeting you, I know what I missed. I think you're very much like her."

She tried not to feel the burst of pleasure his compliment gave her. She knew it was one of the highest he could pay her. He might not know that, but she did. Eliza might have been the only person he loved in the world.

"Thank you." What else was there to say? His voice was softer, like he was drifting, not hurting so much and she renewed her efforts, massaging his scalp and then his temples. She enjoyed touching him, having his head in her lap.

"Who taught you to be so compassionate and kind, Shylah? Did you have a mother figure? Someone who looked out for you when you were a baby?"

"We had a series of nurses." Her earliest memories didn't have anyone who resembled a mother. "But when I was around three or four, I realized that everyone else came and went but Bellisia and Zara. Even the other girls were moved around. When we were seven, this new house mother came in. Whitney always called them house mothers."

Her fingers massaged the worst spots right at his temple where his head throbbed to the beat of his heart. Each press against his skull drove the demons away. He couldn't explain that to her, but he didn't want her to stop — and she didn't.

"Keep going, my sweet little peony," Draden murmured. "I love the way you smell."

He sounded drowsy, and her heart turned over. She didn't even correct him referring to that hated flower name, which, strangely, she was beginning to like. She was more than susceptible to him; she was already falling fast, and she didn't even care. Not when they both were going to die in a few days. Falling for Draden seemed the only sane thing to do.

"Her name was Helena and she was everything we could have wanted in a mother. She showed us what our lives could have been. She was about forty-five, and I think she must have always wanted children because she treated us as her own." She had to smile, remembering those bright days. "Helena believed in laughter and she taught that to us. How laughter could change every situation into something good. She did too. We loved her, and we learned what love was."

His fingers stroked caresses over the back of her hand. "I feel that in you. Your skin is like the petals of that flower I love so much. Soft. Beautiful. Perfect."

He was drifting. She could tell, and her heart reacted, thundering in response to his touch and his unguarded compliments.

"Go to sleep, Draden, we'll figure it all out tomorrow."

7

Shylah Cosmos was an unexpected gift. Draden moved like a ghost in the forest, so silently, insects rarely were disturbed. He *felt* his way, even moving fast. Having someone with him he suddenly cared about could have been his worst nightmare, but Shylah was as much a ghost as he was. He couldn't find fault with her at all. She had the same feeling for placing her feet carefully, no matter what kind of pace he set.

She was at home in the trees. She was a gazelle on the forest floor. Her instincts were dead-on. Draden had feared she would slow him down or he would worry so much about her that his attention would be divided, but he found himself treating her the way he did his fellow GhostWalkers. He gave her his highest respect by not questioning where she was at any given moment. He moved with his normal speed and never once checked to see if she could keep up, after their initial start.

Shylah seemed to be in perfect sync with him, as if they had been hunting the enemy for years together. That strengthened his belief that the woman had been paired with him. Whitney had the idea that a pair of soldiers, male and female, could be sent out together and they would be just as successful as a unit of soldiers if they had the right weapons. By that, he meant if *they* were the right weapons.

They had both fallen asleep the previous night, his head in Shylah's lap, her hands in his hair. It should have been uncomfortable for him. He'd never spent a night with anyone since he was twelve and learned how vulnerable he could be in sleep. Even with his fellow GhostWalkers, he set himself a little apart and spread a few traps around him. He always slept with weapons at his fingertips, and he woke several times to check his surroundings. With Shylah, he just slept.

She was the most relaxing person he'd ever been around. When he did stir, it was because she moved, sliding down onto the mattress with him. He'd simply rolled onto his side, his body around hers, his arm curling around her waist. They both slept.

Once in his arms, Shylah made no noise

and didn't move. He woke first and looked down at her face, her flawless skin with the dusting of freckles across her nose and under her eyes. The feathery fan of lashes. She was on her side as well, and her hand was tucked under the pillow. He lifted the edge with two fingers to see her fingers curled around the hilt of a knife. Her gun was within reach of her other hand. They'd slept all of the night and most of the day away.

It was taking a chance to go after the MSS in daylight hours, but he didn't have much time left. He was hot, sweat dripping occasionally, and his mind still felt chaotic. In spite of that, Draden had found himself smiling. He was infected with a killer disease and he was waking with a smile. He assessed his body carefully because he needed to be able to handle himself in a fight. Other than the vicious headache, he was still functioning. The site of the dart entry was swollen and red. His temperature was definitely up. His muscles hurt, but strangely, the effects of the virus weren't nearly as harsh as he'd expected. Still, he needed to get this done.

They'd had a good evening, although Shylah had cooked up another really foul-tasting ration before they went back to sleep. Thinking about it, even that had made him laugh. Now, in the light of day, they were making their way through miles of forest back to the village the MSS were using as cover.

It was drizzling, a long slide of silver falling through the canopy. He glanced back at her, looking through the tree branches. She looked beautiful, running along a particularly thick limb. She was sure-footed, moving fast, scanning ahead of her as well as below her. He saw her gaze move upward. He liked that. Most people would have assumed no one could possibly be above them. It was unlikely, but they could do it so that meant someone else might be able to as well.

He held up his fist and she froze, which meant she always kept him in her vision. She was giving him a million reasons to fall in love with her. When she stopped all motion, she went completely still, blending into the foliage around her. He knew exactly where she was, but it was difficult to see her. He sent her a small grin, just because she made him want to smile, and then he was all business again. They were back in MSS territory. The village the terrorist cell had taken over was just ahead, a quarter mile in from the river.

He'd stirred up a hornet's nest the last

time he'd been to the village. By killing the men in the infirmary as well as the commander, he'd signaled to them that he could walk into their homes and kill them at will. He'd taken out the majority of their guards. Worse, he'd turned the table on a boatload of those hunting him. Now, they were everywhere, moving through the forest in numbers, looking for any sign to track him. They seemed to be hunting in pairs, which made his job easier, but first, he had to figure out who had taken over as commander. That man would know if they had any more of the virus.

He waited for two MSS members to pass under the tree he was crouched in, and then he began to move forward again, toward the village. The sound of the barred eagle-owl had him glancing over his shoulder. The laughing hoot, very distinctive, was a perfect replica. They were funny-looking creatures with a soft whistle and a call that sounded like the bird was happy and calling out to make certain everyone knew it.

Shylah signaled to him that she would track and dispose of the two MSS members. *I'll hunt here while you go into the village and find out everything we need to know.*

He'd made it clear he didn't want her with him when he interrogated the new commander, but he hadn't expected her to actively take on those hunting in the forest. She wasn't asking his permission either. He wasn't in charge. She'd made that clear more than once. Shylah was an independent thinker, was used to working alone. Whitney had shaped her into his torpedo, and she went after the enemy; she wouldn't sit at home waiting for Draden to get back from his task.

Draden nodded. *Not going to tell you to be careful, woman, but won't be happy if you fuck up and one kills you.*

Her soft laughter slipped intimately into his head, stroking his body like the touch of her fingers. He'd fallen under the spell of her fingers and now, to have that sensation in his mind was almost erotic.

No worries. I've got this, unless you're worried about getting out of there with half their army on your tail. I'm not certain how many times I can pull you out of the river.

Very funny. Although true. He had nearly blown it. They wouldn't be expecting him to return to their community, which gave him some advantages. *Give me an hour. I should be able to find him, break him and get out of there. If they still have the virus, we'll need to get it back. That's more important than killing every one of them.* It was, but he still intended to do as much damage to them as possible. *And Shylah, once you breathe on them, they could get infected. You have to kill them.*

I'm perfectly aware, Draden. She held up the mask and gloves he'd given her and then slipped them on.

He heard the resolve in her voice. She knew what they were dealing with. She had accepted her fate — that she would die from the virus. He hadn't quite gotten there when it came to her. He was still determined to find a way to save her. He was counting on Trap and Wyatt. Once on a task, they might spend hundreds of hours, with little food or drink, just working to find answers. Draden counted on his friends' intense concentration and brilliant minds to come through for him.

Good hunting, sweetheart.

Same to you.

Then she was gone, fading into the trees. He crouched on the branch, wishing he had the time to track her, to see her in action, but he had to make certain to get any virus left out of the hands of the MSS. In his opinion, no one should have such a weapon, something that could wipe out the majority of the population of the world, but he couldn't control everything. He could go after this group and he could point his fellow GhostWalkers in the direction of the three men who had deliberately created and then sold the virus, allowing the MSS to set it loose on innocent people.

Draden was forced to move slowly as the new commander had spread his men out, so that they walked along the forest floor in twos. A few checked out the trees overhead, but that was rare. As he approached the village, he was tempted several times to drop down and kill a couple of the enemy, but he couldn't tip them off that he was anywhere close and about to infiltrate their stronghold.

From the branches of the closest ironwood trees and further camouflaged from view by the abundance of supplejack vines wrapped around and hanging from branches, Draden watched the flow of the village. It appeared, at first, as business as usual. There were people moving in the marketplace, but after a few minutes, it was evident to him that only men were out, and no one had taken the boats for market. The village traded and sold goods from their boats out on the river, rather than depending on others to come to them.

The men pacing back and forth seemed to be concentrated around the commander's cabin. The man taking over had moved in and doubled his guards, thinking that would make him safe.

Once Draden understood the flow of the guards, their patterns and the way the rest of the village was moving, he leapt from the tree, landing on legs that acted like springs, an inheritance from the big cat genetics Whitney had given him. He donned the gloves and mask he'd found in the remote lab and remained still while he allowed his senses to give him the necessary information to begin his infiltration of the village.

It wasn't hard to look the part. He needed clothes and he chose a soldier approximately his own height and weight. He took the guard as he approached the river with his automatic carelessly thrown over his shoulder. The man was too busy eating and drinking as he walked his rounds, certain that the enemy wouldn't be foolish enough to come back.

Draden left him in the heavy brush, removed his mask and then walked boldly back to the village. He cradled the weapon as if it were his best friend — and right then it probably was. He moved with absolute confidence, keeping his face hidden in a hood, presumably to avoid the steady downpour. No one challenged him as he went past the guards right into the heart of the village.

He skirted the small marketplace, snagging a papaya off the rickety table of one of the local farmers. The man made a rude gesture but didn't stop him, and two nearby soldiers snickered. Calmly, he pulled out a large knife and peeled the fruit, dropping the peelings as he walked in the general direction of the commander's cabin. Again, he wasn't challenged, not even as he got close enough to see into the windows.

There were three guards rotating around the structure and they were bored beyond words. One was smoking. A second stopped briefly to chat with the smoker before continuing his circuit. Draden paused, in plain sight, digging his knife into the papaya to remove the seeds before slicing off a piece and putting it in his mouth. The juice ran down his fingers and he licked at them, seemingly enjoying the fruit. All the while he timed the guards' rotation.

They couldn't be on all sides of the house since there were only three of them. In spite of the rain, the sunroof had been left open and that was his entry point. He knew the roof would be slick, but it would get him inside. He waited, mentally running over each move in his mind, perfecting it until there were no mistakes. There was always the potential for that unfortunate, unforeseen complication that could fuck up a perfect operation, but other than that possibility, his plan was nearly foolproof.

The second the guards broke apart, he was all business, gaining the porch as if he owned it, swinging up onto the eaves, holding the automatic so it didn't clank against the wood and long fronds making up the roof as he made his way up the steep pitch to the open sunroof. He'd chosen the darkest side, where the shadows from the forest would help him blend in.

He glanced down into the interior and then entered, again without hesitation. He had memorized the layout after studying it before, and the moment his feet hit solid flooring, he went low and looked around, a full sweep, to ensure he had entered without being seen. Adrenaline pumped through his body, heightening his senses until each was razor sharp.

Movement came from the bedroom, and he took a moment to sweep the rest of the small house to ensure he and his target were alone. Satisfied, he once more put the mask on to be certain he wouldn't leave any of the virus behind and headed for the other room. The commander sat at the desk, head in his hands, pushing at his hair over and over. He didn't look happy.

Draden walked right up behind him and removed his sidearm. "Don't make a sound or I'll shove this knife right through the base of your skull." He spoke in the local dialect, and immediately the man stiffened.

"I speak English." The man stared straight ahead feeling the tip of Draden's knife. It wasn't in any way trifling. He preferred smaller knives, but when you wanted to make a statement, you did it big. He wanted this man cowed and willing to talk.

"I suggest you listen and obey every word. Do not cry out for help. If you do, I won't kill you outright. I'll gag you and slice you into little pieces." To make his point, he trailed the tip of his knife from the base of the man's skull down along the left side of his spinal column, cutting through the clothes and leaving a thin streak of blood.

The man nodded his head.

"Your name?"

"Intan Lesmono." The new commander mumbled it. There was a tremor to his voice. He kept his eyes fixed on the wall across the room, holding himself very still.

"I'm a little pissed, Intan. Not only did you wipe out the people of Lupa Suku, but you infected me. Do you know what that means to you? If I sneeze on you or breathe too hard, you're going to die a very ugly, painful death. Just like the death you condemned those people to."

Lesmono shook his head. "Not me. I didn't have anything to do with that. I swear . . ."

"I saw them. Men. Women. Children. All dead. And they died hard."

Lesmono made a choking sound. "I know. I didn't have anything to do with it. They needed money . . ."

"Who? Who needed money?"

"Agus Orucov. He grew up here. We all know him. Worked for a big shot in the U.S. and they had a falling-out. He claimed he developed the virus, but his former boss somehow cut off their funds."

He was talking too much. Telling him things he wasn't asking for. Either he expected company, or he really was horrified that they'd wiped out so many innocent people.

"They had a buyer, big money, but they need some kind of vaccine against it. They thought they had it, but something went wrong. They tested it on a couple of Orucov's enemies. That's the way he is. He holds a grudge. They were in school together as kids, and he still is angry at them. Maybe he thought the vaccine would work, but it didn't."

That explained the three men who had died before those in the village. "Where's the rest of it? You still have more of it."

A sob escaped Lesmono's throat. "I don't know how to get rid of it. I don't want it around me, my men or these people. This was my village. I grew up here."

"You knew the people of Lupa Suku." Draden made it a statement.

Lesmono nodded, his head hanging. "Yes." It came out a whisper.

This man had taken charge, but he wasn't happy with what had gone before him. Draden wanted to feel sorry for him, but he didn't. Lesmono hadn't done anything to stop his former commander from killing innocent people.

"Where is it?"

Lesmono pointed a shaky finger to the door that was on the side of the desk where he sat. Draden's heart gave a powerful jerk of shock. What the hell were they thinking?

"Take it out."

Lesmono shook his head. "I'm not touching it."

"Open the door." To emphasize that he meant business, he let Lesmono feel the very, very sharp edge of his knife, by tracing another path from the base of the skull down the right side of the spinal column, leaving a second trail of blood.

Lesmono reached down and pulled open the door. There was a small desk refrigerator built inside. Keeping the knife at the base of the new commander's skull, Draden opened the refrigerator door. A small metal case was inside surrounded by ice packs. Clearly no one knew what they were doing with the virus.

"Take it out carefully. I'm already infected so I could care less if you accidentally drop the thing." Draden kept his tone matter-of-fact.

For the first time, Lesmono turned his head slightly toward the window, and Draden felt him fill his lungs with air. He was far more afraid of the virus than he was the knife. Draden slammed the blade through the base of his skull. The new commander fell forward and face-planted onto the desk.

Draden checked the case. It was filled with ice, and sitting in a bed of cooling foam was a plastic ampule containing only a couple of drops, but that was all that was needed to wipe out a good portion of the world. Drops. He shook his head as he closed the case. What were the three men thinking? It was insanity.

Tucking the case inside his shirt, he moved in silence across the room to the other living space where the sunroof remained open in spite of the rain falling. The earlier, soft rain was now falling at a steady pace and the floor was saturated. He easily made it to the roof but had to lie prone, stretched out in plain sight while the guards made their rounds. Then he was on the porch and back on the ground, walking away, hood pulled up and his weapon in his arms.

Without hurrying, he made his way through the village. Because he acted completely confident and in control, no one challenged him. He kept to himself. He could speak the language, but he didn't look like a native and he wasn't taking chances, especially now that he had the virus. He would have used any means necessary to gain the information he needed on the whereabouts of the remainder of it, but he'd gotten a lucky break in finding the commander had a conscience.

He headed away from the river, back toward heavier forest. Somewhere, Shylah was hunting. He wanted to join her, but he needed to get the ampule back to the remote lab and inform Trap it was there.

Joe would send someone immediately to collect it. He had the times Whitney had the use of the military satellite. He had about three hours. Tigers could easily leap ten feet straight up and he used that ability to get into the trees where the arboreal highway afforded him fast movement without detection.

He had been careful to close the cabinet in the desk, leaving the commander slumped in his chair for his men to find. He knew he was already going to be gaining a reputation, a phantom in the forest, one darted with the virus but sneaking into the village and killing whenever and whomever he felt like.

He began to make his way back through the trees the same way he had come, hoping to find evidence of Shylah's work. When he reached the place they had split up, he went ten feet farther, and just under the tree he saw two bodies. The men lay facedown in the rotting vegetation. He couldn't see how they had died. Their injuries had to be in the front. That made him frown. She'd faced them. She hadn't shot them because the sound of the bullets exiting the gun would have reverberated through the forest and carried back to the guards surrounding the village.

Curious, he leapt to the ground and turned one man over. There were two small wounds at the left side of the neck — two holes with thin metal needles sticking out of them. She had severed the external and internal carotid arteries and had either thrown the needles or used a blowgun. Either way, it took tremendous skill to hit exactly where she needed to with such a small weapon. He inwardly whistled low, gaining new respect for his partner.

You within reach? Telepathy was only as good as the distance they could maintain it, which, sadly, as a rule, wasn't that far. The GhostWalker teams carried small radios just in case that bridge between them failed. He had a strong connection with Shylah and hoped it was still available to them.

Yes.

That single word seemed to fill the places in him that were so lonely. He was getting used to her being with him. He liked that. Liked that at the end of his life, he wasn't alone. He was determined to save her, but knowing he was dying now that he'd met her was both a glimpse of heaven and hell — and he wasn't a fanciful man.

You want these needles back?

He didn't realize how much affection he had for her, and it was growing fast. He'd just met her, yet it seemed as if they'd known each other years. A part of him felt she would always have been a mystery to him, elusive and enigmatic, but at the same time, she was comfortable as if they had been together for years.

Yes, please, they're difficult to make.

He'd bet his last dollar she made them herself. He removed the needles, wiped the blood off carefully on the victims' clothing and took a moment to examine them. They were lightweight yet had balance to them. He wrapped them up and slid them into his pocket. He closed it with the Velcro to ensure they wouldn't fall out in his hurry to catch up with her.

He was able to move a little faster than she could because each time he came upon members of the MSS, they were already dead. He removed eight more of the needles from four more victims. Her accuracy was amazing.

How often do you practice? He couldn't keep the admiration from his voice. Or the excitement. She was everything a woman he would want was. Mystifying. Deadly. Soft-spoken. Humorous. She looked like an angel and kissed like sin.

Stop. We're connected. There was laughter in her voice. *You can't think things like that.*

Why? It's the truth. You might as well know. It isn't like we have all the time in the world. This headache is very persistent. You know that's the first sign. His temperature indicated he was infected as well, but he refrained from acknowledging that.

Stop being a baby. You hit your head very hard. There's still a big lump there. Quit thinking in terms of saving me and think about saving us.

He was definitely catching up to her. Two more bodies. Her count was going to rival his if he didn't look out. The MSS was going to have to start recruiting again.

I have a hard head. No concussion.

You don't know that. What are you? A doctor?

Laughter spilled into his mind. It wasn't nearly as funny as she thought it was, but he couldn't help laughing because she really felt like sunshine spilling into his mind and she made him happy. He'd forgotten happiness.

Have you run out of your needles yet?

I don't run out. Those little things have saved my life on multiple occasions. They're easy to conceal and a breeze to use.

You sound like a salesman and not a very good one. They aren't a breeze to use unless you practice day and night. I throw knives. I'm nowhere near as good as a couple of others because I don't spend every waking minute practicing.

Give me a sec.

He increased his speed as he hurried through the trees toward her. She'd come upon a couple of the terrorists. He could feel the difference in her. Laughter faded away and she was all purpose, all determination. A professional. He didn't want to distract her, so he stayed very still in her mind, curious to know how she dealt with the taking of lives.

Shylah was filled with compassion and kindness. He felt it each time she entered his mind, or he poured himself into hers. She wasn't the type of woman to hunt and kill, yet she was extremely efficient at it. Looking into her mind, he realized she didn't see a man with a family, someone's son, husband or father. She viewed them as killers. She held the peaceful people from Lupa Suku in her mind. He felt the blow, almost as physical, the one she felt when she surveyed those men, women and children. She exterminated those who participated in killing as these men had done. She thought of them as rats, deadly, hate-ridden rats. Rats willing to do anything for money. She kept remembering the way the villagers' bodies had looked, bloody and exposed, swollen in the heat, as if they'd exploded.

He detested that for her. She mourned for those lost people. Taking out those responsible for their deaths was her way of honoring them. She didn't flinch from the kill, not even for a second. Coming up on the next pair of soldiers, she hit the first one, and before he could do more than slap his hand up to his neck, she'd hit his partner. A second needle entered right after the first one to ensure she'd made the kill.

Two more down. I'll retrieve these needles and then wait for you.

Shylah, don't. Stay put. All at once he had a bad feeling, something he never ignored.

The forest had gone quiet. Something hostile moved toward her. She didn't argue, and he was grateful.

Tell me what you see.

Not good. Not good. There was excitement more than fear in her voice. *It's their tiger, Draden. Lupa Suku protected a tiger here. They traded with poachers to keep them from killing him. He's gorgeous. Truly regal. There's only about four hundred left in the entire world and I'm looking right at one of them.*

Stay away from him, Draden was compelled to caution. She sounded too excited. He had the feeling she might jump down any second and introduce herself. *Did you know that their feet are slightly webbed to enable them to catch their prey in the water better?*

He's smaller than most tigers but looks powerful. Heavier black stripes defining the orange. He looks to be about three hundred pounds.

Draden increased his speed. He wanted to catch a glimpse of the rare animal, but more importantly, he wanted to make certain his woman didn't decide she was best friends with a tiger.

Again, laughter poured into his mind, this time like warm honey. *He's looking up at me. Draden.* She breathed his name, reverence in her tone. *You have to see him. There's intelligence there.*

Tension slipped in. A wave of darkness spread through him and he feared he knew what it was. He had a visceral reaction to her observation. Primal. The male cat in him provided him with all kinds of gifts, from his radar to his jumping abilities, the ferocity when needed, but it had negative consequences as well. He recognized jealousy and the need to claim her as his.

It's the epitome of idiocy to be jealous of a tiger, but I am. He might as well admit the truth when she could read his ridiculous emotions through their connection.

Her soft laughter slid into his mind. It wasn't laughter at him, rather an invitation to join in, to laugh at the two of them in the impossible predicament they found themselves in.

If he was female, no doubt I'd want to run her off, Shylah admitted, that warm laughter heating his blood. She immediately created more intimacy between them by putting them both together, admitting she would share those same emotions.

Draden found himself smiling. Somehow, she created a burst of sunlight to spear through the darkness that had suddenly grown in him. Just with a few words and that soft laughter, she had dispersed jealousy and given him back his dignity.

You were dignified even when you were jealous.

That made him laugh. She was bringing out things in him he hadn't known were there. *I don't think anyone is dignified if they're displaying jealous traits. Just so you know, that's a new one for me. I've never been jealous before and it kind of sucks that it was over a tiger.*

More laughter spilled into his mind, a burst of radiant joy. He'd stuffed the mask and gloves in his pocket and knew she'd done the same. With the mask on, one was far too aware of the predicament they were in to think about laughing. *I nearly fell out of the tree. Uh-oh. He's looking up at me again. He walked over to the bodies and he sniffed them and now he's looking at me. I'm trying to look like I've never been hungry in my life and have no intention of eating his roadkill.*

He continued moving fast. If there was a problem with the tiger, better he took care of it than her. She would regret having to kill the animal for the rest of her life. He wouldn't like harming the big cat, but he could get past it, especially if by doing so it meant saving her from having to. As he moved closer, he felt the laughter drain out of her, leaving her mind serious and then going from serious to horrified.

Draden, he's caught in a trap and he's going crazy.

Draden could hear the tiger, roaring his challenge, pain wracking the furious snarls that rose to almost a howling pitch.

Don't you go near it. You stay in that tree, I'm almost there.

I should have been looking for signs of poachers. They always leave signs to warn others the area has traps laid. There were tears in her mind, but not in her voice. She was angry. *He's ripping at the tree trunk the cable is anchored around. So many of them have died just like that, starving, chewing at their own legs. Draden, I have to do something.*

"I'm here," he said softly, stepping onto the branch where she clung, her horrified gaze fixed on the wildly fighting tiger.

The noose was wrapped around its right back leg and the animal fought back, attacking the tree in a frenzied attempt to get loose. It clawed at the trunk, leaving deep rake marks in between biting at its paw and leg and even the trap.

"Do you have anything nonlethal on you? Something we can dart him with? Put him out? Neither one of us can help him when he's like that. It's too dangerous."

"They should have something at the ranger station," Shylah said, still not taking her eyes off the thrashing, fighting animal.

Even Draden, who attempted to be nothing but hardened steel, felt a little heartbroken when watching the animal struggle to survive. He was trained to be a heat-seeking missile, going after the enemy, not to take on any other tasks along the way. But he was also GhostWalker special forces, and that called for thinking independently. In this case, his thinking veered toward wiping out the poachers along with the terrorists.

"You had to have studied the region before you were dropped in," he said, deferring to her greater knowledge. He had come to get in and get out, not for an extended stay, and the only other information had been provided by Malichai. "What hazards besides the tiger are we facing?" He was calm, matter-of-fact. When Shylah continued to stare silently down at the raging, fighting animal, he poured command into his voice. "Shylah, I need data now."

She looked up at him, blinking rapidly, and his heart stuttered when he saw her lashes were wet. She nodded twice, clearly forcing herself under control. "Poachers set multiple traps in the same area. They knew this tiger frequented this area. There are probably eight or nine more traps on the ground. They leave signs to warn others that they've already laid the traps. I should have been looking. I was concentrating on the enemy."

"Stay in the trees then and make your way back to the station fast. I'll keep watch over him and examine the ground. I should be able to find the other traps and remove them while I'm waiting for you. Maybe I can find a way to calm him down." He said it more to soothe her than because he believed that he could.

She nodded. "You might be able to. In the park where you see tigers more often, when one is trapped, often the others protect it, or at least that's what quite a few of the natives think. So, who knows? When the rangers try to remove snares, they can be risking their lives going into tiger territory. He might view you as a protector."

Draden doubted it. He was more of a hunter, a predator, and the tiger most likely would scent that in him. Still, darting a big cat was dangerous. Exotics were difficult to take down without killing them because there was no set dosage even if they were the same weight and age. He only knew that because he had worked at a zoo for a short while in his younger years, before he'd found the comfort of the nursery and the rows of peonies that soothed him when he couldn't contain his anger. The zoo veterinarian had often talked to him about the dangers of taking down a large cat.

Adrenaline poured through the big cats and they fought the drug until the very last moment before they dropped, and then they could easily go into cardiac arrest. Even if the rangers had ketamine to knock the tiger out, he wasn't certain of the dosage. Worse, he knew the vet always had yohimbe on hand to reverse the ketamine, and he didn't have a clue what to do with that drug.

"Forget trying to get back to the ranger station. I'm going to clear the traps from the area and you can help me do that. You should be able to scent them. Or feel for them before you reach them. Talk to the tiger while we do the clearing. Get him used to the sound of your voice."

"What do you plan to do?" There was suspicion.

He wasn't about to tell her his insane plan. Instead, he dropped down from the tree and began to move in an ever-widening circle with the raging tiger as the center. The tiger stopped raking the tree and turned to face him, snarling.

"Yeah, you don't like me much, do you?" He sent Shylah a smirk. "He likes you though, and I'm way too close to you. You're giving off the vibe."

"What vibe?" Shylah demanded, daring him to say it aloud.

His smirk turned into a grin. "The very sexy and oh-so-alluring, I'm-so-ready-to-get-laid vibe."

She tossed her head so her hair, which had been in a tidy braid, went flying. Ten-drils of hair had pulled loose on her wild run through the branches of the trees and she looked every bit as exotic and beautiful as the tiger. "This is not true." She narrowed her eyes. "And dangerous of you to say so."

He sent her a quick grin. She was so damned adorable and just as sexy. "I must have been mistaken."

"You were."

He laughed, and she did too. For one moment their eyes met and his heart clenched hard. He needed to keep his head in the game or one or both were going to be mauled by the tiger.

"Keep talking to him. He likes your voice." Draden liked it too, but he refrained from mentioning that. "You're female and he senses that. I'm a male, a rival, and he'd like to shred me. Talk to him, get him used to the sound of your voice."

All the while she talked, he searched for the snares. There was a pattern to them and within a short period of time he had discovered six more. He removed them while she continued to talk to the tiger. He moved into position while she occupied the animal's attention.

What are you doing? Shylah kept talking in a soothing voice, working her way close to the animal, but staying just out of its range.

The tiger was calmer, staring at her, but

showing teeth to let her know she'd better not get too close. Draden didn't hesitate. If he did, he would be killed. He was on the tiger, using his enhanced strength, his arm choking the animal, holding it to the ground while it fought and tried to turn its head to sink its teeth into him. One leg was tied up, but it tried to rake with its other three.

You're insane, Shylah whispered into his mind, but she'd already leapt into action, working fast to try to untangle the cable from around the tiger's paw.

Adrenaline poured through Draden's body. He could feel the hot breath of hatred exploding against his arm, but the tiger couldn't reach him with claws or teeth. The difficult part was the dismount. Taking the tiger to the ground had been easy because the tiger was completely focused on Shylah. Now, it was completely focused on him.

Ready? Shylah's voice shook.

Not yet. When I give the word, you take the cable all the way off then leap for the tree the instant he's free, he instructed. *And don't give me any shit either. Just do it. I'll tell you when to take it off. Understand?*

Yes.

Good. Then get ready. They both had to be ready.

He had to be ready. He had to be able to

count on her to do exactly what he said because his attention couldn't be divided. He didn't want the tiger to touch him. Not one single rake on his skin. He was uncertain how the virus was transmitted because he couldn't study it. The remote lab was a good one as field labs went, but it wasn't as safe as he would like it to be, not when he knew Trap would be sending for blood and virus both and the military lab he would be using would be far better equipped, with far better safety protocols.

Of course, Draden should have taken the virus straight to the remote lab, and called in transport, everything else be damned, but there was that quiver in Shylah's voice that had turned him inside out. For the first time, knowing he did something completely out of character for him, something that was important to the rest of the world, that he'd done what he'd wanted to do, felt damned great, even with a tiger's teeth inches from his face.

I'm ready. No argument. She was a partner a man could depend on.

He took a breath, let it out. "Listen, buddy, we're trying to help you here. Just give me a minute to get into the tree before you start trying to chew on my spine, rip off my leg, gut me and eat me, okay?"

Draden. Shylah breathed his name into his mind. Softly. Aware. Touching him somewhere deep.

He didn't wait. *Now.* He let go and sprang away, all in one motion, leaping for the tree branches overhead. They were high, some twenty-five feet, but his hands gripped a twisting limb and then he was up, standing beside Shylah. He slipped one arm around her and held on to the trunk with the other. No doubt the tiger could leap the distance. They had to be ready to go higher or get to the next tree.

The tiger stood up slowly, shook his head and then turned his gaze on them. Those eyes were piercing. Wholly focused. They stared at one another for a few moments, but instead of leaping at them in murderous fury, the animal turned away from them and slipped into the heavier brush.

Shylah's smile was worth the righteous chewing out Draden was going to get when he made his report. He bent his head and kissed her. Quick. Barely there. Meaning it. Hoping she felt what he did. When he lifted his head, she had stars in her eyes, and he had the satisfaction of knowing he'd put them there.

8

"You're insane," Shylah whispered.

She hadn't spoken a word on the way back to the remote lab. Not a single word. Draden had tried. He'd dropped his arm around her shoulders, pulling her to him, but she hadn't reacted, not even to pull away. She'd kissed him in the trees, but once on the ground, heading toward the remote lab, she had withdrawn.

It wasn't like he could blame her. He knew why she was upset. It was insanity to tackle a tiger and put it in a choke hold. "I'm strong, Shylah," he reminded. "Enhanced."

"The tiger could have killed you. Its teeth were inches from you. Inches, Draden."

"I'm living under a death sentence," he reminded gently.

She cast him a singular look from under her lashes, and his heart clenched. Her brown eyes looked liquid, the lashes wet and spiky. "You aren't alone. You aren't one anymore. It's the two of us. Together. We do this together. That was the plan. That was your promise and I count on you."

His first thought was to defend himself. He'd freed the tiger instead of killing it for her. She'd wanted the damn thing alive, and he'd given her that gift. She hadn't hesitated, not one bit, to help him do it. She'd almost begged him to keep the tiger alive. Still, she was right. She'd probably expected him to find a way to put the animal out and he hadn't explained why it was so dangerous. He wasn't sorry he'd saved the animal and he wasn't going to lie to her and tell her he was. There were so few of the tigers, and the male was in its prime or getting there.

More, he knew she'd been happy about it, that kiss had told him so.

He remained silent, trying to puzzle out what other men might say or do to defuse the highly charged situation. He didn't know the first thing about relationships.

"That wasn't fair," Shylah said, her face turned away from him as they walked. She studiously kept her gaze on the thick grove of trees marking where the clearing was. "I practically forced you to save the tiger and I don't have the right to be angry about your methods."

He knew for certain that wasn't true. "You aren't angry, baby, you're hurt," he pointed out. "And scared. Both of which you have every right to be." The last thing he'd expected was an apology from her. Those tears. Her averted face so he couldn't see them. She turned him inside out without trying. "I knew I could do it and I wanted to do it for you. I'm not going to pretend to be noble and say I was risking my life to save the endangered tiger. I risked it for you, but you're right, I was risking a lot. I should have talked it over with you first, so you'd be comfortable with it."

Mostly he hadn't told her his plans because he'd been afraid that he'd choose to kill the tiger instead. That he would fall back on his training, the thing that made it easy for him to avoid all people as well as controversy. He'd spent years keeping to himself and staying quiet, barely acknowledging those around him. It was entirely new letting Shylah so completely into his life. He'd deliberately opened himself up to her, made himself vulnerable. And if he was being completely honest with himself, he knew he wouldn't have done that — certainly not so quickly — except that he was going to die, and he had nothing to lose.

"I knew I had the speed and strength. I'm

as flexible as he was. But I should have taken the time to explain myself to you."

"You knew I would have argued."

He shrugged and pulled her closer, molding her body against his, needing her forgiveness. His entire life, he hadn't cared if he'd upset someone or made them angry. No one had mattered. He'd found a place inside himself where he was safe, where no one could get to him. But she could — she had. Evidently, he wasn't as safe as he'd thought.

"Say it, Shylah. I need to hear the words." He did. He'd let her in, and he wasn't the least bit sorry he had. Every moment in her company was worth the feeling of vulnerability.

"You're touching my mind. We're connected."

"I don't care, sweetheart. You know what I need."

I forgive you, but please don't do something like that again unless I'm ready for it. I could barely breathe.

The words, sliding into his mind, were vibrant with her emotions. Dripping with sensitivity. Weeping with her reaction. Intimate beyond measure. Because she murmured forgiveness into his mind, she gave more of herself away to him. She was feeling very fragile, so much so that when they entered the remote lab and he switched on the computer to be able to talk to Trap, the moment she caught sight of Bellisia, she backed out.

I can't talk to them yet.

Draden glanced at her sharply, assessing how close to tears she was. Too close. She wouldn't be able to keep it together for her friends.

I'll cover for you, until you're ready, he promised as he put the ampule he'd taken from the MSS into the freezer. That gave her time to exit before anyone really caught a glimpse of her. The camera was pointed toward him. For him, it wasn't about whether or not the freezer was even cold, it was about containment. If the generator went out and the freezer went to room temperature the virus would be contained in that airtight box until it died.

I'll try to be fast.

Take your time. They're going to want to talk to you.

I want to talk to them, I just don't want to cry in front of them.

He sat down in front of the computer. The screen was split in two. Ezekiel was on one screen with Bellisia looking over his shoulder, but he didn't see Zara anywhere around. Joe, who was still in Indonesia, was looking at him from the other screen. Wyatt and Trap appeared just over his shoulder, both looking exhausted.

"Azami Yoshiie moved one of their satellites for us to use," Joe said. "She's married to Sam Johnson, a GhostWalker from Team One. Her family owns Samurai Telecommunications, so we were able to get a satellite for our exclusive use. The Indonesian government has sent their military into the area to keep everyone away from the lab and you. They'll stay away as well. Their orders are very clear."

Joe glanced over his shoulder for a moment, which told Draden he wasn't alone and someone, most likely high up in the military, was monitoring everything said.

"That's good," Draden said. "We're taking out as many of the MSS as possible. They're well entrenched in the village, but the people don't want them there." He didn't want the military sending soldiers in. There would be a slaughter.

Joe turned his head to talk to someone behind him out of sight. When he did, Shylah slipped up behind Draden, her arms around his neck, chin on his shoulder. Draden's heart slammed hard in his chest before settling into a strong rhythm. She was showing the others they were together, a team. He reached up and covered one of her hands with his.

"Shylah!" Bellisia called out, uncaring that Ezekiel remained in front. She was tiny, but she just went around him, so she was practically sitting in his lap.

Trap heaved a huge sigh, which Draden wanted to laugh at. He didn't. Not with strangers around, but he wanted to. Trap didn't have much use for niceties and having Bellisia hog the computer when he obviously wanted to talk about the virus was almost more than he could take.

"I'm right here," Shylah said. "We're good. Wish we had some decent food."

"We're arranging for food," Joe said. "You ladies have the floor for a couple of minutes and then we have to get down to business."

Bellisia rolled her eyes, but she didn't sass Joe. It was never a good idea, and she'd been there long enough for Joe to have assimilated her into the team. She was the best they had in the water, lethal as hell, but she also knew, when push came to shove, Joe was in command.

Bellisia touched the screen and immediately Shylah put her palm up as well. Smiles faded, and they stared at each other.

"Where's Zara?"

Hearing her voice, Draden tightened his hand around hers to give her strength and to let her know he was with her.

"She was sent away with Nonny, Pepper, Cayenne and the three little ones. If someone is planning to set loose a virus on our teams, Team Two has the facility to protect our loved ones," Ezekiel said.

"That's a good idea. I wish you'd gone with them, Bellisia," Shylah said. "I need to know you and Zara are safe. *Both* of you."

"We need warriors here, Shylah," Bellisia was gentle. "You know what I can do. Around here, there is a great deal of water."

Shylah turned her hand so that her fingers threaded through Draden's, seeking comfort. His hand wrapped around hers, surrounding it, holding her to him.

"I know, Bellisia. I wouldn't have left either, but that doesn't stop me from needing to know what Draden and I are doing isn't for nothing. You're family. My only family, you and Zara. I like knowing you're safe. Picturing you happy with your husband. Zara as well."

"I am happy," Bellisia assured. She glanced over her shoulder at the man standing behind her.

"Trap, why did you send Cayenne with them? I would have thought she would have come with you or stayed there to protect our homes," Draden said. Trap had to have sent her. Cayenne would never have left him any other way. She obeyed one man only. She was a wild card, and Joe knew it. She trained with them and she protected their home and families, but she was always with Trap.

Trap suddenly looked uncomfortable. "She'll kill me if I say anything."

Bellisia gasped and glared at Trap through the computer screen. "She's pregnant. You wouldn't send her away for any other reason. She's pregnant."

"That true, Trap?" Joe asked, his tone annoyed.

"Yeah. She's been pregnant for a while. She didn't want anyone to know, and she doesn't really show much."

"Is she seeing a doctor?" Joe demanded.

"Nonny is seeing to her."

Trap ran his finger around the neck of his shirt. He was wearing a T-shirt so Draden couldn't help but laugh. "You're going to be a father, Trap."

Trap gave him a look that would have made anyone else drop dead right on the spot. "Fuckin' gonna put a cap in your head," he warned.

Draden shrugged. "Not much of a threat

when I'm dying anyway."

"Might help you along," Trap said.

"We're being monitored," Joe reminded. "Wrap it up, ladies."

Draden felt Shylah's breath catch as she pressed her front to his back tightly. "We saved a tiger today, Bellisia. The Sumatran tigers are so rare, maybe only four hundred remain in the *entire* world and we saved one today. Or rather, Draden really did. You should have seen him. I never saw anyone move so fast."

Draden tightened his hand around Shylah's in warning. She either ignored it, or she didn't realize why he didn't want her to go there.

"We were coming back from encounters with the MSS. I'd gotten a few, and Draden had managed to retrieve what was left of the virus. The tiger was right below me, looking up at me, and he took a couple of steps right into a poacher's snare. He went crazy, attacking the tree and rolling and raking, snarling. He would have starved or chewed through his own leg. It was truly horrible."

"That's awful," Bellisia said. "How in the world were you able to get the snare off of him?"

"It was a cable and the more he fought

the tighter the noose drew. Draden dropped down from above, right on him, driving the tiger to the ground. Somehow, he managed to put him in a headlock while controlling his movements with his legs, holding him down so I could remove the snare. Then we had to time both of us getting away before he could put a scratch on either of us. It was the coolest thing ever."

Draden kept his eyes on Joe's face the entire time Shylah was relating the story to Bellisia. He knew why she did it. She wasn't thinking about the sickness they carried in their bodies or the fact that he had an ampule with drops of the deadly virus on him when he'd done such a foolhardy thing. She wanted to spend time with her friend. Losing that contact meant they were another step closer to dying.

"Wrap it up now, Bellisia," Joe ordered.

She shot him a look but obediently blew a kiss to Shylah. "You're loved, girl, you know that," she whispered.

"Same," Shylah said, sounding choked.

Bellisia removed herself from in front of the camera to stand beside her husband. Ezekiel wrapped his arm around her, and both stayed in view of the camera.

"Did you have the virus on your person when you rescued that tiger?" Joe demanded.

Shylah stiffened. She started to straighten, but Draden kept his hand on hers, holding her against his back and shoulder.

"I did."

"What the hell kind of dumbass move was that? You know how deadly that virus is. What were you thinking?"

He shrugged. "I wasn't thinking of much other than giving my woman a gift. She's dying, and I can't save her. I want her last days to be as happy as possible under the circumstances."

"What kind of bullshit excuse is that?" Joe demanded. "You're talking about a possible worldwide pandemic if this thing gets out. You know better. Your first duty is to your country."

Shylah pulled her hand away from his and wrapped her arms tighter around his neck, nearly choking him while she glared at the screen. "I think giving his life for his country is about all anyone can ask. You don't have much compassion in you, do you? I guess that's what makes you such a good commander, but frankly, neither one of us has to do anything you say. Not one damn thing."

"Baby," Draden cautioned.

"No, we don't, Draden. We're the ones

here facing this thing." She was fierce about it. "We're dying. Everything we give them is a damn gift they can accept with a freaking thank-you instead of tearing strips off you."

No one, in as long as he could remember, had stuck up for him. Certainly not with the ferocity of a tigress. She was making it known, just as he had, that they were a couple.

There was a small silence. Joe probably had half the Indonesian military behind him, certainly the commander of their elite special forces. Draden doubted if they would have responded to such insubordination gracefully, but Joe did. He was the sort of man who stayed cool under even the most embarrassing situations and having Shylah rip him a new one in front of an audience had to be right up there.

"I apologize, Ms. Cosmos." Joe even managed to pour sincerity into his voice, although Draden was certain he wanted to take Shylah into another room and give her one of his renowned dressing-downs. "It must be very difficult to be in the position you're in, aware of what's coming. Both of you are courageous and deserve respect. On the other hand, we have to protect the public. We can't have even a couple of drops of that virus get out. I am certain you can see my position."

That was Joe. Apologize, but let everyone, especially Shylah, know he was right. Draden wasn't about to allow him to make her feel small. He interrupted. "We've taken out a good number of the MSS, and yes, we're wearing masks and gloves when we hunt. We'll take as many of them down as possible for you. Our strategy is to make the village as unfriendly a place for them as possible so hopefully they'll move out of there and the Kopassus can deal with them."

Shylah leaned her head against his back. He could almost feel her weariness and need to have the strangers gone. It took nerves of steel to face what they were facing, and she didn't want to waste what time they had left being chastised and fighting with command. He wanted to wrap things up, but he really needed assurance from Trap first.

On the screen, Joe glanced over his shoulder, nodded to someone off-camera and then turned back. "That can be coordinated. Right now, we're close to you. We'll be coming for the blood and virus and we'll bring you food and supplies. They're keeping everyone away, so you shouldn't run into any civilians. When you want them to take over, let us know. The Kopassus will be on standby."

"The MSS haven't come this far into the interior. So far, we've been safe from them," Draden reported.

"The Indonesian military will help with that. They've thrown up a ring around the remote lab and the ranger station. You will be able to move in and out freely, heading toward the village to do as much damage as possible to the terrorists but they won't be able to get to you. Be careful, both of you. Don't take chances that could spread the virus."

"We won't. Clear kills only," Draden agreed.

"Are you showing any signs of infection, Draden?" Trap asked. "Symptoms can appear within two days and you received a healthy dose."

Draden appreciated the concern on Trap's face. The man was his best friend, but he rarely showed emotion. He nodded and rubbed at the back of his neck. "My head's pounding. I've had a headache for over twenty-four hours."

"He isn't showing any signs," Shylah denied, her head appearing over his shoulder again in the camera's vision. "He hit his head really hard and clearly has a concussion, which he denies."

Draden's lips twitched. He tried hard to suppress his grin. She looked cute. Earnest. On-camera her freckles showed up as pure gold. He had an unexpected urge to wrap his arm around her neck, lean back and kiss the hell out of her. Pure temptation.

Trap ignored her. "Do you feel nauseated?"

Draden tried not to wince. He'd worked with Trap on social cues, but they didn't seem to take if he wasn't there to remind him. Trap lived in his own world, one few understood. He was a brilliant man who could be generous, but most of the time he didn't give a damn what others thought of him. Nothing softened his hard edges but Cayenne, his wife. Even then, the GhostWalkers thought of her as a miracle, that she could live with his eccentricities. Trap had Asperger's, but with his IQ he should have been able to learn to read others, he simply didn't care enough to do so.

"Only when Shylah cooks for us."

She burst out laughing, just as he knew she would.

"Don't tell me she's feeding you the rations Whitney's nutritionist concocted for us," Bellisia asked.

"Is that what it is?" Draden countered.

Both girls laughed. Joe managed to smile.

Trap didn't so much as change expression. He was all business, his mind already immersed with finding a way to keep the two of them alive.

"I need to know what the point of entry was, specifically, Draden."

"Left thigh quadriceps, more to the side, but injected right into the muscle."

"Was there a burning sensation? Do you have any infection at the entry site?"

"There was a burning sensation, but no infection," Draden responded, resisting the urge to rub the spot.

"What about swelling?"

"Some, about the size of a golf ball." He didn't want to discuss it with the possibility of Shylah overhearing. It was very red. "I'll photograph it for you and send. Will measure as well. It isn't particularly large, Trap."

"Itching? Rash on either of you?"

"No. No rash yet, but we'll both conduct a thorough examination each morning to make certain." He rubbed his temples wishing the headache would recede. When he sat, the pain seemed to get worse, but he knew it was because being inactive made him concentrate on it more.

"Any swelling in lymph nodes?"

Draden was careful not to look at Shylah. "Yes, this morning."

"Shylah?"

"I haven't checked her yet but will."

The idea turned his stomach. He kept his expression blank and his tone matter-of-fact, but he found it much more difficult to think of Shylah infected than him. He knew he was infected, but he just couldn't help wanting a very different outcome for her. The longer he was with her, the more he felt that way. Having Trap ask any question about her, especially in that clinical voice, left him shaken. He knew it was necessary, but that still didn't make it any easier.

"Have either of you experienced problems with movement?"

He felt Shylah's fingers dig deeper into his shoulder. The questions were bothering her as well. They'd been out a good portion of the night in order to cover the distance to the village the MSS had taken over. They were both tired and hungry. The morning light seemed dazzling as it streaked through the trees, growing brighter and brighter until he felt it behind his eyes as a sharp, piercing spear. Birds sounded off, calling to one another, more and more species, until the symphony turned to cacophony, jangling on the nerves.

He looked over his shoulder, one eyebrow lifted in inquiry at Shylah. He wanted to get the inquisition over with, so he could lie down. He still had to make certain everything was ready for pickup.

She shook her head. "I didn't have any trouble and I was running along tree branches in the dark."

"She also dispensed with a few of the MSS tonight," Draden added, trying to sound as clinical as Trap. It was nearly impossible when he was referencing Shylah. "I didn't have problems with motor skills either."

"Physical exhaustion? Fatigue? Where are you with that?" Trap asked. "Give me a scale."

Draden was so tired he just wanted to sleep for hours. Maybe days. That was alarming to him. He was used to running for hours without becoming tired. He glanced up at Shylah again. "I'm very tired, Trap. Extremely tired. I'd say an eight. I'm running a low-grade fever as well."

"He took a very hard blow to the head," Shylah pointed out immediately. "He's been going ever since. He's been back and forth to the village, which is miles from here, and he hunted and killed I don't know how many of the MSS, but the numbers are staggering. Of course he's tired. Anyone would be. Even someone enhanced. I'm tired and

I haven't done near the work that he has."

Draden slid his arm around her waist, uncaring who was watching or if they got it on camera.

"I'll have everything ready for pickup," Draden assured Joe. "We're signing off. Both of us are exhausted."

Joe nodded. "We'll be in the air in twenty. ETA, forty-five."

"Trap, I'm counting on you to get her out of this," Draden said.

Her fingers tightened on his shoulder. She leaned in. "Both of us, Trap."

Trap nodded and was gone. Draden turned off the computer and leaned back in his chair. "I'm damned tired, Shylah."

"Me too. I think I've been running on adrenaline." She stepped back to allow him to stand up.

"You might want to be careful chewing Joe out," Draden said. "Just in case."

She shrugged, not looking in the least repentant. "He's not my boss. You and I both know the chances of us making it out of here are slim to none. In any case, even if I do make it out, he shouldn't talk to you like that."

"He was right. If the tiger had killed me and someone found that ampule containing the virus before our people, it could have been a catastrophe."

"I'm well aware of that, so thank you for the extraordinary and, in this case, costly gift. I loved it. But that doesn't mean he should talk to you like that when you're giving your life for them to try to see the progression. You explained you were going to record everything. Leave them blood samples every day. We both know this is going to get very ugly. He knows that as well."

Draden put all the carefully labeled blood samples in a carrier and left them in the freezer along with the ampule containing the virus and then held out his hand to her. There was little point in locking the lab. Anyone could break into it. They had military aid now, the Indonesian government providing them with soldiers to keep everyone away. Draden knew that ring of security around them was to contain them as well, but he didn't point that out to Shylah. She was intelligent enough to figure it out for herself.

He closed the door and they walked together back into the forest, taking the shortcut to the ranger's cabin.

"Shylah, the three virologists, the ones creating the viruses for Whitney — where were they getting their funding? Once Whitney cut them off, they had to get money from somewhere. You've been on their trail for a while. Who is he? Their moneyman. You have to know."

She sent him a small, under-the-lashes glance, but then she nodded. There wasn't a reason to hold back information anymore. They needed truth between them and in any case, someone else had to take up the search for the three men and whomever they planned to sell the virus to.

"I knew from the phone messages we'd intercepted that they were discussing selling the virus to a man by the name of Ethan Montgomery. He was born in Mississippi and went to school with Tyler and Cameron Williams. Montgomery is extremely wealthy and has skated on that his entire life. Every time he got in trouble, and that was usually with the Williams brothers, his daddy bailed them out by paying everyone off."

"Shylah, you should have told Joe. You can't keep valuable information like that to yourself."

"I didn't. I sent it to Whitney."

He wanted to shake her. He actually counted his steps to cool his rising temper. He took a deep breath and let it out, not breaking stride as they moved through the thick vegetation. "You're infected with a virus Whitney had his three madmen create specifically to target you. To kill you. That was his intention, and he's actually accomplished it. You do realize that, don't you? This is Whitney's fault."

"It wasn't his intention to create a virus of this type."

He stopped dead at her defense of the man, forcing her to halt as well. "Don't do that. Whitney deserves a bullet in his head, not your defense."

"I'm well aware of that, Draden," she said. "I'm not defending him. I'm stating a fact. He repeatedly ordered them to stop working on this virus when they told him a hemorrhagic one was the only type that might actually have a chance of infecting me. I knew they were working to find a virus, and that they'd 'accidentally' created what could be used as a biological weapon, but I lost track of the fact that this started with me."

"He told you that or you wouldn't say that as if you know what was said. Don't let Whitney fool you, Shylah. You should know by now he lies. More, he would want a biological weapon. He wouldn't be able to stop himself. That man would never pass up the chance to know if the virus would work on you. They were testing it in your blood, after all." Draden began walking again, needing the outlet of physical activity because the anger and the desire — the *need* — to actively hunt Whitney down and kill him was so strong.

"I'm well aware of Whitney's character, Draden. I've studied him. I know his every character flaw and his need to develop weapons."

Draden fought back a retort. She would have taken the time to study Whitney if she considered him the enemy. He let a few moments go by, breathing deeply for calm. "Why did you report to him?"

"Your team and the Indonesian government as well as the World Health Organization will all be hunting the Williams brothers and Orucov. Probably every law enforcement agency around the world as well. While they all do that so openly, Whitney can quietly send assassins to hunt and kill Montgomery. That's the only way to take Montgomery down. It's even money that the moment the guy knows or even suspects that someone is after him, he'll be in the wind."

"Would Montgomery let the virus loose on the world? What kind of man is he?"

She pursed her lips, considering the questions for a few moments before answering. "From everything I've discovered about him, he's a mean, spiteful, spoiled bully. Would he release the virus? Yes, I think he actually would, but, only if he was protected from it."

"So, if he already has the virus, everyone's in trouble."

She nodded and then sighed. "I probably should have told the others, but your Joe rubbed me the wrong way."

"He's a good man, sweetheart. And so is Trap. I honestly believe Trap and Wyatt have a shot at figuring out how to get you out of this mess."

"I don't know why you keep saying that."

Draden swept his hand down the back of her head and settled his fingers on the nape of her neck as they approached the two steps leading to the porch. His touch was possessive because he felt that way. He didn't mind being a little primal.

"This virus was designed by the Williams brothers and Orucov. They constructed it. We have their original files. Some are password protected and I'm betting those are the files Trap needs to deconstruct the virus. Even if he can't get into them, he'll find a way. He'll do it in time to save you. I know he will."

Just as she had before, Shylah moved in front of him to examine the silky strands she'd left across the stairs and doorway. The strands looked like those of a normal spiderweb. Delicate. She turned to face him, leaning her back to the door, her hands on her hips.

"I understand that. What I meant was, why would you believe Trap can find a way to save me, but not you? Why do you keep putting it that way?"

Draden shrugged, looking at her face. He thought her face was the most beautiful thing he'd ever seen. That flawless skin. Her freckles. Her generous mouth and large dark eyes. He wanted to kiss her, not discuss dying with her.

"They injected me with the virus, giving me a larger dose, if you will. It's more concentrated in me. You have a little more time." He stepped closer to her and framed her face with his hands. "Maybe I want you saved so much I don't let myself think of anything else happening. Whitney's virologists were having a difficult time coming up with a virus that would infect you, so your immune system is very good." Hopefully that would buy her a lot more time. He was counting on Trap and Wyatt.

"I want you to remember we're in this together, Draden. I need to feel I'm in this with you, not by myself."

"You know if you're with me, Shylah, you're just plain fucked. There isn't any getting out of this for me." He wanted her to understand that and start looking toward Trap to find a way for her to live.

"I'm with you, Draden," she said softly. "I'm right here with you every step of the way."

He slid the pad of his thumb over her perfect skin. Had there been hurt in her voice? "Baby," he said softly. "I'm not trying to push you away. I'm trying to save your life. I want you to live. You're extraordinary. The world needs you."

She shook her head. Tears glistened on the tips of her lashes. Yeah, he'd hurt her. He slid his thumb over her lips needing to stop the trembling.

"Do you really believe that?"

If she kept blinking and sending those tears trailing down her face, he wasn't going to be responsible for what he did. "Absolutely."

"I kill people, Draden. I can justify it and call it everything but that, but I kill people. That's hardly extraordinary."

"Of course, it is. Men like the Williams brothers, Agus Orucov and Montgomery are willing to wipe out the population for money or power. Someone has to track them down and take them out. The world does really need you, Shylah."

There was a long silence while she stared into his eyes, and he felt as if he might be drowning. The sensation was so real he held his breath.

"I don't want the world, Draden. I just want you. Here. Now. Whatever we've got in the time we have left."

He heard the sincerity in her voice. She knew what she was facing just as well as he did. She'd seen the evidence, the results of such a horrific virus. His heart clenched. No one had ever wanted him, not in his entire life. His own mother had thrown him away, essentially traded him for drugs. It had started there and gone further downhill.

He leaned into her and took her mouth. Gently. His body stirred, a familiar ache now, when she was close. She had captured his heart and he didn't ever want it back. The taste of her was wild, hitting his veins and spreading like wildfire. He'd never felt so alive and it was rather ironic that he was dying.

He lifted his head reluctantly, knowing that each time he kissed her, he was sealing her fate. He stroked his thumbs down the path of her tears and then brushed kisses over her eyelids. "Let's go inside. We both need to lie down for a little while."

She nodded and turned away from him to open the door. They both knew no one was inside. The webs had been intact and neither one of them felt their radar going off as it would have with an intruder, but they still paused to double-check before stepping inside. The habit was ingrained in both of them.

Draden loved that he didn't have to remind Shylah, that she was already in sync with him about their security. Another person might have been so overwhelmed with the thought of dying that they couldn't cope, but Shylah was determined to make every second count — and she wanted to spend that time with him.

Once inside the ranger cabin, Shylah went to her backpack. No one would suspect a young woman hiking in the forest to be a seasoned assassin.

"You've had some time to poke around. Why do you think Whitney's virologists took off before they figured out a vaccine? Was it the fact that the World Health Organization had been called in? Or that the Indonesian government were sending their elite to Sumatra?"

"Why do you think they didn't find a vaccine?"

He shrugged. "No evidence at all. None. No notes, no entries, no coming close."

"I think they were panicked," Shylah said. "For sure. They didn't even take the time to wipe the computer. They ran. That makes me suspect it was more likely the MSS were hunting them. Either for more of the virus, the vaccine or because they hadn't realized it was that lethal. It makes more sense that they were being hunted. I tracked them to the MSS village, remember? Their tracks showed they left without hurrying, but they never returned to the lab, they fled, using the river as an escape."

"There's no sign of the MSS beyond those two villages."

"Not yet, but the commander of the MSS could have easily said something to the three of them that made them feel threatened enough to run."

Draden nodded in agreement. The action sent a burst of pain radiating through his head. "I'm really damned tired, Shylah," he confessed. "More than I've ever been in my life."

"You're injured, Draden. You need to eat better and sleep the entire day today. That head injury was far more severe than either of us guessed."

His gaze was on her face while she reassured him. He would have believed her more if worry hadn't been there so plain in her brown eyes. He glanced down at his watch. He only had a few minutes to rest before he would have to meet the helicopter and Joe. He knew he wasn't going to have Shylah come with him. This time he was going to make it clear that he wanted her saved. There had to be a way, even if that meant physically removing her to a hospital somewhere.

9

Draden waited in the shade of a tall dipterocarp tree as a helicopter landed in the clearing and a crate containing food and other supplies was set in the grass. Men in the military garb of the Indonesian army raced back to the helicopter, and Joe emerged wearing a hazmat suit. He let Joe come to him. He didn't like being out in the open with so many soldiers carrying weapons, most loosely trained on him. He couldn't blame them. Many had probably seen the effects of the virus and wanted to ensure he didn't get anywhere near them. Even so, it was the first time he felt like he was truly infected and a danger to innocent people.

After Draden deposited the virus and blood samples in Joe's container, the commander of his unit stood for a moment just looking at him. It wasn't difficult to read the mixture of compassion and sorrow in his eyes. "I'm so sorry, Draden."

Draden nodded. What was there to say? He knew how fucked-up it was to die from any hemorrhagic virus, the disease devouring his insides until every organ was nothing but liquid. "I've got a bullet. I'll hold out as long as I can to give Trap and Wyatt and whoever else is working on this enough data to increase the chance of saving Shylah. She isn't showing any symptoms and it's possible she has more time than I do."

Joe took the package from Draden. "We could airlift you both to a hospital. You'd get better care."

Draden knew he wasn't going to die like that, with everyone peering down at him like he was a science project. He'd seen it before, that undignified exit of life and he wasn't about to go out that way. If he was in a hospital, he wasn't going to be given a gun. "Not going to happen, Joe. You know me. I'd force these soldiers to kill me first. I'm not running around infecting anyone. I'm wearing a mask and gloves when I make kills. I had to go into the village in order to retrieve the virus, but I was careful not to contaminate anyone."

"Stay close to the lab. The sicker you get, the more likely you are to have doubts about staying out here," Joe cautioned.

"I won't. You know me better than that. I do want you to give me a day to convince Shylah to go back with you. She won't do it now, but I can convince her it's best for mankind or some crap like that."

"Draden . . ." Joe's tone was even more cautionary.

"She might make it. I'm almost positive her blood is the one labeled P-one through -five. I think they were looking at her. Her given name is Peony. Whitney hired the three scientists to create viruses specific to each of the girls. Bellisia had one in her. Zara had two capsules placed in her. Shylah says she's never gotten sick. Not ever. Not even with a cold."

"You think this virus was designed to specifically target her immune system?"

"Yes. And that makes her all the more valuable to all of you. It's possible she's immune and you can create a vaccine and therapy for this virus using her blood."

"Are you trying to convince yourself or me?"

Draden knew he wanted Shylah saved at any cost. It was possible he was convincing himself she was the answer because he was falling for her and didn't want her to die in the worst possible way. He shrugged. "I don't know the answer to that, but judging by the fact that not one person got out of that village alive, it has to have a fast replication cycle. Twenty-four to forty-eight hours tops, and I'm already showing signs. No one tried to get to the boats or to walk out. I made certain no one got out. I searched in every direction for miles. There were no tracks. I checked the infirmary where the MSS are holing up. No one was ill. There were no whispers of a terrifying disease. No rumors have gotten out yet."

"We believe the attack on the doctors was an attempt to get the maximum publicity for the Milisi Separatis Sumatra so they could emerge as a terrorist organization that could strike fear in the hearts of every enemy. They had a virus capable of causing a pandemic and weren't afraid to use it. It was decided not to give them that publicity and so far, they haven't come forward to claim the deaths."

"I killed their commander. The new one was reluctant to make himself and his men a worldwide target."

Joe nodded. "It could be as simple as that."

Draden shook his head. "I don't think it's simple. There's more going on here than Whitney's three crazy scientists getting pissed because he didn't like the virus they created. Whitney sent Shylah to track them down and kill them. In the process of doing that, she found they were corresponding with a man by the name of Ethan Montgomery. He comes from Mississippi and went to school with the Williams brothers. He was purchasing the virus from them. Whitney may or may not have sent a hit team after him. I think Montgomery has been supplying his friends with money."

"Whitney paid them very well."

"Not when they didn't deliver a virus that would kill Shylah. According to Shylah, and I know we have to take this with a grain of salt because Whitney lies, he specifically told them they were not to create anything resembling the Marburg or Ebola viruses. I don't think that's necessarily true. Whitney might very well have wanted to have the ultimate weapon, but first he would have wanted the vaccine. Who knows? At this point it doesn't matter. You have to find them and take them out. And you have to get that virus back."

"We've got people on Whitney's scientists," Joe said. "I'll put someone on Montgomery. The most important thing for us now is to save your life and Shylah's."

Draden didn't think Joe was a very good liar. "Were those we extracted able to collect tissue or blood samples from any of the people in Lupa Suku for the labs?"

Joe shook his head. "No, the MSS ambushed them before any of the work could actually get started. They said it was bad, Draden."

"It was. I burned the bodies and the village to the ground. I didn't want to risk animals feeding on them, or monkeys getting near them. I felt it was the safest thing to do."

Joe indicated the supplies stacked on the ground. "We've brought fresh food and medical supplies. I'll be back tomorrow, so let us know if you need anything else when you call in."

Draden stepped back and saluted his friend and commanding officer. He had no idea what condition he would be in when he woke up in the evening. "It's been an honor to serve with you, sir."

Their GhostWalker unit didn't stand on formality as a rule. They were different, and they would always be apart from society. They only had one another, so they were more friends than one having authority over the other unless it was military business. He felt it was important for Joe Spagnola to know how he felt about the man.

Joe looked stricken, but his back was

ramrod stiff. "Fight, Draden. Trap and Wyatt and the others will work day and night to pull this off for you. You have to know that. And get some rest. You're running on empty."

That much was the truth. Draden shouldered the bags of supplies and made his way back to the ranger's cabin. Shylah waited on the porch for him. The light hurt his eyes, but it didn't matter. She looked beautiful there, waiting for him. His breath caught in his throat and he just stood at the bottom of the stairs staring up at her.

Her smile faltered. "Is something wrong?"

It was the absolute best question she could have asked. They were both infected with one of the worst viruses on earth and were sentenced to a horrific death, and she greeted him at the door, a smile on her face, and then asked if anything was wrong. What the hell kind of woman was she, and what had he ever done to deserve her? Nothing that he could think of, but it didn't matter.

He was well aware he was weaving a fantasy around her, and she was doing the same around him. That didn't matter either. If his arms weren't filled with the supplies, he would have swooped her into them and carried her across the threshold.

"No, sweetheart. I think they sent us real

food here. We're not going to have to eat those nutritional" — he coughed a couple of times and made a show of clearing his throat — "rations Whitney sent you with."

She laughed, just as he knew she would and then stepped back through the open door, allowing him entry. It was only then that he saw she had a rifle lying close to her thigh, out of sight when he'd first walked up.

"Who was that for? Me? Or Joe?"

"You I like. Joe, not so much."

"He's a good man, Shylah."

"Maybe so, but that good man had a sniper in the tree just over your left shoulder. If the shooter made a move against you, he was dead. I let Mr. Badass sniper see he was in my sights."

Draden didn't like that. "Don't risk yourself like that. I mean it, woman. He would have radioed to someone on the ground to cover you."

"I would have gotten the shot off."

He didn't know whether to kiss her or yell at her. Since there was no use in yelling, and nothing to say because he would have done the same thing, he brushed a kiss along her temple as he slid past her and set the two bags of supplies on the floor beside the refrigerator.

"I'll cook unless you really want to," Shylah said. She pawed through the bags and then began to put the various items away. "I'd rather you rest."

"I don't like that you're having to do the lion's share of the work in the kitchen." He didn't. He wasn't that kind of man. "Why don't we make a meal together and see how that works out." He liked the idea of the two of them in the kitchen. It seemed intimate to him.

She smiled at him and then washed her hands. He couldn't help but notice that her weapons were never far from her. "I like that idea. Do you know what you'd like for dinner? They've given us fresh produce."

"Anything but those rations Whitney sent with you. Are you absolutely positive that he isn't trying to slowly torture and kill you with that stuff? Because it's nasty."

She burst out laughing, the sound filling the little cabin. Something in him settled, something he hadn't known was tense, knotting his gut and leaving him edgy. She had already washed and was deftly slicing two chicken breasts before indicating he wash vegetables.

"Do you have any favorite recipes?"

Her voice slipped over him, soft and mellow, making him even more comfortable.

Being with Shylah was soothing in any situation. This one, doubly so. "You're a miracle, woman." Draden meant it. He couldn't imagine most people reacting the way she was in the circumstances.

"So everyone tells me." There was a note of teasing laughter in her voice.

He felt those intimate notes slipping under his skin settling around the area of his heart. He let her direct him how to cut up the potatoes and then grill the vegetables while she worked with the chicken, stuffing it with thin-sliced cheese and long strips of red pepper. Soon, the room was filled with the aroma of cooking food.

Draden found himself wondering what childhood would have been like for her. "Who cooked for you?"

"We had a series of cooks in the kitchen. Some let us come in, others not so much." She shot him a mischievous smirk, her dark eyes dancing at him. "The ones who didn't allow us in the kitchen didn't last long. We weren't shy about playing pranks on them. The meaner they were, the worse the pranks."

He leaned against the counter and watched her hands as she worked. He liked her hands. They looked almost delicate. Every movement was graceful. Looking at her, one would never suspect her lethal training, or the way she could get the job done so efficiently. He liked that. He liked that he was the only one who saw her. Who knew her.

She was so adaptable. She fit into any environment as if it were her home. Draden had seen her moving fast in the forest. He'd come across the men she'd killed. Now, in the kitchen, she was all feminine, soft and graceful, laughing intimately and making him feel as if he had a home for the first time in his life.

"Is that where you learned to cook?"

"I only can make a few special dishes. Zara is the one who really can cook. She excels at it. She really likes it. I wanted to know how it all worked. From there, I learned how to make a few dishes and that sort of satisfied me. I actually don't mind the rations when I'm out in the field."

He could understand that now that he'd spent some time with her. She was all about efficiency. The rations Whitney provided were fast, efficient and nutritious. She needed fuel when she was hunting. She needed to concentrate and focus on the hunt. He liked that about her as well.

"Have you ever thought much about the traits you'd want in a man if you were going to settle down and get married?"

She frowned at him as she put chicken on each of two plates. "It never occurred to me I would ever have the chance to find a man. Whitney always plants the capsules in us before we leave for a mission. If we don't return to him, we're dead. Luckily I've been given several weeks in order to track these men down. In his world, we can go into a breeding program to make him a little supersoldier, but we never thought in terms of settling down and getting married or anything remotely resembling that. What about you?"

He watched her add vegetables and the potatoes to the plates before placing them on the table. He liked having her there. Just her movements were soft, with no hard edges. That graceful, fluid motion she had that resembled a cat was all feminine now, not at all reminding him of that hunter in the forest. The more he was around her, the more the demons in him quieted.

"I've never even entertained the idea of having a home and family until I met you. As a rule, I don't like spending too much time with anyone. I think being at Wyatt's home helped with that. If not for him and Nonny, I probably still wouldn't have any idea of what a home should be."

They both sat at the extremely small table. "This looks delicious, Shylah. And it makes the house smell really good."

"I'm not guaranteeing anything but that it looks, smells and tastes better than rations."

He gave a little smirk of derision. "That's not much of an endorsement. Anything would taste better than that crap."

She laughed, just like he knew she would. "Tell me about the home you went to."

"The Fontenots. Wyatt Fontenot is a member of our team. He grew up with several brothers out in the swamps of Louisiana. His grandmother raised them. We all call her Nonny, and she's incredible. I didn't have a clue that women like Nonny existed."

Shylah was like Nonny. She would stand with her man, carving out a home and fighting by his side when necessary in the worst of circumstances.

"Nonny took all of us in when she didn't have to. When you're with her, you feel welcome. You feel like you have a home. I didn't even know I was missing that until I walked into her house. For the first time something reminded me of being with Eliza when I was a kid. Nonny's kitchen smelled like this place does. Filled with warmth. With welcoming. That house is like that because of Nonny. This one is like it because of you. I really want to thank you for giving me this experience."

She sent him a small smile. "I can't say I haven't had fantasies, Draden."

His cock jerked unexpectedly at that word. *Fantasies.* She'd given him a few of his own. "Those would be? Because you have to know, I'd be willing to fulfill every single one of them."

She threw her head back and laughed. Her hair went everywhere, falling around her face in soft waves. Her eyes danced and that generous mouth of hers drew his attention. He was dying, and he felt more alive than he ever had. Every cell in his body was alert and focused entirely on the woman seated across from him.

With her head thrown back, the graceful line of her neck was exposed. Her small white teeth flashed at him and amusement danced in her eyes. He had the sudden, mad desire to stand up, sweep all the plates and food off the table and lay her down right there like some primitive caveman. "You're giving me ideas best left alone, sweetheart." He put a bite of chicken in his mouth to keep from doing anything crazy.

"I'm glad I'm not the only inappropriate one," she said.

That was another thing he loved about her. She always made him feel as if they both were in the same boat. That if he was suffering for want of physical intimacy, so was she. She didn't take offense at his thoughts, admissions or actions. There was such freedom in that. He found Shylah Cosmos amazing. The fact that he'd been given such a gift at the end of his life both angered him and appeased him.

"I like this, Draden," she continued. "I'm going to pretend that we're living together."

"You don't have to pretend, sweetheart. We are."

"You know what I mean. I'm letting myself fall for you. All the way. I want that. You're definitely the kind of man I would want."

His heart clenched so hard it was a physical pain. He chewed, taking his time. "What do you mean?" He did his best to sound matter-of-fact, matching the conversational way she was being so honest. Neither had anything to lose. What was the possible use of hiding or misleading each other?

"If I was going to choose one man to spend my life with, it would be you. I like everything about you."

He liked that a hell of a lot. More than he realized. "I feel the same way about you," he admitted, forcing himself to take another bite of the delicious chicken. He made himself taste it. Savor it. Because she'd made it for him. That felt a lot like caring. He knew, because that was the way Nonny's food tasted. He knew, absolutely, that Shylah had taken special care to make this meal for him. Maybe she had because she thought it might really be his last, but she'd poured herself into it.

"Where would you want to live if we could live anywhere?"

He had never given that much thought. He sat back, chewing on the chicken and studying her face. It was slightly flushed. She was feeling the emotion underlying the intimate, revealing conversation they were having. Exchanging fantasies, but yet, they were real to him now because they all had her face. Her scent. He even had the taste of her in his mouth.

"I've gone all over the world and I know this sounds a little ridiculous, but I've fallen in love with the Louisiana swamp. It can be as hot as hell and humid like the tropics, but the beauty there is indescribable. I like the remoteness of it. The way a man can see what's coming at him and yet disappear if he wants. You can get by if you need to, living off the land. It isn't an easy life, but it's a good one."

"That surprises me. I don't know why, but it does."

"I went out there with few expectations. I honestly didn't care where I was. My unit was there, my fellow GhostWalkers, and we protect one another. Wyatt's grandmother was there, and she was becoming known to our enemies. Then Wyatt found Pepper and his three little girls. That gave us all another purpose to stay there. The girls are still young enough to bite when they get upset, and their bites are lethal. The swamp is a good place for them right now. It allows them freedom and keeps others safe."

"Your voice changes when you talk about the place. I can tell you really love it."

"I do. I didn't think I could love anything or even anyone, but Nonny has this way about her. She made me realize that there were good people in the world. She made me see that we were a family of sorts — the GhostWalkers in my unit — and that we had an extended family in the other GhostWalker units. I liked that. I liked belonging to something important like that. I also found I liked knowing I had the ability to protect Nonny, the three little ones and Pepper."

"What made you think there weren't good

people in the world, Draden?"

He almost missed that carefully worded question because she spoke so softly and used the same tone she'd been using before. He felt his gut clench. "That's for another time, sweetheart." He rebuffed her gently, not wanting her to think he wasn't willing to share with her. After all, who was she going to tell? Even if she judged him harshly, he'd be dead in a few days anyway. "When we're lying in bed in the dark."

She didn't look hurt. She gave him a faint smile. "My mysterious man is always so intriguing. I think I might like your swamp."

"We're all sticking close. We all have money. Whitney's daughter has shared a fortune with us, but Wyatt is loaded, and Trap is ridiculously loaded. Apparently, Gino is as well. Who knew?" He shrugged and sent her a small grin. "I'm sitting pretty as well."

"I take it that means all of you have enough money to purchase the land and make it defensible."

He laughed. Actually laughed. His woman was practical in some way others weren't. She didn't say build a house. Or furnish it with the best. It was all about defense.

"I found this really nice acreage just to the south of Trap and Cayenne. I liked it because it gave me privacy but allowed me to get to the fortress we're all setting up at his place in a very short period of time." He could run it in minutes and the trees, dripping with moss, provided him with good cover.

"Did you ever consider you might have a partner to share your home?"

"Not until I met you. Well, technically, I hadn't actually met you. I leapt over you when I was running for the water. You were lying on that little raised knoll, but in the depression. You looked up at me and I remember thinking I wasn't going to make it to the river because I was going to have a heart attack instead."

She shifted in her chair, pushed the empty dinner plate aside and leaned into her hand as she put her elbow on the table. Her large, dark eyes never left his face. "I knew you saw me."

"I didn't know you were there until I jumped over you to keep from stepping on you. You had a pair of binoculars in your hands, but you didn't move. You didn't flinch, not even to protect yourself. You kept your hands down. You just watched me with those eyes of yours and for a second, I felt like I was drowning. I knew then it was you."

"That's the most beautiful thing anyone's

ever said to me. I like that you knew."

He stood up to gather the dishes and take them to the basin-type sink. He liked that she didn't argue with him about his knowing. She just accepted it. He wasn't even going to bring up Whitney and his inevitable pairing. Or the fact that he'd considered killing her right then.

"When I woke up and realized that you had given me mouth-to-mouth, I wanted to shake you. And yell at the top of my lungs how unfair life was. You know, a child's reaction."

She cleared the rest of the table while he washed the dishes. "I had the same childish reaction when you told me you were infected. At last I'd found someone I was truly interested in, and you were telling me you were going to die. That sucked."

"I've been thinking about that." Draden didn't want to think about her leaving, but he was desperate for her to have a chance to live. He had to get her to agree to leave. He knew the others would get her to a hospital and do everything they could to make certain she lived. "If you were at a hospital, there's a chance they could use your blood to develop a vaccine or a therapy to treat the virus. Joe could pick you up tomorrow and take you to a hospital." He risked a look at her.

Shylah stood absolutely still, her face a mask of shock. Rejection. Anger. Hurt even. It was all there. She didn't say a word. Instead she left him standing there at the kitchen sink and went straight out the door. She didn't exactly slam it, but she closed it very, very firmly, just loud enough to make him wince.

Outside, light spilled through the canopy and lit up the entire morning. He stood at the window and watched her sink down onto the porch stairs. She seemed to be rocking herself back and forth for comfort. It was the first real sign he'd seen from her that she was close to a breaking point. One couldn't see the results of a filovirus and the way they caused severe hemorrhagic fevers in humans and not be terrified. He wasn't being stoic. He was as terrified as a man could get, but he had trained himself to stay ahead of fear. He ran. He was running now, killing as many of the MSS as possible to give himself purpose while the virus took effect.

Shylah had to be just as scared, maybe even more so. She didn't want to be alone, not in a hospital surrounded by strangers, any more than he did. He didn't want to go out feeling like a helpless, terrified lab experiment. He wanted to choose that moment when he lifted his hand and ended his suffering. Before he did that, he was determined to record every step of the disease's progression, so Trap and the others could hopefully find a way to stop the virus from spreading across the world.

He dried his hands while he thought it all through. He didn't want her to die. That was his hold-out hope, the one he needed to make it through this without breaking. Maybe she needed him. He hadn't considered that she might need him. Another thing he hadn't considered was that maybe being there for her was more important to him than what he needed. He had told her he would stop pushing her away and then he'd just done the same thing again.

He tossed the towel on the counter and went out to her. He didn't say anything, he just sank down onto the stairs beside her, thighs touching. Reaching over, he took her hand and slowly, one by one, opened the fingers she had curled into a fist. He was grateful she didn't pull away from him. He lifted her hand to his mouth and brushed a kiss there before pressing her palm to his heart.

They sat together for a few minutes in silence. He listened to the birds and insects.

They were great sentries, the birds in the air and the insects on the ground. Loud, the insects nearly drowned out every other noise, but the birds rivaled them with their cacophony of sounds. Some were melodious, but all too often, one sounded off on a particularly jarring note. Still, he liked to hear them.

"I'm sorry, Shylah. It won't happen again." He brought her hand to his mouth again, pressing kisses to the center of her palm. "It's important to me that they find a way to save you. I think I became a little obsessive about it and I didn't stop to think how it could look to you. I'm not rejecting you. Just the opposite. You mean something huge to me. Huge. I can't think about much of anything else but keeping you alive."

She was silent, staring out into the trees, her long lashes drawing his attention. Her profile was as beautiful as when he was staring straight at her. Up close he could see the dusting of gold across her nose. He loved those little freckles and he'd stared at them so much he knew the exact position of every single one of them.

"I've been preparing to die for a long time, Draden. I was always going to choose a time and let go on my own terms. There was no escaping from Whitney, not without dying a nasty death. He let us all know that. It was get killed in combat, and I'm not capable of aiding that along, or die of a virus. I knew he was having those individual strains created to target us. We always knew we weren't worth anything to him or anyone else there."

Everything male in him reacted to that. His entire body rebelled at the idea. He wanted to get physical, punch something, break necks. Kick the shit out of someone. She was worth so much — the world — and yet she hadn't been given that. "Baby." He tried. How did one tell her? Emotion rose to choke him, and he had to turn his head away. Whitney was the most fucked-up being he'd ever encountered, and he'd met his share of vile individuals.

"I wouldn't have chosen a virus like this one. I'm scared to death. I am. But I would much rather be here with you. Have this time with you. Die with you, rather than live a life of what amounted to slavery to Whitney. We talked about it, the three of us: Bellisia, Zara and me. We couldn't stay there forever. We agreed to escape if the opportunity presented itself, even if that meant death. We were going to live free for a few days, a week or two, for whatever time we had. This is my choice. *You* are my choice.

Don't take that away from me."

She turned her head and waited until he looked at her. He felt himself falling into her eyes. Under her spell. The emotion welling up was sharp and terrible. Fierce. Overwhelmingly strong.

"I love everything about you. I told myself that was what it was. All those parts separately, that I loved them. I watch you. I'm inside your mind. I see who you are. I've decided it isn't about loving everything about you. It's simply about loving you."

Shylah was the most courageous human being he'd ever met. His blood thundered in his veins, roared in his ears. His heart beat so hard it felt like it would come through his chest. He remained silent until he was positive he could keep his voice under control. Emotion was still choking him. He wanted to wrap her up in his arms and hold her close, keep her safe.

Draden waited until he could breathe. Until the lump in his throat dissolved. "Do you think you could have fallen in love with me if the circumstances were different? Not as extreme? Knowing we had all the time in the world?" He waited a heartbeat. "Because I know I would have fallen like a ton of bricks. Just as I have now. I know it with absolute certainty."

He pressed her palm to his lips again, brushing kisses there before moving her hand back to his heart. He kept his gaze fixed on hers, wanting her not only to hear the truth in his voice, but to see it on his face and in his eyes, because he'd never said anything truer.

"You would have been my choice. I would have taken longer to get there. I would have been suspicious, and I would have fought it, but I would never have walked away from you. I know that's the reason it's so important to me to believe Trap can save you. I *need* you to be safe. Out there, in the forest, I know you're skilled and you have every chance to be the victor in combat. But this virus, it's the devil, Shylah. It's evil and it consumes a human being from the inside out."

Her eyes shone at him. He could see an answering light there and it shook him more than he cared to admit.

Shylah leaned closer to him. "We've got now. Together. We can decide for ourselves what we're going to do until one or both of us goes down. In the meantime, we can be us, locked in our own little cocoon. We'll give them our daily reports and our blood, but they shouldn't expect anything else from us. We'll do what they ask, but I'm not leaving you. I won't do that, Draden."

"I've got the headache already, Shylah, a fever and extreme fatigue. My lymph nodes are swollen. This has to be a fast virus, or it wouldn't have killed all the villagers that quickly. I'm surprised I'm not sicker faster, but I know I'm infected."

"You have a headache from the blow to your head, Draden. And you've been going nonstop. You've not had much sleep since I've been with you. And I don't know when you'd slept last before you were ordered to rescue the doctors and soldiers. People get sick when they're run-down."

He couldn't deny that what she'd said was true. He hadn't had a lot of sleep prior to being sent on the rescue mission. They had been there instructing and also learning from the commanders of the Kopassus, an exchange of information in the hopes of taking down the terrorist cells in Indonesia.

He shrugged. "Let's go back inside. I'm not getting the vibe that anyone is watching, but we are ringed by soldiers. I don't like the idea of them spying on us." He stood up and held out his hand to her. "Come inside, baby. I won't suggest you leave again and I'll make it clear to Joe, you're staying with me."

She nodded as she stood. "You make sure

you do that, because I won't have any problem forcing them to kill me if they try to take me."

"They aren't going to take you." He meant that. No one would lay a hand on her. "You need to accept my apology and then let it go. That's the way we're going to do things when we're together. I'm going to fuck up and apologize a lot. You're going to forgive me and let it go."

She laughed, just as he hoped she would. "I presume letting it go means I don't get to bring it up later."

"Exactly. Clean slate every single time." He held the door for her.

"I see. I'm slightly worried about that term, 'every single time.' Does that mean there are going to be a lot of times you screw up?"

"I'm afraid so. I don't have a lot of experience in the relationship department so sadly for you, I'm going to blow it. On the other hand, you don't have a lot of experience either, so you might not even notice when I screw up. At least I'm hoping for that."

She looked around the room. "You finished the dishes."

He gave her a tentative grin. "Thought it best to let you cool off. I've seen Cayenne when she's pissed. She's very creative with silk."

"I think I'm going to like Cayenne."

"Trap shocked the holy hell out of me when he said she was pregnant. I know for a fact she's been on two missions with him and held her own. She didn't look pregnant when I left to come here. She probably would have had the baby in the forest, and then killed and wrapped an entire army of enemies with a newborn in a front pack."

Her mouth twitched. "How do you know what a front pack is?"

He tried to look serious. "I read."

"You saw it in a picture, didn't you?"

"Pepper bought one, so she would have her arms free to work with the three little vipers," he admitted. "Don't ever tell her I called her daughters that."

He sat on the edge of the bed and pulled off his boots. "Let's darken this room so we can sleep." Every muscle in his body hurt. He didn't tell her that, because, like him, she had to have some illusions to make their little fantasy work for as long as possible. He did note it for Trap, glancing at the time. "I want to look you over for rashes, and I need to examine your lymph nodes as well."

"It's easy to get rashes here, especially when I was lying in the grass."

Alarm skittered through him. "Shylah?" He waited until she turned around, her hand on the screen ready to pull it down to darken the room. "Do you have a rash somewhere?"

She shrugged. "I was lying in the grass when you raced toward the river. I'd been there for some time. Of course I have a rash. It's like your headache, no big deal."

Now his heart was pounding in earnest. "Come here." He pointed to a spot right in front of him, between his thighs.

Shylah pulled a second shade and then stepped back, toward the window. "It's really nothing."

"If it's nothing then you shouldn't have any problems letting me look at it."

"It's on my stomach. My shirt must have pulled up while I was lying on the ground watching the village."

"Come here," he reiterated, this time using his commander's voice. He didn't pull rank even within the unit, but he could. "Shylah, right now." He was going to examine her lymph nodes first. He had to know she was safe.

10

Walking out of the forest into the clearing with the morning light surrounding them gave Draden a feeling of déjà vu. He was absolutely exhausted, having spent the night killing as many of the enemy as possible. The entire time he had tried not to worry about Shylah. He'd examined her before they went to sleep and she had a rash that had spread up her tummy to just under her breasts and then down below her navel. Worse, he'd detected several swollen lymph nodes. He told himself that didn't mean anything. Lymph nodes could swell for a variety of reasons, stress being one of them.

The ranks of the Milisi Separatis Sumatra were becoming very depleted. He and Shylah had worked as a team to annihilate the enemy, taking out as many as possible. She hadn't hesitated once. He didn't want either of them to unintentionally expose the villagers to the virus, so he had deliberately taken out the MSS guards and scouts *outside* the village. Members of the terrorist cell were still hunting for the two of them, spreading out into the forest, this time in greater numbers, making it even easier to do more damage. By morning, Draden was certain the Indonesian soldiers could infiltrate the village now to make certain the inhabitants were safe from the terrorists.

They were both tired, but when he mentioned it, she had simply responded that it was to be expected. "I want to talk to Whitney," he said as they approached the remote lab.

Shylah had bent down to touch the delicate trip line running across the ground in front of the stairs. The sun coming up shone on the web, revealing the lines stretching across the stairs and around each window. There was a neat burrow situated to one side of the stairs, as if a funnel-web spider resided there. Insects walked across the trip line alerting the spider to prey. In this case, those lines would serve as a warning if the remote lab had been penetrated.

Her head jerked up. She slowly straightened. "Why?"

He detested the suspicion in her voice. "Shylah, last night I told you I loved you. It wasn't bullshit and I didn't say it because we're both infected. I told you that because it was the truth. I don't lie as a rule, and I damn sure will never lie to you. We made a pact and I'm going to honor it."

"You can't trust anything Whitney says to you."

"Believe me, I'm well aware of that. I agreed to be psychically enhanced but that wasn't the only thing he did to me." He had been furious, and it had just proved to him all over again that no one could ever be trusted. Now, he was oddly grateful. He liked the fact that his woman was his perfect match, or at least seemingly so.

He didn't have the spider strain, but clearly it wasn't as strong in her as it was in Cayenne. Shylah made use of her ability to spin silk, but she wasn't compulsive about it. He'd seen beautiful lacy curtains, all made of silk, hanging all over Trap's bedroom. There were silken streamers hanging from the ceiling. Cayenne often wrapped herself in silk and rested away from the team, her gaze on Trap, every cell in her body tuned just to him.

"I have a few things to say to Whitney."

"I have nothing to say to him."

"It may be the last time you ever have the chance to tell him what an asshole he is."

She turned away from him and started up

the stairs. "I have no desire to give him that kind of satisfaction. He's heard it his entire life, and it just makes him feel superior. If you feel the need to talk to him, by all means call him."

She stood at the door, examining the silken lines that crisscrossed in the very functional pattern of the funnel-web spider. Frowning, she ran her finger down the door. "Someone's been here, Draden."

He came onto the porch immediately, stepping right behind her, close, so his larger frame covered hers. Just in case a rifle was trained on them. He touched her shoulder. "Ease around to the southern side of the building. There's more cover there. Act like you're looking for more breaks in the web."

She didn't argue with him, she jumped off the porch and made her way around the corner of the building. Draden took his time examining the door. The silken lines were broken, snapped off when someone had opened it. He glanced back at the lines on the stairs. Not a single one had been broken. Someone had known not to disturb those webs.

He stood slowly. *Joe? You close by?*

There was a long silence and then he felt the presence slide into his mind. *Waiting for the two of you to come back. I came by earlier, opened the door and looked inside.*

There was another hesitation, and Draden's alarm went off.

I'm sorry, man. Trap says both of you are infected, but he says you're fighting it. He wants more blood ASAP.

In terms of fighting it, what does that mean?

He says your immune systems are working overtime and the virus is being killed at a rapid rate. You both are fighting it off actively.

They had it. Both of them. They carried that death inside of them. It was an eerie feeling. *So, you're saying we're both carriers.* He hated that even more. The idea of being responsible for infecting anyone, even his enemies, was abhorrent to him.

That's not what I said. Just get inside and get me some blood. You know how obsessive Trap is, he wants it like yesterday. He's been at me all night.

"Shylah, it was Joe. Trap sent him for more blood."

You go on inside and stay away from the windows.

Her voice sounded warm and sweet like honey. Wild honey. His breath hitched. *You don't have a knife up against my commanding officer's throat, do you?*

Of course not. I have a gun pointed at his

head. He doesn't know it. I was careful to stay out of sight.

He knows it. Joe's a GhostWalker, just like we are. Nothing gets close to us without our knowledge. For God's sake, woman, you're going to get my ass thrown in the brig.

You're too trusting. If orders came down from the top to kill you, don't you think he'd do it? He would in a heartbeat. We're dangerous to everyone.

No, Shylah, he wouldn't do it. Joe's my friend. I don't trust many people, but I do trust him. I'm going inside. Come and join me. You're giving me a hell of a hard-on and I can't do anything about it because we're both infected with this nasty virus.

There was silence. Too long. He paused, hand on the door. *I should have said, our bodies are fighting it off.* For the first time he let himself really breathe. Really think there was a possibility to live. *Joe's a tolerant man, sweetheart, but no one likes a gun on them.*

You know how to ruin a girl's fun.

Even knowing Joe was lethal as hell and any minute might lose his patience — although he wasn't known for that — Draden still felt like smiling. He had the impression of Shylah pouting, and that made him happy. Just talking to her made him happy. The fact that she would circle around, hunt and find the man watching from the forest, was a complete turn-on. He liked that his woman would be his partner.

He waited for her on the porch. She walked into the clearing, shoulders back, head up, straight as an arrow, completely unrepentant. She even gave him a little smirk. He wrapped his arm around her neck and kissed her. Kissing her was an experience that could get out of hand fast. She was addicting. Hot. Her mouth a kind of paradise he hadn't experienced until he kissed her, and now he didn't want to stop.

For God's sake, Draden. I swear I'm going to put a bullet in your leg if you keep that shit up. I'm hot and hungry and I've got Trap calling me every ten minutes. You ever experience Trap when he's in full-blown research mode? Get inside and give me your blood. Now. Consider that an order.

Draden debated. Kissing Shylah was worth getting shot. Still. He lifted his head, looking down at her dark eyes and the golden dusting of freckles he loved. He wanted to spend time kissing every single one of those spots. "Joe's getting antsy. Let's get inside and take our blood, give it to him and then we'll contact Whitney."

"I don't have anything to say to Whitney," Shylah reiterated. "But since I've been kind of mean to your friend, I agree we should give him the blood." She looked away from him, deliberately concentrating on the door as he opened it to allow them both inside. "You said we were fighting it off. What does that mean?"

"I honestly don't know what it means, sweetheart." Draden kept his voice gentle. She needed gentle. The news was overwhelming emotionally. They'd both tried to prepare themselves for the ordeal of dying a horrific death and now they'd been handed hope. He wasn't certain if hope was a good thing, not knowing the virus was inside of them, attacking their bodies every way it could. "Trap is good at what he does, and he's sharing everything we give him with the best in the military. Everyone is working to try to save us." He washed his hands and pulled on gloves. He didn't want to tell her that of course their bodies would attempt to fight the virus. That was what immune systems were for. They both needed hope.

She gave him her arm. "You do know if they find a way to save us, I can never meet your commanding officer face-to-face after the things I said to him."

He flashed her a grin. "I think he'll be so glad we're both alive that he'll forgive you the comments. The gun aimed at him is a different matter."

"We've got weapons aimed at us," she said, wincing as he took out the needle. "I don't mind them going in, but I hate it when they're pulled out."

"I'll try to be more careful." He hated hurting her. A stick with a needle wasn't anything, he knew she'd say that to him. But it was to him. He had the feeling she'd had a lifetime of needles and experiments with no one caring whether or not it hurt her. "Shylah, if we survive this, I want you to stay with me."

Her gaze jumped to his face. It was clear, from her expression, she hadn't expected there was a chance of survival and she hadn't thought what would happen if she didn't die.

"I'm never going back to Whitney."

"I wouldn't want you to go back to him, but if you survive this, you have choices. I know Lily, Whitney's daughter, would give you the money for a clean start. She's helped out all of us. Hell, I'd do that. I don't want you to think you don't have choices, but when you think about what you would want to do, think about staying with me. Making a go of it, the two of us. The things we talked about yesterday, we could make them real."

They'd lain on the bed together, talking for hours. Laughing. Putting together a mythical household. Designing the rooms. Talking about what their days together would be like. How many children they wanted.

He had stretched out, full length, head propped up with his hands, looking at the woman he knew would forever have his heart. Not once during those hours had he thought about dying. Not one single time. He'd thought about their life together and how they were so well matched. He'd found himself finding ways to make her laugh just to hear the sound.

Later, as the day had lengthened, her voice had become drowsy, and he'd found those huskier notes sexy. She'd slid deeper into the bed, lying beside him so that her scent enveloped him. Although his body had reacted, he'd found it soothing, even comforting, to have her lying so close. He'd wrapped his arm around her waist and pulled her against him. They'd fallen asleep like that. He had never trusted a woman — or anyone, for that matter — to sleep close to him, let alone in the same bed. And yet, already, he was completely relaxed with her. He couldn't imagine being without her, and now, if they survived, it was a very real possibility.

"I have to find the Williams brothers, Orucov and also Montgomery."

She didn't. Every cop in the world would be looking for them, but he understood. She'd started out hunting them and she wasn't about to hand that task over to someone else. She would go after them. He would have done the same.

"Of course you have to find them, Shylah." He concentrated on taking enough blood of his own to satisfy Trap. "I wouldn't expect anything less from you." He glanced up and caught the relief on her face. "Do you think I don't know who you are? You have to find them. I'm the same way. We started this. Let's end it together."

"You'd go with me?"

"Yes. And my team will want to help as well. We're very good at what we do." He flashed her a grin. "You'll have your chance to boss Joe around since you'll be lead."

A faint smile curved her lower lip and emphasized the bow of her mouth. It was all he could do not to lean down and kiss her.

"I'm not about to antagonize that man any more than I already have." The look on her face was too mischievous to be believable. "Of course, if I ended up back with you in the swamp, he'd probably find a way to retaliate."

He liked that she hadn't shut down his plea. *Blood is ready, Joe. Anything else Trap wants?*

Shylah's gaze jumped to his face. "You're talking to him telepathically."

"Joe's a strong telepath. He can build bridges for those not as strong. I'm telling him we've got the blood ready for him and asking if he needs anything else."

Report on any symptoms developing.

Draden had inspected Shylah's rash and lymph nodes. She'd looked for the same on him. By necessity, it had been a semi-intimate inspection. His hands had moved over her body, trying to be impersonal, trying to remember he was a doctor, but he registered everything about her on a very personal level. She was so soft. Inviting. Tempting. His.

There'd been nothing clinical about it when she'd inspected him. Her hands had lingered on him. Stroked caresses over his skin, forgetting to find the nodes he had told her how to look for. She'd been tempted as well. He saw it on her face, felt it in her touch. The examinations had taken much longer than necessary because they were paying more attention to learning each other's bodies than searching for telltale symptoms of the virus.

I'll send him the report via email.

Coming to the door.

"Joe's coming in."

Shylah immediately stepped to the side of the door so that when it opened, she couldn't be seen. She had her Glock out and pressed against her thigh, all business, backing him up as Draden went to the door to give Joe the blood. He liked her efficiency. He worked well with the GhostWalkers, as a member of that team, but having Shylah as a partner was eye-opening. She seemed to anticipate every possibility as he did, and she took steps to protect him more fiercely than any person ever had.

He opened the door and Joe was already there, wearing the hazmat suit. Draden handed him the carrier with the blood.

"Your woman is a tigress, Draden," Joe greeted. "You just remember that if you ever get out of line."

Draden grinned him. "She is, isn't she?"

"She have a gun pointed at me?"

"She was born with a gun in her hand, so my guess? Yeah. It's probably aimed right in the middle of your forehead."

Joe shook his head. "I can't wait to meet

her officially. Trap is being closemouthed, but you know him. He's showing some signs of excitement. He hasn't slept and won't eat. Cayenne usually keeps him from being so insane during these times, but she's gone. Everyone wants to get her back just to keep him under control."

"Is she really all right?" Draden liked Cayenne. He especially liked her for his friend. Trap was a good man. He did forget to eat and would go far too long without sleep when he was onto something in the laboratory. He grew surlier and more edgy with every passing hour. Cayenne had a way of taking all that away but still letting him stay on track.

"She is. Apparently she's had very little pregnancy sickness. She doesn't show at all. I wasn't too happy when I found out she was pregnant, especially when I found out how far along she was. She didn't say a thing, not even to the other women. Nonny would never give up a confidence. She actually went on two missions with us in her condition. I'm not sure how Trap got her first, to stay behind, and then to leave with Pepper and the girls, but he managed it. Now we're all paying for it."

"Sorry about that," Draden said, half genuinely sympathetic.

Joe shook his head. "Fight hard, Draden. And you're finished going after these MSS bastards. The Kopassus are planning to take them down. You've done your part, now rest and let your body fight this thing."

"Does Trap really think it's possible?"

Joe hesitated.

"It's easier to know the truth, Joe," Draden said. "We have to be prepared. If I go down and Shylah's left, she has to have a plan and vice versa."

"Trap plays things close to his chest. He and Wyatt have been working night and day. They barely eat. They don't talk unless they're barking orders to one of us. I'm staying close to you with a couple of the others, so communication with them is not in person. Gino's taking the brunt of their craziness. Malichai and Diego are backing me."

Draden could hear the caution in Joe's voice. Their eyes met in understanding. Joe, Malichai and Diego were staying in the vicinity to protect Draden and Shylah just in case someone in the government decided they were too big of a threat and decided to kill them.

"If we're cleared, Shylah will continue hunting Whitney's three scientists and Montgomery. I would like to accompany her and also ask that our team help us in any way they can lend support."

"I expected as much. Given her penchant for pointing weapons at innocent substitutes, I figured she'd want the chance to go after the real thing."

Shylah's soft laughter slid into Draden's mind. Warm, like honey, filling him up when he hadn't known he was empty. He had never been known for his sense of humor, but being around her, that mischievous amusement had managed to feed that side of him. He smiled a lot more and, to his shock, laughed with her.

Draden talked for a few more minutes with Joe and then watched him leave. He could feel the soldiers who had surrounded the clearing, but he couldn't spot them. That made him uneasy. He didn't trust them. They weren't part of his unit and they could get trigger-happy. He wouldn't blame them. Many had families. If they had seen the effects of the virus, they would be terrified of it being unleashed on their population. They had to be nervous. He just hoped that those guarding the area had nerves of steel.

Shylah leaned against the wall, her eyes dancing when he came back inside. "Your commanding officer has a sense of humor."

Draden nodded. It was impossible to resist her when she was in this mood. "He says we're done going after the MSS."

"I heard, but I'm not convinced he's right. Did you notice each time they hunted us, their circle has been cast wider? Tonight, they very well could make it to the ranger's cabin."

"They'd have to go through the line of soldiers between us."

"The soldiers I've observed are more concerned with keeping us confined than paying attention to anything coming at us."

That much was probably true. Again, he couldn't blame the soldiers, but it made for an opening the enemy could slip through.

"Call Whitney, sweetheart. We may as well get this over with. Once he's on, just hand me the phone and then, no matter what I say, stay quiet. And, babe, expect me to lie."

She had her cell out and she glanced up at him and gave him a faint smile. He could see she was stressed. She didn't want any contact with Whitney at all. He was the boogeyman. He'd held absolute authority over her for her entire life. Defying him was difficult. It said a lot that Shylah was willing to die — that she would choose a horrific death rather than go back to him.

She handed him the phone and then

paced as far from him as the little room would allow. Draden put the phone on speaker.

"Peony?" Whitney's voice was gruffer than Draden remembered.

"Not Peony, Whitney. Draden Freeman here. We don't have a lot of time and I need answers to some questions. I'm in the remote lab. Peony has been infected with the virus. The fact that she has tiger DNA that has merged with human DNA has changed the structure of the cell, so the virus had a difficult time adhering to the cell. It takes longer to infect her, but the virus is taking hold. She's going to die, Whitney. Trap needs to know her genetic makeup. All of it. You can't leave anything out because we don't have time."

"Are you certain she's been infected?"

"Absolutely. I'm here with her, looking right at her."

"You sound anxious."

"Don't play games. I know you paired us. That aside, anyone seeing the results of this virus would feel anxious. She's valuable to the world and you know she is. Whether she's under your command or a GhostWalker unit's, she's too valuable to die. Our children alone would make her of value, let alone all the training she has."

Whitney heaved a heavy sigh. "There is no cure for the virus."

"They were working on a vaccine, weren't they? The Williams brothers and Orucov. You had them working on a specific vaccine."

"There is no use in explaining that we need biological weapons to match what other countries are secretly developing. With those weapons, we need vaccines to ensure our soldiers are protected at all times. I don't expect you to understand."

"Why? I'm a soldier. I'm also a doctor. I've seen the effects of these viruses and the fear always is another pandemic." Draden poured sincerity into his voice. "Of course, we need vaccines against the viruses. We need therapies to treat them. Studies have to be done. I'm not arguing the point. What I'm trying to do right this minute is to save Peony's life."

"You have to accept that is impossible."

"If you accepted most things were impossible there wouldn't be GhostWalkers. I don't accept that we can't save Peony, and neither does Trap. We're focused on stopping this virus from eating her alive, but we don't have much time. Trap can map out her entire genetic code, but you've already done that, and it saves us time."

"I'll send it to both of you, but I need reassurances that you'll return Peony to me."

"You know if I gave those to you, I'd be lying. I don't want to play games with you. She's worth saving and she's just as valuable to our country staying with me, maybe even more so, than she is with you. You're either going to help or you're not."

"I'm sending to Trap and to your personal email."

If it was supposed to shock him that Whitney had his personal email, it didn't. He ignored the subtle bragging.

"Do you have further data on Montgomery? Did you give Peony everything on your three scientists?"

"She has everything I have, but I can send those files to you in case she didn't have a chance to turn them over. I don't have much on Montgomery, other than he's completely worthless and his family has spent far too much time bailing him out of every bit of trouble he's ever gotten into. He paid his way through college, getting others to do his work for him. One professor was paid half a million dollars to give him top grades because he didn't attend any of the classes."

"We'll find him," Draden assured.

"You do this, Draden, and I'll send you

everything I have on you."

"I told you already, you want to show that shit to anyone, do it. I won't be blackmailed. You caught me in your net when I was young and stupid. It didn't turn out so bad. I like what I do, and I'm good at it. I don't give a damn if you want to hold it over my head for the rest of my life because I just plain don't care if they come for me."

"That's easy enough to say because you haven't had to face a trial."

"I've always refused to be blackmailed by you. I always will refuse. If you want to turn whatever evidence you have of my insanity over to the cops or the military police, do it. I will never be blackmailed. I will never accept a sword hanging over my head. I won't be owned by anyone, least of all you. And Whitney, I won't allow Peony to be either."

Draden's eyes met Shylah's. She had to know, sooner or later, that he was no saint and never would be. He loved her, but if she was going to stay with him, she had to know the worst of him. He wanted honesty between them. That was why he wanted her in the room when he spoke to Whitney.

There was a long silence. "I destroyed all the evidence against you the moment you became a GhostWalker, Draden," Whitney admitted, grudging respect in his voice.

"You're too valuable to our country and you've contributed far too much to turn you over to shallow-thinking people who would condemn your actions."

"I appreciate you thinking that."

"I was particularly pleased with you returning to school and completing your education." Whitney sounded like an uncle talking to a favorite nephew.

"It was important to help Trap and Wyatt," Draden said, as though making a concession by admitting it to the man. "Now, with Peony having this virus, I need more than ever to help them find a way to help her."

"I've sent you everything I have on Peony. I also sent a copy to Trap," Whitney assured.

Draden pointed to the computer, leaned down and wrote out his email address and password on a slip of paper and handed it to her.

"I want you to know, Bellisia and Zara have adapted well into the GhostWalker program. They are assets as well. You might want to rethink this plan you have of planting a virus in the women before you send them out. Losing any of them could lose us valuable assets at the wrong time." Draden had to keep him on the line as long as possible. He needed Shylah to assure him that they had her information.

"We need soldiers, not women," Whitney said.

"I agree," Draden said. "But without the women we aren't going to have the soldiers. You set up a genetic experiment. Let it unfold. That's all I'm saying."

"It has to be with the strongest of them," Whitney said. "Women are weak. They fold under pressure as a rule. I test them over and over before it's decided to use their genetic material to create a true soldier. Only the strongest deserve that honor."

Draden kept his eyes on Shylah. She'd pulled up his email and turned to nod before she copied the file and saved it to a flash drive. Whitney might have a way of infiltrating, retrieving or destroying the document, and they needed it. She gave him the thumbs-up, and he breathed a sigh of relief. If he had to kiss Whitney's ass in order to save Shylah, he didn't mind. If he had to pretend to think Whitney was the coolest guy in town, and agree with his bullshit theories, then so be it.

"I've got to wrap this up and talk to Trap," Draden said.

"Call if you need anything else, and, obviously, if Peony gets worse. I also need reports on the progress of the vaccine."

Draden's breath caught in his chest. "You

have more of the virus. You're storing it. Are you crazy? If it gets out, you saw the results. It could go global in a matter of hours under the right circumstances."

"It's safe."

"It isn't safe. You just had three men breach your storage facility."

"They created it."

"Because you couldn't find a virus that would kill Peony."

"Peony never, ever, got sick. Fortunately, she believed me when I told her I planted a virus in her before she went out, and that brought her back to me. If she had known she was free, I would have lost her."

"Because you couldn't make her sick, you were angry with the three you were paying to create something specifically targeted to her."

"*Only* her. The virus was only supposed to kill her. She has a specific code and that should be able to be attacked under the right circumstances. They should have been able to create a virus without going so far. If we don't have immunity from the virus, it renders it useless as a weapon."

"Montgomery doesn't think so."

"Greed supersedes patriotism more often than not. You can't put people in positions of power and expect them to turn it over to you. They know you're smarter than they are, and they want to be able to prove to themselves that you're not. You and I both know that."

Stroking Whitney's ego turned Draden's stomach, but he needed as much information as possible. He wasn't about to end the conversation on a sour note just in case they might need more information from him later.

"I expect people to do their job when I pay them a fair wage."

"People are assholes, Whitney. I'm sure you've learned that by now. I have to go. I have very little time. Peony's got a gift for tracking and we need her to run these men down."

"Keep sending reports."

Draden had enough. He hit the end button and turned to face Shylah. There was no condemnation on her face, but then he didn't expect to see it there. He knew her now. He knew she waited on judgment. Because she hunted criminals, he thought she might see in terms of black and white, but she seemed to listen to everything with an open mind. Still, he had committed murder. There was no getting around that. It had to be said.

"Just tell me," she said.

"Not here." The little room reeked of the three scientists and what they'd done. He didn't want to confess to her there, where their evil lingered.

She was the one who held out her hand, signaling to him that she was willing to hear him out, just as he knew she would. He enclosed those delicate fingers in his much larger hand, needing the connection. Even when he'd asked her to stay if they both lived, she hadn't answered him.

They walked together across the clearing, back into the forest along the trail leading to the ranger's hut. "We needed those files, Shylah. I would have sold my soul for them."

"I'm aware of that." She glanced up at the sky and then looked to the trees. "The birds are usually very vocal this time of day."

"Soldiers surrounding us."

It was after noon and should have been bright and sunny. The early morning had held promise, but already the oppressive heat had come and with it, dark, ominous clouds. They moved overhead with the building wind.

"Obviously, but it could be the weather," she commented. She didn't push him to get started on his explanation. He was certain most women would.

"A storm is coming in. According to Malichai, who likes to give us all kinds of trivial facts about weather when we're on a helicopter and can't get off, Indonesia has frequent storms, but they aren't nearly as intense as those in some other countries."

She sent him a tantalizing smile, one that held a hint of laughter, but also something deeper. "Good to know."

Her smile did something to his insides. He'd been tense. His gut in knots. That one, brief smile tied them together. It felt like an intimacy between them. That smile was his alone and he knew that.

He was falling deeper with every minute in her company. Trap and Wyatt. They *had* to save her. He knew others were working to find a vaccine or at least a therapy to aid the two of them, but he counted on his fellow GhostWalkers. Trap was renowned in the field, Wyatt, a close second. At least he knew the two tenacious GhostWalkers wouldn't stop trying.

They approached the ranger's hut as they always did, very cautiously. She checked the webs, he checked their surroundings. Nothing had been touched. Once inside, she headed for the small shower. It was mostly cold water, but after hunting killers all night through the forest, he knew she always showered, cold water or not. He stood at the window and watched the storm coming in.

Just as in the swamp he called home, it was warm — almost hot, yet it was growing dark, and in the distance, he heard the first roll of thunder. Drops of rain fell through the canopy, turning the leaves of the trees a beautiful silver. They hit the roof, drumming loudly, and he knew the drops were probably warmer than the water pouring over Shylah's body.

The moment the thought came to him, he tried to push it away. The image of her naked, all soft skin and nothing else, just a few feet from him, was difficult to get out of his mind. They couldn't go there until she knew everything she needed to know about his past.

Still, she had those breasts. Full. Round. High. When they lay in bed, his hand had cupped the undersides and his thumb had grazed her nipple. She had the kind of nipples he could play with for hours and never get tired of. He wondered how sensitive she'd be when his mouth was on her. His tongue. His teeth.

If you don't intend to do anything about it, stop thinking about putting your mouth on me. That's hard to ignore.

He spun around. She stood just outside

the shower, wearing a tank top and jeans. She dried her hair with a towel, but the water had dripped down the tank, or she hadn't dried her body properly, because he could see through the material and she wasn't wearing a bra.

"Seriously, woman? You're tempting enough."

"We might die anytime, Draden. It might be the only time I have to be with you."

"You aren't helping."

"I don't necessarily want to help you."

"We have things to talk about before we ever go there."

She tilted her head to one side. "Are they things that would make me not want to have wild, crazy sex with you in the middle of a thunderstorm?"

"Most likely."

She gave a little sigh. "Maybe we should postpone you telling me."

"Maybe you should behave yourself."

"I thought all men jumped at the chance when they're offered sex."

"I'm looking for more than just sex from you, so we're doing this right."

She rolled her eyes. "Fine, go take a shower and then we'll talk."

He studied her face. He wasn't certain he trusted her to behave. "I'm taking my shower, but when I come out, we're talking."

"There's all kinds of ways to talk, just in case you didn't know," she muttered, sounding rebellious.

He was set on having her for the rest of his life, no matter how long or little that was, but he could see, if she agreed, he was going to have his hands full. He took the towel from her and stalked into the little shower that made him have to stoop over to get any water on his head.

11

Shylah stood at the window, listening to the sound of the water, knowing it was falling on Draden's naked body. He'd been as close to a perfect gentleman as he could possibly have been. She knew he was attracted and that the chemistry between them was explosive. They both had tried to respect the fact that they were in a bad place and not complicate that with sex.

When he kissed her, she couldn't think. Her brain just shut off. She hadn't known it could be like that. In her wildest imagination, she hadn't considered that the attraction between a man and a woman could be so fierce. They had so many things stacked against them, and now he had some deep, dark secret that Whitney, of all people, knew.

She had to respect the fact that Draden was determined to tell her before he touched her, because he believed whatever that secret was, it would change her mind about him. If he was a traitor, a spy for Whitney, that could change her mind, but she knew that wasn't it. Draden's loyalty was 100 percent to his team. The GhostWalkers were his family. She heard that in his voice every time he talked about them. That was impossible to fake.

Rain hit the roof harder, drumming so loudly it nearly drowned out the sound of the shower, or he'd turned it off. She remained staring out the window at the tops of the trees as they swayed back and forth in the wind. Dancing. It was beautiful. A little primitive. The air was hot and humid. Sultry. Her body seemed to have caught some of the intensity of the storm. She felt a little wild and out of sorts. Edgy. On the verge of something big.

She felt different when she was with Draden. She'd learned to live in the present a long time ago, to enjoy every moment she had. Time was a luxury, something she knew she could run out of very quickly, so she made sure each minute counted for something. She allowed herself to experience every emotion. When she was happy, she wanted to recognize that. When she was sad, she let herself be sorrowful. Now, she didn't know what she was. It was impossible to recognize the feelings both emotionally and physically because she'd never had them. But she liked feeling the way she was.

She'd been around men, but no one had ever made her feel the way he did. When he looked at her, she grew hot. Needy. Hungry for him. Each time his fingers brushed her skin, her body reacted, every nerve ending on fire. And when he kissed her, the world fell away and there was only his taste and his heat. The flames pouring into her and down her throat, spreading like a wildfire. He was addicting without even trying.

Shylah loved to look at him. Just look at him. She could do that all day. He was the epitome of male perfection. Rugged, without being too contrived. Jaw-droppingly handsome without being so beautiful he bordered on feminine. When he smiled, he took her breath away, those strong white teeth showing the perfection of his smile.

She wanted his touch on her skin. His mouth on her breasts. She wanted him inside her, sharing her skin. Making them one. She didn't believe that his friends could save them, and she wanted to know what it felt like to make love to someone who was her absolute match. Draden was hers. The one. The only. She didn't know how she knew it, but she did know that nothing in her life was truer.

Water slashed across the window and the wind hit the little cabin with a force that rocked it, drawing her attention back to the storm. The shower went off abruptly, but she didn't turn around. She liked the storm and would have gone outside on the porch to witness its approach if she had more clothes. She was traveling light out of necessity. Whitney always arranged for weapons to be waiting at her destination, along with the necessary permits to carry them.

Sometimes she traveled under various identities, but she didn't care what anyone called her, unless they addressed her as Shylah. That was real to her. Now, Draden had her rethinking her name, Peony. Who wanted to be named Peony? It was a ridiculous name, but Draden made it sound sexy. When he whispered that name in her mind so intimately, she melted inside.

What would be so wrong with having sex, Draden? She poured need into her mind. Hunger. The image of her kneeling at his feet, his cock in her mouth.

He groaned. She almost smirked at his reaction. He wasn't nearly in as much control as he pretended to be.

Woman, you're a handful.

She brought her hands up under her breasts, her fingers performing a small massage, thumbs sliding over the twin peaks. Just that light touch sent streaks of fire racing straight to her sex, lighting her up.

I think I'm more than a handful. Can you feel me? This is where your mouth should be. She was taunting him, trying to force his hand. She knew better. She knew she should hear what he had to say before she succumbed to other needs, before she made up her mind, but she didn't want to chance missing out on him.

My mouth needs to be somewhere else.

At once she had the image of her legs over his shoulders and his mouth feeding at her sex. It was so erotic she squirmed, nearly feeling him there, his tongue lapping and stroking, his teeth teasing. It was too much to think about.

Devouring you, he corrected. *Eating you like candy. Claiming what's mine.*

It was a dangerous game the two of them were playing, when he had seemed so determined not to get physical. *Claiming what's mine,* she echoed. *I like that. I like feeling as if I belong with you.*

He came up behind her, his arms sliding around her, tight, under her breasts, holding her while they both stared out at the storm. It was nearly upon them now, lightning forking across the dark, purple sky, lighting up the canopy for a few seconds before it went dark again. The clouds were thick and nearly black, rolling and heaving as if in fury.

Draden's mouth went to her neck, kissing her, teeth scraping back and forth. She shivered a response, her sex clenching, needing him more than ever. He suckled there for a moment, and then kissed his way to her shoulder.

"I really want you," she admitted. "We both have the virus. Your friend said so. If we both have it, it doesn't make any difference what we do. Right?" She wasn't above asking for what she wanted. She didn't believe they were miraculously going to be saved, no matter what his friend said. She knew he didn't believe it either. It wouldn't matter who asked first, once they both were dead.

He pressed his body tighter against hers, so she could feel the evidence of his desire imprinted in her skin. "Go lie on the bed. We're going to talk, and I want to look at you while we do."

Staring at his reflection, she lifted her chin. He didn't seem to realize that his thumbs were sliding back and forth across her nipples. Each touch sent that sweet, sweet wildfire roaring through her veins to settle between her legs.

"Fine. We'll talk then." She moved out of his arms, but she drew the tank over her head and tossed it onto the small kitchen table as she passed by it. He wanted to look at her, then he was going to look at all of her. Every last inch of her.

Deliberately she swayed her hips seductively as she walked away from him to the side of the bed, unzipping her jeans as she went. Keeping her back to him, she shimmied the denim down her long legs, bending at the waist to pull them off, first one leg, and then the other. She'd practiced the move a hundred times, pretending she was dancing for her man. She wasn't certain what effect it had on him because her back was turned, but the books she'd read and the instructional videos had assured her that her man would love it.

She heard his breath hiss out between his teeth and a small groan escaped. Both made her smile. She was making progress. She flipped her hair over her shoulders as she sank down onto the mattress, leaning back on one elbow, one knee drawn up while her other leg stretched out at an angle.

His gaze dropped from her breasts to her gleaming sex. It was all she could do not to touch herself, but she forced herself to wait for the right moment. She knew one would come. The front of his jeans held a large bulge, thick and definitely long. She kept her gaze fixed there.

"I'm waiting for your explanation of the delay."

"Can you pull the blanket up?" There was a hint of desperation in his voice.

She smiled and licked her finger. "No, I can't." She slid her finger over her right nipple. It was already erect, and the light touch made her shiver.

"I need your complete attention, Shylah."

"Believe me, honey" — she made her voice purr — "you have my complete attention."

He was wearing only his jeans. His chest was all muscle, his abs out of a magazine. She licked her lips and then put one hand on top of her knee. Waiting. Eyes on him. Watching him start to sweat. Tiny beads she wanted to lick off of him. As a seductress, so far, she was batting zero. If this didn't work, it would definitely be okay if she died because she wasn't certain she could live with the humiliation of rejection.

"Damn it, Shylah, I murdered several people and Whitney knew it. He had video of me killing them. That was what he threatened me with. That's what I've been living with all these years, knowing at any moment he would use it because I refused to be blackmailed."

There was an abrupt silence with only the sound of the rain hitting the windows and drumming a wild rhythm on the roof. His breath moving in and out of his lungs. Her breath coming slow. Her heart pounding to match the wild wind, not because of his confession, but because she wanted him desperately — even more now that he'd made his revelation.

She could see he expected condemnation from her. Turning away. Rejection. He expected it because everyone he grew to care about left him, just as his mother had. Now he was sure that because he had committed such a heinous crime, she would leave him too.

She tapped her fingers on her knee in a little letter of love to him, of solidarity. She wouldn't. She loved him. More, and maybe most importantly, she knew him. She knew his character. He was incapable of the cold-blooded murder of an innocent. He could say whatever he wanted to say, but if he killed another human being outside of the enemies he faced in the service of his country, he would only kill for self-preservation or in the defense of others. She knew that as surely as she knew it about herself.

She met Draden's eyes, willing him to go on. He wanted her to know what he'd done and because that was so important to him, she would listen. But if he thought she would turn from him because he had blood on his hands, he was wrong. Whitney had sent her out before to track an enemy of the United States. She'd done her research and read the files on whomever the target was before she was sent. Ultimately, she'd been the one to make the kill. The responsibility lay with her.

"I don't feel remorse for what I did," Draden continued. "I didn't even care that Whitney had been secretly watching the people and caught me on tape. I was modeling with several others, working my way through college. Some of the girls were young. It was some big private fashion venue with all designer clothes, so a lot of very wealthy clients. We were to go through the rooms in various apparel and the clients could decide to purchase if they chose. That was the gig, and I'd been to quite a few of them. At the time I was very popular."

Shylah didn't interrupt to say she knew why. He was beautiful. Just watching him talk, watching the passion move across his face made her heart beat harder. He made her go damp with need.

"Afterward, we were paid right there, under the table, all cash. I couldn't remember where I left my jacket, so I went hunting for it. When I came back to the room where we'd been rounded up to get our money for the night, there were five men standing over the girls, yelling at them in another language. It seems these girls were brought into the country illegally and were used virtually as slaves by these people. They had no rights and were supposed to turn over every bit of their earnings to them."

Shylah sat up straighter. She was well aware of the way illegals were often treated, but she'd never witnessed it. She took a deep breath and slipped off the bed, reaching for the nearest shirt. It was one thing to try to be seductive when she was working against a virus and a storm. It was another when he was talking about virtual slavery.

"The five of them were very powerful people. I think one was a congressman, and two of them were his brothers. The other two were originally from another country, and the five of them were making a lot of money from their scheme. The girls had been trying to hold on to some money each time to save to leave. They were being beaten severely. I walked in on it."

She couldn't imagine what she would have done had she walked in on several grown men beating young girls. She pictured them as teens, maybe early twenties. She would have lost it. Apparently, Draden had.

"I remember running toward them, and one came at me, swinging. I saw he had brass knuckles on. He'd actually hit the girls with them. It made me crazy. I hit him hard, right in the throat and kept going straight at the next one. I went through them all. The girls were screaming, and I told them to get their money back and get the hell out of there. I remember checking pulses and then realizing that I didn't care if they were dead or not. I didn't know what to do, so I just sat there, waiting, I think, for the cops to arrive. I'd forgotten I'd arranged a ride back to the university. I didn't have what others called friends, because I barely talked to anyone, but this one guy was persistent and nearly always picked me up from my gigs."

He swept his hand through his hair. "He came to get me, found the bodies and I told him what happened."

"Was that Trap?"

"No, it was Joe. He sent his father to help me."

His loyalty to Joe made sense now. Joe had helped him at a very critical time. She didn't know why Joe hadn't called the police and distanced himself from Draden, but he hadn't.

"What did Joe's father do?"

"He got rid of the dead bodies."

That was a bit of a shock as well. She gave him a faint smile. "Is that how you ended up in the military?"

Draden nodded. "Yes. I just followed everyone in. Trap. Wyatt. Joe. Gino. And then I found out Whitney had a tape of me killing everyone. Joe actually found the camera before the bodies were taken away, but it was too late, my part had already been sent to a remote location. Fortunately, Joe's dad and Joe were never captured on it."

"They've never told anyone?"

"As far as I know, they never have. Joe is close to Gino, but I'm not certain even Gino knows. If he does, he's never said anything."

"What about Trap? I can tell you really matter to him."

"Trap's kind of like me in that he's essentially a loner. Or he was. Wyatt got in there, probably because he's smart like Trap and they could bounce ideas off each other until all hours of the night. He let me in because I don't talk much to anyone. And

Cayenne. That woman is all about Trap and Trap is all about her."

"In what way?"

"No one will ever tell Cayenne what to do, with the exception of Trap. She's lethal as all get-out and a little scary." For the first time since he'd decided to reveal his past to her, he flashed her a little grin. "I can see why that sort of thing gets Trap hot and bothered."

She would have rather he got hot and bothered when she was playing the seductress. Clearly, she was using the wrong tactic. She had mad assassin skills, but she clearly lacked the ability to get him excited enough to want her. Or maybe she just wasn't reading the situation right. Perhaps she needed to let him see she could wrap him up in silk and tie him to the ceiling. Or better yet, build a funnel web and cocoon him in a burrow.

She sighed. That smile of his was dangerous, at least to her. She walked over to the window again to watch the wash of water spilling across it in great gusts. It wasn't droplets that hit the glass, it was more like a mini-waterfall. She traced the pattern on her side of the glass, not looking at him. The storms in Indonesia were rarely intense. They had thunder and lightning, but this was quite strong. The gusts of wind hit the cabin and rattled the windows. The rain hit hard, pelting the glass and roof, threatening to drive right through the structure. Unease crept down her spine.

It wasn't that she didn't like storms — she did. She often sat outside and watched them coming at her. This one was unusual for the area. Lightning was overhead now, streaking across the sky and lighting up the rolling black clouds. This was the type of weather where all the creatures hid, making certain they had somewhere dry to ride it out.

"I think you did what any of us would have done under the circumstances. In any case, it was self-defense. They couldn't let you go after what you'd witnessed. You do understand that, don't you?"

She remained facing the glass, trying to see through the storm. It was midday and yet dark enough to make it hard to see much of anything. That bothered her on an elemental level.

"It doesn't matter whether they would have or not. I detested them. I detested that people who already had everything they could possibly want would step on others who had nothing. Would use them and crush them. I'd lived my life mainly in the streets and found out the hard way that people who could have helped just hurt us."

"Do you believe Whitney destroyed that video?" Shylah swung back to face him. "If you don't, I can go back and find it. I'm pretty good at getting in and out of tight places."

"You're not going back there." His features darkened to match the storm raging outside the cabin. Fury burned in his eyes.

"I said I *could* go back, not that I planned to." Unease slid through her again. She glanced toward the window and then rushed to her jeans. "I think we need to check outside. I don't know why, but I can't shake this feeling that something's wrong."

He didn't argue, already dragging a T-shirt over his head and catching up his weapons, shoving them into the loops on his jeans. She was doing the same.

"Is there a back way out of here?" There hadn't appeared to be when he had explored the space. He'd looked for exits, but the building didn't appear to have another exit.

"We'll have to go through the window at the far back. That's the biggest one and I think you can fit. I don't know if anything's outside that shouldn't be, Draden. It could just be me getting a vibe from this storm."

"I must be getting the same vibe you are,"

he said. "It isn't strong, which leads me to believe the threat is some distance from us, but it's there."

"There's a ring of soldiers around us, supposedly guarding us," she said, catching up a small pouch and pulling the drawstring over her head. "Maybe they decided they were too scared to allow us to live."

She didn't care about the reason — she only knew that her heart was pounding, letting her know they were in trouble. She hurried toward the back of the cabin, thankful Draden wasn't the kind of man who wanted to tell a woman she was crazy or full of nerves. He hadn't even asked questions, and he was right behind her. She felt his breath on the nape of her neck.

She listened for a moment first, and then she pushed the window up cautiously. The rain hit her upturned face, droplets gathering on her lashes.

"I'll cover you."

She didn't turn to look at him, but she wanted to. She took a breath and let it soothe the adrenaline rushing through her veins. She dove out, headfirst, her hands in front of her to cushion the dive. As she hit the soft ground, she somersaulted and came to her feet, stepping to the side to give Draden room. The moment she was in position by the side of the building, she let her eyes adjust and then gave the forest a long scan for danger.

I've got you covered.

Her concentration was mainly on the eastern side. Her radar went off in that direction. *To the east. Something's coming at us via that route. Your friends didn't warn you about company, did they?* A purge? Was that the reality? They had the virus, and everyone wanted them dead. Whitney might even decide he had to kill them for the sake of the world.

She should have heard Draden come through the window, or at least land when he hit the ground. He was a big man and it didn't occur to her that anyone, even a GhostWalker, could get through that window without a great deal of noise, but he'd managed. One minute she was covering the forest and waiting for him to launch himself through and the next he was right beside her.

He signaled to go up into the trees. She nodded in understanding. The closest avenue of escape was a good twenty feet away, a tree whose strong branches reached out toward neighboring trees, providing access to the arboreal highway. She was tempted to sprint for it, but she held herself in check, mainly because Draden was holding his closed fist in the air, the universal military sign for freeze. She waited, inhaling, the storm crashing around them.

Hit the ground, baby. Lie flat and don't move. The next flash of lightning is going to rip across the sky. Stay focused on the trees just to the left of that little dip where the vines are thick.

She eased her body all the way flat, feeling the water saturating the shirt she wore and her jeans. She hadn't put on underwear and the water soaked right through the material to her skin. It wasn't cold and with the heat, it made her feel sweaty and dirty instead of clean.

She didn't take her gaze from the cluster of trees just to the left of the dip, but she did ease a dart out of the bag that hung around her neck. Very slowly she placed the blowgun between her teeth and loaded it. Already she could see the shadows fanning out from those trees, at least six of them. They didn't look like soldiers to her. She had excellent night vision, at least six times better than most humans'. She knew Draden had just as good or better. She was equally certain the approaching enemy couldn't see them.

Be ready. Draden sounded as if he were

counting down.

The hair on her body stood up and then lightning forked across the sky, spear after jagged spear spreading through the heat and clouds. It registered that they were members of the Milisi Separatis Sumatra as the one in charge turned his head to look up, exposing his carotid artery. She blew the dart and reloaded to blow the second one before the lightning faded, the sky going dark as thunder boomed, shaking the ground. She had to wait for the perfect time when the wind was between gusts before she took the shot.

Two men dropped simultaneously. She'd shot her target twice, something she often did just in case she missed the first time. She glanced over at Draden. He wasn't there. He'd silently taken out the second man, but she wasn't certain how and she had no idea where he was.

Chaos erupted and two of the MSS soldiers fired their weapons at the cabin. One knelt beside the commander and felt for his pulse. He remained kneeling, looking carefully around. She stayed very still, certain that none of them could spot her lying in the rotting vegetation. The scent of wild orchids mixed with spice and fruit. It wasn't altogether unpleasant, but it impaired one of her main senses. Still, she tried to use everything available to her.

If she shot again, it was possible they could get a fix on her direction. She was certain they had come across the bodies of their companions, one who had died with two holes in his neck. She was certain Draden had retrieved the darts, so for all she knew, they thought a vampire was on the loose. She wanted to laugh, but the air was charging once again. She'd reloaded immediately and was ready for the next display of lightning.

Once again, it lit up the sky and the dark clouds. Rain fell in silvery sheets, obscuring the vision of the members of the MSS, but Shylah was ready and had already marked her target. She shot just as the first streak spread across the sky in broken, jagged veins. She shot a second member and then got off a third shot, hitting her last target twice before he went down.

She saw that Draden had been busy as well. He managed to get two more. She thought she saw him in the trees directly above the members of the MSS, but then the shadow was gone, and the night shook with the boom of thunder.

The two remaining soldiers went back-to-back and began to creep back into the forest. She didn't take the bait and remained perfectly still. Sure enough, they backtracked, coming in from a different angle. Shylah didn't wait for the lightning strike. Both faced her, straight on. Very slowly, she removed the short dart and replaced it with one of the few longer ones she carried. Holding the gun steady between her teeth, she loaded it.

Her target abruptly stepped forward, his automatic in his arms, looking up at the tree above him. She shot him, this time hitting him square in the chest, right over his heart. It might not be an instant kill shot, but it put him down. The other one spun to face the cabin and then he went down.

Draden jumped from the branches above them, landed in a crouch and she saw his knife gleam for a moment in the silvery rain when lightning once again lit up the sky. The storm had moved past the cabin, but the light was bright, almost shocking.

I'm going to backtrack to see if they killed the guards, or if they got through them. You need to radio Joe and tell him we were under attack.

Give me the difficult job, she groused.

His soft laughter slid into her mind and she found herself as warm on the inside as she was on the outside. She knew he wasn't a man who laughed much. She liked that he laughed with her.

Not a chance, baby.

Fine. But sex is out. You had your shot at it and now it's off the table.

Sounds like a challenge to me. I'm going to think up a million ways to get you to change your mind and you're going to love every single one of them.

Now the laughter was completely and deliberately sensual. It stroked over her skin like the touch of fingers. She felt it deep, where she didn't want him. Where she'd made up her mind to keep him out. She felt completely vulnerable to him all over again.

Big talker.

I can see I have my work cut out for me to change your mind.

She got to her feet and jogged around to the front of the cabin. She had set spider-webs radiating out from the trees, just a few trip lines. She bent automatically to check one anchored to the funnel web in the ground, just a few feet between the forest and the front porch. As she touched it, it shivered. She froze. The wind could be shaking it. The rain could be tearing it down, but it felt like something hit it. Something not of nature.

Draden. I think we've got more company.

They came at us from more than one direction. Where are the soldiers? Did you find any of them dead?

I think they're gone. I haven't found a single body.

Her breath caught in her throat. *Were we set up?*

Looks like it. If there aren't any bodies, either the soldiers were called back, in which case, we're genuinely in trouble, or they were given orders to let the MSS through, in which case we're still in trouble. Pick your poison, sweetheart. Wait there. I'm making my way back to you. Can you get into a position where you can get eyes on them?

What kind of question is that? Of course I can.

Shylah looked around her. The closest tree to the house was a distance away. The rangers didn't want trees coming down on top of the structure. The road leading in to the ranger's cabin was drivable only partway. All materials and supplies had to be brought in by another method, usually domestic ox or horse. She could crawl across the open clearing and hope no one spotted her, but the storm was passing and with it, the dark clouds. Already light was spilling around the cabin.

As with most of the houses in that area,

the cabin had been built on stilts to allow the breeze to help moderate the temperature as well as keep the structure above storm-water runoff. Because she'd studied everything she could about the country, including the architecture, she knew building on stilts was practical, keeping the occupants, food and everything else free from damp and rot.

The ranger hut was built like a longhouse with a beam, post and lintel structure system that took the load straight to the ground. The walls were made of non-weight-bearing wood rather than bamboo. Instead of nails, mortise and tenon joints and wooden pegs were used in the construction, which did give her a little pause as she went up the side of it. She knew, as a rule, the construction was extremely strong, but she was trusting her weight to be held — guns waited for one wrong move.

Rain sheeted off from the sharply inclined roof while the large overhanging eaves prevented water from entering the house and kept the occupants cool in the heat. The ranger hut had several large windows for cross ventilation. Shylah had to avoid them and get around them without being seen as she made the climb to the roof.

The roof was built with materials readily

available close to wherever the structure was situated. In this case, the roof was traditional, a beautiful thatch art piece, made of sugar palm leaves, grass and straw. Lovely, difficult to climb. Once she made up her mind, she didn't hesitate. She was forced to spread her weight evenly so as not to break off the various materials painstakingly woven together.

It took time and patience to make her way, and while she eased up one side and over to the next, she heard the MSS soldiers whispering to one another as they converged on the ranger's house. *In position.*

I'm in the tree behind them. We've got them in a cross fire.

He was more exposed than she was, not that the roof materials would protect her, but the idea of Draden being in danger made her heart go crazy, which, she reminded herself, was ridiculous when it had been confirmed that they both were infected with the virus. It didn't matter that they were told their bodies were fighting it. She was certain the inhabitants of Lupa Suku had fought it as well. Maybe it would be better for Draden and her to go out in a blaze of glory fighting terrorists than letting a virus consume them from the inside out.

You ready?

Yes. I'll take the two on the left. I've got a good angle on them.

Don't miss, baby.

She gave a little sniff of disdain. *Keep that advice for yourself.*

His soft laughter took the last of her nerves. She already had the blowgun loaded and she blew, a short, strong blast that sent the dart straight and true. It hit the soldier in the side of the neck and his hand went up, clapping over the protruding projectile, driving it deeper to sever the carotid artery. Simultaneously, another dropped straight to the ground.

Shockingly, elite soldiers from the Indonesian special forces, dressed in hazmat suits, emerged from the forest. Each held a semiautomatic, and from their body posture, was no-nonsense about using the weapon. Every one of the MSS soldiers threw down their gun a good distance from them.

Joe's with them, Draden informed her. *He realized something was wrong when the soldiers returned to their base, which isn't far from here. He immediately went to the commander and demanded to know who issued the order to bring them back. That commander had to relieve the one above him of command.*

The MSS has infiltrated their military? That

shocked her.

She knew someone with money was behind the organization, but the MSS were still relatively new and until now hadn't caused much in the way of actual trouble. The idea that they might have been secretly working to infiltrate the military and get some of their members in high places meant they'd been working for a long while to place their people before they ever made their first moves.

Stay still, sweetheart. I've let Joe know where we both are, and he's informed the Kopassus commander, but that doesn't mean one of them might not get trigger-happy. We'll let them take their prisoners and all dead bodies and go.

She couldn't help but let him feel the faint laughter she couldn't hold back. *Life with you is never dull, is it?*

I like to give you the occasional adrenaline rush.

Tone it down a little. I'm tired and hungry. And this roof is making me itch.

You little complainer. You were the one staring out the window getting the uneasy feeling. I was fixating on your tits. You have some gorgeous ones, by the way.

Now you say that. Had you said it then, we wouldn't be in this mess. You could have had your wicked way with me, but now I've come to my senses and am determined to continue down the path of the good-girl assassin.

She kept her gaze fixed on the scene playing out below her. The Kopassus were tying their prisoners' hands behind their backs and not being very gentle about it. She didn't blame them. The soldiers had to have seen the dead in the village of Lupa Suku as well as their wounded and fallen comrades. The MSS had murdered the World Health Organization's doctors to bait a trap. Who did that? The WHO were men and women who had dropped everything and come at a call for help from the Indonesian government. The soldiers had every right to be angry with the prisoners. She didn't feel in the least sorry for them, no matter what was in store for them.

Did you warn Joe to tell them to burn the bodies? I used a blowgun.

Of course. They know not to take chances. The MSS prisoners will be quarantined and their blood tested.

She was suddenly very tired. Exhausted. That alarmed her. She knew fatigue was one of the symptoms of the onset of the virus. She forced herself to examine her body for any other signs. Her muscles ached. Everywhere. Arms. Legs. Shoulders. Especially her neck.

She tried to slow her pounding heart. For a moment she debated telling him. If she said it, the probability of the virus spreading through her body became real. She knew she was going to have to. He had always been so honest with her and she'd tried to dismiss it, to find other explanations for his symptoms. How had he been so matter-of-fact?

She closed her eyes and drew in air, trying to remain calm when she wanted to panic. Strangely, her body actually prepared for flight. It wanted to run, to stay ahead of the certain death sentence. She forced herself to think, to get past the chaos in her mind. Blood thundered in her ears, drowning out the sounds of the cicadas, something nearly impossible in the Sumatra forest.

She understood why Draden hadn't wanted to have sex with her. She felt — disgusting. For the first time, it was real to her that she was infected, and the virus would liquefy her organs and eventually kill her.

Shylah?

The moment she heard his whisper, that soft, intimate sound, she pulled away from him. Not pulled. Jerked. She knew this reaction wasn't about dying. It was solely about the way she was going to die. She couldn't face him until she got herself under control. The moment the soldiers faded away, she was going to go for a long walk and try to get some of the adrenaline to leave her body, so her fight-or-flight reflex wasn't so strong. She just couldn't face Draden, not until she was every bit as calm and accepting about the virus as he was.

12

Draden leapt from the trees the moment the Kopassus cleared out. As a rule, he would have waited for a few minutes, even a half hour, to ensure they were really gone before he moved. This time he took Joe at his word, that everyone was in helicopters and the soldiers were back, circling the ranger cabin so they were safe from intruders.

Something was wrong with Shylah. She'd withdrawn from him, and she'd never done that before. Not once. She'd been open and honest almost since the moment they met. It was that trait that drew him to her. He knew something had to be wrong and she was falling back on her normal way of dealing with things — alone. He knew because he was that way.

Baby, talk to me. He tried coaxing, using their intimate connection.

There was something beautiful about being in each other's mind. No matter how alone, the moment the other poured in, there was warmth and happiness. She filled all those empty places in him where he struggled with human connections. He hoped he did the same for her. She'd always responded. Always.

She wasn't hurt. He would have known. He raced across the small open space to the house and up the porch. She'd come down off the roof, he'd seen her slide to the side of the building in order to climb down the side. She wasn't inside. He swore, biting profanities out between his teeth. He should have been watching her instead of the soldiers.

Not kidding around with you, woman. I need to know you're safe. Talk to me.

There was a small silence. He counted every one of his heartbeats. Waiting. He'd never had this experience before. This was a first. He'd never cared about someone this way and her silence — leaving him not knowing what was wrong — nearly drove him insane.

Damn it, Shylah. I'm coming after you. You have to know I am.

He began casting around for her tracks. She'd sprinted for the forest. It was still light and with the storm mostly gone, there was only drizzling rain. The sky was overcast. The air muggy. His shirt and jeans were plastered to his body.

He was back in the forest, looking for signs of her going up into the trees. It was her favorite mode of travel. There were none that he could see. He found a partial print along a narrow animal path. A few feet farther in, he saw a twisted leaf on a large fern.

The first stirring in his mind was tentative, as if she could make the connection but was being extremely careful not to give too much of herself away.

I just need a little time to myself. I'm not used to sharing so much of myself with anyone.

That was total bullshit and he knew it. She wasn't a bullshitter either. *I'm not accepting that excuse. Give me something I can get behind.*

There was silence. From her lengthened tracks, he could see she had begun running. *Where are you going?* Now his heart was in his throat and he was running too. He was fast. He ran every night. Sometimes, for most of the night. He could catch her, but he didn't know if he could catch her in time.

Damn it, Shylah. The soldiers will shoot you before they'll let you through their line. They're there not only to keep others away, but to keep us isolated. If you violate their perimeter, they will shoot you. You answer me.

I'm well aware of them. I don't need you to tell me that. I'm just running, Draden. You of all people should understand.

Was that what she was doing? Just running? Then why would she abruptly leave him? Stop him from connecting with her? It wasn't his imagination. She had withdrawn. He was catching up to her because she wasn't running fast, she was jogging to cover distance and clearly didn't want to tire herself out.

I'm coming up on you. You don't want to talk, we won't talk, but I'm running with you.

She didn't respond, but he got the impression of tears and that cut like a knife. She didn't want his company. That was just too damned bad.

Then she was there, in front of him, her long legs sure on the narrow path. From behind her, he could see her perfect rhythm. Her clothes, like his, were soaked. As he moved up for a moment to check her features, he could see the white tee she'd pulled on earlier was his. Now it was soaked and see-through. Completely. It might as well have been nonexistent. She wasn't wearing a bra and both hands pressed her breasts tightly to keep them from bouncing.

Tears tracked down her face and she didn't try to hide them. She didn't even look at him, just stared straight ahead as she doggedly put one foot in front of the other. He swore to himself he would keep his mouth shut. He wouldn't say one word. She was entitled to her privacy. After about two minutes he was all but grinding his teeth. Three more minutes and he was exploding.

He caught her elbow and pulled her to a halt. "You're killing me. *Killing me.* Damn it, Shylah, whatever this is, we're in it together."

She wouldn't even look at him, instead, she stared at the ground, the tears refusing to stop. Desperate, he did the only thing he could think of. He caught her hair in his fist, pulled her head back and his mouth took hers. He didn't expect a response and at first, he didn't get one, although the chemistry between them exploded in his mouth. Her taste was on his tongue. Addictive. Fiery. So hot he needed more.

Then she leaned into him, her body melting into his, all soft, pliant. Her arms slid up his chest to circle his neck and her mouth moved beneath his. Instantly, he knew he was losing control and he wanted to. He wanted to crawl inside of her. She set him on fire. His skin, his cock and his soul. All of him. Every inch. He hadn't known kisses could do that until he experienced kissing Shylah. He hadn't even been into kissing that much. It had always been more for the woman, but now, he devoured her.

When he lifted his head, she pushed her forehead against his chest. He held her, his arms tight around her, trying to tell her without words that no matter what, he would be there for her.

No matter what. He glanced down at the top of her head. *Sweetheart. You don't have to look at me, but are you experiencing symptoms? Do you have a headache? What is it?*

Her body was warm, but it was hot in the forest and the rain hadn't cooled things down. If anything, they were sweaty and muggy. In the trees they'd been protected somewhat, but the wind wasn't in the least cool and on the roof, she would have felt like she was being blasted by a furnace. They'd just run, that would heat their bodies as well.

He felt her head move. She was nodding, but she still didn't look at him. *Exhaustion. Fatigue. Whatever you want to call it. I can barely lift my arms up. It came on fast. And my body hurts, all my muscles. I've never felt like this before.*

She'd never been sick. Shylah didn't get viruses. His heart skipped a beat and then began pounding. She wasn't supposed to get sick. Trap had said they were both infected, but they were fighting it off. She wasn't supposed to get sick. He hadn't allowed himself to think of that possibility. He tightened his arms around her as if that would save her. It didn't matter that he knew they'd both been infected. He wasn't prepared for her to get sick.

"All right, sweetheart. Let's get back to the house. We were up all night and traveling back and forth, all those miles separating us from the MSS village . . . It's tiring. Isn't that what you keep saying to me?"

She nodded her head, still very close to his chest, close enough that he felt the deep breath she took. He knew the moment she got herself together. He knew Shylah Cosmos was the woman for him. In the absolute worst of circumstances, she would stand. He let her step away, but he reached for her hand.

"I think we should get married."

She tilted her head to look up at him, but her mouth curved into that smile that always teased every one of his senses. Amusement. She could feel it and give him that same sense of playfulness and joy that she seemed to have in abundance. "I think you're a little crazy, Draden."

"It makes sense."

"It makes *no* sense. Why would we get married?"

"Because when I die, I want to go out as your husband." He'd put the idea out there because he knew she'd smile, but once he voiced it, he found he wanted to marry her.

She walked in silence for a few minutes, not shooting him down, but clearly giving it some thought. "Do you think we have time for that? We're in Indonesia. Even if we got married, would it be legal?"

He grinned at her. "We're going to be dead before it matters, but I think yes. I've heard it can be done."

"We're not really thinking of doing this, are we?" She looked up at his face as they walked.

Draden pulled her under his shoulder, needing to feel as if he were protecting her. He loved looking down at her face. Shylah was back to being herself, that woman who accepted who and what she was as well as who and what he was. She saw him, that man who kept himself isolated, so separate from the rest of the world. She saw him for what he was, and she liked him anyway. Not only liked him but was falling hard for him. He felt it each time he connected with her mind to mind.

To keep her from thinking about dying, he was willing to talk marriage and everything else in between. "Why not? We can do whatever the hell we want to do." Now that they were both symptomatic, he doubted they had more than a day or two at most, but they could plan. And dream. They had to have something to take their mind off the ugly way they were going to go.

He realized he really did want to die her husband. If they had one day or one hour, it didn't matter. He wanted that time with her as the man in her life.

She shook her head, her eyes still bright from tears, but she was grinning as she glanced down at the path. "I should say yes and then if we both survived, you'd be stuck."

He nudged her with his hip. "So would you. Be stuck, I mean, with me. And I'm a much bigger pain in the ass than you are."

"That would depend entirely on who you ask. If you consult Whitney, he would tell you, without a doubt, that I am."

He liked the smugness in her voice. Shylah was getting back to her normal self. She was so much like Nonny, she could have been her daughter. "I can imagine you with me in the swamp, helping to raise our sons, shotgun right at your side, everywhere you go."

"Daughters."

"Baby. Really? I'm a manly man and I have manly sperm, the kind that only throws sons. Way, way too much testosterone for the female children. You're going to have to let that dream go."

"I have my heart set on daughters, so you're going to have to tone down the male craziness and get the feminine vibe going."

"I don't want to crush your heart, sweetheart, but, aside from the fact that it would be impossible for a man like me to do that, it's just plain not happening. I'd kill any idiot who was dumb enough to try to date a daughter of mine."

"If they were anything like me, you'd be more than happy to pay someone to take them off your hands." She giggled.

The sound sent his stomach on an emotional roller coaster. He could feel answering laughter welling up. "We're having boys. A whole bunch of them."

Deliberately she heaved a sigh. "Both then, and that's the final offer."

"You drive a hard bargain. A couple of girls and the rest boys."

" 'The rest' being how many?" Suspicion had crept into her voice and onto the expression of her upturned face.

He grinned at her. "Maybe seven."

"I'd have to shoot you, Draden. All kidding aside, I think you need to remember I have very special skills. Weigh that very seriously before you give me another number."

He forced himself to look sober. She was terrified, but willing to walk into fantasyland with him to keep from losing her mind. He was so in love with her he couldn't think straight. Neither of them needed to worry about what was said. Like Shylah, he knew that even if their bodies tried to fight the infection, in the village, there had been a 100 percent kill rate. Their odds weren't good.

"You have a very good point. I'll go with three."

"Since they're mythical, I'll agree to that."

"You'll go hunting and fishing with me."

"I'm not certain how I feel about killing animals." She frowned. "What does it involve? Besides pulling the trigger."

"You skin the animal —"

"Whoa. Stop right there. There's no skinning. I draw the line at skinning. I don't want to skin and eat a poor animal after shooting it. I think that's out."

"You're an assassin for God's sake."

She tilted her head again, giving him that little snippy look she had that was supposed to put him in his place but only made him want to kiss her.

"Nevertheless, there's a huge difference between a nasty human being and a defenseless animal that's just minding its own business."

"You buy meat in a market."

"I don't. I've never been in a market. When I'm hunting a target, they don't ordinarily go into a market."

"Fine. I'll do the hunting and fishing. With the boys. And our daughters."

"You do that. I'll read a book while you're gone." Her eyes lit up. "I've always wanted to garden. I can grow our vegetables. And I'll cook."

"We can share those chores. Cooking, dishes, that sort of thing."

"Good you said that. Cooking I'm okay with, the rest of it, we do together."

They were once again at the small clearing where the ranger's house sat. He didn't want to stop with their fantasy, but he needed to examine her and record his findings. He'd get that out of the way and then go alone to the remote lab and let Trap tell him whatever needed to be said. The absolute truth because he liked the idea of marrying her. Dying as her husband, as part of a couple who belonged together made sense. He wanted that, and he wanted to give her that. It had started out as a joke to take her mind from their reality, but once spoken, the idea appealed to him. More than appealed.

"You're on," he agreed and opened the door for her.

Shylah went ahead of him. He loved to watch her walk. She was tired. He could clearly see her fatigue in the way she carried her body, but she still had that erotic, feminine sway. She peeled off the wet shirt the moment she was inside. He turned her around and instantly saw the rash that spread across her stomach and breasts. It was red, raised bumps and angry looking. He used his phone to take pictures.

He kept all expression off his face as he examined the lymph nodes in her neck, under her mandible, on her arms and chest. Her lymph nodes were swollen, and it was all he could do not to cry. She held very still as he examined her, as if she were holding herself together by a thread. He took her temperature, wanting to get the examination over with as soon as possible. It was high, but just barely, as his was.

"Why don't you take another shower and lie down for a few minutes. I'll go have a mini-consultation with Trap, and when I come back, I'll try my hand at cooking. After we eat, we'll get some sleep."

Shylah nodded. When he turned away from her, she caught his hand. "Thank you, Draden. You pulled me back from the edge."

"You would have gotten there. I just got you there a little sooner." He bent his head to hers, cupping her chin in his palm, looking into her dark eyes. "I think getting married to you is a really good idea. Let's plan it and do it tomorrow, even if we can't make it legal."

Her tongue touched her upper lip, tracing the intriguing bow. The corners of her mouth turned up. She had a small indentation when she smiled, a little dimple that came and went but fascinated him.

He brushed kisses over the dusting of gold across her nose and cheeks. She had amazing bone structure and he kissed along the line of her high cheekbones. Shifting his hands to frame her face, he brought his mouth down on hers. The world dropped away. The fact that they were infected with a terrible virus disappeared.

There was heat. Fire. Perfection. The moment his lips rubbed against hers, soft and sensuous, the flames leapt and burned. Electricity arced from his skin to hers. He kissed her over and over until neither of them could breathe. When he finally lifted his head, it took effort not to just pick her up and carry her to the bed. Instead, he found medicine for the rash and aspirin for her headache. Kissing her was paradise but taking care of her was more important to him.

Leaving her to shower and nap, Draden made his way to the remote lab, trying not to think about living without her. He should have thought about dying, about having to kill her and then himself to avoid the effects of the hemorrhagic virus. Instead, with every step away from her, he tried to picture what it would be like for both of them to survive and split up. He couldn't face that bleak future any more than he could face the idea of dying in such a vile way.

He wanted that future the two of them talked about. He wanted the fun of planning a ceremony and looked forward to being with her and working out the details.

Wyatt Fontenot appeared on the screen when Draden called. In the background, he could see Trap bent over a worktable. Trap reminded Draden of a mad scientist, but then he always did when he worked in a laboratory. The human race lost him to whatever intriguing medical mystery he was working on. Unless Cayenne was around. The woman had a way of making him eat and sometimes sleep. Several times a day Trap would look around him a little helplessly, and she'd hand him whatever it was he needed. Other times he'd just look at her and the two would disappear for an hour and he'd come back looking refreshed.

"Shylah's developed a large rash that's spread across her body. She's fatigued, and her muscles ache. She's running a low-grade fever and her lymph nodes are swollen." He tried to be clinical. "I still have the headache and I'm very tired. I have a small rash on my arms, belly and chest. My muscles are extremely painful and my temp has gone up a degree."

Wyatt nodded. "That's to be expected, Draden. You're both infected, but your bodies are fighting it aggressively." He turned away from the screen to talk to Trap.

At first Trap kept his back to Wyatt, but he suddenly swung around and stalked across the room to appear in front of the camera. "Tell me exactly how Shylah is feeling. What's happening to her?"

"She's never been sick, Trap. At least that was what Whitney told me when I talked to him. I forgot to tell you, I spoke with him. That's how you got the file on her. It did get to you, didn't it? I received it, so I thought you would have."

"Yes. I've been working on sorting out what the two of you have in your makeup that would have you both fighting so aggressively." He waved his hands in the air. "I need to know about Shylah. Her symptoms."

"I've sent you a picture of the rash. She has a low-grade fever and her lymph nodes are swollen throughout her body. She's showing signs of fatigue, and her muscles ache. She's never complained about anything in all the time we've been together. I can see that she's scared."

Trap waved that away. "There's no need to be yet. I'll check the new blood samples. Just hang in there. We're working night and day on our end."

"Thanks, Trap."

There was no need to profess gratitude, Trap was already gone, consumed by his work. Wyatt's face was there again. "We really think with what Whitney sent us and the file on Shylah, we've got a good chance of figuring this out," he said.

"Time's running out, Wyatt. We want to get married. Can you get an expert on all things Indonesian and get the ball rolling to make it happen? Who's the resident expert on Indonesia?"

"That would be Malichai," Wyatt responded. "Give me a minute and I'll have him here."

Draden took the opportunity to look for information on the Internet while Wyatt was away from the computer. They could be married in Indonesia. That much he'd learned by the time Malichai sat in the chair Wyatt had vacated.

"You doing all right, bro?" he asked.

Draden nodded. "For having a killer virus in me, I'm doing surprisingly well. Need to know about getting married in Sumatra."

"You have to have a religious ceremony, Draden. You both have to be the same religion. I believe six religions are recognized. Hindu. Are you Hindu?"

"Very funny."

"I've got to ask. What about Islam or Catholicism?"

"Neither. And she isn't either." He hadn't asked her, but he was certain she wasn't.

"There's Protestant Christian, Buddhist or Confucian. Take your pick. You need one to make it legal. Buddhists, Christians and

Hindus hold the ceremony first, and then it must be recorded with the Civil Registry. They issue the marriage certificate. You would still have to register that in Louisiana."

"I see. We'll figure it out tonight and do the paperwork. Can you get Joe to push it through for us?"

"You're serious about this? You're actually going to marry her?" Wyatt asked, leaning into the camera around Malichai. "You aren't going to die, Draden. We're not going to let that happen."

That was easy enough to say. He thought they might be a little delusional. Trap and Wyatt were good, but so were a few hundred other virologists, microbiologists and scientists. No one had yet come up with a vaccine for Ebola and it wasn't for lack of trying.

They talked for a few more minutes, but he was in a hurry to get back to Shylah. He didn't like being away from her. Images of her sprawled out on the bed, her long legs bare, her body naked after her shower, kept creeping into his mind. He signed off quickly and hurried back to her. He half hoped she'd be in bed, just so he could remove the blankets.

Before he opened the door, he knew she

was cooking. The aroma coming from inside the house was amazing. Joe had managed to get his hands on chicken, and clearly she was making full use of it. She stood at the stove. "I thought I'd make soup. I wanted something light. I used the chicken again and tons of veggies. Is that all right with you?"

She wore a pair of soft Capri bottoms and a racer-back tank that clung to her every curve. She looked more delicate than ever. For some reason the simple, comfortable outfit enhanced her fragile bone structure and emphasized her firm, defined muscles and soft skin.

He went right to her and leaned down to kiss the nape of her neck, so inviting with her hair piled on top of her head in a messy knot. "That smells wonderful. I'm suddenly starving."

"Me too."

There was the smile in her voice that told him she approved of him kissing her. He wrapped his arms around her middle, his fingers threading together just under her breasts, so he could nuzzle her neck. She smelled as delicious as whatever she was cooking, and for a moment he buried his face in that sweet spot between her neck and shoulder and just inhaled.

"Do you have a religious preference?" he asked, his mouth against her skin.

She burst out laughing. "So much for whispering sweet nothings."

"We have to have a religious ceremony to get married."

Her hand paused in her task of adding seasoning and she looked back at him. "You can't be serious, Draden."

"I absolutely want to marry you. I want us to plan the ceremony and what we're going to say to each other and then tomorrow, I want to do it."

She turned back before he could read her expression. Staring down at the soup, she shook her head. "I don't see how it's possible."

"Wyatt said our immune systems are fighting the virus off like crazy, so I know we'll have the time. We can do it. I know we can."

"Do you have any idea how special you are, Draden? How extraordinary a man?"

She made him feel as if he were the best man in the world and she'd never be able to see any other — and she most likely wouldn't.

"I'm going to let you think that, Shylah, because I want you to marry me. And if you knew about the thousands, maybe millions of good men out there who are all so much better than me, you'd run away fast and find someone else."

"I don't think that's true."

Shylah regarded him with that sober look that turned him inside out. She looked cute as hell with her freckles standing out on her face and her eyebrows drawn together.

"Stop staring at me and come eat. The table's set and dinner is ready. Zara used to fix this recipe, so I know it tastes delicious."

He took the pot from her and ladled up the soup into the bowls already set on the small table. He lit the candle she'd put there. The storm was long gone, and night was falling, the birds calling to one another one last time and the cicadas and other insects took up the jarring symphony. Frogs took up the chorus, so the surrounding forest was filled with sound.

"What religion are you, Draden?"

She was looking down at her soup, cooling off a spoonful by blowing on it. She still had an appetite and he was grateful for that. Still, he had a sense of urgency. Now, it was important to him that they marry, that she carried his name when she went. That he was there with her to the very end. He liked being her man. No. It was much more than that.

He had always shied away from feelings,

preferring to keep himself closed off rather than put himself out there where he could be destroyed emotionally. With Shylah, everything was so different. He could say anything to her. She understood and accepted him even when he told her the worst of himself. He was comfortable with her. She could take care of herself, but he felt protective of her.

"Draden?"

He sent her a grin and then took a bite of the soup to keep from having to answer her question.

She made a face at him. "Seriously? Whitney conducts illegal and immoral experiments every single day. He uses children for those experiments. He doesn't believe in a hereafter. He certainly didn't want us to believe we were worth anything to anyone. He had us study religion, but only as a means to understand the anger and fanaticism that brought nations to the brink of war, or war itself."

"I can see that."

She played with the soup in her bowl, swirling the liquid around with her spoon. "I leaned toward the simplicity of Buddhism. The teachings made sense to me, but I certainly didn't have the opportunity to explore the teachings with anyone who was in the religion. What about you?" she challenged again.

"I never got involved in any religion," he admitted. "Living on the street, I certainly went to my share of churches, but it was because they fed the homeless or allowed us to sleep in their churches during storms or on extremely cold nights."

He shrugged and took another bite, this time the taste getting through to him. "This is good, woman. I might have to let you do all the cooking."

"I only know how to cook a couple of things, other than the rations, but I'm certain Whitney would send them to us if we wanted them. It might be better than killing and skinning an animal. What kind of animal, by the way, and don't you dare say a rabbit."

He couldn't help laughing. "You sound so belligerent, like you're going to get a gun and shoot and skin me just for even suggesting hunting. Who knew you were so squeamish?"

Her head went up and her eyes blazed fire at him. "I am *not* squeamish. It isn't that. If I had to hunt for food for you, me or our children, trust me, honey, that animal would have to go down. My point is, it isn't my thing and I don't *need* to do it."

"No hunting. I'm on board with that. Are you the same about fishing?"

"How long does it take to catch a fish?"

"You had to have laid hours in the grass watching that village."

The soup was delicious, and he was making headway on it. She hadn't eaten that much. She took small spoonsful. She hadn't yet eaten any of the vegetables out of the bowl that he could see.

"It isn't the same thing. That was work. Isn't fishing considered recreation?"

"It's work. It's manly fishing, bringing home dinner."

"I'll try it, but only because it matters to you."

"Damn straight it does. Our daughters have to see their mom is tough. It's not like you can take them on a hunt with you for your job." He hit his forehead with his hand and the action, while supposed to be funny, sent pain jangling through his body.

"What was that for?"

"I forgot. What are we going to do when our kids have parents' day at the school?"

"What's that?"

"They take their parents and proudly tell the rest of the class what their jobs are. Can you imagine? This is my mother. She kills people. This is my dad. He's a doctor, but mostly he blows things up and silently creeps up on guards and slits their throats."

She laughed. "I guess we'll have to work on that one."

"Buddhism it is," Draden said decisively, ignoring the fact that Buddhism was synonymous with peace and their professions were the exact opposite. "We'll study that religion quickly tonight and then have the ceremony tomorrow. We can put that together while we're in bed and send for whatever we need in the morning. Joe can bring it to us."

"You really are serious. You want to get married."

"Don't you?" He leaned across the table, capturing her gaze. "I want to marry you more than anything. Do you feel the same way?"

"I don't know the first thing about it, but I know I love you and if this is what you want, then we'll do it."

She said it so casually, as if it weren't a monumental gift. No one had ever told him they loved him, not since the woman he called mother had died of cancer. Even that seemed a brief period of time. Eliza had taught him there was such a thing as love. Shylah, Bellisia and Zara had taught one another.

He reached across the table and took her hand, his thumb sliding over her bare ring finger. "I want to give you the world, Shylah, because you deserve it. I want my ring on your finger and my name with yours. I've only told one other woman I loved her, and she deserved to be called mother. She would have loved you and taken you in as a daughter. I think Nonny will do that when she meets you."

"I truly wish I had the chance to meet both of them," Shylah said. "I'm so happy that you were able to actually meet Zara and Bellisia. They're my family. At least I know they're taken care of."

He brought her hand to his mouth, kissed it and then leaned over to blow out the candle. "I'll do the dishes, sweetheart. It's only fair when you did the cooking."

"I'm not opposed. I'll go look up what a Buddhist ceremony entails, and we can design one. But really, Draden, you can't just pick a religion."

"What are they going to do to us? If we don't make it, I don't think they're going to follow us to our graves to reprimand us."

She laughed and helped him clear the table. He didn't make a big deal over the fact that she'd barely eaten when the soup had been so delicious. She'd been eating the nasty rations Whitney had sent with her, but now that they had decent food, she wasn't hungry. That alarmed him. He deliberately dropped back a step to watch her walk to the sink. Her shoulders were down, and she seemed to be hunching just a little.

His little peony would never complain. No matter how bad it got, she wouldn't say anything to him unless she thought it was needed for Trap and the others to find a vaccine for those left behind. She would forever remind him of that classic flower. She had no rival with her elegant beauty and that unforgettable, delicate scent.

"Are you still hurting, Shylah?"

She sent him a quick smile. "I'm doing fine, Draden, considering what we're expecting. Just a little off. Are you certain you don't want me to do the dishes while you shower? I don't mind."

She wouldn't, because like the flower, she was dependable. She would stand with him for as long as he wanted her. Draden was an intelligent man. Even if he'd met her under different circumstances, it wouldn't have taken him long to realize he would want this one woman at his side for the rest of his lifetime and beyond.

"Lie down, sweetheart. I'll be quick. We can plan our ceremony."

She flashed another smile at him and went straight to the bed. He cleared the rest of the table watching her without seemingly doing so. She flopped down on the mattress without her usual grace and instead of sitting up to wait for him as she'd done since they'd been thrown together, she curled up into the fetal position and closed her eyes. His heart jerked hard in his chest, rebelling. Knots tightened in his belly. There was no getting around the fact that Shylah, for the first time in her life, wasn't feeling good.

He took his time with the dishes and his shower, wanting her to fall asleep. When he finally went to bed and eased in beside her, she rolled over and wrapped her body around his, practically sprawling over top of him. She seemed even warmer than earlier, but he told himself that was because the air was still muggy from the storm.

13

"What are you doing awake, Shylah? I thought you were already asleep," Draden whispered. "You're exhausted."

"I can't go to sleep. I think I've gotten used to staying up all night and don't know how to actually sleep when it's dark." There was a quaver in her voice. Small. Barely noticeable, but it was there and Draden didn't like it.

He smoothed his hand down her back to the curve of her bottom and rubbed gently. She was afraid, and he couldn't blame her. She'd just seen an entire village, men, women and children wiped out in a horrific way, and now she was facing that same death.

In the stillness of the night, there in the dark, it was impossible to hide from the brutal truth. That virus was inside of her. Unseen, but already wreaking havoc on her body. It was in him as well. For a moment panic welled up, and his heart rate accelerated. He fought dread and terror back, pushing them away. That way led to insanity and an ugly death. He had to be in control not only for himself, but for Shylah. His sweet peony. His delicate flower.

"We're all right, sweetheart. It's just the two of us here and for tonight we're both just fine. More than fine." He brushed kisses along her forehead and inhaled that perfect, tantalizing scent that he would always associate with her. Elusive. Subtle. Not all peonies had a scent, but the ones that did were unforgettable. Like his woman.

She rubbed her cheek along his chest. "It's close tonight, Draden. Crouched like a monster ready to pounce if I close my eyes."

"Now, I'm here, baby. Nothing is going to get you. Besides, I can see your gun sticking out from under the pillow." He tried to ease the tension in her, massaging her bottom and teasing her to get her mind off the fact that they were both going to die in the next few days.

"I can't shoot the virus unless I'm killing myself."

He closed his eyes. He couldn't think about anyone putting a bullet in her brain, and he didn't want her thinking about it either. "I'm still holding out hope that Trap and Wyatt will come through for us. They've put together a team of virologists and they're working around the clock. I believe they aren't the only ones." He moved his hand up her spine to the nape of her neck, kneading the hard knots there in an effort to comfort her.

"You're amazing, Draden, and you don't even know it. I hate that you have the virus in you as well, but if I had to go through this experience, I wouldn't want to do it with anyone else."

Her voice rang with sincerity. He didn't know why he was inexplicitly pleased, not when the virus was consuming him just as fast, but he was. "We're getting married tomorrow. I've already asked Joe to facilitate the paperwork and have given him a list of items to find for us. Did you ever think about your wedding day and what you'd like to have there?"

"It never really occurred to me that I would have the chance to marry. I did fantasize about it but never thought it would actually happen." Her fingers absently trailed across his heavy muscles. "I wanted flowers. Lots of flowers. I think more and more brides have opted not to have flowers because they can be very expensive, but I thought they brought something special to the wedding. Bellisia laughed at me, but Zara agreed. So, mostly, when I thought about a wedding, I thought of flowers."

"That's strange. I never thought much about getting married either, but when I did, it was always the flowers that seemed significant to me too. I thought it was just because most of the few good memories I have come from the time I worked in the nursery."

She murmured a wordless sound of agreement and nuzzled his throat. "I like ceremonies. Rituals. Especially the ones that involve big family celebrations — probably because I never had a family of my own. Once I was in Russia. I had tracked this agent to St. Petersburg. He'd come to the United States and poisoned a defector — a man who just wanted to be able to be free to perfect his artistry. The man also was very wealthy and believed in everything Whitney was doing. He gave a great deal of money toward Whitney's experiments. You can imagine how angry he was that this agent interrupted that flow of money."

She fell silent, but he felt the fan of her long lashes against his skin. Her hand, stroking caresses and drawing letters over his chest, was sending little streaks of fire through him. He caught her wrist to still the movement.

"Keep going." He wasn't trying to distract her. He was genuinely interested in everything she had to say. If for no other reason, he loved the sound of her voice.

She shrugged. "It's silly really. I was following him along this narrow backstreet and went around a corner to the main street. I couldn't be obvious, so I stopped to stare in the window of the building. There were all these people inside."

Shylah nuzzled his chest, lifted her head and looked into his eyes. "It was a large, extended family celebrating a birth. They'd all gathered. Men in suits, looking so handsome. Women in dresses, their hair up, makeup on, a true occasion, you know, where everyone wants to look their best. Children of various ages were running around, looking good in their dress-up clothing. But clearly, it was a *family.*"

His heart turned over. There was underlying sadness in her voice. She had never had a family and she knew she never would.

"I remember they had this very cool tea service. I noticed it because it was hand-painted and it had blue peonies on it. Can you imagine?" Now there was a smile in her voice. "Me, noticing peonies? It was this incredibly beautiful, clearly vintage tea service. I'm certain it must have been in their family for a generation or two. It was the way they touched it, so gently, almost reverently."

He heard the wistfulness in his voice. "Describe it for me."

She laid her cheek on his chest again. "I actually went back later, snuck in and took pictures, so I could look it up. It was a Russian samovar and was hand-painted with the blue peonies. It was a traditional Russian tea set, with a tray, teapot and warmer. The spigot and tap was this glorious gold, as were the legs of the warmer, spout and handle of the teapot. The tea glasses were crystal looking but the holders were hand-painted with the blue peonies and had gold filigree. It was so beautiful, Draden. I looked at that and thought about generations celebrating their own special occasions the same way, and I wanted to cry because I knew I'd never have that. Not in a million years."

The wistfulness in her voice was heartbreaking. He wrapped his arms around her, trying to protect her from her life, from the virus, from knowing they were going to die an agonizing death. He wanted something, just one thing, to be perfect, to be everything she wanted before she was too sick to enjoy it. Before she died.

"I was there to kill someone, and that family was celebrating life, celebrating the birth of a child. That was the first time I realized that some people had something truly beautiful and it was called family. I wanted that for myself — and that tea set. It was elegant and beautiful, and it represented that bond they had as well as their connection to the past."

"Family isn't always blood, baby," he said. "I was lucky enough to have a woman take me in as her child and teach me what family really is. We didn't have much, but we had each other. She sang a lot, and every night she sat on the edge of the bed and told me stories. They were always about knights and dragons. Good versus evil kind of stories. I guess that was our ritual."

He rubbed her back and hips, trying to ease the soreness out of her. "On Sunday mornings, she would make me eggs and pancakes with bacon. The pancakes were always cut in the shape of a shield. I know she didn't have a mold, but she did it for me because I loved the idea of the two of us having a shield. She carved two dragons facing each other and words like *courage, bravery* and *integrity* into the pancakes. She said that was our crest. The way we lived."

He was silent a moment, allowing his memories to flood his mind. It was painful to think about his mother, those long months of her illness while she wasted away in front of him and he was helpless to save her. "She kissed me every night. Every single night, even when she couldn't get out of bed and I went to her. She would always say good night and tell me she loved me."

Just whispering that much to Shylah, sharing something he fiercely guarded, something so private he held close, was difficult. Those days of happiness had been brief, but he treasured every one of them. He'd locked those memories away, keeping them safe from what he'd become, what the streets had shaped him into being.

"She sounds beautiful and amazing." There were tears swimming in her eyes, and dripping off her lashes, but she smiled at him.

"She was. Even when she was dying she was beautiful. This light came from inside her." He stroked more caresses down the back of her head, fingers tangling in her thick hair. "I've seen that same light in two other women. Nonny, Wyatt's grandmother, and you." It was the highest compliment he could pay her, and he hoped she understood.

She lifted her head and brushed his jaw with kisses. The little wisps of fire trailed down to his throat. He tightened his arms possessively. Yeah. She knew.

"I really love you, Draden. I don't want you to think you weren't loved after you lost her, because you are."

"Not for my looks?" he teased.

"Mmm," she hedged, her dark eyes dancing at him. "I have to think about that for a minute or two."

He waited until she rubbed her cheek on his chest and then he nuzzled the top of her head, strands of her hair catching in the stubble growing along his jaw. He liked that. Liked that they were in the same bed. He enjoyed being with her.

"The photograph of that tea set. You still have it?" He knew she did. He could tell the tea service represented family and love to her, things she wanted but had never had.

She stretched her arm out lazily, reaching with her fingertips to draw her phone to her. He watched her put her passcode in and then she found the photograph and showed it to him. Draden had never paid much attention to things like women's china, or even the ritual of drinking tea, but he recognized a beautiful work of art when he saw it.

"I love that. I can see why they'd keep it in the family."

She looked at the photograph and lovingly ran the pad of her finger over it. "Isn't it beautiful?"

The wistfulness in her voice was his undoing. His chest hurt from the need to change her life. As far as he was concerned, she'd suffered enough just being in Whitney's hands, let alone everything else that had happened in her life. He really did want to give her the world.

"It is, Shylah. I've never seen anything like it." He brushed more kisses on the top of her head, deliberately picking up more strands of her hair so they'd tie the two of them together. "I love that it has peonies painted on it."

"I do too," she admitted with some reluctance and then she sent him a smile, her eyes bright again. "How many tea services have you actually seen?"

"You don't know, it could be thousands. Don't be judging me." He gave her a little shake. "You wanted flowers in your wedding and a tradition of some kind. What else? All girls dream of dresses. You must have."

She turned her face away from him. "Zara smuggled in a catalogue of wedding dresses once. We were oohing and ahhing, being silly, and trying to decide which would look the best on us when Whitney came in with his smirking supersoldiers."

Draden didn't like the change in her voice. "What happened?"

"They made a lot of fun of us and tore up the catalogue a page at a time. Zara was beaten and taken to the isolation cell. Whitney hated her so much. She was gentle and kind. She didn't like hurting others. She really couldn't take pain, and that made Whitney think she was weak. He inflicted pain on her as often as possible saying it would build up her tolerance, but of course it didn't."

"What it did was make her strong," Draden said. "She was in China. Some of our team went in to rescue her. She'd been horribly tortured, but she didn't break. Whitney was ridiculous to look down on that woman."

Shylah looked at him, clearly horrified. "*Horribly* tortured? What does that mean?"

"I shouldn't have used that word. She's all right now, sweetheart. You saw her. Doesn't she look happy and healthy? Believe me, Nonny fusses over her. She will you too when she meets you." He said it without thinking because he wanted Nonny to get to know Shylah.

"I wish I could meet your Nonny. She sounds extraordinary."

"She is. Wyatt is a lucky man having her. But we got off subject. We were talking about wedding gowns. Did you have a particular favorite before Whitney broke up the party?"

"I didn't have a chance to look closely. I wanted something elegant but with color to it. Bellisia had assured me that there were some dresses that weren't perfectly white."

"Why didn't you like white?"

She shrugged, and clearly sought to try to find the right words to tell him. "I loved the lace and buttons. The beautiful beads. Even the cut of the gowns. But I wanted something that said who I am, and I've got way too much blood on my hands to ever wear white."

There it was, the real reason. He looked at her statement from all angles before responding. Denying it wasn't even close to the truth, wouldn't work. She wouldn't believe him. She had killed, just as he had, in the service of their country, but her feelings were legitimate and he couldn't ignore them.

"What color did you want to wear?"

She traced little patterns on his chest,

driving his body crazy. He caught her hand and brought it to his mouth, nibbling on her fingertips while he waited for her answer.

"Something elegant. On my wedding day I would like to look elegant. I'm tall enough to pull it off and I've got a good figure, so with the right dress, I could do it. I don't know about walking in heels, I always thought if I had to wear a long dress, I'd go barefoot rather than fall on my face wearing heels."

"What color?" he persisted.

"Probably champagne. Or gold. Wouldn't that be pretty in a gown? A champagne or gold gown with lace. French lace maybe. Have you ever seen French lace?"

"I was a model, sweetheart. Fabrics and lace were a must to know." He said it in the voice of one of the most famous designers, snippy, sarcastic and arrogant.

She laughed, just like he knew she would. "Well, that's what I always envisioned."

"It sounds beautiful."

"What about you? Did you ever think about getting married and what you would like?"

"Briefly. I never thought I'd meet a woman I could love or who would ever love me enough to want to marry me and spend the rest of her life with me. I had no idea I'd find you and you'd give me such a compliment as to say yes."

Her soft laughter turned to a giggle. "The rest of my life isn't that long, so I don't know how big a compliment it is. One day? Two?" She rubbed her chin along his chest. "Stay humble, my man."

"With you I have no choice."

"Wedding ceremony."

"Flowers. Especially peonies. I pictured them everywhere."

"You did not. You're making that up."

"I'm not, Shylah. They were my comfort flower. My mother always wore a scent that was the real deal and smelled like peonies. I tried to find it one time, but most of the perfumes that say peony don't smell like them at all. That's probably why, when I worked at the nursery, I gravitated toward that section of the greenhouse. Sometimes I slept there." He made the confession in a low voice.

Her arms slid around him, and she kissed a line of flaming little darts all the way down his chest and back up, leaving behind a trail of fire.

God, he loved her. It was that simple and that profound. He looked up at the ceiling, his woman snuggled over him, and knew, if he had to die at least he'd had her for a time. At least he knew she existed and that she was his partner in every way. She was the one for him. He wasn't alone and never would be as long as she was alive. He didn't kiss her because that would lead to other things and there was still a very small chance that her body could fight this thing off. He knew he was infected and didn't want to risk increasing her exposure. A part of him knew he was kidding himself, but he had to believe she would survive and get better, even if he didn't.

"I guess you can call me Peony," she whispered. "If it comforts you."

"*My* peony," he emphasized. "And it's only for us, no one else." He liked the intimacy of having a special name for her no one else knew but the two of them. He also liked that she got the significance of the flower to him.

"I love that, Draden. You turned that horrible name to something beautiful. I like that it's just ours."

"I do as well."

"So, lots of flowers. What else?"

Her voice held a drowsy note that trailed over his body like the touch of her fingers. He threaded her hair through his fist and then moved down to her nape where he began another slow massage. He knew she was tired and he wanted her to go to sleep.

"I want to watch you coming toward me. Walking up a path scattered with petals. I want to see your face when you come to me. That's important."

"Then that's what we'll do." She yawned. "I'm really sleepy, Draden."

"Then stop talking, woman, and go to sleep."

"I love talking to you, but I'm so tired."

He remained silent, willing her to go to sleep. He had a lot of work to get done and not very much time to do it. It didn't take long before she was out. He waited an extra twenty minutes and then carefully slid her off of him. She woke with a sleepy protest, but he soothed her back to sleep, promising to be right back.

Draden dressed in jeans and a T-shirt, keeping his gaze on his woman. She had been unexpected. Exhilarating. She made him feel alive just when he should have been at the lowest point in his life.

She must have felt his stare because her head moved slightly, and she lifted those long lashes of hers and blinked at him several times sleepily. "You need me to get up? I can go with you. Are we on alert?"

Her words were slightly slurred. Drowsy.

Sexy as hell. She definitely did it for him.

"No, baby." He bent to press a kiss against her temple, sealing himself there. "I'm just checking things. Be right back."

"Be safe or I'll be upset with you."

As threats went, it wasn't too worrisome, especially when she looked so beautiful lying there in his bed. "I'll be safe. Go back to sleep and don't shoot me when I come back in."

Her lips curved, but she didn't even lift her lashes again, already settling back into sleep now that he'd reassured her.

The rain had stopped so he wasn't going to get completely soaked, which, after the first drenching, he was grateful for. He slipped Shylah's phone into his pocket and hurried out to make his way back to the remote lab.

The forest was dark, but the moon spilled a silvery light over the canopy, giving the leaves a metallic gleam. The wind had died down to more of a breeze, ruffling the leaves and needles so the trees appeared to dance, swaying to the symphony of the ever-present cicadas. With his acute hearing he could hear the rustle of rodents in the thick vegetation. He spotted an owl as it dropped down on silent wings, talons outstretched. The bird missed and pulled up, screaming its disappointment, the sound adding to the evening's dramatic mystery.

He'd always preferred the dark. He often ran by himself, shrouded in fog in the swamp, the night creatures his warning system as he let the demons in his head have free rein and then fade away from sheer exhaustion. Since he'd been with Shylah, those demons had, for the most part, stayed silent. She seemed to be a guardian. A shield of sorts. Shylah was pure magic. If they had to die, he was going to give her everything he could before that happened.

Inside the lab the computer powered up immediately. Joe answered his call within thirty seconds. "You alright, Sandman?" Joe asked, calling him by the name his team often used.

"Have a request for quite a few items. I need you to pull out all stops. Money isn't an object. I'm sending you paperwork to access my accounts, but you know I'm good for it. Don't care what you have to spend. My next call is to Trap and Gino, asking them to help with the money until you can get into my accounts."

"No worries."

"I have a list. Some of the items are specific, so you're going to have to work all night, but I have to have them by tomorrow. I'm sending the list now."

He waited a couple of minutes, picking up a pad of paper and sketching how he planned on changing the lab into a place where he could marry his woman.

"Draden." Joe's voice held caution. "This is crazy. Some of this stuff is insane. How do you expect me to get this here by morning?"

"Afternoon. She's very tired, and I'm going to do my best to black out the windows so she'll sleep. Then we'll have a good breakfast before I meet you. At that time, I'll put everything together. I know it doesn't give you much time, but Trap has a jet that can go anywhere in hours. It's expensive as hell, but he'll be thrilled to make the pilot work for his keep."

"You sure this is what you want? I believe Trap and Wyatt when they say the two of you are fighting this virus off. You don't have to do anything drastic yet."

"We're infected. What part of that didn't you get? Of course we're fighting it off. We both have unique and very strong immune systems, but that doesn't mean we won't fail, just like everyone else. I hope like hell we don't, but live or die, I'm doing this because I want to do it. No matter what, she's the one."

"Getting married is permanent, Draden. You don't even have a prenup."

He wasn't used to spilling his feelings and it annoyed him that he had to keep reassuring his friend that he knew what he was doing. He'd never given a damn about the money. On the other hand, he knew he was asking the impossible. Even expecting it.

"Don't need a prenup. I know this seems extravagant, and I know it won't be easy to pull off, Joe, but it's important to me."

Joe sighed. "I get that. I'll get it done for you. I don't know how, but it will be done."

"As soon as possible," Draden pushed.

"You got it. I just want you to hold out hope."

"I do. I am." He wasn't. He didn't like the rash spreading over Shylah's body. It hadn't been there before, and it definitely was worse. In the beginning, when she wasn't showing any signs, he had convinced himself that she was going to be fine. The moment Wyatt had told him they were both infected, but fighting it off, he had to fight spiraling into depression and anger. He didn't think about himself. He knew he could put a bullet in his head when the time came, but Shylah . . . That was an entirely different matter. He had counted on her winning.

"I need to talk to Trap, Joe," Draden pushed. He wanted Joe to get started. Joe was the one who had to do most of the work, arranging for the jet to pick up any item wherever it was in the world and get it back in time. It was a huge undertaking. He also had to arrange for an official to perform the ceremony as well as push the paperwork through. His task wasn't easy, but Joe always got things done and Draden was counting on that.

Joe signed off after giving his reassurances that he would find as many things on the list as possible in the time allotted to him. Draden called Trap and Wyatt next. As always, Trap remained in the background, working, his back to the camera. Wyatt took the time to sit and regard his friend with a hint of shock on his face when Draden explained what was going on.

"This is a little sudden." Wyatt was far more cautious than Joe had been. "Are you certain you don't want to give this a few more days?"

"I've never been more certain of anything in my life."

"Your bodies are fighting it off somehow," Wyatt said. "We just haven't figured out how. Your cells are doing crazy things. We'd like more of your blood tomorrow to see what, if any, progression."

"I'm getting married tomorrow."

Trap didn't turn around, but he must have been listening. "Still need the blood, bro."

Draden sighed. They did need it. Even if it was too late to save Shylah and him, if the virus was let loose on the world, those working around the clock to find a vaccine and a therapy would need their blood.

"I'll make sure you get it. I need your jet, Trap. And any money Joe needs to make things happen the way I want. I've got money in my account, but Joe may need a death certificate to access it after I'm gone. You know the drill with the paperwork we all filled out. He knows to pay you back."

Trap glanced over his shoulder, annoyance written on his face. "Shut the fuck up, Draden. We're friends. You need the jet, it's yours. My woman won't buy herself a pair of shoes and I just spend money on equipment. I think we're good." Sarcasm dripped. "And you're not going to die, so make certain you want to spend your life with her, because she's going to live through this too."

Draden understood it was Trap's way of showing he cared. He wouldn't say the words and he wouldn't act emotional. He'd contribute what he could, and he'd work until he dropped to find a way to save them.

Trap didn't act like the nicest of men, but he was solid, and he'd never stop until he found a way to make things right.

For some reason, Trap's reaction to his request choked him up when nothing else had. He had insisted Shylah would live. He was adamant. Trap had already turned away from the camera, head down, studying something in front of him without giving Draden a chance to respond.

"You thinkin' of takin' the jet and makin' a run for it?" Wyatt asked, dropping his voice as if they were co-conspirators. That only made his Louisiana accent more pronounced.

"I've got Joe running all over the world looking for things for my woman. I want to surprise her."

Wyatt's eyebrow shot up. "You really are fallin' for this woman."

"Already gone," Draden admitted. "I fell hard, and I want the world for her. If we lose this battle, Wyatt, I want her to have something extraordinary. And I want her to know she was loved."

Just saying it out loud to one of his closest friends had him choking up again. What the hell was wrong with him? With dying came some clarity. "This isn't just for her. I want this for me as well. I want to have this day with her. If there's any way for Bellisia and Zara to be with us, not physically, but with her, so she doesn't feel so alone, I would very much like to give her that as well."

Wyatt nodded. "You know, computers aren't my thing, but we've got a few people who know what they're doing. Flame, my sister-in-law, is hell on wheels with a computer. She should be able to put something together for us. Azami is loaning us the satellite for as long as necessary and we've got the use of it anytime. We can do this, for you, Draden."

"Thanks, man. I want to marry her at sunset. It's beautiful here when the sun is just sliding out of the sky and the forest is beginning to stir."

"You're going to want it light enough for all of us to see, especially if Zara and Bellisia are watching. Bellisia is in Louisiana, and Zara is up in the mountains of Montana. We're here in Sumatra."

"I'd forgotten about that. We'll set the ceremony for a half hour before sunset. That way we'll have both. I put cameras on the list for outside and inside. I think I can hook it all together. At least I hope so."

"If you can't, and you promise Bellisia a wedding, you may as well stay right where you are because if you don't come through, she'll end you herself. Zara will be sweet about it, but knowing you disappointed her, it will be Gino who will come after you."

Draden couldn't help smiling and it felt good. Wyatt called it exactly the way it would be. Gino would probably punch him for making his woman sad, and Bellisia would at least pretend to do him in.

"I don't think I've actually seen you smile before," Wyatt observed. "This woman must be the real deal to teach you how to smile."

That brought him up short. He didn't smile often, but he did smile, didn't he? He honestly couldn't say. At Nonny? He'd brushed a kiss on her cheek before he'd left for the mission. They all had said good-bye in their own way to her. No, he hadn't smiled. The triplets? The three beautiful little girls with their dark curls and large eyes and quirky little ways? They were all three geniuses, which wasn't too surprising considering Wyatt was off the charts and Pepper was extremely intelligent. No, he didn't smile around them either and he should have. He liked them. He thought the three were little troublemakers and funny as hell, so why didn't he smile?

He had begun his modeling career early when he'd been "discovered," and in those shoots he hadn't smiled. They hadn't wanted him to smile and he hadn't felt like it. He'd been living two lives. One on the street and one in the world of cameras and high-powered men and woman who'd looked at him as a commodity and nothing more. He doubted if they'd even known his name. The money had put him through college, so he'd let them take his picture, but he'd avoided any contact with anyone who might uncover his earlier days. The publicity would have been good for his career, but he hadn't wanted anyone knowing his business.

"I didn't want your woman to see my smile. I was protecting your marriage." As comebacks went, it was lame, but it was a good first try. He heard the way Malichai and Mordichai razzed the others. They were good at camaraderie. He was still learning what real camaraderie was, not the fake smile and pretend, like he'd taught Trap. He wished he had the time to work with Trap more and do a better job of explaining so the man would understand — like he was just getting — that friends and family were important enough to make an effort with.

"You wish."

"How is she? She was so sick, we were all worried. You must hate being away from her." Draden felt guilty about that, although he didn't know why.

"I don't like it, but she's strong. I talk to her and the girls several times a day. The girls are having fun there. It's a different environment. I should have thought to take them to a place that would be safe for them and expose them to other surroundings. As for Pepper, she doesn't do well being separated from me, but she knows it's necessary. She always says to give you her love and that she's thinking of you."

"She's like Nonny. Lots of heart." It was true. Draden realized he judged all women by Nonny now. Pepper took care of them all the way Nonny did. She had no mother and no one to guide her, so she patterned herself after her favorite woman. Pepper was very close to Nonny. He wanted that for Shylah.

"That's a nice thing to say, Draden," Wyatt said. "I'll pass it on to her. She loves Nonny and that will be the best compliment anyone could ever pay her."

"What about Cayenne? How is she doing without Trap?"

"She hasn't killed anyone yet, but she won't FaceTime him. She's wrapped herself up in silk and refuses to talk to anyone other than Pepper and Zara. Zara seems to be able to get her to eat and drink a little."

There was a hint of worry in Wyatt's voice that Draden picked up on immediately. Trap didn't turn around, nor was there any indication that he heard, but Draden knew better. Cayenne was his world. He was sacrificing a lot in order to stay there and work while his pregnant wife was far from him. She was the most lethal, self-sufficient woman Draden could imagine, and yet entirely dependent on her husband. The dichotomy was very strange.

"Can you and Trap work in Montana? It might be safer for you there. If the Williams brothers and their friend Orucov are heading that way then all of you would be safer to get out."

"Do you think that's a real possibility?"

"I haven't found enough on them to get a reading for what they might do, but Shylah thinks so and she's been tracking them, so she knows them better than anyone else. She thinks it's a possibility. Right now, all we know for certain is that they left in a hurry. The last sighting was in the village with the MSS, but they disappeared, using the river as an escape route. We discussed the fact that they despise Whitney and may decide to take out a GhostWalker team in retaliation, but we have no evidence pointing to that conclusion."

"Word was put out and law enforcement everywhere is looking for them. Airports, any point of entry, have been notified."

"Why don't you all pick up and move to Montana? Trap could be with Cayenne and I wouldn't have to worry that you're a target."

"We need to be close to you, Draden. We can't afford the time it would take to get the blood samples flown to Montana, or Louisiana for that matter. I'm working with Trap and I'm used to him being a bear. The girls and Nonny will take care of Cayenne. We'll all get through this. You're the only one of us Trap acknowledges as a brother . . ."

That got a snort of derision from Trap, but he didn't turn around.

"Other than me, of course," Wyatt added.

Trap did turn around. "I'd like you a lot better if you'd help instead of gab all the time. You're worse than an old gossipy woman."

Wyatt flashed a grin. "Now he's in for it. I can't wait to tell Nonny what he just said. Not only is it sexist, but he's just insulted my *grand-mere.*"

"I didn't. She doesn't gossip."

"She would tell you that women don't gossip any more than men do. She's been to the Huracan Club and she's known Delmar Thibodeaux all her life. He's the biggest gossip in the bayou or swamp. Probably in all of Louisiana," Wyatt said.

Trap scowled and shook his head. "You can add your name to that list," he muttered as he turned back to his work.

Wyatt laughed, and Draden felt lighter just listening to it. Wyatt had the Fontenot laugh, the one Nonny had. It was genuine and invited others to join in.

"I'll let you go, but think about having Ezekiel move everyone to a safer place," Draden said.

"We've got everything in place in the swamp to get them if they come close to our territory," Wyatt said. "We've got the home court advantage there. A stranger shows up out there, we know about it almost immediately. Zeke'll get them, Draden. You concentrate on fighting this thing and having a good day with your woman."

"Will do." Draden ended the call and sat for a long time listening to the night sounds and letting peace steal into him.

He had a lot to do to make the wedding special for his bride. The remote lab was going to need a complete makeover, and he'd start there. He was still going to have to get blood from Shylah, but he didn't intend to allow her into the lab until their marriage ceremony. He'd take it in the ranger cabin, freeze it there, and then hand it off to Joe. Having made his plans, he got to work.

14

Shylah woke to the sounds of birds. It sounded like dozens of them right outside the cabin. There were lilting sounds, whistles and a strange call that sounded like "took, took," as if the birds were tattling on one another. Each seemed to be vying for who could be the loudest complainer. After the strange call, the birds would erupt into maniacal laughter. She lay listening to it, wondering what kind of bird made sounds like that.

Draden was wrapped around her, his body close to hers, one arm circling her waist. She remained relaxed, enjoying the way he felt, his hands large, taking in her bare skin where her shirt had ridden up. His fingers were spread wide, as if to get the largest expanse possible. She didn't know if that were true, but she loved that it felt that way.

There was something amazing about being with Draden. In part it was the way he made her feel about herself. She was always very aware of her attributes. She didn't need Whitney's validation in order to feel good or bad about herself. She didn't have that kind of nature. She'd always felt bad for Zara, who could have used even one compliment from the man. Or Bellisia, who didn't think she was attractive because Whitney had told her so practically from birth.

Shylah had no idea why she was so self-possessed, but she was grateful. She had no trouble making up her mind to defy Whitney and take whatever punishment he doled out. Through it all, she had quietly accepted that one day he would ask her to go after someone she didn't think deserved it and she'd have to end her life by allowing one of his viruses to kill her. Because she'd always known that was how her life would end, she hadn't been as horrified when Draden had first told her he was infected. The way the virus killed was horrific, but there was always a bullet, and she was pragmatic about that.

Now, having met Draden, she knew what love for a man really was. She loved Bellisia and Zara, but it had never occurred to her that she would meet and fall in love with a man. It wasn't in the realm of possibility for her. Now, at the end of her life, he was there with her. He was strong, a rock really, for her to lean on when she needed it.

She'd never had a breakdown before. That had been scary, to cry without the ability to stop it. Crying on Draden should have been humiliating, but it had been comforting. He didn't seem to look down on her at all for that slip. She was determined it wouldn't happen again.

Slowly, reluctantly, she began to slide out from under his arm. At once that relaxed, heavy arm tensed, and he pulled her back against him and nuzzled the nape of her neck with his mouth. His breath was warm, teasing strands of hair, teasing nerve endings.

"Where are you going?" His voice was a sleepy protest.

She loved the way he sounded when he was only half-awake. He'd been out a good deal of the night. She'd woken up twice and found the bed empty, but she still wasn't feeling well and she hadn't moved, although she'd worried. It was strange being sick. She couldn't remember a time in her life when she'd fallen ill.

"The bathroom," she answered honestly.

"Come back to bed," he said. "After."

Her body reacted to that husky, sensual note in his voice, but she wasn't going there again. She'd already tried seduction and she hadn't been that good at it.

"Go back to sleep, you were up most of the night." She was noncommittal, hoping he'd leave it at that.

She felt his lips whisper against her nape and then his arm loosened enough that she could slip out from under him. She stood up and stretched. The birds were having a field day, the various species calling out loudly, singing or laughing hysterically. The windows were screened, so less light could slip through, but she moved closer in order to identify the various flocks.

The birds making the most noise were the strangest she'd ever seen. They looked like something out of the dinosaur era. Each was large, with dark brown feathers on the upper body and white feathers underneath. The tail feathers appeared extremely long, almost doubling the size of the bird. The strangest thing was the bizarre protuberance on its head. It was a thick casque, perched much like a helmet atop the upper half of the bird's head. The beak was yellow and red and the casque was definitely red or reddish orange.

Fascinated, she stared out the window at the strange birds as they called out, ate figs and laughed at one another. She had no idea what they were, but she knew they had to be rare. These birds seemed as if they were immature, maybe just recently out of their nests, juveniles rather than adults. She'd been there a few days, going back and forth from the coast to inland into the forest and she'd never encountered them. She wanted to take the sighting as a good omen. They were comical and made her feel happy, brightening her day immediately.

Reluctantly, she turned away from the birds and went to the small bathroom with its little shower. She knew she shouldn't spend too much time using up the water, but it felt good on her aching muscles. She scrubbed her body and was a little surprised that the rash had faded. She knew little about viruses, but she thought as she progressed, getting sicker, the rash would spread. Most of the raised bumps were gone so that the red dots were mostly under the skin.

She washed her hair, taking her time with that as well, rinsing several times. She felt better than she had the night before, as if just sleeping took away the horrible burning in her eyes and skin. Shouldn't that have gotten worse as well? She wasn't nauseous, she was hungry when the night before she could barely manage a few spoonsful of soup.

She wrapped a towel around herself, stepped out of the shower and began drying off and inspecting the areas that had been red and bumpy the night before. The rash was definitely fading. She should have studied more about viruses and how they progressed because, at that moment, she didn't feel in the least sick.

She went to her backpack and pulled out her underwear and a fresh pair of jeans. Today, supposedly, was her wedding day. She wanted, like most brides, to look her best, but she wasn't hung up on details. Being with Draden made her happy and marrying him was something she'd never dared to dream let alone actually have come true. She didn't know how Draden expected to pull it off, but the fact that he wanted to marry her and was making it happen was enough.

Her heart hurt it was so full, and she pressed her hand over it. Draden. Who knew there were men like him in the world? He made it exciting to wake up in the morning. She looked forward to the day. To their shared laughter. Their conversations. The intense attraction between them. Who wouldn't fall in love with him?

She pulled a T-shirt over her head, her nicest one, so she'd at least look halfway decent if they really had a ceremony. It took a while to tame her hair. Thick and wild, the waves curled every which way, but not as anything as well behaved as actual spirals. The color wasn't actual blond either, more like a dark honey color falling in a rebellious riot past her shoulders. She wasn't certain there was any way to style hair like hers. She often put it up, but the weight combined with the fineness had it tumbling down after a few hours and not in an artful way. That had never mattered before.

Now it did.

She stared at herself in the mirror. She rarely wore makeup and didn't have any with her. She'd brought cream for her face and that was about it. It hadn't mattered until she met Draden. He didn't seem to notice, but she wanted to look her best for him. Shrugging, she brushed her teeth and once more stared out the window at the strange birds. She counted thirteen of them. They were definitely eating the fruit on the great pile of twisted vines and branches on the forest floor. She had no idea where the stack of vines had come from and she peered out, trying to see if there was an abundance of fig trees around them.

"Good morning." Draden came up behind her, pressed a kiss to her neck and went past her to the bathroom.

She watched him walk away from her. He was naked, and he had a beautiful body. All muscle. She'd never paid that much attention, but she was fairly certain someone should sculpt him, immortalize him for all time. He had that good of a body. With his face, that bone structure, strong jaw, straight nose and beautiful, compelling eyes, it was a little intimidating to be with him.

"What's going on in your mind?" he called out to her. "It's our wedding day."

Shylah spit into the kitchen sink and rinsed out her mouth several times. "I was thinking that you're so beautiful it could be a little intimidating being your wife. Fortunately, I'm very confident, so you're going to be stuck with me."

"I like the idea of being very traditional."

She heard the water running as he washed his hands. Something in his voice made her suspicious. Draden didn't seem like a traditional sort of man.

"Traditional how?"

"Since the virus could take hold anytime" — he came out of the bathroom and leaned one hip lazily against the wall — "and we have to say 'until death do us part,' I thought we'd keep the original wording of the marriage ceremony."

She sensed a trap, but she'd never been to a wedding. She wasn't about to commit until she knew what he was talking about. "Why do I have the feeling you're up to something?"

He grinned at her, which shot his attraction up another million watts. If he didn't put clothes on she was going to jump him. Since he hadn't made any advances, she thought he was going to be traditional and not have sex with her until they were married.

Shylah made a face at him. "Now I know for sure that you're up to something. I'm not agreeing to anything yet. Take your shower while I ponder this."

"There's no cheating."

"How could I cheat?"

"You have to stay in the cabin because I'm fixing things up for our wedding outside." He disappeared into the shower and then stuck his head back out. "You could fix me breakfast. I need something hearty. I have a lot of work to do in a short amount of time."

"I think you just want me to feed you."

He laughed, and the sound moved through her like a wave of pleasure.

"That could be true."

"Look out the window before those birds go away. There's thirteen of the coolest-looking birds I've ever seen eating figs off those branches."

"I cut those branches last night and twisted them together. I wanted an arbor over the door to the lab, so I got a few things done last night."

"You should have woken me up, Draden."

"You weren't feeling good and I wanted you to rest. How are you feeling now?"

"Much better."

He stuck his head back out, his gaze drifting over her. "Your color looks better."

"The rash is better too. At least it was when I went into the shower. The heat brought it out again, but nowhere near what it was when I went to bed. It's still a little itchy, but my eyes aren't burning. I think that must have been from all the crying." She hesitated, but it had to be said. "I'm sorry about that."

"I want to see the rash."

"Later. Shower now, inspection later. And look at the birds, tell me if you know what they are."

"You're more of a wildlife expert than I am." He disappeared again. There was silence and then he whistled softly. "Those are helmeted hornbills, or something like that. They're critically endangered. If I'm right, they generally stay up in the canopy. I cut down all these fig branches and they've come for the figs. From what I understand, and I'm quoting Malichai here, usually they stay in pairs. And, my beautiful bride, they bring good luck."

"Why would so many of them be here?"

"They have to be juveniles. The female is sealed into a nest built into the hollow of a tree. Only a tiny hole remains so the male can feed her while she incubates the eggs. Wouldn't mind sealing you up somewhere Whitney can never find you."

"Ha ha ha. Very funny." Sarcasm dripped, but she was laughing. *Laughing* when she knew a virus was eating her up inside. How did he do that? Make her life better than it ever had been just with his presence? Just by the way he looked at her? Maybe those birds were a good-luck symbol after all. If they weren't, Draden was.

Before anything, she wrote the story of Draden and the dragons. It was fun to draw again. She wasn't nearly as skilled as she wanted to be, but she could create illustrations for his story. She didn't have colored pencils, but she knew that wouldn't matter to him — the gift itself was hopefully magical to him.

Shylah went to the refrigerator and peered inside. Joe had brought them all kinds of supplies. She wanted to make a really good breakfast for Draden. One he would remember. What had he said his mother made him on their special Sundays? She made pancakes with their special crest. It was in the form of a shield, with two dragons facing each other and words like *integrity, bravery* and *courage.* She could do that. She had some art skills.

What else had his mother made for him? Bacon and eggs. That seemed like a lot of food, but if that was what he ate with his mother on Sundays, then they would have that for breakfast. She wanted to bring him memories of his happiest days to make the day special for him. More importantly, she wanted to give him a sense of his mother celebrating his wedding day with him.

He wanted her to stay in the cabin while he worked outside, and putting together a wedding gift was something she could do. She had a good imagination, and she'd read enough stories to write one about dragons and white knights. She could illustrate it as well. She would do her best to make him feel as if his mother was with them.

She worked quickly to have as much done

as possible so when he emerged from the shower, toweling his hair dry and coming toward her, she pointed to the bed. "Dress please. It's later than I thought. I have a few things I want to do in here."

He sent her his cocky grin, the one that sent a shiver of excitement sliding down her spine. She couldn't help the answering smile. They might not have a single tomorrow, but they had this — their wedding day. It didn't matter if it was legal or not, she would mean every vow she took . . . "Vows. There's something in traditional wedding vows I'm going to object to, isn't there?"

She narrowed her eyes at him when he looked innocent. She didn't trust that expression on his face for one minute.

"Everyone exchanges vows in a marriage ceremony, sweetheart."

He turned away from her but not before she saw he was fighting laughter. Definitely the vows. "I'm going to write my own vows." She declared it as she began shaping a shield out of some thin metal strips she'd found. She'd washed the strips over and over, but they were perfect, thin enough to bend into the shapes she needed. She wasn't clever like his mother, cutting it after the pancake was made. She needed a mold, even one of her own making.

She'd already put on coffee and the aroma mixed with the smell of the bacon and eggs she was frying. "You can set the table," she called over his shoulder as she worked on the pancakes.

"I'm an old-fashioned kind of man, Shylah," he protested as he pulled the two plates off the rack and put them on the table with silverware. He poured both of them a glass of orange juice and then himself a cup of coffee. "Those ceremonial vows have been around for hundreds of years." He looked far too earnest to be believable.

Clearly, she should have been researching marriage vows. She flashed him a look meant to intimidate him, but he only grinned at her. That grin sent a flutter of need through her sex and a shiver of excitement down her spine. The man did it for her. He didn't have to do much more than smirk and she was lost. She shook her head, unable to keep from smiling, and turned back to finishing the pancakes. She'd warmed up the syrup Joe had sent, hoping that's what one did with maple syrup. She'd never had it before, but she'd tasted it and it was good. Sweet, but good.

She put the eggs and bacon on the table in front of him and then carried the pancakes, butter and syrup over. She added the small little story about two fiery dragons willing to sacrifice everything to save those they loved. Strangely, her heart was pounding. What if he didn't like that she'd copied his mother? What if he didn't understand making his pancakes into a shield was meant as a gift for their wedding day? She didn't have much to give him and this was the only way she could think of that might include his mother in their wedding.

Holding her breath, she put the plate of pancakes right in front of him and then put the warm syrup and butter next to his coffee. She could barely force herself to look at him, but she did. His eyes were on the stack of shields with the two dragons and the words carved into them. She'd made shallow indentations, and some were better than others. The metal strips had been used for the shield and dragons, although truthfully, her dragons didn't come out as well as she would have liked. The words were hand done.

His face had gone pure stone. He didn't say a word, just stared down at the pancakes for what seemed an eternity. Then swallowed hard. Blinked several times and finally, slowly, very slowly, lifted his gaze to hers. "Shylah." He breathed her name. Barely above a whisper.

"You like it." She made it a statement because he clearly did. She leaned down and brushed a kiss on his temple. "I wanted her here with us today, and I couldn't think of any other way to give that to you."

She turned to make her way around the small table to her chair, but Draden wrapped his arm around her waist holding her there beside him and turned, so he was facing out away from the table. He tugged until she was between his thighs and he could press his head against her stomach, both arms circling her waist. She wrapped her arms around his head, emotion choking her. The intensity of love she had for Draden was overwhelming.

Shylah held him, the man who was always so strong. So confident and sure. The man she'd fallen so hard for and didn't even know when it happened or how. Tremors ran through him, so fine she barely felt them, but because it was Draden and she registered all things Draden, she felt them. She stroked caresses through his hair, feeling her own eyes burn. They were one step closer to being together permanently, and one step closer to death.

Finally, he lifted his head, his eyes staring into hers. There was liquid turning that dark blue into a fathomless sea. There was also stark, raw love looking back at her. Even though she had never experienced that kind of deep, intense emotion from a man, she recognized it and her heart turned over. The burn of tears in her eyes was nearly overwhelming. She had to blink rapidly.

"Thank you, sweetheart. I can't imagine a better gift." He reached up to capture the nape of her neck, applying pressure so she had to bend down. "Mine will be in the closet, so no peeking."

His hands framed her face, his touch tender. His mouth took hers, and instantly the fire between them flared hot and bright. In contrast to the gentle way he cradled her face, his mouth was rough, demanding, a takeover. She couldn't think when he was kissing her over and over. Devouring her. There was only feeling, the arcing electricity that jumped between them, the spread of heat that rushed through her bloodstream, the melting that made her feel boneless. His mouth was pure fire and there was nothing better.

When he broke the kisses, his gaze moved over her face and then he pressed his forehead against hers. "In case I haven't said so, I'm so in love with you."

"The feeling is mutual." She was astonished she managed to get the words out when her body had spiraled completely out of control. She wanted him with every breath she drew.

He held her for another minute, as if he knew she clung to him because her legs were unsteady, and her knees were wobbly. Eventually she took a deep breath and made it to the chair opposite. It took effort to slide into it with dignity instead of just plopping into it before she fell.

"Taste them before you get too excited." She needed to find a way to bring down the intensity of emotion filling the room. "I followed the recipe on the package Joe sent. They might not be edible."

"It really wouldn't matter to me one way or the other. Shylah, do you realize no one has ever done anything like this for me? No one. Not since she died. I've never received a present in my life, and certainly not one like this."

She smiled at him, feeling shy. She'd been so afraid she was stepping on a wonderful memory. She watched him take a bite and then he was smiling and indicating for her to eat.

She was expecting the pancakes and syrup to taste like cardboard, but they actually tasted really good — good enough that they might be a favorite if she lived long enough to have more than one meal of them.

"It's weird, Draden, but I don't feel sick at all this morning. Not like last night."

"And the rash isn't worse? It didn't spread?"

She shook her head. "No, it faded. It almost looks like it's just under the skin, and it's definitely not burning like it did last night."

Something moved across his face. Hope? She couldn't tell. Maybe they both needed hope. The virus could take longer to incubate than either of them thought, but if that was the case, how had it killed an entire village so quickly? No one had escaped that they could see. That meant it had to bring its victims down fast.

"I'll take blood samples, our temperatures and pictures of the rash to send to Trap. He shares with the others working to deconstruct the virus. I talked to Trap last night. Well, not Trap. He grunts a lot and ignores me. I talked with Wyatt. They think they're close. With the notes Whitney's three virologists left behind in the computer, they had a jump start on it."

She took a bite of the bacon and eggs and chewed, watching his face. Draden was easily the handsomest man she'd ever seen. It was difficult to imagine him in the service, particularly the GhostWalker program. He had rugged good looks, so it wasn't that, but he belonged on a poster hanging on the wall, not in an Indonesian forest waiting to die.

She looked down at the small stack of pancakes on her plate with the two dragons on them. Draden and Shylah. In her mind, those mythical creatures represented the two of them and the fire between them. When they had to, they could do battle, but when they weren't committed to a fight, they were together, the shared fire between them.

Draden got her laughing before the end of breakfast and she didn't even know how. He did it so easily, telling her funny stories of Trap and Cayenne. How they were both so antisocial, yet so devoted to each other. He talked about Nonny and the other members of his team. He made them each so alive and vivid, she felt as if she knew them and could recognize the individuals without an introduction.

She told him of her escapades with Bellisia, Zara, stories of deliberate defiance and pranks, sometimes on Whitney. Zara thought up most of the mischief, but it was Bellisia and Shylah who carried it out. She loved watching him laugh.

"You have to tell me about these traditional marriage vows, Draden." She wanted to share whatever he was up to with her "sisters." She planned on leaving them a letter and she wanted it to be funny and upbeat.

Draden sent her another mischievous grin. "There's a little line that says you will honor and obey me."

She blinked, her lashes hiding her eyes for moment while she thought that over. "Is that true? Did women say that to their husbands?"

He nodded. "I'm teasing you, Shylah, I don't expect obedience. Honor maybe, but you're independent and you think for yourself."

"Do you think the words really meant that a woman had to obey her husband?"

"I don't know what other people's interpretation is, but for me, you should just be you. Say what's in your heart. That will be enough for me."

She loved him all the more for that, for the sincerity in his voice. He had been teasing her, but he made it clear hearing her vow to obey him wasn't at all what he wanted. She wasn't going to have a single regret for her decision to marry him.

When they finished, they did the dishes

together and then he photographed the rash, frowning as he did so. "I can't believe it's faded this quickly. It looks more like an allergic reaction than a reaction to the virus. You were lying in grass and then on the roof. The roof was made of some kind of leaves. It's possible you were having an allergy attack, Shylah, not showing early stage symptoms of the virus."

She shook her head. "Trap told you I was infected."

He ignored that, his frown deepening as his fingers moved over her lymph nodes. "A little swollen, but nothing like last night. You ate."

"I was very hungry when I woke up this morning," she confirmed.

"You still have a slight fever."

He took her blood efficiently and then his own. He inspected the site where the dart had entered his thigh. It was clean. No redness. "Do you have a headache?"

She shook her head. "What about you?"

"It's definitely better. I thought my head might fall off a couple of days there, but it's hurting a lot less. More like a regular nagging headache than my head is about to explode."

"You had a concussion, Doc." She couldn't stop the grin. "I don't have a fancy degree with a million letters surrounding my name, but I did a better diagnosis than you."

She didn't want to let herself hope, but it was impossible not to have that sudden flare. She didn't look at him, but kept her gaze fixed on what he was doing. He was very thorough in taking mouth swabs and blood. He was meticulous in documenting exactly what their temperatures were and adding pictures of her rash and the entry site on his leg. He was painstakingly scrupulous about everything, unhurried, taking the time to double-check everything.

"I have no idea what's going on, my beautiful little perfect peony, but those birds did bring us good luck. Maybe there's something to that little whispered rumor after all." Using the satellite Azami Yoshiie had made available to them, he sent off the data to Joe and Trap and then put the samples away, so he could give them to Joe when he arrived. "Stay inside while I get things ready outside," Draden cautioned.

For some reason his comment about getting things ready outside wiped out the terror at the thought of infection and the small flare of hope this morning's findings had given her, replacing it with thoughts of their wedding. Of marrying Draden. Her heart beat overtime all over again, and she nodded. "I've done my flyaway hair as best I could and unfortunately, jeans are all I have. No makeup either." She touched her mouth a little self-consciously.

"I've taken care of that. Joe's bringing a dress and makeup and my wedding gift to you. I'll get it to you immediately."

Her heart jumped at the possibility. "A dress? As in a wedding dress?"

"A more traditional dress for a Buddhist wedding. You're going to love it, Shylah. I sent Joe several examples and let them choose which one. I think he was consulting Bellisia and Zara. You'll have a beautiful dress." He made a little grimace. "They're also sending me a traditional outfit as well. I thought if we were doing the ceremony, we should do it right."

She hugged herself, happy that Bellisia and Zara had contributed in some way, however small. She wasn't going to let anything mar this day. Not one single thing. "I love the idea. I know we have to do this ceremony, but how do we make it legal?"

"There will be a civil one as well and Joe will take care of that end of it. He made me the promise, and Joe never lets anything stop him when he wants something. He'll make certain it's legal."

In spite of her assessment of Joe after he'd reprimanded Draden so harshly over saving the tiger, she was beginning to think he was a good man and an even better friend. "That's good."

"Stay inside, Shylah."

She wanted to smile at the note of command in his voice. He did that a lot. By now, he knew from their time together and the stories she'd told about her relationship with Whitney that she tended to decide for herself what she wanted to obey and what she wouldn't. This time it was easy to nod her head in agreement.

Draden worked hard on the bower surrounding the door to the lab. He had already twisted the fig branches together. He used green, leafy vines to bind the branches and then filled them with fresh orchids. The arbor looked amazing by the time the helicopter got there and Joe emerged along with three other soldiers, all wearing hazmat suits. Even that didn't deter his happiness.

The supplies kept coming; everything he'd asked for, Joe had managed to find. He handed Joe the samples of blood and saliva and then saluted, agreeing once again on the time of the ceremony. That was critical.

He needed the rest of the time to set everything up and then get ready himself.

Draden decided the small wedding cake couldn't be a surprise because he wanted it in the cabin's refrigerator rather than in the lab. He took Shylah her dress and the cake. His present for her was already wrapped and he put that in the closet and ordered her not to touch it. Then he went to work. The first thing he did was set up cameras so that those watching the ceremony could see his bride walking toward him just as he would see her. He set up screens, so she could see Bellisia and Zara were there with her.

He went at each task the way he did everything, working fast until it was done. He decorated the inside of the lab. He'd already put equipment away and now he hung the large reed woven mats in colors of deep rose, red, black, green and yellow on the walls, draping them so that they covered every dingy nook and cranny. He put up the small shrine to Buddha in keeping with tradition. He placed the candles, incense, the small statue of Buddha and a floating garden of peonies at the far end where they were in plain sight of the cameras, so the observers could see they were following the Buddhist tradition as closely as possible. Joe had told him the monks would give them their blessing and an official would make certain they exchanged their vows properly.

After transforming the small room as best he could, he glanced at the time. He was cutting it close. He had just enough time to shower and get dressed. When he got back to the cabin, he knocked to make certain she knew he was coming in.

Shylah's hair was swept up in a swirling updo with tendrils falling inevitably out. It was impossible to tame her hair completely, and he liked that. He thought she looked sexy with the heavy gold bracelets adorning her arms and the necklace of fiery rubies around her neck to match the red of her nails. She wore only a tee, so he wouldn't see her in her wedding dress.

Mindful of the time, he showered, taking a few extra minutes for himself under the cool water. He didn't want to get there too early and blow their time with the others. He dressed in his brocade gold *bhaku,* rich with tiny red embroidered protections scattered artfully, the shirt with sleeves that fell to his ankles. His waistcoat was ivory brocade with beautiful golden embroidery outlining it. His trousers matched the golden *bhaku.* It was strange to dress so differently, but the clothes made him feel formal and that the ceremony had weight to it. He wanted that for Shylah. Something memorable whether they lived or not.

He glanced at the time. "Don't forget that after the actual ceremony, we have to do the paperwork with the clerks. That will make it legal. Use your name. Peony Cosmos."

They had settled on Cosmos because that was the last name Bellisia and Zara had helped her choose when she was sent out of the compound.

"I want this to be legal. It's important to me. The government is cooperating because of our sacrifice." He winced when he said it. He didn't want to think about dying, only living with her.

"You explained the process. We'll get it done." She smiled at him, a smile of reassurance. "I want our marriage to be legal as well."

He loved her all the more for that. "I want you out there in ten, Shylah. Make your way to the lab precisely at six. When you're near the lab, I'll start the music for your walk to me."

She nodded, her eyes bright. His heart turned over. He had started out marrying her because it was what *he* wanted, but now he wanted this day, this ceremony for her. She'd given him a wonderful gift, bringing his mother to his wedding day, now he wanted to give her something equally as special.

He brushed a kiss on her cheek, careful of the makeup artfully used. As a rule, she wore no makeup and he thought she was the most beautiful woman in the world without it, but he'd been in the fashion world and knew makeup was a woman's armor. "You look beautiful."

"I'm not dressed yet."

"You look beautiful."

"You look sharp. The material is wonderful. And I love the color."

He wasn't a purple or red kind of man. Gold was the only color he would consider when it came to the traditional garb of the groom. He hurried out, thinking he should be nervous, but he'd never been surer of anything in his life.

Back at the lab turned wedding gazebo, he tested the cameras a final time to make certain they were working, then completed the video connections to Zara in Montana and Bellisia in Louisiana. Teams One and Two were in Montana with Zara. They were all watching, some standing, some sitting, but all crowding in to watch the ceremony. He spotted Nonny and even Cayenne sitting on either side of Pepper, each holding one of Wyatt's little girls in their laps. To his astonishment, the third team, the urban GhostWalker unit out of San Francisco, were also there.

In Louisiana, Draden's team had all assembled, Ezekiel and Bellisia in the front. To his surprise, the men were in their dress uniforms. For some reason that brought a lump to his throat and he found himself swallowing several times.

Lastly, he conferenced in the video feed there in Sumatra. Trap and Wyatt stood with Joe and the monk and the high-ranking officer from the Indonesian government officiating over the service in Indonesia. Behind them were the other members of his GhostWalker team: Diego, Gino and Malichai. Draden knew they were somewhere, set up quite close. Trap almost never wore his dress uniform and it was shocking not only to see him there, but that he, like the other members of his team there in Sumatra, was dressed for the occasion.

He was surprised that several of the members of the Kopassus were there. He saw all eyes turn past him and without looking, he knew she was there by the reaction. He switched on the music and slowly turned to look at his bride.

His heart nearly stopped and then began

to pound. Shylah emerged in her beautiful finery. Her *bhaku* was lace and ivory, the sleeves long and the neckline a golden lacy choke collar. The rubies at her throat matched the tiny red embroidered protections scattered in the lace of her *bhaku,* just as they were in his jacket. Her sarong was pure shimmering gold matching the gold lace of her top. Dazzling rubies blazed at her ears and thick gold bracelets gleamed on her wrists.

She wore a headdress of gold with crimson gems woven in. She'd painted her nails and lips a matching scarlet and accented her eyes with a dark charcoal, enhancing her natural beauty. She robbed him of his breath. He forgot everyone watching and just stared in admiring fascination at her. Unexpected emotions choked him. He'd never thought, not once, that he would ever find a woman of his own.

Then Shylah was coming toward him on the path he'd made for her with his own two hands. The path was scattered with orchids and peonies, the flowers he'd cut in the forest and the ones Joe had brought to him. His own little peony. He was mad, crazy in love with her. She had the bouquet he'd left for her. He had made it himself, using the white and red roses Joe had brought, embedding them in a sea of peonies. He stood under the arbor he'd painstakingly built for her.

By the time she climbed the steps to him, he could barely breathe. He took her hand and led her inside to the shrine. He'd studied the traditions, and he bowed and picked up the matchsticks. He lit half the candles and incense and handed Shylah the long matchsticks so she could light the rest. When that was done, he turned to the basket of flowers he'd collected, and the remaining ones Joe had given him, and they offered the flowers to Buddha.

He turned her toward the cameras, and for the first time she saw the screens and the people watching. He knew the exact moment when she saw the familiar faces she most longed for. Her breath hitched, and she looked up at him, blinking back tears. Zara covered her mouth and bit back a sob. Bellisia pressed her head against Zeke and closed her eyes briefly, attempting a shaky smile when she opened them. To Draden's shock, his fellow team members were visibly shaken, even Trap, the stoic, expressionless friend he loved like a brother.

Draden took Shylah's hand as both bowed their heads for the monk's blessing. Once the prayers were complete, they faced each other as the official asked them to recite their vows.

Draden cleared his throat. "I've lived a lifetime in the last few days, and no time in my life has ever been better. I give you my heart, Shylah."

He couldn't look away from her, his entire attention riveted on her. Love was welling up so strong, he could hardly bear it. "I promise you that no matter where our journey takes us, I'll be at your side."

He choked up and had to breathe deeply to continue. All the while he stared down into her dark eyes, drowning there. Going willingly. "I'll be faithful and always supportive of you, putting you and our family first in my thoughts and in everything I do. I will always be yours and stand by you in sickness and in health."

The catch in her breath and the tears glistening in her eyes was nearly his undoing, but he held it together by a thread. His voice was clear in his declaration because he meant every word. "If tomorrow never comes, today has been all I've ever wanted or needed. You are my life. And you will be after I've taken my last breath."

He wanted to believe in another life where he could have his woman for more than the short time it appeared they had left, but if he didn't ever get that, he would celebrate every second with her now.

Shylah looked up at him, her eyes swimming in liquid, making them so dark brown they looked like chocolate. "I love you with all my heart, Draden, and I'll always be your woman. You made me dare to dream, to feel real emotion. You make me laugh when the world is crashing in on me. You showed me what love was when I had no real idea."

She swallowed hard and a tear like a beautiful diamond dripped down her face. Her voice was soft but clear. Trembling but firm. "I take you as my husband and promise I'll be faithful and always at your side throughout our life together, whether that's in sickness or in health."

Her voice shook and Draden stepped closer to her, tightening his hold on her hands. The little tremor sweeping through her body made him want to gather her close and shelter her for all time in his heart.

Shylah took a deep breath to get control. "This love may not have the luxury of burning long, but it will burn bright. You will always be the man for me, the true love of my life."

The look she gave him was radiant, although tearful. He slipped the ring on her finger, the one he wanted there because he was a traditional kind of man. Who knew? He gave her the ring to put on his finger. When he worked, he probably wouldn't be wearing it, at least not on his finger, but he'd have it on a chain around his neck.

They were pronounced man and wife, and then he was kissing her, vaguely hearing the cheers in the background. She had given herself to him as fully as he'd given himself to her.

15

After talking with all their friends via computer, Draden gathered his woman into his arms and kissed her thoroughly again before dancing to the music playing in the background. Holding her in his arms, close to him, gave him a sense of peace, or rightness, and brought every cell in his body alive.

"It's a damn good thing I'm wearing this jacket," he declared, pulling her even closer as he whirled her around the room. "I wouldn't want to put all the soldiers on alert."

She laughed, the sound more like music than the song playing. She had removed the headdress for the dance and her hair was tangling in the stubble already growing on his jaw, although he'd shaved that morning. He loved that, the way those gleaming strands wove them together. He'd never believed in soul mates until he'd found her.

She was it for him. She always would be.

"I rather like the idea that you want me."

He heard the little note that didn't ever belong in her voice. The one that said she wasn't as confident as she let on. He looked down at her. "Look at me, sweetheart."

She kept her head pressed against his chest for a moment, clearly gathering courage, and then her eyes met his. Shyness was there for certain. Where before she'd been a bold seductress, now she was unsure of herself. Had he done that?

"I've wanted you every minute of every day. Sometimes, baby, it was pure hell keeping my hands off you. I held out hope you didn't have the virus. You weren't exhibiting a single symptom while I was. I know we kissed and that should have cemented the fact that you were infected, but I couldn't be sure. If I'd acted on the way I felt, and I was the cause of your death, that would have been the worst possible thing I could imagine. Loving you and causing you to die. I wasn't getting worse, and I knew they pumped me full of that shit. There was a chance I was fighting it off."

"So, you decided you had to protect me." Her long lashes fanned her cheek, drawing his attention to her delicate bone structure and the smattering of freckles that he wanted to kiss one by one.

"Absolutely I did." He couldn't help himself — it was sheer indulgence, but he did kiss every freckle of gold that matched the gleaming metal at her throat.

"You're so crazy, and you missed a few big opportunities."

The teasing note slid down his spine like fingers. His cock reacted, growing harder. The ache was becoming a distinct pain. "We've got to go. Get out of here. I need you alone."

"I'm not protesting." Her eyes took on a mischievous glint and that quirky mouth of hers gave him a million ideas. "I'm the one who practiced all sorts of things and I believe you're going to benefit from my studies."

"We're out of here," he said to the camera.

A cheer went up, and he made a point of waving at them to let them know he'd been waiting long enough to be alone with her. It was all he could think about. Shylah teasing him only made him need her that much more. He shut down the cameras and music and held out his hand. Shylah placed hers in his without hesitation.

Night had fallen while they were inside, and the sounds were soothing after all the noise of conversations and well-wishers.

Neither of them had been around other people for a few days, and he hadn't realized how they lived with just the sounds of the forest. He was used to the swamp sounds, which meant he spent more time in it than out of it.

"I want the chance to show you my home. The swamp is beautiful in its own way, Shylah. I like being away from everyone, all the noise that drowns out the sounds, that brings peace. I go out at night and run so I'm part of what's out there, instead of being locked indoors."

He took his time, enjoying walking with her close to him. The moon spilled down on them, making the gold in her dress shimmer and gleam. Every now and then a beam caught on the rubies at her throat and ears, turning the gems into fiery blazes. Even that caused a reaction in his body. He forced himself to walk slowly, to take in everything, to memorize each moment with her. He never wanted to forget even the smallest detail about their day.

"Thank you for this, Draden. I have no idea how you pulled this off, but it was the most beautiful, amazing day any woman could possibly wish for."

He brought her hand to his mouth and kissed her knuckles. "I wanted you to have a wedding day, Shylah. You deserved it."

"You brought Zara and Bellisia to the ceremony."

"I can perform magic once in a while." They moved together on the narrow path leading to the ranger's cabin. It was in sight now, the moon giving it a kind of halo in the high humidity. The air felt sultry. Hot. Or maybe it was his need of her. He wanted out of his clothes, and he wanted her out of that beautiful, formfitting dress.

On the porch of the ranger's cabin were two cases clearly holding food. As another surprise, Joe had catered a small dinner for the two of them and the cases had been set on the porch of the ranger's cabin by two soldiers dressed in hazmat suits. They were long gone before Draden and Shylah arrived.

Draden picked up Shylah, skirted the cases and opened the door. He carried her over the threshold, promising himself if they got back to the swamp, he would do it again to officially welcome her to their home. She settled her arms around his neck and when he went to put her on her feet, she kissed him.

He was already hot and the moment her lips moved against his, his head seemed to explode. He barely managed to kick the door closed before he was carefully undoing the *bhaku* and casting it aside, still kissing her. Over and over. He couldn't stop. Couldn't get enough of her. He managed, while he kissed her, to shrug out of the jacket and his own *bhaku,* leaving just his golden trousers. If he wanted her, he had to lift his head and take care of business, but his mouth had other ideas.

Shylah was left with just the golden sarong and the ruby necklace and earrings. Her skin had a glow to it. Shylah had high firm breasts, full and rounded, and he didn't hesitate. Both hands cupped the soft weight and he kissed his way down her chin to her left breast. She tasted like heaven.

"Take the sarong off, sweetheart, and then my trousers." He wasn't going to sacrifice one minute of having her body to a mundane task, although removing her clothes could be sexy as hell under any other circumstances. He toed off the loafers he'd worn to speed up the process of getting rid of anything between the two of them.

Shylah gasped when his fingers tugged at her right nipple while his tongue and teeth worked her left. Her breath hitched and then rushed out with a little keening cry that got him right in the cock.

"Hurry." It was a command. An order.

Almost a plea, but he felt her hands drop to his trousers, loosening them so they would drop around his ankles where he could kick them off.

She stepped out of her sarong, leaving her in nothing but her gold and ivory heels and the rubies and gold bracelets on her wrists. She hadn't bothered with underwear. It was too hot, and they were constantly washing out clothing. He kissed his way down to her belly button. He spent time there, licking along that sweet treasure before lifting her to carry her to the bed, under the large overhead fan.

He hadn't turned on any lights, but he didn't need them. The moon was nearly full, and the cabin was surrounded with windows on every wall, so the silvery light spilled across the bed and her body. He came down over her, framing her face and kissing her again. Devouring her fire. That mouth promised paradise and then delivered in the form of flames.

Then he was at her breasts again, this time leaving his mark. She cradled his head and arched her back, giving him full access to her without hesitation. Her soft cries of encouragement fed his hunger. His hands couldn't stop moving over her, shaping every curve, taking his time, memorizing her so that he'd know her body anywhere, light or dark, she was imprinted on his brain.

He wanted his last memories to be of this, the softness of her skin, the sounds she made, the way her fingers felt in his hair as she held him to her. Shylah was perfection, her body moving under his. The soft cries she made, those sounds he wanted to hear in his mind before the end came.

Her fingers stroked along his back, sending waves of pleasure down his spine. Then they pressed deep and her nails were biting into him as his teeth scraped and his tongue stroked. He kissed his way down her body, using hands and mouth to know every inch of her intimately. Her legs were slender and went on forever. He especially loved that about her. It felt to him as if he could wrap his hands around her thighs and he did just that, pulling them apart, giving him access to what he wanted.

His first taste was amazing. Exquisite. Wintergreen. Delicate. Her entire body jerked and shuddered. A little gasp escaped, and he glanced up to look at her sprawled out on the bed before him like a feast. Her face was flushed. Her full breasts swayed enticingly with every movement. Her hips bucked, the long legs bent and spread wide, his hands clamped there like shackles around her thighs. Her lips were parted, breath coming in ragged gasps, the color sweeping up her body to her face. The gold around her throat and wrists gleamed in the moonlight and the fiery gems blazed at him.

He would never forget the sight of her, waiting for him. Eyes a little dazed. The sound of her soft keening surrounding him. She didn't plead out loud, but he saw the aching hunger in her eyes. She didn't know what she wanted, but he did. He settled between her thighs and licked up the inside of her leg. His teeth scraped and then nipped. Her hips bucked hard.

"Settle, my beautiful wife." He breathed warm air across those honeyed curls. "I intend to indulge myself. I've waited a very long time for you, and I'm going to make sure you're just as needy as I am." He wanted to make certain everything he did brought her pleasure.

"I'm not complaining." Her voice shook. So did her body.

He took his time, nuzzling her, pulling her erotic scent into his lungs. There was the elusive perfume he had come to associate with her. Wintergreen. Peonies. His personal peony. His tongue moved over her, swirled around her clit and then, when she gasped, plunged deep. She cried out and he took advantage of his strength, holding her thighs open so he could feast. He created a suction cup with his tongue, and then flattened it.

Draden was careful to be gentle, giving her time to get used to the unfamiliar sensations racing through her. Several times she cried out and her hips bucked ferociously, her breathing more ragged than ever, encouraging him to continue. Each time it happened, he added a little something more. His tongue. His hand cupping her. Fingers circling her. Thumb flicking. Every stroke took her higher. Gave him more liquid honey.

Love welled up, mixing with lust, a shocking turn-on that shook him past anything he'd ever felt before. Each stroke of his hand on her soft skin, the taste of her in his mouth, the way she filled his mind, made him feel complete. The intensity of feeling every single sensation rushing through his body when he was so utterly focused on her, determined to give her the best possible experience, only brought him more pleasure than he'd ever known.

Each time she got close, he backed off. He needed her desperate. She was tight. Too tight, and he wasn't a small man. He waited until the sounds she made were little chanting demands. Her body was flushed and moving without direction, always seeking his mouth and fingers — his strumming thumb. She thrust with every rhythm he created. Only then did he take her over. She went hard, the orgasm sweeping through her, ripping like a powerful tidal wave.

Her low, keening cry sent heat spiraling through his body and a rush of desire down his spine. He was on his knees, his cock lodged in her. He needed to see her eyes and she opened them, shock on her face as he steadily pushed through those tight, hotter than hell muscles. Her body reluctantly gave way, opening for him when he demanded.

Already the friction was so much it was scalding. Fiery. A velvet fist gripping him hard and squeezing rhythmically. He hit the thin barrier and felt her wince for the first time. He gripped her hips and surged through while her body was still rippling with the aftereffects of her orgasm.

Shylah gasped, her mouth forming a round O. Her eyes went hazy. He stopped moving and she instantly protested, thrusting up to impale herself on his cock. He filled her, stretching that tight channel, closing his eyes to savor the feeling of being inside her. Paradise. He'd known that was what she'd feel like.

He was gentle, taking his time, each stroke a long, slow build to send streaks of fire racing through her. He lifted her bottom, his hands on her hips, guiding her as he moved in her. Every surge forward jolted her breasts, so they swayed and danced, heightening his pleasure. Her stomach muscles rippled with life. Her breath came in ragged explosions and her eyes went wide and dazed. He was a visual man. Seeing his woman with that dazed, almost shocked pleasure on her face, feeling her response, her body moving with his, those tight muscles massaging a burning friction into the shaft of his cock, heightened the sensations racing through his body.

Draden moved a little faster, thrusting deep and hard. Fire streaked up his cock and spread through his belly. She matched his rhythm as if born for sex with him. He couldn't look away from the beauty of her face. The way it was flushed and sexy. The way she watched him as if he were the center of her universe.

"You good?" He needed her to say it. His body was making demands, feeling the ferocious fire building between them.

"More than good."

He took her at her word and began to move the way he needed, holding her hips, fingers digging deep as he surged into her over and over, deep, hard thrusts that sent lightning crashing through him as her tight channel gripped and milked with greedy determination and strength. His cock swelled and pushed at the soft tissue, adding to the exquisite friction.

He felt her body ripple, a delicious warning and then her sex clamped down on his so tightly he could barely move, strangling his cock, working it, determined to get every drop of his seed. Heat spread through him like wildfire. His cock kept swelling, fighting back against the tight restriction. He kept moving, chasing the lightning, letting it have him. His balls were on fire, twin roiling cauldrons drawing up tight. His body strained, from his toes to his head. Then his cock was jerking hard, emptying itself into her, coating the walls of her sheath so the burn was scorching beyond what he'd ever known.

Her body took his like a tsunami, sweeping them both out and away, tossing them into a star-studded galaxy, while her tight, hot channel continued to work him, draining him dry and leaving him absolutely spent with sheer pleasure. He collapsed over top of her and the action sent another strong ripple through both of them.

His lungs burned. Hers had to, but he couldn't move, letting her take his weight for several long moments while he fought for air. She didn't protest, although he knew he weighed enough to crush the air from her lungs. He loved the feel of her soft body under his. It felt as if she'd melted into him and they wore the same skin.

His lips found her throat and then moved up to nibble at her chin, her dimple and finally her mouth to take the last of her air. Only then did he find the strength to rise up on his elbows, his hands framing her face.

"I love you, Shylah Freeman. With everything I am, with everything in me." Ordinarily he might feel ridiculous saying something like that to a woman, but it was the truth and he felt compelled to give her that. "You're never going to have cause to think you made a mistake."

"I know that, honey," she whispered back. "I absolutely believe in you — in us. We're good together."

"Whitney may be a complete madman and an absolute fucking wreck of a human being, but he gave me you," Draden said. "I'd still put a bullet in his head, but I'd thank him first."

Shylah muffled her laughter against his shoulder. "That sounds like you. I'd be right there with you."

"Are you starving? You haven't eaten since breakfast."

"I am, but I don't think I can move."

He gave a little groan as he rolled off of her. His cock slid free and sensations shook him as the sensitive organ pulled free of her tight grip on him. "That feels so damn good, baby. Unbelievable."

"Mmmhmm." The sound was both amused and an agreement. "I'm going to just lie here, but I think I've sprung a leak and our bed is going to be a mess. Still, I'm not moving."

He forced himself to sit up. His legs felt shaky, but his body was buzzing with life. So alive. Every cell. "I'll get something to clean you up and then we're eating, because as soon as possible, we're doing this again."

She rolled onto her side to watch him get a washcloth wet with warm water. Propping her chin on her hand, she regarded him steadily. "How soon?"

"Don't know. Minutes. Hours. Depends. That was pretty wild. But just looking at you gives me a rush." It was the damned truth. She was staring hungrily at his cock.

Just the way she was looking at him with such enthusiasm and demand sent heat spiraling through his groin. "Put your knee up, sweetheart."

Draden caught her knee himself and gently washed between her legs, reluctantly removing his seed from her. He hadn't realized he would want to see that evidence of his possession gleaming on her thighs, or how much it would turn him on all over again. She lay looking up at him, her face soft, eyes on him, but she didn't speak.

He took her hand, his thumb sliding over his ring on her finger. As far as he was concerned, it was the perfect ring for her. He'd wanted a fancy red diamond for her. The one he'd chosen was purplish red surrounded by small white diamonds. He would never tell her what it cost because she'd never wear it if she knew, but he'd had that vision in his head for her ring. Red matched the fire in her. On his wedding ring there was a single tiny matching diamond, because he wanted her brand on him.

The pad of his thumb moved back and forth over the ring, and all the while he looked down at it. "You happy with this choice?"

"I love it. I've never seen anything like it."

He tugged until she stood up. She was a

little wobbly at first, and he wrapped his arm around her waist. "We need to eat."

"I think you're right. I'm starving, but I'm too weak to make it to the table." She rubbed her face on his chest like a cat.

He caught her hair in his hand, crushing the silky strands into his palm. "I love you, Shylah. Thank you for marrying me. It was important to me."

"It was to me as well."

She looked up at him again, all wide-eyed, something close to adoration on her face. His heart stuttered in his chest. To have a woman like Shylah looking at him with that expression was almost more than a man could take. He took her mouth because he was helpless to do anything else. Around her, he was certain, he wasn't going to have a tremendous amount of control.

He kissed her, tasting love in her kisses. Fire. Her passion for him was every bit as strong or stronger than her passion for life. She lived life large, and clearly and she loved him with that same intensity, as he loved her. Shylah didn't hold back. She wasn't coy or embarrassed about showing him how she felt, and that was more of a turn-on for him than anything else ever could be. She wanted him, and she let him know she did.

When he lifted his head again, his gaze blazing down into hers, she gave him that same little rub on his chest with her face, a cat purring her love. "I need to get dressed, but it feels like too much effort. I think my arms and legs have turned into spaghetti."

"You don't need clothes to eat dinner with me," Draden pointed out.

She looked a little scandalized. "You want me to sit at the dinner table nude?"

"You're wearing heels and jewelry. I don't think you need anything else." He grinned at her. "Are you afraid the neighbors are going to stop by unexpectedly?"

"Is this going to be a regular thing? Dinner and no clothes?"

He nodded slowly, his eyes moving over her body. He'd never get enough of looking at her. "We might lose a few dishes now and then when I sweep them on the floor and have you for dessert."

Her tongue darted out to moisten her lips. "I suppose sacrificing a few dishes isn't such a bad idea." She took a step toward the cases he had opened. "What did Joe send us?"

He pulled out the dishes. Two beautiful white plates rimmed with gold. Crystal champagne flutes rimmed with gold. Gold silverware. A white tablecloth with golden threads woven through it. He handed it to her, and she smoothed it over the little wooden table. Her hands lingered over it.

"Draden, this is so perfect. I can't believe you did this for us." Tears shimmered in her eyes, and his heart clenched.

"I can't take credit for the dinner. The team sent the rest to us." He handed her the plates and stemware. "Which means Joe."

The bucket of ice with the chilled champagne bottle in it he placed on the table himself. The food smelled and looked amazing. The heated plates were covered in silver warmers and Draden placed the items on the china. Prawns served in ginger and lime sauce were in one server. Filet mignon, potato and mushrooms in another and grilled asparagus in a third. At once the aroma filled the room and he found himself starving.

He seated her in the chair across from his, leaning down to kiss the vulnerable nape of her neck before opening the champagne and pouring it into the two flutes. Her fingers brushed his semihard cock and, just like that, his body responded.

"You do want to eat our wedding dinner, don't you?" He put the flute into her hands.

She nodded, but her eyes were on his

groin. Her tongue slid out and she licked her lips. "I don't know. I think so. You look like dessert to me."

She was deliberately putting images in his head, building them carefully with erotic, descriptive words. He could see them in her head and that had never happened before — *seeing* instead of hearing. Her fingers were already settling over his hip and urging him closer to her chair as she took a sip of the bubbly golden liquid. Not once did her eyes look up. He knew better, but he allowed her to pull his body in close. His cock had grown as hard as a rock.

"Baby," he cautioned.

She ignored him and leaned forward, her breath on the smooth, now throbbing head. Her tongue slipped out to taste him. A cautious foray. Just that took his breath. She got bolder and licked, as one would an ice cream cone. Without warning, her tongue swirled around the sensitive head and then she licked from base to tip. Her hands cupped his balls, gently squeezing and then her mouth was there, exploring, sucking gently.

Draden was certain his head was going to explode. He put down his champagne flute before he forgot he had it in his hand and caught her hair gently with his fists. Gripping. Not guiding. She didn't need guidance: she wanted to be in charge. To explore. He gave her that because her tongue was talented, and every stroke had little explosions going off in his cock.

Then her mouth engulfed him, and he was in a tight, hot, wet tunnel, her tongue swirling up and down his shaft and then flicking the tip, rimming it and then going back to the base with that swirling motion that kept left him without a brain. Her tongue flicked under the crown, hitting the exact spot that threatened to end everything before it began.

She pulled her mouth off of him to wrap one hand around his cock while she took a mouthful of champagne. He stood above her, and she had to lean again to reach him. Keeping the champagne in her mouth, she sucked him gently into that hot tunnel. At once, bubbles burst around his shaft and the sensitive head. He'd never felt the sensation before and it felt like a thousand tongues lapped at him. He couldn't help thrusting a little deeper. To his shock, she took him deeper, sucking and lashing him with her tongue.

"Look at me." He had to see her eyes.

Her lashes lifted, and he was looking at his wife. Her lips were stretched wide around his thick shaft and her mouth worked as she continued to suck. Her brown eyes shone with pleasure, with something else as well. He could see lust mixed with love. Bright. Hungry. Needy. She was enjoying herself almost as much as he was and that added to the pleasure roaring through his veins. She'd said she'd practiced, and she hadn't been kidding. She had all kinds of techniques and just when she was in one rhythm, she'd suddenly switch it up.

"Keep looking at me, Shylah. I'm going to blow. You might want to stop."

Her eyes said there was no way she was stopping. More, she suddenly just swallowed him down. Took him deep. There was no warning, just the sudden squeezing of his shaft, those muscles working in her throat and the sight of that, the feel of it, sent his body exploding like a volcano. His cock jerked hard. Over and over. He stepped closer to her, his fists tightening in her hair, his first aggressive move, as he pushed his cock even deeper and held himself there, hips thrusting as lightly as he could control it.

It felt like every cell in his body went up in flames. From his toes to his head the fire swept through him. His spine nearly bowed under the explosive pleasure. He poured into her. Blasted like a rocket. The muscles surrounding him squeezed and milked. When he loosened his hold on her, she pulled back gently. Her tongue slid up his shaft. Swirled so lightly, the sensation helping to bring him back from wherever she'd flung him.

She lifted her head, took a swallow of champagne and then another mouthful. Once again she took him in her mouth and the bubbles surrounded his sensitive cock, licking at him nearly as gently as her tongue had.

He took several deep breaths before he could find his voice. "What the fuck, Shylah? Where the hell did you learn that?"

She sat back, a smug look on her face. "I had a lot of spare time, and I read. There are tons of interesting articles on technique, and I told you, I practiced. A *lot.*" She stroked her fingers over his cock and balls. "I didn't think I'd ever find the right man to give my expertise to, but then you came along."

He leaned down and kissed her. She tasted like champagne and sex. It took another minute to find the strength to walk to the other side of the table and it was only a couple of steps. "Here's to your expertise, sweetheart. Feel free to practice anytime. You blew my head off."

"I take it that's a good thing." She sounded complacent, and he knew she was well aware what she'd done to him.

His woman was a ferocious little tiger in and out of bed. She wasn't in the least embarrassed. She was proud of herself and very confident. He really liked that. "I'm going to eat a lot. I think I need to keep up my strength."

She nodded. "That's a good idea. I don't think you're going to get a lot of sleep."

He burst out laughing. "That's my line, woman."

"You created the monster." She cut a small piece of the filet. Her expression changed. "Draden. Whoever cooked this, we have to take him home with us. Seriously. Even if we have to kidnap him. Or her. It had better not be a woman. You'll fall in love with her."

He took a bite. The meat was so tender it nearly melted in his mouth. "I have to agree, but you don't have anything to worry about. I could give up food for what you just did."

She ate in silence for a few minutes. He glared at her. "This is where you give me that same reassurance."

Amusement lit her eyes and that quirky,

sinful mouth of hers curved, bringing out her dimple. "Is that what I'm supposed to do. Let me think about that. This is pretty good. Flavorful. Melt in your mouth. Remember I had to eat those rations for a good portion of the time."

Her teasing found its way into his heart just the way it always did. He tried to look stern. "I hope your reading included the better elements of BDSM."

Her eyebrows shot up. "Are there better elements? Of course I read about it. We all did. It was intriguing reading, but if anyone's tying anyone up . . . I've got the silk."

He shook his head. "That is not where I was going with it. Think about lying across my lap, my hand on your bottom."

She took a bite of the prawns. "What would your hand be doing?"

"I have a vivid imagination. I can think of all kinds of things to do with you lying across my lap and your bottom presented to me as a gift."

She squirmed a little in her chair. "Now that actually sounds intriguing. This is really delicious, Draden. Far better than what I made for you."

Draden frowned and shook his head. "You made me pancakes this morning, sweetheart. Nothing can ever compare with that."

He waved his fork at her. "Save some room for our wedding cake."

"I'm thinking more about the present in the closet than the cake," she admitted. "It isn't like I ever got presents. Zara smuggled us things, but we didn't celebrate birthdays or Christmas like other people do. It's been kind of exciting to think about what you could have gotten for me."

She leaned toward him, drawing his attention to her full breasts and the jewelry she wore that emphasized the full curves. She looked so beautiful sitting there, her eyes bright, his ring on her finger and his marks on her pale skin.

"Then we'll hold off on the wedding cake and the rest of the champagne until we're back in bed. I have plans."

"Plans?"

He nodded. Sitting there looking at her sweet little body, images poured into his mind. He could eat cake off of her. Paint that frosting everywhere and lick it off. Drink champagne out of her belly button and treat her to the same sensation of bubbles she'd given him. He was suddenly looking forward to going back to bed — soon. He hadn't thought it possible that after two hard, very explosive releases, he could get hard, but his cock was already trying.

"Um, hon, I'm kind of in your head right now."

He was entirely unrepentant. "I do have some great ideas, you have to admit."

"I'd be down for most of that. Putting cake in places it might not come out is not only a little shocking but could be a little scary."

Her nipples were twin hard peaks. She liked his ideas. Even the scary ones for her.

"I'd have fun hunting every last crumb," he assured. "Are you finished?" He couldn't wait to show her what he'd gotten her for her wedding present. He didn't think it topped the pancakes she'd made for him, but then nothing would ever top that when it came to gifts.

"I've got an imagination too," Shylah announced.

That pulled his attention right back to her and made his cock jerk hard. The tablecloth slid over his sensitive groin, causing him to groan softly. Her lashes swept down and then back up, guileless and innocent when he knew she was being anything but.

"You're not letting me read your mind," he pointed out. "I'm very interested."

"I want to give you surprises, Draden. You

do things for me, I'm planning on giving you as much as possible because you deserve it."

She shook him every time. He wasn't a man used to having a woman want to give him anything. "Just make certain you tell me when you have needs or wants, Shylah. You're a very nurturing person and I don't want to ever take advantage of that."

She burst out laughing, the sound melodious, filling the room with fun. "I'm an assassin, Draden, or have you forgotten? Not too many people would call me nurturing."

"Then they'd be wrong. That's exactly what you are."

Color swept into her face. "You say the nicest things to me, Draden. I don't always know how to take your compliments, but I really appreciate them because I can tell you're sincere."

He reached over and collected her plate. She'd eaten most of the food. He'd eaten all of his. That registered. They'd both *eaten.* Neither had stomach problems. He took a long look at her body. The remnants of the rash that had been there that morning were gone. His marks were on her body everywhere. Her breasts, her belly, her thighs. No rash. Only him. He fucking loved that he was all over her body more than he could possibly tell her. Hope blossomed again. Maybe Trap wasn't bullshitting him after all. Maybe they really were fighting off the virus. By now, it should have consumed them — or at least him. He'd been shot full of it.

He let her rinse and stack the dishes while he put everything else away. The champagne and ice bucket were set up by the bed. He put the cake there as well. It was small, but elaborate, the flowers peonies, just as he'd requested. He added more ice to the bucket and placed the flutes close.

Shylah sent him a small smile. She was standing by the closet where he'd stashed his present. She wore her heels and jewelry and nothing else.

"You look so damned hot, I don't think we're going to go very long before I've got to have you, woman."

She ran her fingers over the rubies that lay on the curve of her breasts. "I'm all for that, because every time I look at you, my mouth waters. I love the way you taste. I love the way you feel inside me when we're moving together. And I love you in my mouth, heavy on my tongue, my lips sliding over you, feeling the shape and texture of you. So, yeah, I'm really happy you find me hot and want me because I want you the same way."

There it was. His woman. Laying it out for him. Giving him truth and making him feel like he was the luckiest man on earth. He moved past her to open the closet door, but as he went by, his hands lingered on her breasts, finding her nipples and tugging gently, rolling them for just a moment before he leaned down and drew the left one into his mouth.

She was delicious. That shiver that went through her. The way she cradled his head to her. The way she arched her back, giving him more. He spent a few minutes on her left breast and then gave the same intimate attention to her neglected right one.

He took her hand gently and slid her palm down her belly. He lifted his head and looked into her eyes. She didn't pull away when he continued the journey between her legs. He used her fingers to circle her clit and then curled them inside of her, dipping deep. When he pulled her hand free, he brought it to his mouth and sucked the liquid from every finger, taking his time, savoring her taste. All the while he looked into her eyes. Watching her watch him.

Her breath turned ragged. Her other hand cupped his balls, fingers gently stroking him as she watched him suck. "You're so sexy,

Draden. Everything about you. I love that you're so responsive to me."

His eyebrow shot up. "You do that, baby, not me. Your body's wet and ready. I can scent your need."

Her smile went wider. "Like a cat in permanent heat, maybe."

"I can only hope."

She bent to kiss his sac, running her tongue over him, her hair brushing his cock and making it swell all over again. He waited until she straightened before kissing her again. *The rate we're going, we'll never be able to get to the present.*

Will I love it? Feel intense gratitude? Need to show you that gratitude by allowing you to do whatever you want with the cake and champagne?

He hadn't thought of that. His cock hardened into what felt like titanium. *I believe you will love it that much.*

She pulled back first, her lips curving into that quirky smile. "Bring it on, Draden. I've never had presents, and you've already given me more than I could possibly deserve, but I can't wait to see what you've gotten for me for our wedding."

He opened the door to the closet without another word. He wanted to see the look on her face when she opened it. "Sit on the bed, sweetheart."

Shylah looked up at his face and then walked over to the bed in her high heels. He watched her walk away from him, her very firm and shapely ass moving suggestively. His heart thudded. His woman. She was going to kill him with her long-legged, ass-swaying, very elegant stride. Who would ever suspect she was lethal as hell?

She sank onto the bed and crossed her legs, swinging one foot while she looked at him expectantly.

16

Shylah pressed her lips together, more excited than she wanted to be. She didn't want Draden to ever think she wanted gifts from him. She didn't need them. The day had been — extraordinary. She had never, in her wildest imagination, ever considered that a man would look at her with an expression of adoration and love the way Draden looked at her. She couldn't have dreamt in a million years the way it felt to have him touching her body, his hands, mouth and cock so worshipping, sending the most amazing sensations rushing through her body.

She wanted to experience that same feeling with him over and over. She knew there was so much more, and she couldn't conceive of it, but she was more than willing to follow him wherever he led for as much time as they had together. And she was still hoping there would be a lifetime's worth. She didn't feel sick in the least. Tired, but that was to be expected with the way they had come together. Nothing would make her happier than to live a long, long life with the man she loved.

She gave a little shiver of delight and hugged herself tightly, eyes glued on the gorgeous man at her side. Hers. Husband. Forever. They had tied their lives together in a way that meant she would never be alone. They belonged together, to each other, and had a bond for all the world to know. It was wondrous. Almost unbelievable. Like champagne bubbles, but in her soul. She felt — effervescent. And so in love.

Draden stretched to retrieve the package from the shelf in the closet. Muscles rippled beneath the smooth expanse of skin. Defined muscles. He was totally ripped, front and back. Every muscle could have been carved out of stone. He had to have been born with the kind of body that naturally built and maintained muscles easily. Even with his continual training, genetics had to play a part.

"I like looking at you," she confessed as he turned toward her. The box in his hand was enormous and looked heavy. It didn't make sense that her heart was pounding, but it was. She touched her tongue to her upper lip, moistening it. She really couldn't imagine what he'd gotten her.

Draden put the box on the bed and stepped back. She didn't look at the present, she was too caught up in the expression on his face. He really liked giving her things. He was excited and a little anxious. She ran the pads of her fingers down his thigh. The one the MSS had darted. The swelling was down, as was the redness.

"Draden." She breathed his name. "Look at this." Her fingers stroked over the entry site. "It looks far better than it did yesterday. You heal fast."

His eyes remained on her face, almost as if he were afraid to look, to believe, but eventually his gaze flicked down to his thigh. She heard his swift intake of breath.

"Maybe Trap wasn't giving us a line of crap, Shylah. Maybe we have a chance. A real one. We gave him our blood. He'll be able to tell if we're still fighting it off or if it's replicating too fast."

She reached for the present, not looking at him. "If we do manage that kind of a miracle, will you regret marrying me? You can always ask them not to file with the registry." She kept her voice strictly neutral.

"I meant every damn word of my vows, woman. If you're thinking of walking away from me, you can think again."

She glanced up at him, hearing the underlying hint of anger in his voice. She realized immediately how she'd sounded. She was insecure, but he really had to be. His birth mother had sold him. The woman he'd called mother had died. He'd withheld his trust from just about everyone else until she came along.

Shylah sent him a tentative smile. "I'm glad you feel that way, because I was going to remind you what I do for a living." She frowned suddenly. "What do you think the private sector pays for assassins?" Her hands paused on the wrapping paper and she looked up at him.

Those incredible blue eyes of his were darker than ever. "You plan on staying with me?"

He clearly wanted her to say it straight out. She felt like he was holding himself in.

"Of course I plan to stay with you. Don't be a blockhead. I'm just as nervous as you are. I've never been in a relationship, but I love you more than life. I'm in all the way."

He studied her face for what seemed forever. The expression on his face was so blatantly loving that she felt heat rising, spreading through her body. She loved that he would let himself be so vulnerable with her. "Did you just call me a blockhead?"

She pressed her lips together to stop a smile. "Sort of. Maybe. You kind of deserved it for already doubting me."

"You were doubting first."

Damn. He had her there. She had started it. Instead of confirming her culpability, she began to carefully remove the wrapping paper from the box.

"Shylah."

She heaved a sigh but didn't look up. "Okay, fine. I'll admit I might have started the entire boneheaded conversation. What did you say about once it was over, it was over?"

"That was when I screwed up, not you."

She laughed because she couldn't help it. "You're so crazy. I can't get the box open. Whoever sealed it didn't want what's inside to see the light of day." She frowned up at him. "It isn't Whitney's head on a platter or anything ghastly like that, is it?"

"I should have thought of that." He caught up a knife from under the pillow and slid it carefully around the top of the box.

The contents were wrapped in Bubble Wrap and packed carefully in foam. She eased the first big piece out, glancing up at his face. His breath hitched. Hers did as well. Whatever he'd gotten her meant a lot to him. He hadn't just had Joe pick something out. This was specific, from Draden to her.

Very slowly, her heart beating far too fast, she began to take the layers of Bubble Wrap from the object. Blue peeked out at her. Gold. It was shaped almost like a vase, but had golden feet and two scrolled golden handles. Then all air was trapped in her lungs and she could barely breathe as the last of the Bubble Wrap dropped away to reveal the Russian tea set warmer. It was exquisite, covered in blue peonies and gold.

The samovar was metal, but painted in exotic, bright colors. There was the traditional body base and chimney, the tap and key, which were gold as were the rings and vents and the drip bowl. It was beautiful beyond measure. The fact that he had found it for her, this exact replica, was astounding and made her want to weep with joy.

"How?" The tea set looked exactly like the one in the picture she had in her phone, the one she'd watched a family use to celebrate the birth of a child.

His smile started in his eyes, a warm rich color of navy blue enveloping her with love. The corners of his eyes crinkled and then his mouth curved. Her heart clenched hard in her chest, so hard she pressed her hand there, watching his white teeth flash at her and the lines in his face soften so that he almost looked boyish. This smile was reserved for her alone and it was full-blown, wide, bright and heart-stopping in its joy.

"When it comes to you, Shylah, I'm magic."

She moistened her lips and handed him the samovar warmer. "I believe you are, Draden." Her hands were shaking as she unwrapped the gold and blue teapot. "Can these be used? I can actually put boiling water in this little teapot?"

"Yes, and the samovar has been converted so it can actually be used as an electric kettle. That's the newer thing, to take the vintage and rework them. I was fairly certain you'd want to use it."

"Are these the cups?" She unwrapped a crystal glass that set down into a base, a hand-painted metal holder with golden filigree. It was beautiful.

"Six cups. I saw you run your finger over them in the photograph and knew they were important to you."

Blinking back tears, she nodded and pulled out the tray. It was as intricately and beautifully painted as the samovar and teapot. For a moment she held it against her bare breasts, wrapping her arms around it and just looking up at him, knowing her heart was in her eyes.

"Thank you." What could she say? There weren't words to answer a gift like this. "You're the most amazing man in the world, Draden, and no matter what happens, no matter how ugly it gets if this virus takes us, being with you and getting to know you is worth anything I might have to go through."

Draden's hands were gentle as they cradled her face. He bent down to kiss her. Instantly butterflies took wing in her stomach. He could do that to her every time. Melt her, the moment his lips brushed tenderly over hers. Who knew that her man could be so tender and so possessive at the same time?

He deepened the kiss, and her stomach bottomed out. He tasted like Draden. Hot. Carnal. Dark passion. Pure fire. She barely noticed that he took the tray from her hand and put the box down on the floor. His mouth never stopped moving from hers. Between her legs, she was already damp and needy, her clit pulsing with desire to match the dark hunger building in his eyes. He caught her legs and spun her around on the bed, so she was fully seated there.

"Scoot up against the headrest, sweetheart." He put a pillow behind her back.

He was up to something, and that sent a quiver of anticipation rippling through her feminine sheath. She did as he asked without hesitation. When he got that dark look of lust, of sheer carnal hunger on his face, there was no resisting him.

He poured champagne into a flute and handed it to her. He poured one for himself and sank down onto the bed beside her, holding the crystal glass up. "To my woman. My everything. Here's hoping we have our forever, even if we live it in just a few hours."

They touched flutes, and both sipped at the golden liquid. The bubbles slid down her throat, reminding her of the way she'd held it in her mouth to surround his cock to let the bubbles lap at his sensitive crown. Her mouth watered for more of him and she couldn't help looking to make certain he was as ready for her as she was for him.

He shifted in the bed and then took her drink from her hand, placed it on the end table and caught her hips. Without saying a word, he yanked her down on the bed so that she was sprawled out. His hands circled her thighs and pulled them apart.

"What are you doing?" She regarded him from under her lashes, watching his face. His expression tightened her stomach muscles in anticipation. There was no doubt now that he had something up his sleeve.

Draden bent his head to her stomach and brushed warm kisses there. Everywhere he touched her skin, her nerve endings jumped and sent licks of electrical pulses straight to her core. "Can you bind your wrists to the headboard with silk?" He whispered the question against her belly button, breathing warm air over her skin. Her nipples tightened. "For me, baby? Would you do that?"

She glanced back at the two wide posts. The idea was a little shocking. It wasn't like she would be placing undue trust in him. Draden wasn't the kind of man to ever harm her. She could loosen silk in seconds if he did anything that frightened her, and she couldn't imagine him doing anything remotely coming close. If the sensual lines of dark lust carved into his face were anything to go by, she had nothing to lose and everything to gain.

She couldn't look away from those navy-colored eyes as she reached behind her, spreading her arms wide and opening her hands so her palms pointed directly at her target. She felt he already held her captive, just with his compelling stare. He turned her inside out, her body throbbing with need. The stark hunger on his face nearly drove her insane.

Silk wrapped around both posts simultaneously and then she turned her palms to face each other. Silk tightened around her wrists, securing her to the posts. He didn't take his eyes from hers. Her lungs refused to work, and it felt as if he'd been the one to secure her to their bed, not her. Just the act of lying there, seemingly helpless, added to the pulsing excitement coursing through her body.

His palm rested between her breasts, fingers spread wide. "I love that you give me whatever I ask for, baby." His hand slid down the length of her, from breast to belly and then lower so that he cupped her mound, his palm sliding over wet lips, pressing so that the breath hissed out of her.

She couldn't speak. She had no idea what he intended, but the moment the silk was around her wrists, he appeared more relaxed, as if he had all the time in the world, and she supposed he did. She didn't. Every nerve ending in her body was hypersensitive, waiting for his touch. Waiting for anything he would provide.

Shylah couldn't take her eyes from his face. Now that he had her body stretched out in front of him like a feast, he leisurely raised his champagne flute to his lips and took a drink. His tongue slid along the rim of the glass suggestively, and her sex clenched hotly. She could see the advantages of such a situation right away. He didn't have to do much but sit there staring hungrily at her body as if it belonged to him. As if she were his own personal play-ground. She went up in flames, and he drank champagne.

The silence stretched out until she wanted to scream. She inched her thighs closer together in the hopes of rubbing her legs together to get a little relief. His hand came down immediately to hold her leg in place.

"I see we're going to need more silk, baby." Taking his time, he put down his glass and reached for her thighs again, easing them farther apart until her legs were spread wide. "I need you to tie your ankles to the posts for me." His large palms slid up and down her thighs very gently, barely there, just skimming, driving her crazy.

Her heart kicked into overdrive. She'd never felt so vulnerable in her life. At the same time, she'd never been so excited or stimulated. She licked her lips and did as he asked, loosening the silk at her wrists and turning her hands to accommodate his request, although it was awkward to do so. He watched her as if she were the most fascinating woman in the world and he couldn't take his eyes from her. He didn't move to help her turn her hands so she could spin the silk properly, but his eyes narrowed slightly, darkened even more, and the sensual lines in his face carved deeper.

The moment the silk spun around her ankles and pulled tight, she could barely breathe with needing him. She'd never been so happy in her life that she could spin silk. Before, she's always hated that Whitney had made it possible through his genetic splicing, but now, lying there laid out like a feast for Draden made her feel sexy and wanted, especially when he didn't bother to hide the stark hunger stamped so clearly in his face. She tightened the silk on her wrists and waited to see what he would do.

Draden's hand trailed down her body again, starting just between her breasts, ignoring her tight, hard nipples, just missing them so she felt a rush of heat as the edge of his hands passed them. She couldn't help the involuntary thrust upward as she arched her back in an effort to capture the warmth and friction of his skin. It didn't work, and that only added to the need building like a force of nature inside her.

His thumb slid over her, flicked her clit and then slipped into her. Her entire body tightened. Every muscle. She tried to grip him. Hold him to her. He was already gone, leisurely lifting the cake to show it to her. "It's beautiful, isn't it, sweetheart? Blue peonies to match our tea set."

Setting the cake back on the little table, he didn't bother cutting it. Instead, he just took a forkful and held it to her mouth. "Tell me if it's as good as it looks. You have to have a bite or it's bad luck." The fork nudged her lips.

She opened her mouth and let him slide the cake inside. The frosting was delicious, but very sweet. The vanilla in the cake offset the sweetness. She couldn't help licking her lips to get every last bit of the blue peonies. "It's perfect." Her voice shocked her. She's never heard herself sound like that, breathless and needy and so sexy her body reacted to her tone. She sounded like she was enticing him.

He took a bite of cake and nodded. "Very good. Sweet, baby, like you. He took a finger full of the frosting and began painting her mound, and then her lips and clit. Every stroke was designed to drive her out of her mind, and it did. She was panting by the time he smeared it along her inner thighs.

"See how great silk is?" he murmured as he set the cake aside and slowly wedged his shoulders and body between her spread legs. He lifted her bottom and dragged several pillows to place beneath her. His tongue lapped at the streak of sweetness on the inside of her left thigh. She was damp, producing hot liquid, a fiery reaction to his slow, deliberate stimulation. "If we weren't using it, you wouldn't behave yourself and keep your legs spread apart for me." His tongue took the streak of blue peonies on the inside of her right thigh. "Using the silk means you can more easily do what I ask. Isn't that right, baby?"

He paused when she didn't respond, lifting his head, although his hands were busy, sliding up and down her thighs, getting closer and closer to where she needed them, but not quite making it.

"Did you want an answer?" Each word was gasped out. Surely, he didn't expect her to talk to him while he tortured her?

"Yes, I think I do." He lowered his head, but his eyes were on her face as he flicked at the buttercream on her clit.

Each lash of his tongue sent a fiery spear through her body so that she jumped, and her sex clenched hotly. More hot liquid spilled to mix with the frosting. Draden lapped it up, taking his time, ignoring her squirming. Her hips bucked in desperation.

"You're killing me."

"I'm making you feel good."

He was doing that too. But maybe she was going to die before she actually got to the best part. It was entirely possible, she was that far gone. He reached for the champagne. "All that sweetness makes me thirsty. What about you? No?" Gripping the neck of the bottle with his fist, he tipped it up and drank directly from it.

Again, he took his time, looking down at her while she strained toward him. He poured a small amount of the champagne into her belly button. It ran down her belly and his lips and tongue chased after it. Then he took a mouthful and very casually, before she could think what he was doing, lifted her hips higher and using his tongue as a funnel, let the champagne trickle into her. Bubbles burst everywhere. She gasped and heard her own ragged, breathless plea. She was close, so close. She just needed him to take her over the edge. He lapped at the champagne, all the while flicking her clit and then suckling until she wanted to scream her demands at him.

He laughed softly and tipped the bottle to his mouth again. He stretched up to put his mouth over her left nipple. The cold champagne was shocking, along with the contrast of his mouth suckling so strongly. His fingers rolled and tugged on her right nipple, a little harder than before, sending fiery arrows straight to her clenching sheath.

"Feels good, doesn't it, sweetheart?" he murmured, kissing his way down her belly back to between her legs.

"Too good." She barely managed to gasp the two words. Her voice was husky, almost hoarse. Her head thrashed on the mattress and she couldn't still her body.

He laughed and knelt up between her legs, his fist around his cock. He looked starkly male, blatantly aroused, his eyes hooded and lust stamped deeply into the lines of his face. He pushed into her, giving her just the head, letting that broad, velvet tip stretch her.

"Draden."

She just managed to gasp his name, and he surged forward without preamble, his thick cock driving through her tight muscles to bury himself deep. He didn't stop. Didn't give her time to think or give her body time to get used to the invasion. His hips were like pistons, wild and hard, driving into her over and over, so that every exquisitely brutal stroke jolted her body and sent her breath rushing from her lungs.

Flames streaked through her. Spread like wildfire. A spectacular fire with the flames shooting toward the sky in bright colors of red and orange. The sensations ran from her toes to her head, covering her breasts so that her nipples were burning every bit as bad as the tight muscles surrounding his cock. He was scorching hot, never stopping, his pace furious, perfect.

"Give me your legs."

His arms slid under her thighs to lift them up, so he could spread her wider and lean into those hard strokes. She hastily broke the silk, leaving the ties around her ankle but severing them at the two posts. He leaned into her, using his strength, his cock sliding over her clit and deep into her sheath, hitting a sensitive spot that erupted into a heat that rushed through her like rocketing lava. Deep inside a coiling started. Tension winding. Tighter and tighter.

"Draden." She whispered his name as a talisman, or tried to. It came out more of a groan, an entreaty.

That tension in her grew and grew until it was a little terrifying. Looking at his face only added to the erotic intensity. He looked like sex incarnate. His body was hard and hot, his hands strong on her, forcing her legs open. He controlled the movement entirely, which at that point was a good thing. She tried to grind down on him, but she was too far gone.

Desire was so strong it consumed her. Every nerve ending was on fire for him. She was aware of everything about him, wholly focused on him. Utterly. Completely. Every harsh breath he drew. The ripple of his ab muscles, the sheen of sweat on his skin. She watched as they came together and slid apart. He looked big, too big to fit, but still, he did. The fit was tight and scorching hot and the friction was increasing until she thought she was going to go insane or come apart in a million little fragments.

"I'm afraid." She managed to squeak the warning. She was nearing the end of her endurance. The explosion was coming, and she was afraid it might rip her apart.

"I've got you, baby," he reassured, his face a deeply carved, sensual mask of lust and love. "I'll always have you."

She teetered there. Right on the edge. He stroked again and again. Hard. Fast. Deep. And then she heard herself cry out, a long aching scream of sheer bliss. The waves were powerful and took her from her feet up, ripping through her body, the quakes roaring through her, so she was helpless under the onslaught.

Her tight channel clamped down around his shaft, strangling him, gripping hard and taking him with her, ripping the hot seed from his body so that his cock jerked explosively over and over. Long after he stopped, her body still rippled with life, sending shudders of pleasure through both of them.

He collapsed forward, forcing her to take his weight, driving air from her lungs so that it burned to try to breathe, but she didn't try to move out from under him. She liked the way they felt, as if they'd burned so hot their skin had melted together. She felt his heart racing right along with her own, and she liked that he had to struggle to breathe the same way she did. She especially liked that they were still joined together. She wanted to think of them that way, always together. Draden and Shylah.

If they didn't have a lot of time, she couldn't say this hadn't been the best, because it had. He'd given her gifts beyond measure and foremost was the love he'd showed her. She kept her arms around him even when he stirred as if he needed to move.

"Let's just sleep like this."

He kissed the junction between her shoulder and neck, leaving a lingering flame. "You wouldn't wake up. I'd squish you."

"I don't care. I don't want you to move."

Draden brushed kisses over her mouth

and she tried to kiss him back, but it was too much effort. He slid off of her and smiled when she groaned a protest.

"Give me a minute and I'll let you sleep." He sat up and reached to pull the loose silk from her ankles and brushed kisses over the marks before putting her feet back on the bed. "I'll get a washcloth."

"There's no hope for it, honey," she muttered. "I'm a sticky mess and I don't care. I'm going to sleep."

"Not yet. Don't fall asleep." There was laughter in his voice.

She rolled over onto her stomach. "I can't move. I'm never moving again. If you want more sex, you'll just have to roll me over while I'm asleep."

He pressed a kiss into the small of her back and massaged her left buttock cheek. "I don't have to do that. I'll just pull you up onto your hands and knees."

She blew at her hair to get it out of her face, but she didn't move. "You could try, but I'd just collapse. You officially wore me out."

Draden took possession of her wrist and turned her arm over to inspect her skin. He frowned. "Shylah, you shouldn't have marks on you. The point was you controlled the silk. This was pulled way too tight."

"Was it?" Surprised, she lifted her chin just enough to survey the marks on her inner wrist. "It didn't hurt. I didn't even notice. They'll go away." She dropped her head back down and closed her eyes. "Ants are going to eat us alive by morning, but I don't care. I really don't."

"I'm going to wash you up and then strip the bed and remake it. The ants don't get to have you, baby. If anyone is doing the eating, that would be me. I refuse to share, not even with ants."

"I suppose since I don't want to die in true horror fashion, that's a good thing." The moment the words left her mouth she thought about the hemorrhagic virus replicating itself in her cells. She should have been alarmed, but she was just too sleepy and sated.

Draden didn't respond. Instead, he found a washcloth, got it wet with warm water and began the deliberately slow task of cleaning her up. Her nerves were on fire, close to the surface, and her sex was still spasming. Every brush, every stroke of the rough cloth over her sensitized skin sent stronger ripples through her body. Her nipples were hard little pebbles and he clearly couldn't resist bending to kiss them and then suckle gently while she shuddered over and over with pleasure. She didn't stop him though. It felt beautiful to her. Perfect.

Shylah didn't open her eyes, letting the fire just continue to consume her while he worked. She supposed she should offer to wash him, but she was afraid if she tried to move, she'd just collapse. Her entire body felt like a wet noodle.

His arm slid under her legs and behind her back. She tried to open one eye. "What are you doing?"

"Moving you so I can clean the bed. No ants, remember? Give me a few minutes and I'll put you back in bed with clean sheets." He put her bottom in a chair with her knees over the arm so her legs dangled.

"I can't possibly help you, and I should." She pried her eyes open to look at his very intriguing backside.

"You can pay me back later."

She watched him work for a few minutes. He was efficient, stripping the bed of the sticky sheet and placing it in the hot soapy water in the sink. "You do know, I don't exactly have anything to my name, Draden."

He glanced at her over his shoulder. She found his look sexy enough that her body tightened and caused another minor quake right through her core. His eyes moved over her and the sheer possession in them mixed with the raw adoration in his expression deepened the intensity of the ripple.

"You do know whatever I have is yours, right? And Lily, Whitney's daughter, will open an account of your own for you. I deliberately didn't suggest a prenup because it will be upward of a million dollars."

His teasing caressed her skin like fingers. Love for him shook her — nearly overwhelmed her. "You have far more money than that, don't you?"

He shrugged and turned back to inspecting the mattress and floor to make certain every crumb was picked up. The cake went into the refrigerator before he began to make the bed.

"I wasn't thinking in terms of money. You do things for me. Every time I turn around you're doing something awesome, Draden. I don't know a third of the things you know."

He sent her another smoldering look from over his shoulder. "You gave me the best blow job I've ever had in my life. The ultimate. I want that again and again, baby. You can wake me up like that. Put me to sleep like that. Hell, honey, you want to lead me by my cock into the swamp and swallow me, I'm going to follow you and I don't care if anyone says you're leading me around by my cock. It will be the fucking truth."

In spite of being exhausted and ready to fall asleep, Shylah burst out laughing. "You're very orally fixated, Draden."

"After what you did? Hell yeah, I am. I'm not denying it. The look on your face. I have to tell you, woman, you're the most beautiful thing I've ever seen. When you blow me. When you come for me. When you're laughing at me. All the damn time."

She swept back her hair and stared at his broad shoulders and back. "It's kind of hard to think of myself as beautiful when there you are in all your manly glory. Seriously, honey, you could pretend to have a flaw."

He shrugged as he fit the reserve sheet he'd found on the shelf where he'd stashed his wedding present to her. "It is true that I'm without flaw." There was laughter in his voice.

She scowled at him. "I think you're perfect. Well," she hedged, "except for the part where you think you're the commanding officer and really, I am."

"Why do you think that?" He spread out the clean sheet and reached for the pillows, stripping cases off them. "There is no way you have rank over me. I'm a doctor. An officer. How could you possibly have rank over me?"

"I give the best blow jobs you've ever had. *Ever.* And I wasn't even trying." She added the last smugly. "One doesn't reveal all their best techniques going out the gate. I save special things for special occasions. Like bossing you around."

"Fine then," he agreed readily. "You can be in charge."

She laughed again, her heart light. He could send her stomach into slow somersaults or fast-moving roller coasters. He could send a million butterflies winging just by smiling at her. He could make her happy because he knew how to have fun with her.

He came across the room toward her, and she couldn't help but admire the man who was now officially her husband. She'd told him things she'd never told anyone, not even her best friends. She'd done things with him she never thought she'd have the opportunity to do and more, she'd loved doing them with him.

Shylah reached for him, sliding her arms around his neck as he lifted her out of the chair. She pressed kisses over his shoulder into his neck. "Thank you for accepting me." She felt a little shy telling him, but it had to be said. "I don't know why it was more acceptable that Whitney did gene-editing with cats, but I hated the idea of any kind of insect."

"Did Violet Smythe ever visit the compound?"

His voice turned hard, and she pulled back to look at his face. "Yes. She was one of Whitney's experiments and he had her married to a man he wanted to make the climb to president, so the presidency would be under his control. The senator was shot and Smythe was making a bid for vice president, but she sold out the GhostWalkers to Cheng, a dealer of secrets in China. Bellisia went to get the evidence on her. We were certain Bellisia had killed her when we got the news that she'd been bitten by a blue-ringed octopus and hadn't survived."

"She most likely spent a great deal of time sticking her nose into the air and calling you and the others names. She started a secret movement in Washington against Whitney's experiments." He put her into the middle of the bed and drew the sheet up. It was still hot, but he'd turned on the wide-paddled fan above the bed.

"No one knows anything about his experiments." She clutched the sheet against her breasts, looking up at him for confirmation.

"Don't kid yourself. There's an entire faction backing him. Now there's some opposition. They want to keep the original Ghost-

Walkers but anyone with any kind of genetic strain they don't approve of, they want to terminate."

He washed out the sheets and pillowcases and then took them outside to dry. He was fast at repacking the tea set and then putting the food away.

Shylah frowned at him, propping her cheek on her palm. "We really can't just integrate into society, can we?"

His hands stilled. "Is that what you want, Shylah?"

"Not necessarily, but I did say all those horrible things to Joe, and I may have stuck a gun in his face." She tried for humor. The stillness in him warned her that her answer meant something, and she didn't want to disappoint him. She didn't care where they were, or what they did, as long as she was with him.

"Whitney paired Joe with Violet. She got close enough to stab him, nearly killed him too. She wanted him to betray the GhostWalkers and side with her. He refused, and that was it."

"She was a psychopath, Draden. We all knew that. She didn't really feel for anyone, just herself. She used everyone to get ahead, including the husband everyone thought she loved so much. Violet was an actress. I hate that you might be right, and she somehow influenced me not to like a piece of my genetic code." She flashed him a smile. "You made silk something I'll always be happy I have."

"I've got all kinds of ideas for your silk." He started on the dishes.

Shylah made a move to rise. It really wasn't fair that he was doing everything. He sent her a smoldering look that stopped her in her tracks. She decided she really was tired and lay back down. The moment she closed her eyes, he began to hum. He could carry a tune and it was comforting to lie there, listening to the rattle of the dishes, the fan cooling her hot skin, and her eyes closed.

When he slipped into bed beside her, his body curving around hers, she pressed her lips to his throat. "Thank you for the most fantastic day of my life. I love being your wife."

He pressed his lips to her forehead and then rolled her to her other side so he could wrap his arm around her, right under her breasts. His hips cradled her bottom, his cock pushing against the seam of her soft cheeks, a tight fit, but he managed.

"We're going to be fine, you know that, right? If we were going to die, I'd already be dead. This virus was killing too fast in the village for anyone to get out. It's been too many days. We're going to make it." He tightened his arm around her.

Shylah didn't respond. What was there to say? He was either right or wrong. Worrying didn't make it any better. She let herself drift off with the scent of him in her lungs, with the knowledge that she was loved in her head and heart. She woke just before dawn and got down to work, showing him new techniques and driving him right out of his head. Satisfied that he knew she really should be the one in charge, she drifted off again, this time smiling with the taste of him in her mouth.

They woke to pounding on the door. Both were fast, bringing up weapons and sweeping the room. Draden signaled for her to move into a position to take the shot if necessary, forgetting completely that she was running the day-to-day operation. That made her want to laugh, but she stayed completely still, fading into a corner, not a stitch on, watching as Draden stood to one side of the door.

"Need blood, you two!" Joe yelled.

"On my honeymoon," Draden called back. "Go away. We're a little busy." He beckoned to her and pointed to a spot in front of him.

She gave him her snippiest look. He wanted to run the show; he wasn't going to get *two* surprises in the same day.

"I don't care. Give me your damn blood before Trap drives us all crazy. He's got everyone in an uproar because the two of you are fighting this thing like there's no tomorrow."

17

Trap's face came into view of the camera right beside Wyatt. The entire GhostWalker team still in Indonesia stood shoulder to shoulder behind them. It was impossible to read Trap's expression, but the others were grinning ear to ear and Draden suddenly felt as if his legs had been swept out from under him. He pulled Shylah to him, standing behind her, arms wrapped around her, relief shaking him to his core.

Trap cleared his throat several times, and only then did Draden see the emotions trying to escape. "Looks like you two are going to live."

Cheers broke out behind Trap, his team going a little crazy.

Draden took a breath. Drew air into his lungs because he felt dizzy, the relief totally overwhelming. "Sweetheart." He whispered it against her neck. His wife. His woman. He would have time with her. They'd beaten the odds.

His eyes burned, and she turned her head to look at him. There were answering tears in her eyes. They just looked at each other. Drank each other in. The sounds of the GhostWalkers faded away until it was just them. Draden and Shylah. "We've got that lifetime, baby. We asked for it and we got it."

He kissed her. The perfection of the moment, the profound understanding that for the first time in his life, he was handed the prize. Life. Not just life, but living with Shylah.

"Baby." He whispered the endearment softly, love welling up.

"I know," she whispered back. "I can't take it in, but I know what you're feeling. I can barely breathe." Her voice trembled. Soft little tremors went through her body. She was trying to take in the miracle as well.

"We're going to leave you two alone," Wyatt said. "We have to keep taking blood over the next forty-eight hours to satisfy every requirement to declare you free of the virus and to make the point to every organization and government we answer to that you are not carriers." Wyatt still sounded a little choked up, and that drew Draden's attention.

"Wait, how?"

"They used a hemorrhagic virus as a base in order to infect Shylah, one that kills cats," Trap said. "It stands to reason that they'd look at it, because she has cat gene-editing. That virus does have a success rate of survival, which they'd need if she came back to them infected. They tried it on her and it didn't make her sick at all, so they kept screwing around, trying to make it more and more potent. That was the first five vials of her blood you discovered. Each time they tested a version, they'd mutated. Her immune system was far too responsive, so they went a little crazy and then realized they had a biochemical weapon on their hands. Because you both have the same gene-editing, it allowed both of your immune systems to defeat the virus, and now you have the antibodies that we need to make a vaccine."

Draden cleared his throat. "I can't thank you enough. Trap, Wyatt, everyone, for hanging in there with us . . ." He shook his head.

Shylah nodded. "Me too. Thank you, all of you, for sticking with us."

Trap saluted Draden, nodded at Shylah and turned away, hurrying off-camera.

"How soon can we get out of here, Joe?"

Draden asked.

"Whenever you're cleared, so enjoy yourselves while you can," Joe said.

The honeymoon was only two short days, and between laughter and lovemaking, they gave what seemed like every drop of blood in their bodies to Joe and his continual knocking on their door. Both wanted to stay in their little paradise, but Draden could see that Shylah was getting a little restless as she began to feel better and better. She had a job to do and she wanted to get started. No one had found the three creators of the virus. She was insistent she go after them. She knew them better than anyone else and could ferret them out once set on their trail.

Both were declared virus-free by three separate U.S. military labs and a U.S. military helicopter picked them up. The entire crew surrounding them was American military, and Draden stayed on alert. The way they were acting, the crew expected an attack at any moment. They were grim, clearly on high alert, and there were no smiles and no talking.

Shylah glanced at him, but she didn't say a word, nor did she take his hand when they entered the helicopter and chose their seats.

She was the consummate professional. She'd brought along the tea set, but with that were numerous weapons, all concealed. She was as dangerous as any man there and Draden was grateful for her as a partner, not simply a lover and wife. The woman knew how to set herself up for the best possible angle. She could take both gunners and the pilot if need be.

Draden was madly in love with her and part of that was because of this, the way she accepted what was happening around her without fighting it or arguing. They would have been forced into the helicopter had they refused to go. Both went with their armed escort as if they had been expecting them — that and because Joe was with them. He was the only GhostWalker aboard, and he seated himself in a defensible position as well.

Are they with us to protect us and we're expecting company, or are they the enemy? Draden didn't consider any military personnel his enemy, but this was a fucked setup if he ever saw one.

Stay alert. This is about the two of you being extremely valuable. As long as they have you, they have a vaccine for the virus. Both of you carry serious antibodies. We're getting you out of here, but I still don't know what the intention is. I'm hoping it's just a ride home.

Draden tried not to show how coiled and ready he was. He had cat in him and the feral predator came to the forefront when he was threatened. Now he had Shylah, and God help anyone who threatened her, because he wouldn't stop until that threat was eliminated. He'd been afraid of this happening all along if they actually were able to beat the virus.

Why didn't the GhostWalkers pick us up? Shylah asked. Her gaze flicked to Joe's face. Clearly, Joe had bridged the path to Shylah as well and she was included in the silent conversation, but she hadn't yet learned how to talk to someone without looking. That would come with time and practice.

Orders. We've got an escort. Our boys are very much in evidence, which pissed this crew off royally. There was a hint of laughter in Joe's voice, but nothing changed the grim, remote expression on his face. *They're following us in a second military chopper.*

We get any orders from Major General Tennessee Milton? Draden wanted to know exactly how high up they were going to have to go to be safe.

He wants you both safe. Out of harm's way.

That was good news and the reason why his team members were so blatantly escorting the crew picking them up, their chopper running almost alongside.

Shylah and I have to pick up the trail of Whitney's men. That means we go to Palembang. We'll need transportation and backup.

We're ready with that. You had indicated before that she was on their trail. If she's an elite tracker, then we need her to find them before we have an outbreak somewhere else. These men created the virus, and that means, even on the run, they can set it loose anytime they want. Can you find them, Shylah? Are you able to do that?

Absolutely. The reply was stated with full confidence.

We're going to resupply you. I want a list of everything you'll need. While you talk to Trap and the others, I'll be working to get your supplies and transportation. I'll need a couple of hours depending on the list. Make certain you give that to me.

Shylah looked puzzled, throwing Draden a look that told him she'd nearly asked what Joe meant.

No problem. We wouldn't mind a change of clothes and visiting with the man who worked to save our lives.

Don't give that egotistical maniac any credit. I told him you fought the virus off, he had nothing to do with it.

Draden nearly committed the ultimate sin of telepathy — he almost burst out laughing. Trap was an egotistical maniac, but he always came through.

"That son of a bitch Whitney did it, didn't he?" Draden demanded after he'd greeted his fellow GhostWalkers. Trap and Wyatt looked as if they might fall on their faces. The lab was already being broken down and all evidence of the hemorrhagic virus and the antibodies produced in Draden's and Shylah's blood was long gone from Indonesia, flown to the United States along with the computer containing the three scientists' work.

"He did," Trap said tiredly. "We just have to be happy knowing we saved the two of you."

Shylah's lips quirked, remembering that Joe had said they'd fought the virus off alone and Trap hadn't saved them.

"You happy?" Draden demanded.

"It does overshadow the effects of success when we know we were maneuvered into doing exactly what that bastard wanted."

"I *detest* that Whitney managed to get the vaccine, which is probably what he was looking to do all along," Wyatt agreed. "It wasn't hard to figure out that his three little puppets developed a hemorrhagic virus at his command after figuring out that Shylah's immune system was so strong that she could fight off anything. He wanted a vaccine. Now he's got the biological weapon he was looking for."

"Wait." Shylah frowned at them. "Whitney's not in good standing with the government. He's in hiding. He couldn't have really orchestrated all of this. He doesn't have that kind of power outside his compounds — does he?" She looked to Draden expectantly.

"Of course he orchestrated this," Trap said. "Whitney has a lot of friends who believe in what he's doing. He creates supersoldiers for cannon fodder and GhostWalkers to send in to do what no one else can do."

Trap sounded as tired as he looked. He was swaying with weariness, his skin color nearly gray, alarming Draden. He glanced at Gino, Diego and Wyatt. They all shrugged. There was no stopping Trap, and he'd been determined that he wasn't going to lose Shylah or Draden.

"Thanks again, Trap. I know you haven't gotten much sleep, but the fact that you hung in there with me means the world."

Emotion moved on Trap's face and centered in his eyes. He blinked, and it was gone. "It's not like I have a lot of friends, Draden. Not losing even one of them." Trap ran both hands through his hair. "I'm going home and getting my woman. She's pissed at me, and I don't like her upset."

"You don't like her being away from you," Draden pointed out.

"We're all going home," Gino stated. "They were good to us here and happy that we helped break the MSS. Some of us are going into Palembang for a celebration before we take off. Trap will have the jet on standby for us."

"Nice," Draden said. He didn't commit to a celebration. Clearly, the team thought someone was listening in on their conversation.

At this point, anyone could be an enemy. Whitney certainly; now that he had what he wanted, he didn't really need Shylah back, despite what a valuable asset she'd been. The Indonesians? Not enemies, but they probably wanted a pint or two of blood from either Shylah or Draden. The WHO, the CDC, every health organization around the world would be very interested in blood from the two survivors — the only known survivors.

Joe slipped into the room and nodded.

They were ready to escape into the city so Shylah could do her thing and find the creators of the virus.

A port city on the Musi River, Palembang was not only the oldest municipality in Sumatra, it was also was the second largest. The river was spanned by the Ampera Bridge. Currently painted red, the vertical lift bridge was a landmark of the city, connecting two regions of Palembang. No longer opening for ships to pass, the bridge now overlooked the floating markets and lines of houses built on stilts lining the river.

Draden shadowed Shylah through the streets as she maneuvered her way easily through the tourist areas to get to the heart of the city where the locals lived, worked and played. He could barely take his eyes off of her as she threaded her way through the people, smiling at them, open, leaning down to listen to older women or young children as they volunteered information without even realizing they were doing it.

She managed to look as though she wasn't a tourist, but a woman who had chosen the city as her home and knew it intimately. He knew that was one of her gifts — blending seamlessly in, looking as if she belonged, her sunny nature inviting others to talk to her. He was watching a master at work and recognized it. He found he was inexplicably proud of her, as if her accomplishments were his own. He could see why Whitney considered her one of the best trackers on the planet.

He stayed close but tried not to be seen if at all possible. His looks, usually an asset, were just the opposite, drawing attention he didn't want. His body was intimidating, all muscle, a predator moving among sheep, and it showed. She could get far more information without him. She knew the local customs and dressed accordingly. She also bargained for everything.

In the morning she'd gotten them some amazing fruit and pancakes. She seemed obsessed with pancakes, and he liked watching her eat them. She didn't hold back at all from showing her enjoyment. Her laughter rang out often and she was so quirky with her dancing eyebrows and other expressions that she got the most stoic individual to laugh with her.

Draden found himself actually fantasizing about having a little boy with curls in his hair and freckles sprinkled across his nose, holding her hand and laughing with the men and women she approached to ask questions. There were always children ringing her, as if she were the center of the universe, and for him, she had rapidly become just that.

She moved from group to group easily. He never stepped too close. He was going to be remembered if anyone interacted with him. He was a big man and he couldn't do much about his looks unless he wanted to wear a disguise. She'd laughed about that and dismissed the idea out of hand, telling him not to be so vain. It took him several hours of watching her as they moved deeper and deeper into the underbelly of Palembang to realize she had some gift that prevented others from describing her. She was using that same gift to shield him as well.

The moment Draden realized she had to be using some psychic ability, he did his best to remain in the shadows. Using any gift for a prolonged length of time took its toll. Just like the body of a runner who runs miles and is in top shape, but at some point becomes exhausted. In this case, the brain did.

He'd never watched someone like Shylah work before and it was very intriguing, almost as if she were following a psychic footprint rather than a human one. She seemed to follow a path instinctively, skipping groups of people to hone in on some lone man rocking himself back and forth beside a gated wall. From there she went deeper into the city, away from all tourist areas, into places that others might fear.

She obviously had the scent of her prey and was running them down. The three scientists should have been long gone from Sumatra, but while every law enforcement agency was looking outside of the country, she was moving on a sure, set path, totally believing she could find them, even though she was hunting much later than the others.

Night fell as they continued slipping in and out of doorways and alleyways. Shylah offered money in some cases and stood talking for longer periods of times with the informant. More often, she smiled, shook her head and thanked whomever she spoke with politely. Watching faces, more than once, his hand slipped to his knife. She had money and appeared to be a woman alone asking questions in the wrong places. She looked as if she might be easy to rob.

This looks like a good bet. Three men rented a small apartment just south of here a few blocks. They were sweaty, on edge and according to my man, Bakti, here, they were up to no good. One, clearly Agus Orucov, did all the negotiations to get the apartment for a week.

A week? Draden thought that over. Why had they left the forest just to hide out in Palembang for another week? *How long specifically? Seven days? Six? If it's a week, Shylah, we're right behind them.* He couldn't believe that. Why would they stay in Indonesia? They had to know everyone was looking for them. The longer they remained, the more news spread of who they were. What would be their motivation? *Ask him if they had visitors.*

Shylah asked another set of questions. Bakti shrugged noncommittedly. Shylah offered more cash. He shook his head. She added a few more bills. Bakti still refused to cooperate. She was the one to shrug and start to put the money away. Bakti reached out and scooped it from her hand. There was another exchange. She laughed, not holding the slightest grudge against the man for his bargaining.

The dim light spilling from the open door shone on Shylah. Draden could barely keep his eyes off her. Indonesia was a predominantly Muslim community. Women wore dresses quite a bit and covered their hair with loose scarves. Shylah had chosen to wear slim jeans that rode low on her hips and moved with her, allowing her to run or fight quickly. Her tank top was white cotton to protect against the heat, but she also wore a beautiful scarf that went over her head and shoulders to wrap around her upper arms like sleeves. The scarf was made by a local woman and it was bright turquoise and beautiful. The swath of blue wrapped so artfully around her head and shoulders, it gave her an exotic look that called to him.

They were waiting for Montgomery. He came looking for them. I know by his description. Bakti and the others didn't like him and called him inventive names. He was very arrogant but gave them lots of money. Bakti wanted more money at that point in our conversation and was very annoyed when I refused. It appears Whitney's three clowns have still been trying to come up with a vaccine because they asked for a number of items Bakti found suspicious.

Draden didn't like the sound of any of it. *Can we go there?*

He's going to take me there now. More money exchanged hands at that point, and Shylah stepped back to allow Bakti to lead her through the narrow, twisting alley toward the apartment the three men had rented.

I don't trust this man for one moment. He's

been cooperative, and I think he's telling the truth, that the Williams brothers and Orucov rented an apartment there for a week, but he wants money and I have it. He's probably got a bit of backup somewhere. He doesn't think they'll have trouble robbing me, because I'm a woman. I'm actually a little surprised that he hasn't tried to rob me on his own, but I think there's something more here. I'm getting the vibe that he knows Orucov, and I'm coming to believe that Orucov came here to this place specifically for Bakti to help him.

If Bakti and Agus Orucov were friends, it meant that Bakti might take all the money offered but then, when he was certain he had every bit of information Shylah could provide, he might kill her to keep her from hunting his friend. She was well aware that was a likely outcome, but she went with him as if she didn't have a care in the world.

Draden hung back, staying in the shadows, waiting, trusting Shylah to handle the man she followed if he suddenly turned on her. He was patient. If there was a plan for Bakti and his friends to murder Shylah, it wouldn't be the first time such a thing had been carried out in the backstreets and alleyways of any city. They would have done it before and it would be a coordinated plan.

It took four minutes before the first suspect opened the now darkened door of Bakti's house. The man didn't turn on the lights. He came out, walking with a slight limp and carrying a cane as if he might need to use it later. As he passed the neighboring doorway, a second man and then a third emerged. They began to follow Shylah and Bakti. Draden dropped in behind them.

Three men. One walks with a limp. He's carrying a cane I presume will be used as his weapon. They've done this before.

We're in that part of town. Shylah was matter-of-fact. She was a tracker and that meant when she hunted, she wasn't where the nice people of society hung out. She was with the dregs, those making their livings by robbing and killing. *Not too far from here is the local paper man. He can make you any document you want that will pass any inspection, but you have to have the money for him. He's pricey, but worth it.*

How do you know that? And fucking pay attention to that asshole who is going to try to kill you.

He's not nearly as cute as you are.

Shylah, damn it. Don't get cocky on me.

Or as adorable. I bet he isn't good in the bedroom either.

For God's sake, woman, don't think about him in the sack. You only get to think about me there — and not precisely at this minute. I want your entire focus on Bakti and how he's going to kill you, most likely inside that apartment.

Honey, you're not thinking too clearly. He doesn't want to kill me right away. He's got three friends coming to join the party. Not one. Not two. Three. What does that tell you? There's going to be a party and I'm the entertainment. He's going to whip out his knife or gun or whatever and threaten me. Usually not a gun because they don't want noise. I'm supposed to fall apart and be scared, that's part of the entertainment. He'll make me beg for my life. Then he'll tell me what I have to do to stay alive. It will be a very long night for me and then he will happily kill me.

The breath left his lungs. Bile rose without warning. She knew the signs for a reason. She'd been in that exact scenario before.

Honey, I'm here, they aren't. This is what I do.

I suddenly don't like what you do. He didn't. He wasn't a man to tell his woman what she could or couldn't do. He was proud of her. Proud of her capabilities. But this . . . being alone with four men who clearly wanted to rape and kill her, that was beyond his ability to condone.

Most women have to face this kind of threat

at least once in their lifetime. Maybe not with so many, but certainly at least one man. Even without you here, I would kill them all. You know me now, Draden. If these were good men, trying to protect their friend, unknowing of what he had done, I wouldn't harm them. This isn't the case. These men aren't good and they're willing to rape a woman just because they can and then kill her so they don't get caught. Not good. They've tangled with the wrong woman.

He couldn't help the swell of pride. He was that twisted. She was one in a million and she was his. *So, what's the plan?* Because she wasn't handling this alone. This was personal to him. It might not be to her, and he suspected it wasn't, she was too matter-of-fact. To Shylah, men like Bakti were hazards of her work. To Draden they were the worst of all human beings and gave all men a bad name. And this time, it was *his* woman they targeted.

We'll go inside. I'll ask questions, haggle over money. He'll stall to let his friends get here. He'll step up to open the door for them and I'll be right behind him. The moment they're inside, I'll slit his throat. Then . . . game on.

You're not leaving me much time to get there to help out.

I know you. You're bloodthirsty and right now, feeling very um . . . brutal. That's the only word I can think of. You're not going to play nice.

Play nice? He nearly choked, and he envisioned his hands around her neck. Shaking her. *How does one play nice with men like this?*

You kill them fast. They're vermin. You'd probably take your time and not be nice at all.

We have entirely different ideas on "nice" play.

There was a silence. *Draden Freeman. Are you getting turned on because we're talking about doing these disgusting men in?*

No, baby, I'm getting turned on because my woman is the biggest badass in the fucking city. Maybe the world. That is the turn-on. The way you talk. The way you use that knife. I love the blowgun.

Only because it has the word "blow" in it.

There might have been a little bit of truth in that. In spite of the situation, he found himself grinning like an idiot. Still, he picked up the pace, until he was nearly on the heels of his prey. He could see that Shylah had stopped just outside a brightly colored door while Bakti unlocked it and stepped back so she could enter. She went down to one knee on the pretense of loosening her boot, and while she did Bakti took the opportunity to sneak a quick glance down the narrow street in an attempt to catch a glimpse of his friends.

Shylah glanced up and caught the satisfaction on Bakti's face. He was certain everything was going as planned. She stood up and meekly entered the room in front of him. He let the door partially close, but left it unlocked with light streaming from the street through the large crack. He turned on the lights.

Only two bulbs worked and the light was more brown than white or yellow. She risked glancing at that bulb, but it had to be ancient. Why it wasn't burned out ten years earlier, she didn't know. She looked around the apartment. Clearly, it hadn't been cleaned yet.

"Who owns this place?"

Bakti turned away from the door. "I do. I rent to various people by the week. They took it for a week. You can see they've made a mess. There are all kinds of things here I don't understand."

"Sadly, these men are making viruses. This entire apartment could be contaminated. Don't touch anything." She wanted to share that particular wickedness with Draden. It certainly wiped the smile from Bakti's face.

"Viruses?"

She nodded. "The small village of Lupa Suku was wiped out by this virus. The three men created it." She indicated the room. "See the equipment here? This is what is used to make this virus. There's no vaccine. No cure. You must have heard of the Ebola virus. You're an educated man. You know that these hemorrhagic viruses are lethal."

He looked around the room, all the while shaking his head, not wanting to believe her. The door swung open and his three friends walked in. Bakti swung around toward them. The moment he saw them, the doubt was gone from his face, their presence bolstering his courage. She saw his hand move under his tunic to pull his weapon.

She killed him without hesitation. Before the body could topple to the floor, she'd thrown a small blade, no more than an inch long, but it lodged with deadly accuracy into the lead man's neck, severing the artery. He went down hard, blood spraying across the room.

The two men behind him tried to fall back, but Draden was already there. He came up behind the last man, slamming his blade into the base of the skull. That left the one with the limp. He was caught between the two of them.

Draden shoved the dead body and the remaining prisoner into the house and slammed the door. Instantly the prisoner dropped to his knees and began begging loudly for his life, offering all kinds of money and favors.

He's armed, Shylah cautioned.

Draden shrugged. *Let him have his chance. Stay in the background. Let me do my thing.*

Shylah sent him a ghost of a smile, all the while studiously avoiding looking at the dead men. Draden reached down and casually closed their eyes. He stared at the prisoner for a long time in silence. The longer he stared, the more anxious the man became.

"What's your name?"

"Eko, my name is Eko."

"I'm a little pissed right now, Eko. I was right behind you while you were following my wife. I heard all the very unpleasant things you intended to do to her right before you cut her throat. I have to tell you, I'm not happy with you. You have a wife. Maybe I should go find her and do those things to her and your daughters as well. Maybe I should make you watch." He snarled it, deliberately as sinister as the man in front of him.

Eko cried out and rocked back and forth. "No, no, I was only talking big for my friends."

Draden shook his head, deliberately standing directly in front of the prisoner. He knew Shylah was anxious that he was giving Eko a large target, but it was the best form of intimidation, while it also allowed the man to take his chance if he was going to. Better to keep Eko's attention on him, not Shylah.

"I don't think so. It's clear you've done this before. Rented the apartment to women and then raped and killed them. Don't deny it, that will only make me angrier."

Eko shook his head. "They are nothing, these women. Unclean. Nothing. They live to serve men. We would never harm a worthy woman."

Draden wanted to step right into the bastard and cut his throat right then. He took a breath and forced air through his lungs. "If Agus Orucov needed to change his identity, where would he go for the papers? Who would he see?"

Shylah knew already. She'd done her research long before she was in the forest hunting the three virologists.

"Faisal Bataknese," Eko said readily.

Draden didn't so much as glance at Shylah. He wanted Eko to forget she was in the room. *Is that the same man you were told about?*

Yes. He's telling the truth. We still have to track him down.

"Where is he?" Draden asked aloud.

I need to search the apartment. The three may have left clues behind.

Just wait. I need him to make his move without noticing you.

Eko's expression turned crafty. He licked his lips. "I could show you."

Draden pretended to consider it. "I'll think on that. The three had a visitor. An American." He pretended to know all about the meeting. Shylah had drifted around behind Eko, blending with the shadows in the dingily lit apartment.

Eko nodded enthusiastically. "Yes. They had a fight. An argument. It was very loud." He indicated the streets outside. "He gave them money. A great deal. Enough to pay Bakti more so he would take them to Faisal." The sly reminder was blatant.

"How far?" Draden asked.

"Only two streets up. Not far," Eko said. "But he won't do business unless recommended. It is a great deal of money. You pay for the recommend and for Faisal's work." Now he was eager, certain he would not only go free, but get cash out of it as well.

"He's the red door," Draden said.

Eko scowled, shaking his head before he thought. His lips formed the word *tan,* but he clamped his mouth tightly closed before the word escaped. Draden reached down and rifled through Bakti's tunic until he found the money Shylah had given him. He made a show of pulling it free from the dead man's clothes and transferring it to his jeans pocket. Eko's greedy gaze tracked his every move. Deliberately, Draden half turned, presenting a perfect target.

Eko reacted instantly, his hand going inside his robes and pulling out a gun. Shylah was already behind him, a silent wraith. She cut his throat and stepped back before the body could fall.

"You know more about the kind of work they were doing than I do," Shylah said. "If you try to figure it out, I'll try to find something that will point us in the direction they're going." Immediately, she began to go through the apartment, paying close attention to the sleeping quarters.

Draden surveyed the lab equipment. "They had more than one remote lab with them. That's interesting. What do you suppose they argued with Montgomery about?"

"I don't know, but Joe said that Montgomery definitely landed here. He was so arrogant and obnoxious to the locals that everyone remembered him."

"Not very smart," Draden observed. He peered into the microscope to see what the virologists had been studying. The smear was dried and crusted. The vial had P-1005 on the label. His gut reacted. They were still studying Shylah's blood.

"They have my picture, Draden." Shylah came out of the sleeping quarters, holding a small photograph. It was black and white, and definitely Shylah. "Why would they need a picture of me?"

"To show to someone," Draden said grimly. He indicated the microscope. "I'm just speculating, sweetheart, but Trap all but positively agreed with me. They had your blood because they were trying to create a virus you couldn't fight off. Each of the five samples showed evidence of viruses that couldn't infect you. They kept creating more lethal ones in the hopes they not only could infect you, but that you could make antibodies for them. It's very apparent they are selling the virus to Montgomery. Like Whitney, it's useless to him unless he has a vaccine. You're the vaccine."

"*We're* the vaccine, Draden. Just damn.

You think Montgomery is going to send someone after us?"

"I think everyone is going to send someone after us. Half the United States forces are moving into position to guard you. Well . . . us." He flashed a grin. "That's an exaggeration, but we're being guarded. Mostly my team, but everyone else is on alert."

"Great. You didn't touch anything, did you?"

"Not without gloves on. Let's go find this Faisal and see what our boys look like now and what their names are. Joe will call in a team to sweep behind us just to be safe as far as the virus is concerned."

Draden watched as she carefully locked the door to the apartment and then they both slipped into the shadows. He could feel the others close. Gino, for certain. He put off a very lethal vibe. Diego was up on a rooftop with a rifle, no doubt. He was damn good and Draden had never seen him take a shot and miss. It just didn't happen. Malichai was there on one side of the street, with Joe pacing along on the other side. It was a classic GhostWalker urban tactic. They were unseen, unheard and yet in a perfect position to protect their primary objective.

Draden knocked on the tan door. After much rustling inside, Faisal Bataknese answered the door. He looked alarmed, as if he weren't used to being disturbed in the middle of the night — which he probably wasn't. Like Eko had said, he most likely only took visitors known well in advance of their coming.

Draden stepped into him, forcing him to back up, which he did holding both hands in the air, glancing in apprehension behind him toward the interior of the apartment. Shylah entered as well and shut the door softly behind her.

"We're sorry to disturb you, Faisal," Shylah said with a small incline of her head. "Our meeting is urgent, or we wouldn't force our way in. Your family is perfectly safe. If you wish, I'll close the door between your personal apartment and this work space." There was nothing to indicate that Faisal worked out of his home, but Shylah was quickly establishing that they already knew who he was and what he did.

Faisal began to shake his head, putting on his most innocent and perplexed expression — one that had probably served him well in the past, but Shylah ignored his protest and quietly shut the door, indicating to his family he was busy with a client.

"Please don't pretend. We don't have that kind of time, and we don't want to hurt you. We could either turn you over to the government, or if you refuse to give us our answers, force you to do so, but you're a businessman. You stay neutral. You forge papers and your forgeries are amazing." Shylah poured admiration into her voice.

Draden stayed in the background, letting her do what she did, admiring her for the way she used her voice to get the information she needed. There might be subtle threats, and she kept Faisal off-balance switching between respect and threats to keep his attention centered solely on her and what she was telling him.

"Three men came here to get new identities. They were foreigners and they rented an apartment from Bakti. Unfortunately, Bakti and his friends decided the money wasn't enough for them and they are deceased. I'm sure you're well aware these were not good men. Still, they brought you a lot of business. I can compensate you for that as well as for the information I need on the three men who murdered an entire village of your people."

Until that moment, Faisal had been shaking his head, but he stopped and went rigid. "Lupa Suku. They did that."

"How did you know?" The government was supposed to have kept the deaths of those people secret, but Draden and Shylah were both aware that was a difficult thing to do.

"I have friends everywhere," Faisal admitted. He waved his hand toward a chair and collapsed into one himself.

Shylah took the chair opposite him. Draden made certain Diego would have a kill shot through the window straight to Faisal's head. He remained in the shadows, but just to one side of the forger so he could see if the man made a move toward a weapon.

"This virus, was it really as bad as they said?"

"One hundred percent kill rate, and those three men created it." Shylah leaned forward in her chair. "I'm not looking to hurt your business. I know it depends on your silence, but this is too big. Those men are dangerous to everyone, the entire world. Give them to me. No one will know you even talked to me."

Faisal sat for a long time, and then he reached up and rubbed his eyes. "I can't believe I helped them." He nodded abruptly. "Hidden behind the first drawer in this desk is another drawer. I have copies of their IDs still there. You can take them out and examine them. I was going to destroy them but hadn't yet. I keep them for a couple of weeks to make certain they are clear."

"Thank you, Faisal. We'll leave you with enough money —"

Faisal shook his head. "I don't want money for this. It is a betrayal, and yet at the same time, it is what any man should do for his people. Take the IDs and go."

In his eyes, they could see he expected to die right there. Draden moved behind him to cover Shylah while she went to the drawer, putting herself in danger. The moment she recovered the information and altered photographs needed, she backed toward the door. Draden waited until she was clear.

"Thank you." He didn't insult the man by throwing the money on the desk. "The authorities will never know about you from us," he reassured and softly closed the door.

Even knowing Diego had a clear shot if the man made a threat toward them, Draden had to glance back through the window. Faisal had his head down on the desk.

18

Much to the annoyance of the GhostWalker crew, Trap lent his private luxury jet to Draden and Shylah for what he called their honeymoon flight. Draden didn't feel too sorry for the rest of his unit because Trap turned around and rented another luxury jet to fly the team back to the States. They would meet at the Mississippi airport where Whitney's three scientists had flown. They were also getting a U.S. military escort until they were out of Indonesian airspace.

Great identity forgeries took time, and the Williams brothers and Agus Orucov had used that time to try to come up with answers as to why Shylah's immune system fought off viruses so efficiently. By waiting for their new identities, the three virologists had been slowed down and couldn't leave the country, giving Draden and Shylah time to fight off the virus, leaving them only a step or two behind their quarry.

As Draden and Shylah approached the jet, she nudged his shoulder. *We're surrounded by men with guns. Are they protecting us? Or making certain we board the plane?*

They're making certain we get out of here without incident, sweetheart.

Both were armed. No one had searched them for weapons. Draden had the feeling the Indonesian soldiers wanted them gone as much as the American soldiers wanted them out of Sumatra. It was a little nerve-wracking to walk up the steps, feeling as if dozens of eyes — and maybe guns — were pointed right between their shoulder blades.

Once inside, Draden forgot all about the security measures outside of the jet. He even felt a little sorry for the rest of his team. He tugged on Shylah's hand, drawing her into the cavernous and very opulent interior. "This is the way my good friend Trap travels."

A male flight attendant who looked as if he could handle himself in a fight greeted them with a smile. "I'm Greg," he introduced himself. "Let me show you around. There are five cabin zones," he announced, indicating the interior of the spacious jet.

"As you can see each zone is very large and comes equipped with leather couches and very comfortable chairs. Dining is easy on the cherrywood table." He indicated a small intimate table set between two luxurious-looking chairs. "There is a larger table as well, of course. There is a bathroom right here." He opened the doors to a spacious modern bathroom.

Shylah and Draden exchanged silly grins. His fingers tightened around hers.

"I understand you're on your honeymoon. The master suite is ready for you." He threw open the door to a large cabin. The room looked like something out of a magazine. The bed dominated the room, a large queen-size with gleaming gold on the headboard. Gold trimmed the walls. Drawers lined the room leading to the master bathroom.

Knowing Trap, there's probably all kinds of things we don't want to know about in those drawers.

There were several presents sitting in the middle of the bed. Greg walked over and placed them in the drawers. "Your friends sent a few gifts for you. I'll stow them in here for you to look at after take-off or when it's most convenient."

"That's so sweet of them," Shylah said.

Draden couldn't keep a straight face. "Those are potential bombs, baby," he whispered. "Those men are not sweet. Not one of them. It's best to leave them locked in those drawers."

She laughed, the sound like music, filling the cabin. Draden couldn't help noticing that Greg glanced at her. She looked happy, her face lit up, her eyes dancing with mischief.

"I'll protect you," she whispered back.

Draden smirked. If he knew anything about his crew, *she* was the one who would be in need of protection.

"This bathroom has its own walk-in shower," Greg said, throwing open the door.

That's bigger than our private ones at the compound, Shylah whispered into his mind.

"Let me show you the intercom. I'll leave you alone, so you can have complete privacy, but if you need anything at all, just intercom me," Greg said. "We're about to take off, so if you would please find a seat so we can get into the air, they want us off the ground as soon as possible."

"Thanks," Draden answered. He knew Joe had orders to get them out of Indonesia immediately. It was best not to tempt anyone to try to acquire either of them.

He led Shylah back to the middle of the cabin to get seated for takeoff. The carpet was thick and a pristine white with darker ivory tones through it. He wanted to smile, knowing Trap hadn't picked out the colors. He would have waved his hand around and refused to participate in choosing anything but the jet itself. Most likely his assistant, Daryl Monroe, had purchased the jet and outfitted it for his boss. Draden was positive that Trap was one of the few in the military with his own private army of assistants. Gino Mazza had them as well. Draden and Shylah strapped themselves in under Greg's watchful eye.

"Can I bring you a cocktail? Champagne?"

"We're good." The bar was in plain sight. "We'll serve ourselves until we're hungry," Draden assured him. "We're ready for take-off."

Greg nodded and left them, firmly closing the door to the upper cabin. The engines were already rumbling, and the jet began to move slowly to take its position on the runway. Shylah's smile was a little bit mischievous.

"I just want to take my shoes off and bury my toes in that carpet."

"There's no reason why you can't," Draden pointed out.

"I'll wait until we're in the air and out of Indonesian airspace," Shylah said. "Just to be on the safe side."

He looked around the spacious cabin, one

zone flowing into the next other than the secluded master bedroom. "You realize we have about nine hours, maybe a little less. I think I can fuck you in every space. The big dining table, the chairs. The sofa . . ."

"Bed," she added promptly.

He shrugged. "I suppose, but I don't want you to get the idea we're going to be sleeping."

"How do you propose to stay um . . . erect for this marathon of sex?"

"Your mouth. You have this beautiful mouth made for sex."

Her smile widened. "I'm glad you noticed. Are you certain you don't want me to use it right now, while you're rising into the air? You're looking a little . . . needy."

He could almost feel the stroke of her tongue on his cock the way she was looking at him, as if she were more than eager to devour him.

"You're just going to have to wait, sweetheart. Sadly, I've got to consider your safety above my own pleasure."

Her little snort of derision teased along his spine. Draden couldn't imagine what his life would be like without her now. The simplest thing, like buckling the seat belt of a plane and taking off with her, was an adventure. Fun. Sexy. He found he looked forward to every waking minute, so much so that he fought sleep, so he could just stare down into her face. He had gone through what should have been the worst experience of his life, but somehow, because of Shylah, it was the best.

Once in the air, the plane's seat belt sign went off. The cabin lights dimmed, giving the room a soft glow. He was the first to remove his seat belt with the intention of removing her shoes for her.

Stay right there, honey.

There was pure sex and sin in Shylah's voice as it skimmed along his mind, stroking caresses into his brain. Breath catching in his lungs, he obeyed just to see what she'd do.

She leaned down and removed her shoes and socks and then sashayed to the bar. There was no other word for it. As if she were a pro, and by now, he'd believe anything of her, she made two drinks. His was a straight whiskey. Hers was a mojito, with a lot of ice. She handed him his whiskey and took a long drink of the refreshing mint drink.

"I love this jet. We need one just to get around," she said. Very carefully she set the drink in the holder and knelt between his legs. "I think you really need to get started.

If we only have a few hours, we can't waste time." Her hands were already on his zipper. She didn't waste time with his boots, or trying to take off his trousers, she simply opened the jeans and drew the hard length of his cock out.

He loved the way she was so eager for him. He leaned back, eyes half-closed, sipping the whiskey so that fire slid down his throat while she poured fire through his body with her mouth.

"Keep looking at me, baby. I love to watch you. Your eyes. The way your lips are stretched so wide around my cock. You're gorgeous." She was.

The way she worked him, tongue dancing and teasing, her mouth sliding and sucking — she was more than talented. And she did have a surprise up her sleeve, just as she'd promised. Her tongue massaged his cock, and then pressed and flicked just under the rim. The motion sent shivers of heat down his spine. He heard himself groan and he couldn't help but catch at the back of her head, encouraging her to take him deeper.

She did immediately. She had to feel the way his cock was expanding, growing even harder and thicker in her talented mouth. He groaned again. "That's it, sweetheart. Don't stop." He wasn't going to be able to hold off.

Her hands stroked his balls and then slid behind them, pressing and caressing, and that was all it took. She sucked and swallowed and the pressure against her tonsils and throat muscles was all too much. His cock roared to life like a violent volcano. She didn't look away, but kept her eyes on his, so he could see every effort to keep up with his explosion. Her eyes watered, but she devoured him as hungrily as he did her when he had the chance.

She finished slowly and gently, her tongue lapping at him tenderly. Only then, when his body finished shuddering, did he realize he had her hair bunched in his hand and he was holding her tightly over him. One by one he managed to release his fingers.

"Holy fuck, Shylah. I don't think I'm going to survive if you keep that up."

She sat up slowly and reached for her drink. "You'll get so used to it you won't even think about it."

The thought that she intended to blow him that often made him happy. He gave her a silly grin and took a shaky sip of his whiskey. "I could be the luckiest son of a bitch in the world." Because it was the truth.

She laughed. "You are. I'm very curious to see what your friends got for us."

She turned to walk away and Draden quickly got to his feet, zipping his fly as he followed close behind. He reached out, caught the hem of her T-shirt and pulled it over her head. She looked at him over her shoulder, her hair a sexy slide along her back, curling toward her bottom. From behind her, he could see the long line of her back. His breath caught in his throat. She was his wife. Sexy. Sassy. Playful. Willing to fulfill his fantasies and give him hers.

He stepped close and reached around her to catch at the front of her jeans. His mouth moved over her neck while his fingers unsnapped and unzipped so he could catch the waistband and pull the material down her long legs. He left the wisp of lacy thong but urged her forward with his body, so she stepped completely out of the jeans. Unhooking her bra next, he tossed it on the leather chair.

"You're not going to need that for the next few hours."

She turned to him, her hands coming up to cup her breasts, the pads of her fingers sliding over her very erect nipples. "You don't think so?"

"No, I like you just like this. The panties are optional."

She laughed, just like he knew she would.

"It's a little cool in here."

Draden reached out and stroked her nipple, watching the dark haze rise in her eyes. "Cool looks good on you."

She looked down at his hand, his fingers rolling and tugging her nipple, a little rougher than he'd ever done as she arched her back to give him even better access.

"That feels so good, Draden. When you touch me like that, the burn goes straight through me. Like fire in my veins."

"I want fire rushing through your body every second of these hours we have."

"Aren't you getting undressed?"

He pulled his shirt over his head and bunched the material in his hand. "Dressed, or rather partially dressed, I can feel like you're my little sex toy. All about me. I'm just going to order you around and reap the benefits."

Her little laugh was just as arousing as the touch of her fingers. The sound of her, the joy in her, the way she entered into fun with confidence and equal enjoyment, was a huge turn-on for him. Her gaze drifted over him speculatively.

"I think you're *my* sex toy," she countered and swung around, sashaying into the master cabin, her hips swaying invitingly.

"Probably the absolute truth," he conceded. "I'd follow you straight into hell."

"I was hoping for something a little nicer than that, maybe paradise, but we'll see." She tossed her response over her shoulder as she entered the bedroom and then stopped, hands on hips as she surveyed the cabin. "Trap didn't strike me as a gold and white kind of man." She bent over and removed her panties, leaving her body completely bare to him.

"Trap is all about sex with Cayenne. Indoors, outdoors, middle of the swamp, a movie theater, hell, he doesn't even see his surroundings. He only sees her." Draden was certain he was just as obsessed with Shylah as Trap was with Cayenne. And yeah, the sex was a good part of that, but sex was interwoven very tightly with his love for her. "This is probably standard décor, or someone did it for him. I guarantee it wasn't him, although he would go to the ends of the earth to make certain she was comfortable."

She moved across the room to the bank of drawers, her toes sinking into the white carpet. No way had Trap ordered a white carpet, but Draden was already thinking about laying his woman down right in the middle of it and seeing how much give there was in the floor of a jet.

He sank down onto the top of the low cabinets on the opposite side, just drinking her in. He'd spent a lifetime never feeling as if he belonged anywhere until he'd joined the GhostWalkers. Even then, he didn't feel as if he were a fit with anyone and he never expected to find a woman he wanted the way he did Shylah.

"After we find Whitney's scientists, are you coming home with me to stay?" He found himself holding his breath. Waiting. His birth mother had thrown him away. His foster mother had died. Living on the street had been a nightmare. As a teen, it had been difficult to trust anyone, especially when so many'd had their own agenda. If she left him . . .

Shylah turned slowly to face him. She was bare skin, her curves fully on display for him, those full breasts and rounded hips. Her sex. Her long legs. He only saw her eyes. Vivid. Alive. Filled with love. "If you're going to the swamp, Draden, then I'm right there with you. You want to go somewhere else, we go. I don't much mind where we live, as long as you're there with me."

She didn't ask for an explanation of why he was suddenly insecure. She didn't laugh at him or make him feel humiliated, she simply reassured him. Straightforward.

Without hesitation. She gave that to him.

Draden found that love could be an overwhelming emotion at the most unexpected times. He crossed his ankles and kept holding her gaze. "That time at the private fashion gig, where I killed those men. It wasn't the first time. It wasn't even the second time."

She didn't demand to know what he was talking about, she simply stood there, watching him intently in silence. He could tell her or let it go. He knew if he didn't give her anything more than what he'd just said, she'd never bring it up again. That was Shylah. His woman.

"I was twelve, hungry and scared. A man offered to help me. He was living on the streets too and I thought maybe he could show me how to survive there. He took me to an alley where one of his friends was staying as well. They shared some bread with me and clean water, and then laid out their spare blanket between them saying I could sleep there for protection. I hadn't slept in days and I was exhausted."

Shylah sat on the other side of the room, perching on the opposite expanse of white drawers. She didn't say anything, but her eyes never once left his face.

"I was naïve and didn't once think I could

be in trouble. I didn't have anything to steal, so I went to sleep grateful to have found them." He shook his head. "I was old enough to know better. I still had some memories of my birth mother and the life we lived, but I wanted them to take care of me. It was cold, and I was hungry and scared. Still, on some level, I knew better."

He didn't look away from Shylah. From her face. Her eyes. There was no judgment, no condemnation, and he knew there never would be. She waited, listening. Hearing him telling her more than the words he was saying. He was giving her complete trust. Telling her what he'd never told another human being.

"I woke when they attacked me, one holding my hair in a death grip, dragging at my clothes. The other punched me in the ribs twice, saying I was their bitch. He had a knife in one hand and told me he was going to cut me into little pieces if I didn't cooperate."

Draden rubbed at the scruff on his face. "It's like somewhere inside me is this dark being that just rose up and fought back. I don't remember thinking, just doing. They were older, bigger, stronger and probably knew how to fight, but adrenaline kicked in and I didn't care if they killed me. Rage took hold. Icy. Dark. That was how I felt inside. I remember grabbing the knife hand and just rolling, throwing myself as hard as I could to one side, rolling into him, taking that blade with me. The knife went right into him under my body weight as well as his buddy's. It was that fast, that hard."

Shylah's eyes darkened but other than that, she didn't move or change expression.

"The one on my back, holding my hair, nearly ripped most of it out, but I just slammed my head back into him as hard as I could. I was lucky and hit him directly in his face, smashing his nose. He fell back, and I was on him, the knife in my hand. I don't even remember taking hold of it. It was just there. I stabbed him in the throat and ran. It was over in seconds and both were down, dying, I think. I ran in the dark for blocks and then realized I had the bloody knife in my hand."

There was a small silence and he wiped beads of sweat from his forehead, surprised to find them there. Just talking about the incident that colored the rest of his life sent shards of glass digging at his stomach, tying him up in knots.

"I thought about that for years, Shylah. Was I some kind of psychopath to be able to do that so efficiently? I had to ask myself that question. What kid could turn the tables on two fully grown men? I'd never taken a self-defense class in my life. I'd never been in a fistfight. I certainly didn't know how to use a knife. So how had I managed to escape them, and why were they dead and I wasn't?"

"Do you really believe you're a psychopath because you defended yourself, Draden?" Again, there was no judgment in her voice, in her expression or her eyes.

"Not because I defended myself. That was instinctual, the fight-or-flight response. I have the fight reaction instilled in me very strongly. I accept that. But I shouldn't have won that fight, sweetheart."

"You had the advantage, Draden. You didn't think so, but you did. They regarded you as easy prey. There were two of them. Bigger. Stronger. They had a weapon, and both attacked simultaneously. They'd clearly done it before. The last thing they thought would happen was for you to fight back. The moment you did, it was completely outside their expertise. You were fast and made all the right moves, which was your self-preservation instinct kicking in. I would have done the same. Some of us are fighters. We just do whatever it takes to stay alive."

She shrugged her shoulders and stood up, walking across the white carpet to him. He opened his thighs, so she could stand between them. Shylah swept back her hair and leaned down to kiss him. The moment she did, she swept him from those hated, even feared memories, into another place. She did it so easily, her mouth moving against his. Lips soft and inviting. Tongue stroking caresses along his.

Draden stood up, his arms sliding around her, lifting her. She wrapped her long legs around him, aligning their bodies. Her soft skin seemed to melt right into his, until he caught fire. Until that conflagration spun out of control. He kept kissing her as he took her to the bed. Her legs kept him wrapped up tight. Her arms were there, holding him tightly as her mouth gave him everything he needed. Love poured into him and he felt it with every stroke of his body — in every answering move of hers. Her hips rose to meet his as he surged into her again and again. As his mouth took hers until neither of them could breathe. His woman. Perfection. And they still had several hours to go.

The sprawling mansion situated on twelve acres was located right off the water, a good way to escape if necessary. The entire estate was fenced with a high, wrought iron fence that rose twelve feet and surrounded the property on three sides, leaving only the water for an exit. A tennis court, pool and spa were only three of the many luxuries on the outside of the property.

Ethan Montgomery swiveled back and forth in the deep leather seat, sipping on his favorite Scotch as he video chatted with his father. The center screen in the huge control room focused on the distinguished, genteel-looking man he often called "sir." The multitude of screens on either side showed various rooms and hallways as well as outside the mansion itself.

"Are you certain you're safe, Ethan?" the man on the screen demanded.

Ethan indicated the multitude of screens surrounding him. "We've hired the best security there is. This house is a fortress. I can see every single room as well as the outside. The room is locked, and no one can get in. I'm perfectly fine."

"Are you absolutely certain there is no trail of any kind back to the consortium?"

"No worries, sir," he assured his father. "There is nothing to lead back to you or any of the others. Even Cheng is not associated with you. No one in the MSS has ever heard of you. The money was filtered through so many layers it would be impossible to trace."

"You didn't try to hide that you went to Palembang." Calvin Montgomery's voice was strictly neutral, letting Ethan know, as so many times in the past, that he was willing to withhold judgment until he knew all the details.

"It's difficult to hide a plane. The plausible story is, I got an SOS from old friends and flew in to help them. They were acting weird and I didn't want anything to do with them, so I didn't stay long. Witnesses will bear that out. I made an ass of myself so I'll be remembered. No one trying to sneak or fly under the radar does that. Standard story, I'm a party man and I don't creep around in back alleys. I've found it best to let the authorities question me if they have to. I've done the act long enough that I'm totally believable."

"Are your friends going to deliver? We need the virus, but even more, Ethan, we need that vaccine."

"We dangled enough money for them to have fallen for the bait, sir. We kept our end of the deal the few years we had them in our pockets. They want the money. I told them no vaccine, no more money. They were upset and pointed out the cops weren't on my trail."

"I detest whiners. If they hadn't screwed up in the first place, they'd still be working for Whitney and we wouldn't have to recruit more of his people. They could have told him the virus doesn't work on the woman and discarded it while they worked on finding a vaccine." There was disgust in Calvin's voice.

Ethan shrugged. "They got greedy and wanted us to pay them as well as for Whitney to give them more. They always thought they were so clever. They don't matter." Waving his hand dismissively, he looked around the room and stretched his legs out in front of him. "It's why we run the world, not them. What have you done with dear stepmommy Candace?"

"The cheating little bitch? I let her see what happens when she decides to fuck some government official in another country. I showed her his entire family was wiped out. Everyone. Every single one. Not just him and his siblings, parents and grandparents. Everyone he ever grew up with and knew. She got to see the dead with the flies and maggots crawling all over them. He did too."

Ethan's father snorted. "What about him?

Advisor to the president of Indonesia. What a joke. You'd think he could keep it in his pants, but he probably considered the whole affair a good joke on the rich American. We go for a meeting, and my guards tell me she's all over him. Three days in and she's fucking him.

"Before he died, I made certain he knew why Lupa Suku was destroyed, every man, woman and child. He was found dead this morning, and it looked like suicide. She'll know it wasn't because I made certain we had a video of him being hung. I wanted her to see him dying, choking to death slowly. I made certain she knew that every one of those deaths was on her head."

"Sir, you know you have to be safe. She knows too much."

Calvin's expression turned crafty. "I'm enjoying her crude attempts to make it up to me. I like exacting revenge. There's a meeting coming up between the five of us, the World Alliance, and I think she'll be perfect for entertainment. After, when she thinks she's in the clear, I'll strangle her." He held up his hands. "I want the satisfaction."

Ethan sat up alertly, shaking his head. "You know better. You can't do that. It has to look like an accident. There can be nothing to tie this back to you. Have them kill her in front of you, but you can't do it. You're the one who taught me that. We have an alliance. When a favor is called in, we do it. Ask a favor. I'll come to you and do it myself." There was just enough alarm in his voice that it was evident he was serious.

Calvin sighed. "I suppose you're right. And no, you stay there where I know you're safe. I don't want anyone to get the idea that you're involved in this virus business. These GhostWalkers of Whitney's are troublesome unless we can recruit them for ourselves. Violet came to me and explained everything going on. We convinced her we'd back her for the presidency when the time came in return for favors. That was why she took the files on the GhostWalkers to Cheng. It was part of the deal we made with her. There wasn't much there. Whitney plays things close to his chest. We were just lucky the Williams boys worked for him."

"I'm not too worried about the GhostWalkers. They seem like jokes to me. Tyler and Cameron sent pictures of some of these clowns. They look like steroid users. All bulked up, can barely move. Whatever Whitney is doing isn't working. I doubt his supersoldiers could fight their way out of a paper bag."

"Violet did say he was doing all sorts of genetic editing. Or splicing. Or something like that. I don't care what the hell it is, but he's mixing in animals and insects. Hell, someone says he has snake children out in the swamp." There was utter contempt in Calvin's voice. "Cheng has asked that the virus be used on them. He wants them wiped out. He blames them for the death of his brother."

"That's ridiculous. Sir." Ethan rubbed his thumb across the bridge of his nose, whiskey glass in hand, as if reluctant to speak. "Cheng is descending into madness. I've seen these so-called GhostWalkers. Cheng has no evidence whatsoever that they killed his brother. Or that they took him prisoner."

"It's more than possible."

"I doubt it," Ethan argued. "I know the military supposedly has four teams, but what have they really done? Have you gotten any real statistics on them? No one talks. No one. We've offered a lot of money, but no one's gotten footage of them, or given them up other than Violet, and she wanted something huge in return. What *exactly* did she give Cheng? She refused to give the files on them to more than Cheng, after we were the ones to offer to help her in the first place."

"She was paranoid, and who wouldn't be if you thought the GhostWalkers would come after you. Each of us in the consortium offered her money in exchange for information, but Cheng offered the best deal, so she went with him. She wasn't aware of the World Alliance as a whole. We couldn't afford to take that chance with our identities."

"That just proves my point about Cheng. The agreement was for each of us to make an offer to her, without her knowledge of our alliance. Cheng refused to share information with us once he acquired it, even though *everything* is supposed to be shared. Why? He didn't really have anything but wanted us to think so. I believe the military paid a lot of money for a bunch of misfits. Screw-ups, but no one wants to admit it. If they weren't, would the Marines or the Air Force allow them to build fortresses on our soil? No one's worried about them."

Calvin shook his head. "Ethan, when our consortium can't find information on those teams, it doesn't mean they're screw-ups — just the opposite, in fact. It means they're the real deal and we need to be wary of them. We don't want their attention ever turned our way. We work behind the scenes and run the world. We don't want publicity.

We don't draw attention to ourselves. If the GhostWalkers are everything Cheng says, we could all be in trouble. We'll keep a low profile and continue trying to penetrate their ranks. Sooner or later, it will happen, but we have to have patience."

Ethan started to argue but then he sighed and nodded his head. "I hear you, sir. I'll be more careful, and I'll definitely see what Tyler and Cameron have to say about them. They were in Whitney's employ for quite a few years."

"Where are they now?"

"I gave them enough cash to get the identities they needed to get back into the States. I wanted to be home here in Mississippi for a week or so before they arrived. That way it looks as if I went to see them because they put out an SOS, found out what they were doing and got out of there. Just trying to cover my ass."

"That's good. Keep distancing yourself, but we do need them if we're going to acquire a biological weapon."

"If they want all the cash, not just a percentage, they'll be here. I said I'd meet them in New Orleans when they let me know they're there. New Orleans is a party town I frequent, which is great. No one will question my being there. The GhostWalkers

Cheng wants dead have built their homes and a fortress in the swamp just outside of New Orleans."

Calvin rubbed his chin and then sighed. "This is getting too complicated to just call the plays without talking to the others. They're worried about letting this virus loose again without a vaccine. The word we received from our informant in Sumatra was the U.S. military suddenly cleared their labs of everything, all equipment and computers. They took every sample with them and exited in one day. A private jet was escorted by the military off the ground. Right before that, a U.S. helicopter was sent to pick up two people from the forest just miles inland from Lupa Suku. What does that tell you?"

Ethan let his breath out, excitement showing in his expression. "They have survivors of the virus. They can make a vaccine."

"We need to find out everything there is to know about those two. If we can get your friends to make the virus, and we have one or both of the survivors, we've got a biological weapon and that's a game changer. The virus isn't worth anything without a vaccine," Calvin said. "We've got the informant working to find out who the survivors are. They weren't from the village. Everyone was dead. The idiot commander of the MSS filmed the dead, which was stupid, but good for me so I was able to use that footage to show Candace. The MSS surrounded the village as directed to shoot anyone trying to get out. No one did. They were all too sick. It was someone else altogether. We'll find out who." There was utter confidence in Calvin's voice.

"Let me know what else I can do to help," Ethan said.

"I don't care what Cheng wants. Don't let those three test the virus on the GhostWalkers, especially here in the States. That kind of thing will bring us nothing but grief. If Cheng wants them all dead, we'll find another way. We can't take the chance of unleashing something that virulent when we aren't even vaccinated."

Ethan nodded. "I'll talk to them. If possible, I'll bring them to the safe house we have in Biloxi. That can't be traced back to us. We can set up a lab for them. As soon as we get the vaccine and virus, I'll kill them. I'll make certain nothing can be traced back to the consortium, or to us."

"Ethan, this one is hitting very close to home. The Williams brothers were your friends in college. You were in Sumatra to see them. If the cops find them, or the virus is let loose, you're going to be looked at very closely."

There was genuine worry in Calvin's voice. Ethan sent him a reassuring smile. "No one will find the bodies, sir. And even if they look at me, no matter how suspicious they are, they'll never find anything to prove I was in any way responsible. I'm a party animal with too much money and a good lawyer. Trying to wreak havoc in the world would be far too boring for a man like me. I've carefully cultivated that image, and it is believable."

"Just be careful. I want to consult with a couple of the others, they're on standby. I'll get back to you in ten minutes."

"I'll wait for you," Ethan assured him.

His father disappeared from his view, the screen going black. Ethan picked up his drink and wandered over to the large stone fireplace where flames crackled and danced low. The shadows the fire threw on the wall were comforting, and he walked around the room, stretching his legs. He glanced into the dark screen and saw a shadow moving directly behind him. Gasping, he spun around. A tall man stood there. A woman moved into sight, but on his ceiling, clinging with hands and feet. On the wall across from him was another man. It was as if the very shadows had come alive.

He put his glass down very slowly, his heart pounding. "GhostWalkers, I presume." He glanced toward the door. It remained closed and locked from the *inside.* On the screens prominently displayed around the room, he could see his very expensive security guards patrolling the house and grounds. They were on alert, just as he'd instructed, and yet now there were three people inside with him.

His mouth was very dry, and he wished he'd gulped the rest of his Scotch before he put the glass down.

Ten minutes after speaking to his son, Calvin Montgomery, head of the five men making up the consortium that had been making major decisions globally for a great number of years, switched from speaking to the others and went back to his son.

"Ethan." He could see the fireplace and the inside of the room. Shadows from the glowing fire danced on the walls. The control room appeared to be empty. He waited, thinking Ethan had gone to the bathroom or perhaps went to change his clothes for the night.

Five minutes later he glanced at his watch impatiently and then texted Ethan. There was no response. He looked closer, trying to see into the room. A weird shadow rocked ominously on the wall. He tried to see what it was. The heavy blob just swung back and forth, a little darker than the other shadows. The camera was a good one and he could manipulate it from his end. He panned the room and saw porn playing on one of the screens. It was very high quality for a porn film, and for a moment he was caught up in the faces of the two women servicing the man. He thought maybe he might track one of the stars down. The little blond.

Abruptly he jerked the camera from that screen and moved it around the room. What was Ethan thinking putting the video on when they were still working? That was very unlike him. He concentrated on finding the swinging shadow. When he did, his heart stopped, and his mouth opened in a silent scream. His son was stark naked and seemed to have been practicing autoerotic asphyxiation. When he zoomed in on the shadowy figure, he could see ropes or cords wrapped around his neck and other body parts. He hadn't known Ethan was into something as dangerous as breath play, choking himself while watching porn. That was insane. *Insane.* And what the hell was going on with him swinging?

He could see the chair under Ethan's feet. It was right under his feet. Right there. Ethan's feet were sliding back and forth along the seat cushion. What had gone wrong? Was he dead? Alive and still moving? He got on his phone and called the head of security in his son's home, yelling to break down the door if need be. He would be there in minutes. He didn't remember to shut off the camera, he just turned and ran from his control room, calling to the people he trusted most and rushing to his car.

He knew he was too late. He knew he was. His son was dead. Ethan. His greatest asset. His one indulgence. He actually loved the boy and his intelligent, quick mind. How could he ever have gotten caught up in this type of erotic play? It was just insane.

Trying to breathe, he thought about it all the way to his son's home. No way. He would have known if Ethan was into such things. No, this had to be murder, plain and simple. He had enemies, so did Ethan. But if it was murder, how had the assassin gotten into a locked room, through all the security guards and cameras? His son must have . . . No. He wouldn't accept that. Someone had murdered his son. This was a message. Maybe Cheng wasn't as insane as everyone thought.

19

"Nonny wants to come home," Ezekiel greeted. "I think Teams One and Two want to steal her, but she misses her swamp."

Trap flung himself in a chair, looking glum. "They've been gone a week and Cayenne won't even speak to me. I've tried everything, and she won't answer her phone or do a video chat. If I don't bring her home soon, she may not want to come back to me. She's acting like I wanted to send her away. If she doesn't stop this soon, I'm going there and dragging her little ass back and we're going to be talking."

"You can't do that until we find these three scumbags who want to test their virus on us, thanks to Cheng," Joe said. He glanced over at Draden and the newest member of their team, Shylah. "Good work. The papers reported that Ethan was found dead of an apparent suicide. There was no mention of erotic play, and weirdly, three of his security team disappeared. I think Daddy wasn't happy that anyone saw his son like that, but he bought the scenario."

Draden nodded. "We were in the room with Ethan when he was reporting to his father, and the power play they were exchanging back and forth suggested his father might buy into any kind of sexual activity. He's smart though, and he'll figure it out eventually. Unfortunately, Ethan wasn't able to give Whitney's three scientists the order to back down and not test the virus on us."

"Trap vaccinated everyone here," Wyatt said. "The vaccine was tested immediately by the military labs, and it's working. But he can't vaccinate the entire population of the swamp."

"Fucking Whitney got exactly what he wanted," Draden said. "He used us. He took a chance with Shylah's life and he used us to get him his biological weapon and his vaccine. Those in the White House helping to hide him are no doubt very grateful to him and he'll be doubly dangerous now. They'll give him all the more room because he delivered."

"Do you think he intentionally allowed his virologists to escape with the virus?" Malichai asked, stuffing food into his mouth as he did so. Nonny may have been gone, but she'd left behind casseroles and various other meals in the freezer for her "boys." Malichai was forever hungry and no one made home-cooked meals like Nonny. "What do you really think, Shylah? You've been around Whitney more than any of us."

Shylah turned that over and over in her mind. Was it possible Whitney had known all along that the men were talking with Ethan Montgomery? Even accepting money from him? He had to have known. Everything was monitored. Email, phones, computers, any kind of device that sent messages out or received them. He had cameras everywhere as well as audio to pick up conversations. He was able to monitor bank accounts of those he employed. He had people that did that sort of thing 24/7. Even if the Williams brothers and Orucov were smart enough to find a code to use, Whitney would have known, and he would find someone to break it — or would do so himself. He enjoyed playing with codes.

She nodded her head slowly. "He would have known. They couldn't have been working for Montgomery, passing him information over several years, without Whitney finding out. A few weeks, maybe, but it sounded as if they had been accepting pay from the Montgomerys for a long while."

"So, he allowed them to take a few drops of the virus with them," Joe said, shaking his head. "He's partially responsible for the deaths of all those people in Lupa Suku."

"With the way Whitney thinks, the fact that we uncovered the Montgomerys and the consortium and who was funding the MSS is valuable information worth the lives of those people," Shylah said. "People aren't that important. They're disposable, especially ones that cut themselves off from the rest of the world. In his mind, they're part of the problem. They don't contribute in ways he feels are vital."

Joe swore under his breath. "He's won himself more support. If any country protests that weapon, we have only to say we're working on a vaccine. No one knows Shylah and Draden fought it off and survived. The soldiers guarding them knew very little. For all they were told, they were there to try to infiltrate the MSS. The fact that they killed so many of them would lend itself to that explanation."

"Montgomery made it clear he knew two people were taken out of the forest and flown with a military escort back to the States," Draden pointed out. "That was clear in the video chat."

"But he doesn't know who. Chances are very good their informant doesn't know who. Your names were never given out. We had to promise the Indonesian government that if you were infected, you wouldn't be able to leave that area."

"In other words," Draden said, "You were supposed to kill us if we tried."

Joe sent him a lopsided grin and a little shrug. "That may have been mentioned, but I had that woman of yours giving me night-mares. Wasn't about to be the one to pull the trigger." His grin widened when he looked at Shylah and gave her a little salute.

"Glad to have made an impact," she answered with a little bow.

Malichai laughed. "Joe came back telling us about guns to his head and a sniper being threatened. A few more very interesting times as well. I'm a little in love with your wife, Draden, and I fully admit it. Course, my woman's going to just feed me and fan me. No opposition. I don't have the kind of energy a man needs to put up with a feisty woman. I need me a 'yes' woman."

The room erupted into laughter as the GhostWalkers scattered around in various reposes, draped over chairs, lazily leaning against walls or sprawled out on the floor commented simultaneously on Malichai's statement. Most thought he was full of bullshit, but the general common consensus was there weren't any "yes" women for him to find.

"I'm about to start searching," he said solemnly. "I've been contemplating on how to best go about finding this woman. In the interests of not having to work too hard, I've been composing an ad to take out in one of those serious-about-relationship places online." He chewed thoughtfully and regarded his teammates deadpan as he did so.

Mordichai nudged him with his foot. "That the same ad you started a year ago?"

Malichai nodded. "Have to word it just right. Don't want to repeat myself."

Another round of laughter followed and Shylah couldn't help joining in. They were all a little crazy, but it reminded her of spending time with Bellisia and Zara. Bellisia had thrown herself into Shylah's arms and cried, something very unusual for her. She just wasn't a crier. Bellisia was tiny, a gorgeous little pixie, and standing next to her always made Shylah feel like a giant. Before, she'd been a little sensitive about her height. It wasn't that she wasn't confident, but she didn't feel particularly beautiful. Being with Draden had changed that.

She didn't know about her looks, but she *felt* beautiful.

She looked up at his face. To her, he was breathtaking. The most remarkable man in the room, and it wasn't about his looks, although she had to admit she thought he was gorgeous. She loved his personality, the way he communicated so openly with her.

I'm in your head, sweetheart.

His voice stroked caresses through her mind and filled her body with heat. *Well, you shouldn't be. What if I'd been thinking mean thoughts about you?*

You never think mean thoughts about me. I ought to know. I'm always sneaking in to be connected to you.

She knew he did that often. He filled her up with him, making her feel as if they were so close she didn't know where he started, and she left off. The other GhostWalkers' conversations and laughter swirled around them, but they were locked together in their own world.

You never know, I might be upset with you one day and then you'd hear all sorts of bad things about yourself. Mostly made-up, but they wouldn't be nice.

If I hurt you, Shylah, I would want to know immediately and, believe me, baby, I'd rectify that situation on the spot. No matter what, good or bad, it's important for us to communicate.

She loved that he thought that way. From the beginning of their relationship, they'd been honest. She'd told him things she might have been embarrassed to tell him had she known she was going to live, but by both being so brutally honest, they'd given themselves the best start possible. Clearly, he wanted to continue down that same path going forward and she did as well.

No worries, Draden. If you hurt me, you'll get an earful. I'm not one to suffer in silence.

You also believe in retaliation. I learned that on the plane. I'm liking your silk, sweetheart.

She blushed. There was no way to hide the sweep of bright red color creeping up her neck to wash through her pale face. Of course the GhostWalkers were far too eagle-eyed to miss it, and none of them were gentlemen enough to ignore it. The hooting and hollering as well as the multiple suggestions to adjourn to another part of the house only made it worse. Draden didn't seem to mind in the least. *They can't read our minds, can they?*

I don't think so . . . Well . . . maybe Joe. He builds a bridge between everyone who doesn't have telepathy as a natural gift.

She didn't really believe him, but it

sounded plausible, so she snuck a quick look at Joe from under her lashes. Just a peek. He wasn't looking at her. In fact, he had his head turned away from her. Not natural at all. He should be looking at her if they were all teasing her, right? Maybe he really did pick up everyone's thoughts even when he wasn't trying to intrude.

No more teasing until we're alone.

I have to let you in on a little secret, sweetheart, Draden said, wrapping his arms around her from behind and leaning his chin on her shoulder. *Every single man in this room knows we have hot sex. They probably know we have sex a few times a day.*

She glared at him. *They can't know it's hot and it would be impossible for them to know how many times a day.* She scrunched up her face and danced her eyebrows at him, refusing to let him make her blush again.

What part of them all having cat DNA don't you get? Your sense of smell is enhanced. So is theirs. Of course they know. There's no hiding that, no matter how many showers we take.

Shylah *hadn't* thought about that. Her gaze swept around the room. She did have an extremely heightened sense of smell in comparison with a human. Tigers didn't rely on smell for the hunt. Their visual acuity was far more developed than their sense of smell. That didn't mean that the men in the room wouldn't be able to scent her receptiveness to her man.

Draden's soft laughter provoked another rush of color into her face. She refrained from kicking him. *You'd better stop before you find yourself going without sex for a very long time.*

You like my cock too much for that to happen.

That was true and there was no denying the obvious. She was the one waking him up if they both fell asleep and she often initiated the sex, sometimes only a couple of hours after he'd made love to her. She was addicted to the mixture of lust and love he wrapped her in every time he touched her. No matter what he did, it was always mind-blowing and beautiful.

Now who's the one making me blush?

Shylah leaned her head back against him, listening to the easy camaraderie of the GhostWalker team. These men went into combat together, relied on one another to watch their backs. They trusted one another implicitly, and it showed in the way they treated one another. They ribbed one another, but it was always good-natured. Draden belonged with these men and she belonged with Draden. She was going to like her new home.

She concentrated on Bellisia, wanting her to be happy, hoping she was every bit as happy as Shylah was. Each time Bellisia looked up at Ezekiel, he would look down at her with such love on his face, Shylah couldn't help but think the two of them were as happy as she and Draden were.

She reached out to Bellisia. *Are you happy? Does he treat you right?*

Bellisia's gaze jumped to her face. She nodded. *I'm so in love with him it makes me crazy sometimes. I didn't know I could feel this way.*

I didn't either, Shylah admitted. *Draden makes every minute I'm breathing so worth it. I know it sounds like a fairy tale, Bellisia, but he really is amazing the way he loves me. I never thought I'd have this, and it's all the more precious because I thought love and family was for everyone else, not me.*

I was so scared when Wyatt told Ezekiel that you both were infected with the virus. I made up my mind to find a way to get to Whitney if you had died. Now, we're being threatened because Whitney just can't stop.

This little present to the GhostWalkers is from Cheng, at least it sounded like he was the one who ordered it. Even his friends seem to think he's going downhill. They'll probably put out a hit on him and we won't have to take him down.

Bellisia gave a slight shake of her head. *Cheng hurt Zara, Shylah. He would have sold her into trafficking, and Zeke said it was the most vile, disgusting thing he'd ever seen going after Bolan Zhu, his right-hand man and actual brother. Bolan tortured Zara on Cheng's orders. Her feet are so damaged she'll never run like she used to. I'd like to kill the bastard myself.*

"Just what are you two women up to?" Joe asked.

"They're probably discussing some new sex technique," Malichai said hopefully.

There was a sudden silence. Shylah's eyes met Bellisia's and they both burst out laughing.

"Actually, we're discussing killing Cheng and why," Bellisia admitted. "Sorry to disappoint you, Malichai, but we already finished that very provocative and *extremely* kinky technique sharing. Maybe next time."

Malichai sat up straight. His breath hitched. He looked from Draden to Ezekiel. "She's gotta talk. Tell us. Both of them have to."

Shylah shrugged her shoulders and tried to look as nonchalant as Bellisia. "After

Draden is treated to that mind-blowing technique, you can ask him all about it. Maybe he'll share the how-to part."

Malichai groaned. "I'm going to have to hurry and finish my ad."

"The one you've been working on a year," Mordichai reiterated.

"I have to get the wording just right," Malichai defended.

"How many words do you have so far?" Shylah asked.

" 'To the angel looking for me.' " Malichai smiled. "Isn't that perfect, although I thought about changing the word *the* to *my*. My angel. What do you think?"

"I think you're going to die of old age before you ever finish that ad," Ezekiel told his younger brother. Hurry it up for my sake. I'd like a few nephews."

Shylah rolled her eyes. "What's wrong with you men? Are you all about having sons?"

"Wyatt isn't," Rubin Campo declared. "He has triplets, three little girls, and Pepper is pregnant with twins and they're girls."

There was a long moment of silence. Wyatt glared at Rubin. "How the hell did you know that? No one knows. Maybe Nonny. It was a surprise, you blockhead."

"Sorry, man." Rubin made a face at his brother, Diego, and then shrugged his shoulders. "I didn't realize the others didn't know."

"Twins?" Draden echoed.

"Girls?" Trap looked genuinely horrified. "Wyatt, that's *five* girls. What the fuck? We're going to have to kill half the boys in the swamp."

Wyatt sighed and rubbed at the bridge of his nose. "I'm well aware that's five daughters for me. I can do the math." He glared at Rubin. "How did you know?"

Rubin shrugged again. "I just know things sometimes. I can 'see' things. Pepper was obviously pregnant with twins . . ."

"It wasn't obvious to me," Joe said. "She doesn't look big enough to be carrying twins."

Trap cleared his throat. "Are we *all* going to be having multiple births because of the things Whitney did to us?"

Trap was a big man, taller than most of the other GhostWalkers, with blond hair and piercing blue eyes. He was scary looking, until just that moment. Shylah could see fear carved right into the lines of his face as he asked the question. She exchanged a little grin with Bellisia. Let the men be afraid for a change when it came to pregnancy. On the other hand, the thought of having more than one baby at a time was daunting when she didn't know the first thing about children or parenting.

We're so not getting pregnant, she informed Draden. She felt his instant, answering smirk. *I mean it. Until we figure out this having twins thing . . .*

Or triplets. Let's not forget that's a very viable possibility, he supplied helpfully.

Joe nearly spit his coffee out, drawing Shylah's instant attention. She glared at him. *Stop listening to private conversations.*

I would, but the two of you broadcast fairly loudly.

"Trap, you're a fucking genius for God's sake," Wyatt snapped, raking his fingers through his hair in agitation. "Of course, you know it's not only possible but probable. And birth control isn't working for us, so Pepper and I might end up holding the world record for the most children."

"There is an alternative," Malichai said helpfully. "Give up sex."

The laughter was like a sound wave, building in force around the room. Wyatt flung a pillow from one of the chairs at him. "That's not happening."

"One of Cayenne's trip wires just sent out an alarm," Trap announced suddenly. "Several miles from here. But it's our three scientists. The camera picked them up." He lifted his watch to show the others.

The entire group stood, all humor gone. Joe gave the orders. "Zeke, you, Bellisia, Gino stay behind. We're not going to miss, but just in case, you're our last defense."

Ezekiel nodded and glanced at his brothers but didn't say anything. Shylah could see that something, some communication passed between them, but there was nothing to indicate stress or worry in the expressions on their faces.

She stayed close to Draden, not about to be left behind. As far as she was concerned, this was her operation, her responsibility, and she was going to see it through to the end. It took only minutes, and very few of them, for the team to be on the move. To her shock, they didn't go by boat or vehicle, they went into the swamp itself on foot.

Shylah understood why the men Whitney had enhanced were called GhostWalkers. Once in the swamp, they disappeared. It was impossible to detect their presence. The insects continued with their constant cacophony of noise. Cicadas were loud, and every type of wildlife seemed to try to rival the sound. Birds shrieked. Frogs croaked. Coyotes howled. Foxes barked. The swamp was alive with raccoons and muskrats and possums. She hadn't expected to hear so much rustling or the calls back and forth from the multitude of birds. She didn't understand how the men could move so quickly through the swamp without disturbing its natural rhythm. It was as though, when they spread out, they each became part of nature and were accepted there.

She used the trees, following Draden, trying to keep from disturbing the wildlife so as not to give them all away. She was the best tracker in the group, but she didn't need to be here. These men knew exactly where their quarry was, and they were converging from all directions to surround them.

Shylah's heart pounded in fear. She knew the Williams brothers and particularly Agus Orucov were dangerous when cornered, mostly because they were afraid. She didn't want them to infect themselves or anyone else with the virus. She hoped to take them out cleanly, but she knew better. She knew by now they were terrified of the consequences of their actions and they'd be feeling as if they had nothing to lose. Nowhere to go. If they had already heard of the death of Ethan Montgomery — and it had been reported widely — they would know there was no paycheck at the end of the day other than killing the GhostWalkers and possibly acquiring her, which they would know would be nearly impossible.

The entire world was looking for them, law enforcement in every country. There would be no escape, especially when the money ran out. They would be considered pariahs by any friend or family member. They had to know that by now, they were intelligent men. She knew they would be feeling alone, cut off and desperate. Desperate men were capable of anything. She hoped the GhostWalkers would get clean shots at them and take them out fast, but the dread building inside her told her something else — and she'd always followed her instincts.

She concentrated on running along the thicker, twisted branches and when she couldn't, she dropped down to earth, trying not to break stride, following almost exactly in Draden's footsteps. He was fast, his longer strides taking him some distance from her as they ran, but she managed to keep him in sight, which was no small feat. As she ran, mice and reptiles, snakes and lizards slithered and scuttled out of her way. Rabbits hopped to the side and she startled a skunk, although she was more shocked than it was. Before it could lift its tail, she'd leapt over it and was gone.

Keep up. This is treacherous ground. You can fall through. Place your feet exactly where I do.

She didn't need the warning. She realized with every step she took that they were on dangerous, thin ground. Each step left a wet depression behind. The animals had changed as well. Now there were signs of alligators and snapping turtles. She didn't want to meet any of them.

Great white egrets flapped their impressive wings as the GhostWalkers moved through the marsh, but the flock continued feeding on the fish and shrimp they fished for. Waterfowl were everywhere, but the silent men were so calm, giving off so little energy, none of the shore birds rose to give their presence away.

Shylah had to admit, she was enjoying the run through the very interesting and diverse swamp. They raced through a bayou and skirted an island of sawgrass. She felt the others slowing, spreading out more.

Who is your best shooter? The best team, spotter and sniper? She directed the inquiry to Joe and Draden.

Either Malichai and Mordichai or Rubin and Diego. I might give the edge to Rubin, Joe said. *What are you thinking?*

When we get close, tell Rubin and Diego to set up on Agus Orucov. Have Malichai and Mordichai take the other two just to be safe.

She knew it was presumption to tell the leader of the GhostWalkers what to do, but it was her operation. She'd tracked the three scientists from the start and she was going to do her job.

Will do, Joe agreed.

Then suddenly, Draden ceased moving so abruptly he appeared to have been made of stone. She skidded to a halt beside him. The three virologists were just ahead, hastily dumping their backpacks and trying to find cover. Something had tipped them off to the fact that they weren't alone. An alligator slid into the water just to the right of them, startled by the motion of the men as they came to a collective halt.

Shylah knew Whitney's three men couldn't see them, but they obviously knew they were there. Orucov was the most aggressive, just as she was certain he would be.

"You take one step closer and I throw this into the air and release it," Orucov snarled. "I mean it. Back off." He held the glass capsule up in the air.

It isn't passed through the air. Saliva and blood, but not air, Draden reminded.

We can't take a chance that they didn't mutate it, Trap advised.

How long can it live in the air? Joe asked.

The virus in Texas at the research center was still alive when they brought in animals after three years, Trap reminded. *And that was after they eradicated every animal infected and thoroughly washed the lab down with bleach and other proven cleaning agents, using an eleven-day process. If we don't need to take chances, let's not go there.*

Shylah wasn't officially part of the team, but these men were hers to take out. *Let me see what I can do.*

There was a moment of silence. *She's good at this,* Draden reminded. *She knows them better than anyone.*

You're up, Joe made the decision. *But don't get close and don't take chances.*

Shylah didn't hesitate. The longer the three scientists had to panic, the worse their reaction would be. They weren't trained soldiers. They were men who did their work in a laboratory, and being on the run was taking a toll on them. Disheveled and clearly exhausted, with their clothes a mess and beards in various states of disrepair, the three appeared sleep deprived, haggard and paranoid. She couldn't blame them.

She emerged from the shadows of the trees to confront them. Hands on hips to show she wasn't going to suddenly whip out a weapon and kill them, she shook her head. "I can't believe the three of you created such a mess. Whitney is beyond pissed."

Tyler Williams closed his eyes and let out a single croak of a sound.

"Don't be stupid and make this any worse than it already is. You've done what he wanted, so that's something. He understands working for the highest bidder, because he understands money, but you know you should have told him someone else was trying to buy your viruses. He would have doubled the money. Tripled it. Now, because of your very poor decisions, you don't have much in the way of choices."

"There are no choices," Cameron hissed.

Tyler made another sound, this one suspiciously like a child's wail.

"Of course, there are choices. You're all intelligent men. You know there are choices. Agus can throw the vial and he'll be shot dead. That's a choice. My guess is, all three of you will go down in a hail of bullets."

"That's better than being dragged through a public trial," Orucov said. "My family would be humiliated. They'd never be able to raise their heads in public again."

"And you think if you die here today, that still isn't going to happen? Don't be ridiculous. Whitney sent you a one-time offer." She was very aware of Draden going very still in her mind.

"Anything Whitney says is pure bullshit," Orucov snapped.

Cameron put up his hand to caution Orucov. "I'd like to hear what she has to say."

"He'll take you back and see that your names are cleared. You'll be working for him for a very long time — and he didn't specify how long that would be — with little pay and no weekends away from the compound."

"In other words, as his slaves," Orucov protested.

"You'd most likely be treated the way he always treated us. You didn't seem to mind when he kept us under lock and key."

She kept her voice strictly neutral, but she was on high alert, every sense totally focused on Agus Orucov. He was the one with the virus capsule making the threats, and there was pure desperation in his eyes. He looked to be completely unraveling, but not in the childish way Tyler was losing his mind.

Orucov's gaze kept shifting wildly around him as if he could see the GhostWalkers in the shadows. She knew he couldn't, but that didn't stop him from trying. His entire body shook, not just his hand.

"It's not the same," Orucov told her. "We're educated men with something great to contribute to the world. What are you?" Contempt filled his voice. "A woman bred for genetics that aren't even your own. We can't be put in a cage, doing only what Whitney decrees. He isn't smarter than we are, no matter how much he lords it over us."

Cameron took a step closer to Orucov, and Shylah wanted to yell at him to stop. It wouldn't take much to push the scientist over the edge, nor would it matter where the shove came from.

"I want to hear her out, Agus," Cameron said.

"Did she tell you she killed Montgomery? I'm sure she did it. He didn't just die or wake up one day to commit suicide. They have ways of making it look like that." Beads of sweat broke out on the Indonesian's face.

"Montgomery apparently was into autoerotic asphyxiation. He was found with a rope wrapped around his neck as well as other body parts. His father covered that up. No one believes he tried to commit suicide, but there was a porn flick on and he took his kink a little too far." She shared the information matter-of-factly. "I can't imagine how you think I was in any way involved with that. On the other hand, Whitney is giving you three an out. Your reputations will be restored. You'll remain alive. You gave him what he wanted most of all — a biological weapon and the vaccine needed to be able to wield it if necessary. You're really his golden children."

Cameron's facial expression changed. "She's right, Agus. Tyler. If there is a vaccine, he's going to be jumping up and down for joy. We did create exactly what he wanted. He has to be happy about that and we're still useful to him. We just have to eat a little crow for a while and then we'll be back on top."

"What about Lupa Suku? How do we get out of that mess?" Orucov demanded, his voice swinging out of control. "They all died. Every single one of them."

"Yes, they did," Shylah agreed, "but that's on the MSS, not you."

"You have an answer for everything. The fishermen. The MSS didn't kill them."

"That's on your conscience. You know damn well Whitney doesn't have one and he believes one or two lives taken for the good of others is perfectly okay."

"She's right, she's right," Cameron said.

"Whitney does think that. You've heard him say it dozens of times. We didn't create this mess. The MSS did. Montgomery insisted," he added, looking eagerly at Shylah. "He said it had to be that village."

Shylah pitched her voice low and soothing. "Agus, all this time we thought it was you who had chosen that village, but we know it was Montgomery. No one is going to blame you for that."

Orucov stepped back away from Cameron, shaking his head almost violently. "She's lying, Cameron. The minute I hand this over, she's going to kill us, or her friends will. If she's with Whitney, what's she doing with them?"

As he protested, his voice swung out of control, going to a high-pitched shriek. Shylah had never taken her focus from that very real threat. She saw it in his eyes first, that insanity that overcame good sense. Movement started, his arm muscles jerking and dancing before he went for the throw.

Now. Take him out, Rubin. He had been selected as the sniper. Diego was his spotter. She'd been told they were a pair that didn't miss.

She threw up her hands and cast with silk, needing to be more precise than she ever had been in her life. As with her blowgun, like everything else she did, she had practiced for hundreds of hours and that training didn't let her down. The vial went into the air and she followed the trajectory even as she wove her funnel web. She spun fast, marking where the vial would fall and placing the silk cone directly beneath it. The glass hit the funnel and slid down the silk to land safely in the bottom of the basket.

The sound of the rifle was loud, reverberating through the swamp. Agus Orucov's head seemed to jerk back so hard he flew backward, his feet leaving the ground as he went over like a bowling pin.

Shylah calmly drew her weapon and shot Cameron and then Tyler right between the eyes. "Yeah, Cameron, you were directly responsible. All three of you, for every single life that was lost."

Skirting around the bodies without looking at them, she retrieved the silk basket. Draden came up behind her, attending to the dead, making certain their eyes were closed. She could have told him it didn't matter. She didn't want to look at the three men who had deliberately caused so many innocents to die and then expected a free pass.

"You're damned fast," Joe said.

She shrugged and handed the vial

wrapped in silk to Trap. "They all three have backpacks. They dropped them when we came upon them. God only knows what they have inside them."

"No worries," Malichai said. "We'll do cleanup. Not bad for a girl. Zero hesitation."

She heard the teasing note in his voice. For an answer, she threw out more silk, dropping it over his body fast, spinning it in tight circles so he was wrapped and cocooned in the web. She sent him a smile. "Zero hesitation every time. Your skills aren't up to a girl's, my man. I suggest more training."

The GhostWalkers reacted with taunting laughter. Draden whipped out his phone and took pictures along with all the rest of his team. Malichai pretended to take a nap. Shylah ignored him when inside she was laughing. His antics definitely helped to calm the adrenaline pouring through her body.

Draden held out his hand to her and she put hers in his. His fingers closed around hers and they walked away together, back toward the Fontenot home. "Did Whitney really make them that offer?"

Shylah shrugged. "Does it matter? It was never going to happen."

"You didn't tell me."

"What difference would it have made? It was my job to take care of them, and I did. They weren't going to be rewarded for what they did. If they were turned over to the military for a trial, Whitney and his friends in high places still might have gotten them free. They were always going to die."

"You sounded very convincing when you were making your offer."

She glanced at him. "That's why I'm so good at my job, Draden. I do whatever it takes. I make myself believe what I'm saying so they believe it. I used my knowledge of Whitney as well as what I'd learned about them. Tyler and Cameron were weak. They would want to take the out offered to them because they've skated their entire lives. They thought because they were intelligent, that made them superior. Agus Orucov was always the wild card."

His hand moved up her back to the nape of her neck. "You're upset, Shylah. You didn't have to do that. I would have done it for you."

She glanced up at his face. "I had no problems taking them out, Draden. None. Zero. They were dead the minute Whitney put me on their trail. I wasn't certain how you'd react. I'm still not certain. There's a part of you holding back from me. That's part of who I am. I track down the ones that think they can escape justice. I don't hesitate because I believe they need taking out. I absolutely know there is no other way."

"Are you apologizing to me?" He sounded and felt incredulous. "Are you out of your mind? I thought you were magnificent. I was so fucking proud of you I could barely breathe. Not to mention you're the hottest woman in the world. Watching you work is a thing of beauty, Shylah."

He meant it. He meant every word. Relief swept over her. Love swamped her. She wasn't ever going to have to try to hide that side of her. Not from him. He stopped abruptly and turned to pull her into his arms, taking her mouth, pouring love and fire into the darkest corners of her soul.

20

Shylah perched on the counter, drawing her legs up as she watched Zara Mazza add two lemons and two limes, both cut in half, as well as half an orange to salted water in a Dutch oven. She loved watching Zara's face when she was cooking for everyone. Shylah had helped her with the main dishes — Cajun chicken pasta as well as salad and freshly baked bread. The pasta was homemade by Nonny, so they knew it was good. The fresh bread was Zara's, and it was so fragrant they'd been fending off the men all evening.

A voice rose, a hiss of displeasure, Pepper telling Wyatt he could just go to hell. The women exchanged looks with mixtures of concern and amusement. Pepper was always the most accommodating with Wyatt. Anything he wanted, she gave him. She always spoke in low, almost sensual tones. There were never raised voices where Pepper was concerned.

The triplets rushed in, alarm on their faces. Ginger had her hands pressed to her ears. There were tears on both Thym's and Cannelle's faces. It was Cayenne who reached down to lift Thym into her arms to reassure her. Shylah hesitated. The girls didn't know her as well, but she figured it was time they did. The perfect time. She held out her arms to Cannelle and the child immediately rushed to her. Shylah had just been thinking having babies with Draden was out, but holding the little girl made her rethink, just for a moment. The child put her little arms around her neck, snuggling into her.

Shockingly, it was Trap who leaned down and swept Ginger into his arms. "Nothing's wrong, Ginger," he reassured gruffly. "Your mama is having the babies and doesn't always feel good. She's just letting your daddy know that right this minute, she's the boss and he'd better not cross her. Women get to do that when they're having babies. It's all about making that experience exactly what she wants, and she needs to be able to communicate that."

Shylah nearly fell off the counter, even with Draden standing right in front of her, one hand on her knee, the other rubbing

Cannelle's back gently.

"She's yelling. She never yells," Ginger objected with a little sniff.

All three girls looked soberly at Trap for an explanation. Shylah thought that was very telling. Trap didn't talk much as a rule. In fact, he ignored what was going on around him. Most of the time his attention was centered solely on Cayenne or his work. She was beginning to know the other members of GhostWalker Team Four.

Shylah found herself looking at Cayenne, not Trap. Her gaze was fixed on her husband's face. She was pregnant, and actually much further along than she appeared, but she didn't flinch under Thym's weight. She was looking to Trap for his explanation just as the girls were. That, more than anything, really brought home the fact that both Pepper and Cayenne had no knowledge of childbirth or parenting. They were relying on their spouses and Nonny.

In spite of her age, or maybe because of it, Nonny was clearly the center of Team Four. She had the biggest heart, and everyone was always in her home, underfoot. She never seemed to mind. She'd left the cooking to Zara, Bellisia and Shylah while she helped Wyatt deliver. Ezekiel was with them and Wyatt had told two of the others, Gino and Joe, to stand by just in case the babies needed help.

"Trap?" Cayenne pushed for an explanation.

Trap reached out and cupped his wife's face, cradling it gently in his palm. "Labor can be intense. A woman's body has to work to help get the baby out and there's no stopping it once it's really gotten started. When she doesn't know what to expect, it can be a little frightening at first. We looked at the video of birthing several times."

"Everyone was smiling in that video, Trap."

He nodded. "That's true and a little unrealistic. We'll find more realistic ones closer to the birth."

"Does my mommy hurt?" Ginger asked.

Trap used the pad of his thumb to gently stroke over Cayenne's mouth. Shylah could see her lips were trembling. Immediately, Shylah wanted to wrap her arms around the woman and comfort her. She clearly was afraid of the upcoming event.

Pepper's voice rose in another curse. "You can just get out, Wyatt. I'll do this myself."

"Is Daddy being mean to Mommy?" Ginger prompted.

"Wyatt's just acting like a moron," Trap said, brutally honest as usual. "When a man loves a woman the way your daddy loves your mommy, he doesn't like to see her in any kind of distress. She's working hard and can't reassure him that she's all right, so he's kind of acting like a husband, not a doctor."

"Is that what you're going to do?" Cayenne's voice trembled.

"You know me better than that, baby. I'm not as emotional as Wyatt. I'll be just as bossy when you're giving birth as I am all the time." His thumb slid in a little caress over her lips. He stared directly into her eyes.

She must have been reassured by what she saw there because she nodded, and he let go of her face. "Don't forget, Nonny's with your mom," Bellisia said, practical as usual. "So is Uncle Zeke. They're going to help her and pretty soon you're going to have two baby sisters. You're really going to have to help your mommy and daddy with them. Babies can be a lot of work."

Ginger nodded solemnly and shared a look with her two sisters. "We know what to do. Mommy told us. She's been reading books to us and we're going to help her a lot."

Shylah wanted to laugh as she put Cannelle back on the floor. The three girls were very advanced for their age, but they were so little and sometimes little terrors. She had nightmares thinking about having children like the three of them. They thought nothing of sneaking off and playing in the swamp. It took the entire team and Nonny to watch over them. She couldn't imagine what it was going to be like with two more little girls in the mix — especially with the influence of Ginger, Thym and Cannelle.

The water was boiling and smelling very citrusy and good. Zara dumped a massive amount of shrimp into the large pot. The men's gazes were immediately riveted on the food. Shylah started laughing.

"What?" Draden asked, reaching to take several pieces of fresh warm bread from one of the many baskets. He handed the girls each one and then ate half the other in one bite.

"All of you think with your stomachs," she accused.

Draden grinned at her. *Not most of the time, sweetheart. I think with my dick.*

She rolled her eyes. *Okay, that too. I'm okay with that.*

Zara is nearly as good a cook as Nonny already.

Is that a hint that you want me cooking

more? They usually cooked meals together. Construction was going on big-time at the property Draden had purchased. Mostly they camped there, needing to spend time alone together. She loved being his wife. She loved everything about Draden, down to the smallest detail. He could get a little bossy, but she noticed all the men seemed to be that way, some a little more dominant than others. She supposed it was the amount of gene-editing done in each of them.

She especially liked Ezekiel and Gino, the husbands of her best friends. Each was very different from the other but suited his wife perfectly. She had grown fond of Trap, although she hadn't thought she would. He was very distant, but she could see he had great affection for all of them. Joe had become a favorite as well. It was impossible not to like him. Mordichai and Malichai made her laugh, especially Malichai. Ruben and Diego broke her heart at times. She couldn't help feeling their energy and the dark shadows residing in them. They both felt deep sorrow that at times threatened to overwhelm them. She wanted to find a way to make it better for both.

Baby, you're too empathetic. When the Campos are having a difficult time, you need to keep a distance, so you don't take that on your shoulders.

She was listening to the sounds coming from the bedroom. For the most part, Pepper was stoic, not crying out or letting on that she might be hurting. It was only when they could hear the murmur of Wyatt's voice that she protested. Whatever he was telling her to do, she clearly didn't want to do.

Shylah watched as Zara removed the shrimp from the boiling water when they turned pink. She couldn't figure out how Zara could keep her mind on what she was doing when so much was happening around them. Zara immediately placed the shrimp in icy water to prevent further cooking and she did so automatically, as if she were listening to the sounds coming from the other room even while she was making the appetizer for all of them.

"I don't know about this baby business," Gino said, leaning down to brush kisses on Zara's neck. "I have to say, it freaks me out, just a little."

Zara laughed. "Nothing freaks you out. And you're the one pushing for babies." Her lashes swept down as she deftly began peeling shrimp. Shylah immediately pitched in as did Draden.

Gino wrapped his arms around Zara's

waist and nuzzled her neck as she worked. "Lots of babies to keep you home with me."

Zara didn't miss a beat, working as if she were used to Gino keeping his arms around her while she did so. "I'll stay home with you babies or not, Gino."

"Just making sure, princess."

She laughed. "The truth is, you want children."

He didn't argue. Shylah realized Gino did want children with Zara, that it was important to him. She glanced at Draden. *Is having children important to you, Draden? If it doesn't happen, are you going to be upset?* She felt a little anxious over the issue. She wanted to have his children, she already knew that, but what if, because of her genetics, she couldn't? Or something went terribly wrong?

Loving you and living my life with you is important to me. Having children is a natural progression, and yes, I want them. I'd like to have a large family, but that doesn't mean I wouldn't be equally as happy with just the two of us. If you don't want to go there . . .

She did. She liked that he gave her that choice. She could hear that he meant it from the sincerity in his tone. *I'm getting used to the idea and with all these mothers and Nonny around, they'll help me.*

I'll help you.

Shylah sent him a smile because that was adamant. A declaration. She watched Zara pour equal amounts of orange, grapefruit and pineapple juice into several pans. She added fresh lemon and lime juice and then pointed to the fruit she had sitting out on the counter. Gino moved around her without missing a beat and began quickly slicing through oranges, grapefruit, lemons and limes, which were added to the mix in the pan with crushed red pepper. The shrimp were added. She covered the pans and put them in the refrigerator. Gino began the cleanup while Zara washed her hands.

"How long until we get that?" Malichai asked.

"About thirty minutes. The pasta is prepped and will be ready around the same time. If you can keep from eating all the bread, we'll have plenty with a salad." There was amusement in Zara's voice.

Malichai groaned. "I don't know if I can last that long."

Everyone, including the little girls, laughed. Malichai held out his hand to them. "Come on, let's get out of the kitchen so I don't eat all the bread. We can play outside before it gets too dark."

Cannelle grabbed his hand and the three

little girls tried to skip out of the room with Malichai. Mordichai made a face. "I guess I'd better go along and keep them out of trouble." He sounded long-suffering, but Shylah knew better than to buy into his acting.

Ruben and Diego exchanged a long look and then they drifted after Malichai and Mordichai. Shylah knew they wouldn't be playing with the triplets. They'd be outside, on the roof, guarding them.

The group moved out of the kitchen, Draden keeping his arm around her waist. He liked being close to her. She had never particularly liked to be touched, but it was different with him. She found herself needing to feel his hands on her almost as much or more than he insisted. She also reached for his mind often. The way he stroked caresses through her with that psychic touch was both exhilarating and comforting.

"Gino." Nonny came down the hall, her expression all business. "We need you now. She's going to deliver the first one any minute. You'll need to look after the baby with me."

Gino rose instantly, leaned into Zara to brush her mouth with his and then he was hurrying for the bathroom to wash up.

The sitting room was the largest informal

gathering room, but it failed to hold them all so several spilled over into the living room. Wanting to be close to the kitchen to keep her eye on the meal, Zara remained with Trap and Cayenne and Draden and Shylah. Cayenne clearly was worried about Pepper and wanted to be close in case of an emergency.

Shylah identified a bit with Cayenne, in that the woman was a warrior through and through. She had less confidence in herself as a woman than she did as the competent fighter who had earned and deserved a place on the team. Shylah felt exactly the same way. Cayenne was learning at a rapid pace, absorbing everything Nonny was both showing her and telling her. She watched everyone, but mostly paid attention to Trap.

Shylah knew she was taking that same route. After meeting Nonny, she wanted to be like her. She loved the way Nonny's home was so open to everyone and how it felt warm and welcoming. Zara was like that, her skills in the kitchen and sweet nature allowing her to find her way fast. Bellisia was taking a little more time. The concepts of cooking and housework were foreign to her. Fortunately, Ezekiel didn't mind in the least.

The sound of a baby's cry drifted from

the bedroom, and Shylah went utterly still. She lifted her head alertly, her eyes meeting Draden's. They both smiled. Simultaneously, everyone else in the room did the same. It was the first time Shylah had ever heard a newborn and it was an amazing experience. Even Cayenne was smiling.

They could hear Nonny's soft murmur and knew she was assisting Gino with the baby while Wyatt and Ezekiel aided Pepper. It seemed only a couple of minutes later when the second baby clearly entered the world with a soft, mewling cry. Shylah found herself close to tears. She wished she'd been in the room when Pepper had given birth. She would have liked to see it.

No one spoke. Everyone was waiting. Nonny came out looking a little tired. "They're both in good health. Small, but they're a little early. We expected that. Their color is good, their scores even better. She's holding them with Wyatt and then she'll need sleep. They'll be put into the warmers and then you'll be able to see them."

Trap moved first, reaching for Nonny and tugging her to her favorite rocking chair. "We need coffee, Zara. Hot and strong. Nonny's tired."

"I'm already prepared," Zara said and leapt up.

"I can't believe we have two new babies," Cayenne whispered in awe. For the first time that Shylah had seen since she'd joined them, Cayenne touched her stomach.

Trap kissed her fingertips. "We're next, babe."

"Are we ready?" Cayenne's voice shook.

"As ready as we'll ever be. We'll wing it until we figure it out," Trap answered.

"That's what we plan to do," Draden said. "Although with Nonny here, I think we're all going to be fine with this new venture."

Shylah looked at the contentment on Nonny's face. Their eyes met and Nonny smiled her reassurance.

"I hope you're right," she said. "I'm good at certain things, but bringing life into the world was never in my training."

Draden suddenly grinned at her. "We'll practice. A lot. You like to practice things."

Laughter broke out and Shylah tried to pretend scowl at him, but deep inside she felt warm and safe. She felt as if she were home surrounded by an extended family. *You make me happy.*

I love you, sweetheart. Absolutely love you.

She believed him.

ABOUT THE AUTHOR

Christine Feehan is the #1 *New York Times* bestselling author of the Carpathian series, the GhostWalker series, the Leopard series, the Shadow Riders series, and the Sea Haven novels, including the Drake Sisters series and the Sisters of the Heart series.

The employees of Thorndike Press hope you have enjoyed this Large Print book. All our Thorndike, Wheeler, and Kennebec Large Print titles are designed for easy reading, and all our books are made to last. Other Thorndike Press Large Print books are available at your library, through selected bookstores, or directly from us.

For information about titles, please call:
(800) 223-1244

or visit our website at:
gale.com/thorndike

To share your comments, please write:
Publisher
Thorndike Press
10 Water St., Suite 310
Waterville, ME 04901